THE DOCTOR'S SLEIGH BELL PROPOSAL

BY
SUSAN CARLISLE

CHRISTMAS WITH THE SINGLE DAD

BY
LOUISA HEATON

MILLS & BOON

Susan Carlisle's love affair with books began in the sixth grade, when she made a bad grade in mathematics. Not allowed to watch TV until she'd brought the grade up, Susan filled her time with books. She turned her love of reading into a passion for writing, and now has over ten medical romances published through Mills & Boon. She writes about hot, sexy docs and the strong women who captivate them. Visit SusanCarlisle.com.

Louisa Heaton lives on Hayling Island, Hampshire, with her husband, four children and a small zoo. She has worked in various roles in the health industry—most recently four years as a Community First Responder, answering 999 calls. When not writing, Louisa enjoys other creative pursuits, including reading, quilting and patchwork—usually instead of the things she *ought* to be doing!

THE DOCTOR'S
SLEIGH BELL
PROPOSAL

BY
SUSAN CARLISLE

Published in Great Britain 2016
By Mills & Boon, an imprint of HarperCollins*Publishers*
1 London Bridge Street, London, SE1 9GF

© 2016 Susan Carlisle

ISBN: 978-0-263-91531-0

Our policy is to use papers that are natural, renewable and recyclable
products and made from wood grown in sustainable forests.
The logging and manufacturing processes conform to the legal
environmental regulations of the country of origin.

Printed and bound in Spain
by CPI, Barcelona

Dear Reader,

I love an adventure. And Ellen and Chance's story is just that. Take a fish-out-of-water female doctor, a man who has seen too much pain and can't do enough to help the people he cares deeply about, add a developing country, push the two doctors together, mix in drug traffickers chasing them and the fun begins.

I hope you enjoy Ellen and Chance's quest for love.

I want to thank Ron and Susie Woodward for sharing their experiences of working during medical mission trips in Central America. Because of their care many people like those I describe in my book now have better lives. You are both an inspiration to me.

I love to hear from my readers. You can reach me at SusanCarlisle.com.

Susan

To Carol, I love you for being my sister—
if not by birth, of my heart.

Books by Susan Carlisle

Mills & Boon Medical Romance

Midwives On-Call
His Best Friend's Baby

Heart of Mississippi
The Maverick Who Ruled Her Heart
The Doctor Who Made Her Love Again

Snowbound with Dr Delectable
The Rebel Doc Who Stole Her Heart
The Doctor's Redemption
One Night Before Christmas
Married for the Boss's Baby

Visit the Author Profile page at
millsandboon.co.uk for more titles.

**Praise for
Susan Carlisle**

'Gripping, stirring, and emotionally touching…
A perfect medical read!'

—*Goodreads* on
His Best Friend's Baby

CHAPTER ONE

SCREECHING VEHICLE BRAKES caught Dr. Chance Freeman's attention. That would be his three new staff members arriving. They should have been here last night but bad weather had delayed them. He'd needed them desperately. His other team had left that morning and today's clinic had been shorthanded and almost impossible to manage.

Chance glanced up from the baby Honduran boy he was examining and out the entrance of the canvas tent located in a clearing near a village. Beyond the long line of waiting patients, he saw a tall, twentyish woman jump down from the rear of the army surplus truck. She wore a tight green T-shirt, a bright yellow bandana round her neck and tan cargo pants that clung to her curves.

Great. High jungle fashion. He'd seen that before.

Shoulders hunched, he drew his lips into a tight line, stopping a long-suffering sound from escaping. Years ago he'd helped Alissa out of a Jeep. She'd believed in being well dressed in any environment as well. They had been newlyweds at the time. That had only lasted months.

Everything about this new staff member's regal bearing screamed she didn't belong in the stifling heat of a rain forest in Central America. He bet she wouldn't last long. In his years of doing medical aid work he'd learned to recognize those who would stick out the tough conditions and long hours. His guess was that she wasn't one of them. Everything about her screamed upper crust, big city. Pampered.

When had he become so cynical? He hadn't even met her yet and he was already putting her in a slot. It wasn't fair not to give her a chance just because she reminded him of his ex-wife. Still, he didn't have the time, energy or inclination to coddle anyone, even if he desperately needed the help.

From under her wide-brimmed hat she scanned the area, her gaze coming around to lock with his. She tilted her head, shielding her eyes with a hand against the noonday sun. One of her two companions said something and she turned away.

Shaking off the spell, Chance returned to the child. He'd hardly looked down when there was a commotion outside. People were screaming and running. *What was going on?*

He didn't have to wait long to find out. Two men carried another man into the tent. He was bleeding profusely around the face and neck area and down one arm. Quickly handing the baby to his mother, Chance cleared the exam table with his arm.

"Put him here. What happened?"

The men lifted the injured man onto the table. Despite Chance's excellent Spanish, they were talking so fast he was having to work to understand them. Apparently, the man had been attacked by a jaguar while trying to save one of his goats.

A feminine voice asked from the end of the table, "What can I do to help?"

A fragrant scent floated in the air. He was tempted to lean forward and inhale. There was a marked difference between the feminine whiff and the odor of the sweaty

bodies around him. Unfortunately, he would need to warn
her not to wear perfume in this part of the world because
it attracted unwanted insects.

Chance looked up into clear blue eyes that made him
think of the pool of water at the bottom of his favorite
waterfall. The woman he'd just seen climbing off the
truck waited. She'd removed her hat and now he could
clearly see a long blonde braid falling over a shoulder.
With her fair coloring she would burn in no time in the
hot Honduran sun.

"Start with cutting away the clothing."

She stepped to the table. The paper on the table was
soaked with blood. He glanced up to see her face blanch
as she viewed the man who would be disfigured for life
from the deep lacerations.

"Don't faint on me," Chance said through clenched
teeth. "Michael, get over here." He nodded toward the
other table. "Go help there. Michael and I'll handle this."

She moved off to see about the case Michael was
working on. Chance didn't have time to ponder why
someone in the medical profession couldn't handle this
type of injury.

He and Michael worked to piece the Honduran man
back together. It may have been the largest number of
stitches he'd ever put into a person. There would be a
long recovery time.

"We need some help here," Michael called as he finished suturing an area.

The woman stepped to the table again.

Chance glared at her. "I thought I told you—"

She gave him a determined and unwavering look. "I've
got this." She turned to Michael. "What do you need?"

"Bandage this hand," he said.

"I'll take care of it." The words were full of confidence as fingers tipped in hot pink picked up the saline and four-by-fours sitting on the table and began cleaning around the area.

Chance had to stop himself from rolling his eyes. That manicure wouldn't last long here and there wouldn't be another forthcoming either. He moved on to the next laceration. As he looked at the man's arm Chance kept a watchful eye on the new staff member. With the efficiency of few he'd seen, she'd wrapped and secured the dressing and moved on the next spot.

At least she seemed to have recovered from whatever her earlier issue had been. He was used to temporary help, but he still wanted quality.

Many who came to help with the Traveling Clinic were filled with good intentions and the idealism of saving the world but didn't have the skills or common sense required to work in such primitive settings. The clinic served the medical issues in the small villages outside of La Ceiba. Making it even more difficult was that the locals were often hesitant about asking for help.

A jaguar attack wasn't the clinic's normal kind of injury but they did see a number of severe wounds from accidents. He needed staff that could handle the unexpected and often gruesome. If Chance wasn't such a sceptic he'd have given the new woman points for her recovery but he'd been doing this type of work for far too long. Had seen staff come and go.

He was familiar with people who left. His mother had done it when he'd been a child. He'd been seven when she'd just not been there. His father was a world-renowned surgeon and had been gone much of the time. With his mother's absence Chance had starting acting out in an effort to keep his father's attention, even to the point of stealing. That had got him sent to boarding school. Even in that restrictive environment Chance had pushed back.

In a stern voice the headmaster had said, "It's time for you to decide if you're going to amount to anything in your life. Right now I'd be surprised if you do."

He was the one man in Chance's life who had taken a real interest in a scared and angry boy. The grizzled and gruff headmaster had believed in him, had taken time to listen. Unlike his father. Chance had wanted to make the headmaster proud and had made a change after that conversation. He'd focused on his studies. Dedicated his life to helping others. But in the area of personal relationships he had failed miserably over and over to the point he had long ago given up. Those, apparently, he wasn't capable of having.

Why were dark memories invading now? Maybe because the new woman reminded him so much of his ex-wife, Alissa, whose defection always made him think of his mother. Two females who had rejected him. He'd moved past all that long ago. His worry now was how to keep the clinic open. Pondering old history did nothing to help with the present problem.

He watched the new woman as he changed gloves. Her movements were confident now. Marco, a local man who served as clerk, translator, and gofer for the clinic, entered the tent with a distressed look on his face. He hurried to her and said in his heavily accented voice, "I know not where you are. Please not leave again without telling. Much danger here. Not get lost."

She looked at him. "I'm sorry. I saw the emergency and thought I should come help."

"It's okay, Marco. I'll explain. See to the other two," Chance said to the short, sturdy man.

"*Sí*, Dr. Chance." Marco nodded and hurried out of the clinic.

Chance gave her a pointed look. "Please don't leave the clinic area until we've talked."

Her chin went down and she nodded. "I understand. By the way, my name is Cox. Dr. Ellen Cox. Like Bond. James Bond." She flashed him a grin.

She was a cheeky little thing. He wasn't certain he appreciated that.

He finished up with the injured man and sent him off in a truck to the hospital in La Ceiba. He would check in on him when they got back to town. Chance cleaned up and moved on to his next patient, who was an older woman with an infected bug bite. It would be necessary to drain it.

Before starting the procedure, he stepped to the table next to his, where a five-year-old girl sat. Digging into his pants pocket, he pulled out a peppermint and handed the piece of candy to her. She removed the clear plastic cover and plopped it into her mouth, giving Chance a wide, toothy grin. He'd given a child a second of happiness. He just wished he could make more of a difference. What he did wasn't enough.

As Chance returned to his patient, Ellen joined him.

Since she was so enthusiastic he'd let her see to the woman as he watched. "We're going to need a suture kit, a box of four-by-fours and bandages. Supplies are in the van." He gestured toward the beat-up vehicle that had been parked partially under the tent so that the back end was protected from the daily afternoon rain and could function as a portable storage room. Chance waited as she hurried after the supplies.

Returning to his side, she placed the kit on the bed

and a bottle of saline water as well. "I'll get a pan." She was gone again.

Chance spoke to his patient in Spanish, reassuring her that she would be fine and that what he was going to do wouldn't take too long. A few moments later Ellen was back with the pan and plastic gloves for herself.

He helped the older woman lay back on the table.

Ellen gave the patient a reassuring pat on the shoulder and then turned her attention to opening the suture kit, placing it where he could easily reach the contents. Taking the plastic gloves off the top, he pulled them on. She did the same with hers. Removing the blue sterile paper sheets, she placed them on her patient's leg around and under the inflamed area.

Chance handed her the scalpel. She took it without question.

Michael called, "Chance, you got a second to look at this?"

"Go ahead. I can handle this," Ellen said.

Chance hesitated then nodded. He liked to oversee the new staff for a week or so just to make sure they understood the locals and the type of work they were doing but she should be able to handle a simple case.

The patient's eyes had grown wide when he'd left. Ellen moved to his side of the table and began speaking to her in a mix that was more English than Spanish. As she distracted the woman by having her pay attention to what she was saying instead of what she was doing, the woman calmed down to the point of smiling a few times.

Chance glanced Ellen's way now and then to see how she was doing. By the time he returned the patient was bandaged and ready to leave. Ellen had done a good job.

Chance moved on to the next person waiting. She assisted him. They were just finishing when Marco returned with the two other new staff members. He introduced the man as Pete Ortiz and the woman as Karen Johnson, both nurses. Ellen moved off across the short aisle of tables to help Chance's colleague, Michael Lange. Because Pete spoke fluent Spanish, Chance sent him to do triage and Karen stayed to help him.

Working in Honduras on and off for eight years had only made Chance see the needs here grow. There had been a time he'd thought he might really make a difference but the people needed real clinics, brick-and-mortar buildings with dedicated doctors, not just a few coming in and out every few weeks.

He loved this country—the weather, which he much preferred to the cold of the north, the coast. Scuba diving was one of his greatest day-off hobbies. Walking through a rain forest and being surprised by a waterfall was amazing. But most of all he liked the open, generous smiles of the people. In Honduras he had found home.

The Traveling Clinic had been his idea years ago and he'd worked long and hard to gain funding for the idea. The clinic was a successful concept but money was forever a problem. Again tomorrow the clinic would be stopping at a different village and the locals would line up. Some would wait all day for care. The day would start just as this one had. Never enough, and more left to do.

A couple of times during the afternoon hours the sound of laughter reached his ears. Michael and the new doctor seemed to enjoy working together. That was what he'd thought when his wife had spent so much time helping his clinic colleague, Jim. They had gotten along so well she'd returned to the States with him.

The sun was only touching the tops of the trees by the time Chance saw his last patient. Michael was finishing up with his as well. Now all that was left was to break down the clinic, load the trucks, and head for a hot shower. He leaned up against the nearest exam table, finishing a note on his patient's chart.

"Doctor, if you'll excuse me, I need to fold this exam table." Ellen gave him a pointed look as she flipped her hair back, implying he needed to move.

She reminded him of a teenager, looked no older than a fresh-out-of-high-school girl, even though she must be at least twenty-eight to his tired forty-one-year-old eyes. Breaking down the clinic was the job of Marco and the local men he'd hired to help him. As much as Chance was amazed by her zeal, she needed to understand a few things about the culture and dangers here. "Marco and his men will take care of that."

"I can get—"

He lowered his voice. "I'm sure you can but they take their jobs and positions seriously. I don't want them to feel insulted."

"Oh. I didn't realize." She stopped what she was doing.

"Now you do. You need to tread more carefully, Dr. Cox. There are cultural and safety issues you should be aware of before you go off willy-nilly. Don't be reckless. This isn't Los Angeles, New York or wherever you are from."

A flash of something in her eyes he couldn't put a name to came and went before she said, "New York."

He looked at her a second. "There're not only animals in the jungle that could hurt you, as you saw today, but there's a major issue with drug traders. Neither play around or allow second chances. You should never go out alone. Even in the villages or clinic compound, always have someone with you."

"Are you trying to scare me?"

Did she think this was some exotic vacation spot? "No,

I'm trying to keep you out of harm's way." He looked straight at her. "If you don't follow the rules, you don't stay around here long."

Her lips tightened as she glanced toward the men working to break down the clinic. "I'm sorry I upset Marco. I saw the number of people waiting and thought I should get to work."

"You would be no good to them if you get hurt."

"Your point is taken."

"Chance," Michael called.

"Just remember what I said." He walked away to join Michael beside the supply van.

Half an hour later the tent was down and everything stowed in the vehicles. Now their party was bumping along the narrow dirt road toward the coast. Chance rode in the supply van, with one of the locals driving, while Michael was a passenger in the truck. The others rode in the rear of it. The hour-long trip to the resort might be the toughest part of the day. As the bird flew, the distance wasn't far; however, the roads were so rough and winding it seemed to take forever to make the return drive. Chance usually tried to sleep.

For some reason his thoughts went to the young doctor traveling in the truck behind him. She'd worked hard, doing her share and some more. There was no way she was napping while sitting on that hard metal bench. If she complained, he would point out that the ride was just part of doing this type of medical work. Anyone who stayed with it learned to accept the hardship.

Ellen's head bumped against one of the support frames running around the bed of the truck. Taking a nap was almost impossible. She pulled a jacket out of her duffel bag and folded it up then stuffed it between her head and the unforgiving metal.

Looking out through the slats, she watched the fascinating countryside go by. The vegetation grew rich and huge. Some of the leaves were the size of an umbrella. And so green. It looked impossible to walk through. She'd never seen anything like it. The flowers were such vivid colors. A pink hibiscus always caught her attention.

As the plane had been coming in that morning she'd looked down on the coastline of the county. The pristine white sand against the blue-green of the water had made her want to experience it for herself. It was a beautiful country. She already loved it.

Completely different from New York, the city of buildings and lights. She'd worked at an inner-city clinic that saw pregnant teenagers and babies with colds. It was nothing compared to the type of patients and conditions she'd experienced today. It had been exhilarating. Except for that one moment when she'd looked at that man and all the memories of her mother caught in the car had come flooding back.

The Traveling Clinic cared for people who truly needed it. These people had no other way of getting medical care. They hadn't made poor life choices like the drug addicts and drunks in the city. Here they had nothing, and the clinic offered them something they desperately needed. And they still had a bright smile to share.

The type of work she'd done today was why she'd become a doctor. As a child, a car accident had killed her mother and had left Ellen in the hospital for weeks. There she'd learned the importance of good medical care. The staff had loved and given special attention to the little girl who had lost so much. Ellen had determined then that she wanted to work in the medical field, do for people what had been done for her.

The only sticking point had been her father. As a Manhattan socialite and the only child of an overprotective father, she'd worked at being taken seriously when she'd announced she was going to medical school. Ellen desired to do more than chair committees and plan fancy fund-raisers. She'd wanted to personally make a difference, get to know the people she was helping.

When Ellen had started practicing at the inner-city clinic her father had pitched a fit, saying it was too risky and he didn't want her to work there.

"You're acting like your mother. She went in head first and then thought," he'd said more than once to her as she'd been growing up.

Ellen had told him he had no choice. A number of times she'd noticed a man hanging around when she'd come and gone from the clinic. Some days later she'd found out he had been hired by her father to watch over her because he'd been concerned about her safety.

A few weeks later she'd heard Dr. Freeman speak with such passion about his work in Honduras that she had been hooked. She wanted to make that kind of difference, offer that kind of care. The next day she'd applied to join his staff. It had taken her six months but she was finally here.

After her decision to come to Honduras, she'd thought of not telling her father but she loved him too much to just disappear. Instead, she'd told him she was going to Honduras but not specifically where she would be, fearing he'd send someone to watch over her. Again he'd accused her of not thinking it through. She'd assured him she had. For once she wanted to do something on her own, free from her father's influence.

Her head bounced again. The picture of Dr. Freeman's displeased look when she'd frozen came to mind. Her lips formed a wry smile. Later she had seen a small measure of respect in his eyes.

The wheels squealed to a painful halt. Ellen looked out the end of the truck to see a gorgeously groomed area. Where were they? The others filed off the vehicle and she brought up the rear. With her feet on the ground, she looked around. It appeared as if they were in the back parking lot of a resort.

A couple of Honduran helpers pulled her bag, along with Pete's and Karen's, down from the truck. She hadn't met her fellow staff members until the time had come to board the flight to Honduras. Pete was a nice guy who was looking for a change after a bad marriage and Karen was a middle-aged woman who thought working with the clinic would be a nice way to see a new country. Ellen had liked them both immediately.

Their group was joined by the two doctors. She'd enjoyed working with Michael Lange. He seemed fun and laid back. The same couldn't be said about Dr. Freeman. From what she could tell, he was an excellent doctor. Everything she'd heard about him had been glowing. But on the Mr. Congeniality scale he was pretty low. He could work on his warm welcomes. He hadn't even taken the time to offer his name.

After hearing him speak Ellen had expected him to have less of a crusty personality. He acted as if he'd seen too much and couldn't leave it behind. He was as strikingly handsome as she remembered. With thick, dark, wavy hair with a touch of white at the temples that gave him an air of authority, he was someone who held her attention. Even when she hadn't been working directly with him she had been conscious of where he'd been in the tent. She generally didn't have this type of reaction to a man.

"I'll show Ellen to her hut," Michael said.

"No, she's next to me," Chance said. "You see to, uh, Pete and…" He looked at the other nurse. "It's Karen, isn't it?"

"That's correct." Karen picked up her bag.

"Okay. Dinner is at seven in the private dining room behind the main one." Dr. Freeman headed toward a dirt path between two low palmetto plants. There was a small wooden sign there giving arrowed directions to different areas of the resort. "Coming, Dr. Cox? I've got a call to make to the States before it gets too late."

He'd not offered to carry her luggage. If he thought she couldn't or wouldn't carry her own bag, he had another thought coming. Grabbing her duffel, she pulled the strap over her shoulder and hurried after him. The man really was egotistical.

She followed him along a curving path through groomed vegetation beneath trees filled with blue and yellow chattering macaws. She lagged behind when she became caught up in her surroundings. The place was jaw-dropping beautiful. Completely different from any place she'd ever seen.

"Dr. Cox." The exasperation in the doctor's voice reminded her of a father talking to a distracted child. She didn't like it.

"It's Ellen."

"Come along, *Ellen*. I still have work to do tonight." He took long strides forward.

From what she could tell, he had more than put in a day's worth of work. What could he possibly need to do tonight? "Coming, sir."

He stopped and glared down his nose at her. "The *sir* isn't necessary."

"I just thought that since you were acting like a general I should speak to you as such."

"Ellen, you'll find I'm not known for my sense of humor." He continued on down the path as if he didn't care if she followed him or not.

"I'm sure you're not," she murmured. Hefting her bag strap more securely over her shoulder, she focused on catching up. They moved farther into the landscape until they came out in a small grassy opening where two huts stood with only a huge banyan tree separating them. Each had a thatched roof and a dark-stained wooden porch with what looked like comfortable chairs with bright floral pillows.

The space was perfect as a romantic getaway. "This is amazing. I expected to live in a tent and have to use a bathhouse."

"You have a top-of-the-line bath. We work hard and the board believes the least it can do is provide a nice place to stay. The resort gives us a deal." Dr. Freeman pointed to the structure on the left. "That hut is yours. Follow the signs around to the dining room. If you need something, call zero on the phone." With that he headed toward the other hut.

Well, she wouldn't be counting on him to be the perfect neighbor.

Ellen climbed the three steps to the main door. There was a hammock hanging from one post to another. The living arrangements weren't what she'd expected but she wasn't going to complain.

She swung the door open and entered. Her eyes widened. She sucked in a breath of pleasure. Talk about going from one extreme to another. As rough as the working conditions were, the living quarters were luxurious. She'd lived well in New York but even by those standards this was a nice living space.

The floor plan consisted of an open room with a sitting area on one side and the bed on the other. The ceiling was high with a slow-moving fan that encouraged a breeze through the slated windows. A gleaming wood floor stretched the length of the room. The only area of it that was covered was in the sitting area, where two chairs and a settee created a cozy group. A large bright rug of red, greens and yellows punctuated the space.

But it was the bedroom side that made the biggest impression. A large square canopy bed made of mahogany with identical twists carved into each of the four posts sat there. If she was going to spend a honeymoon somewhere, this would be her choice.

She'd come close to a wedding a couple of times but it seemed like her father stepped in and changed her mind just as she was getting serious. It was as if he couldn't trust her to know who and what she wanted. That was one of the reasons she'd come to Honduras. At least here she could make her own decisions.

The open-air shower, shielded from any onlookers by plank walls, was a new experience. At first she found it intimidating but as the warm water hit her shoulders Ellen eased into the enjoyment of the birds in the trees chirping at her. She was officially enchanted.

Half an hour later, Ellen headed down the plant-lined walk in the direction of what she hoped was the dining area. She turned a curve and a crystal-blue swimming pool that resembled a fern-encircled grotto came into view. The resort was truly amazing.

Beside it Dr. Freeman sat on a lounger, talking on the phone. He wore a T-shirt, cargo shorts and leather thong shoes. His legs were crossed at the ankles. He appeared relaxed but the tone of his voice said that was far from the case. She wasn't surprised. Her impression had been that he didn't unwind often.

"Look, we need those supplies. We have to raise the money." He paused. "I can't be in two places at once. You'll have to handle it. And about the staff you're sending me, I've got to have people who'll stay longer than six weeks. No more short term. The people of rural Honduras need a standing clinic." He glanced in her direction.

Ellen continued toward a tall open-air building, hoping it was where she should go. Footfalls followed her.

"Eavesdropping, Dr. Cox?"

She looked back at him. "I wasn't. I was just on my way to dinner. And I told you I prefer Ellen. When you say Dr. Cox it sounds so condescending."

"I'm sorry. *Ellen*."

She now wished she hadn't insisted he call her by her first name. His slight accent gave it an exotic note that sent a shiver up her spine. Not wanting to give that reaction any more analysis, she said, "I'm hungry."

"The dining room is this way." He started up the steps to the building and she joined him.

They entered a large open space with a thatched roof supported by huge poles. A wooden desk with a local man standing behind it was located off to one side. He waved in their direction as they crossed the gleaming wooden floor. Ellen followed him around one of three groupings of wicker furniture toward a shuttered doorway that stood open. Inside were tables with white cloths over them and low lighting. Dr. Freeman kept moving then stopped at a single door and opened it.

"Close the door behind you," he instructed.

Ellen did as he asked. They were now in a small room

where a long table was set in the middle and a buffet area along one wall. The other members of their group were already there, talking among themselves. They grew quiet as she and Dr. Freeman joined them.

"I thought you guys would already be eating."

"Not without you, boss," Michael said with a grin.

"You know better than that. Well, if no one else is going to start, I am." Dr. Freeman picked up a plate off the stack on the buffet table. Everyone else followed his lead and lined up. Unsure of the protocol or the seating arrangement, Ellen moved to the back of the line. A minute or two later, with her plate full of chicken and tropical fruit, she considered which chair to take.

"Come and sit beside me," Michael offered.

With a smile Ellen took the open seat. She glanced at Chance. His eyes narrowed as he looked in their direction.

She and Michael discussed where she was from and what she thought of her hut then he asked, "So, Ellen, what brings you to our little slice of the world?"

She shrugged. "I wanted to work where I could make a difference."

"You weren't doing that where you were?" Dr. Freeman asked.

She hadn't realized he'd been listening to their conversation.

"Yes, but these people really need someone here. I was seeing young mothers and babies. I found my job necessary and rewarding but there was a tug to do something more. Others were there to help those girls but not enough here to help these. I wanted to come here."

"How did you find out about us?" Michael asked.

"I heard Dr. Freeman speak. I knew this was where I wanted to be."

"Well, Chance, you made a convert."

Dr. Freeman shrugged and went back to eating.

"So, what did you think about the work today?" Michael asked.

"It was different, I have to give you that. But I loved it." She glanced toward the end of the table where Dr. Freeman was sitting.

"You might feel differently after a few days of hot, unending work," Dr. Freeman drawled.

"Aw, come on, Chance, don't scare her." Michael smiled at her. "Don't worry about him. The great Chance Freeman has seen so many people come and go here he's a little cynical about all the new ones. Many don't stay the full six weeks. Some have only lasted days. It's made him a little jaded."

"That's enough, Michael."

The doctor's snap didn't seem to faze Michael. He just grinned. Ellen looked at Dr. Freeman. "I don't plan to be leaving anytime soon, Dr. Freeman."

"Dr. Freeman?" Michael chuckled. "We're a casual bunch around here. First names work just fine. Especially after hours. Isn't that right, Chance?"

He leaned back in his chair. "Sure."

After that Michael turned his attention to Pete and Karen, asking them about themselves.

Ellen concentrated on her dinner and was glad to have Dr. Freeman…uh, Chance's attention off her. When everyone had finished laughing at a story Michael told, Chance tapped on the table with the back of his fork to gain their attention.

"Okay, we need to talk about tomorrow. We'll be in the Tooca area. Near the river. This is our first time there so let's be on our toes. We'll need to be at the trucks at four a.m., ready to roll. Get some sleep and be ready for a really long day."

Ellen shuffled out of the dining room with the rest of the group. It turned out that Karen was housed not far from her so they walked back toward their huts together. After leaving Karen, Ellen continued along the path lit only by lights in the vegetation. Thankfully the porch lights were on at her and Chance's huts. One of the staff at the resort must have come by while she'd been at dinner.

Ellen had just crawled under the covers when the light flicked on inside Chance's hut. His silhouette crossed in front of the window. His passion for what he did was a major factor in why she'd come to Honduras. It was obvious he needed nurses and doctors to help him. So what was his problem with welcoming her?

CHAPTER TWO

THE SUN WAS SLOWLY topping the nearest palm tree when the caravan of three vehicles pulled into a clearing near the River Sico. Chance climbed out of the Jeep that had been leading the caravan and walked over to speak to the local village leader, who was there to greet him. Returning to his staff, who were already beginning to set up the tent, he searched for Ellen. To his surprise she was all smiles and asking what she could do to help. The early hour didn't seem to bother her. Did nothing faze the woman?

She'd traveled for over ten hours the day before, put in five hours of work, and had had to wake up at four a.m. and ride in the back of an uncomfortable truck, and she was still chipper. He was afraid her fall would be hard. No one could keep up that positive attitude for long.

Still, he was having a hard time not liking her. And she was certainly nice to look at. Too much so.

Marco and his crew had the tent erected in no time and were working on setting up tables as Chance directed the van driver into place.

Ellen came to stand beside him. "Good morning. Michael said I should see you about my duties."

"Did you sleep well?"

Her brows drew together as if she was unsure of his motive for asking. "Actually, I did. Thanks for asking."

"You're going to need that rest because we have a long, full day ahead of us. We all kind of do what's needed when needed. The lines are blurred between the doctors and nurses here. So you'll know what supplies we have and where they are stored. Why don't you supply each station with bandages, suture kits, saline bottles and antiseptic? Any basic working supplies you are familiar with."

"Will do."

"Under no circumstances do you open the locked box behind the seat of the van without permission. There's a prevalent drug problem here and we have to be careful drugs are not stolen. There's only one key and I have it. If you need something you must see me."

"I understand."

"When you're finished putting out supplies you'll be needed to work triage. People are already lining up."

A steady stream of patients entered the tent over the next four hours. Karen worked with him and she seemed comfortable with all he'd asked her to do. He'd had little time to check on Ellen. When he had, she'd been either leaning over, intently listening to a patient, or in a squatting position, speaking to the mother of a child.

At noon the patients dwindled to nothing. Chance stepped outside the tent, hoping for a breeze. Ellen walked toward him.

"Are we done here?"

Chance let out a dry chuckle and waved his hand to discourage a fly. "Not by a long shot. Everyone stops for lunch. We'll start over with twice the number in an hour.

Marco should have our food ready. Get something to eat and drink then take a moment to rest." ·

With the back of her hand Ellen pushed away the strand of hair sticking to her forehead. Some of it remained and Chance was tempted to reach out and help her. He resisted the urge. Getting involved on a personal level even with something as benign as moving her hair wasn't going to happen.

"You can wash up behind the tent. Remember what I said about not straying from the area." He turned and walked off toward Michael, who had just exited the clinic. Watching out of the corner of his eye, he saw Ellen headed round the tent. ·

"The new crew is really working out," Michael said when Chance reached him.

"Yeah."

"Ellen seems especially capable."

"She won't last long."

"Why? Because she's blonde and beautiful?" Michael said drily.

"That has nothing to do with it."

"Sure it does. They aren't all Alissa. I have a feeling this one might surprise you."

Chance huffed. "It won't matter. She'll do her six weeks and we'll have to train someone else. Just see to it you don't get too attached."

Michael grinned and raised his brows. "Me? Get attached? But there's nothing wrong with a little fun."

"Just don't let it affect the clinic work." Michael was a good guy but Chance didn't need any personal relationship getting in the way of work. He knew first-hand how emotional upheaval could make the working situation difficult. It had been his own issue with his wife and the affair that she had been having with his colleague that had done it last time. He'd lost all the staff and had almost had to give up the clinic altogether. The only way he had survived had been to push forward and devote all his off time to finding new funding for the clinic.

"Have I ever?" Michael said, his grin growing to a smile.

They both knew it had. Michael was known for showing the young female members a good time while they were in Honduras. For some reason Chance didn't like the idea of him doing so with Ellen. "Let's get some lunch before patients start lining up again. I noticed they are coming in by the canoe load now. In the future we need to think about setting up near rivers so that more people will have access."

Michael's look sobered. "We need to think about where we're going to get some major support so that we can build a permanent building to work out of."

"I know. I'm going to have to go to the States soon and start doing some fund-raising." Chance didn't like the dog and pony show he seemed to have to put on for all the wealthy potential donors to get money but understood the necessity. Give them a good time and they would give was the motto. Still, it was so little in the face of so much need.

Sympathy filled Michael's voice. "But you hate the idea."

"I'm more about the work and less about begging for money."

"Maybe it's time to find someone who'll handle fundraising full time."

Chance had tried before but nothing had worked out. "I need to check on a couple of things and I'll get lunch." Michael headed round the tent and Chance entered the clinic to find Ellen replenishing supplies. "What're you doing? I thought I told you to get some lunch and rest."

"Marco didn't have everything set out yet so I came to check on the supplies and get things ready for this afternoon."

"I appreciate what you're doing but I've seen people burn out pretty quickly here."

She looked at him. "Doctor, I can assure you that I am nowhere near being burned out."

"It sneaks up on you."

For a moment she gave him a speculative look. "Is that what has happened to you?"

The statement seared him. "What do you mean?"

"You seem to care about these people but at the same time don't welcome the people who come to help you. You've been trying to run me off from the minute I got here."

Anger rose in him. Was he letting the past boil over that much? "I have not. There's not enough help as it is. Why would I discourage anyone?"

"I'm wondering the same thing."

"I want you to know the facts. And you don't seem the type cut out for this kind of work."

"And you have decided this by…" she cocked her head "…the clothes I wear, the color of my eyes, my shoes?"

"Your age. Your looks. You attitude. In my experience someone like you only comes to a place like this as a lark, running from something, looking for adventure or to prove something." She flinched. So he had touched a nerve. What had brought her here?

"Why, Dr. Freeman, I do believe you're a bigot. And it must be nice to be all-knowing. It doesn't matter what you think. The real question is have you had any problems with the work I have done so far?"

She had a way of cutting to the point. He hadn't. In fact, he'd been surprised at her knowledge and efficiency. He said nothing.

"That's what I thought. Now, if you don't mind, I'll get that lunch you think I need so badly." She stalked out of the tent.

Wow, there might be more to the blonde bombshell than he'd given her credit for. Had he really been that tough on her? Unfair? She had certainly stood up to him. Been a capable doctor. Maybe he should cut her some slack.

By the time Chance had made it to the lunch table Ellen was finished with her meal and headed toward the front of the clinic. "Remember not to go out of sight of the clinic or one of us."

"I'll heed your warning, Doctor," she said in a sarcastic tone as she kept moving, not giving him time to respond.

Despite what she said, it didn't ease his concern. He felt responsible for all his staff but for some reason Ellen seemed so naive that she required more attention. A couple of times the new people hadn't taken his warnings seriously and had almost gotten in trouble. He couldn't let that happen to her.

He returned to the front and took a seat on a stool just inside the tent door. Ellen was sitting on a blanket she'd apparently taken from the supply van. Chance tried not to appear as if he was watching but she claimed his attention. As she sat, a few of the village girls approached. Ellen spoke to them in a soft voice, halting a couple of times as if searching for the correct word. One of the girls tentatively picked up Ellen's hand and touched her fingernail.

"You like my polish?" Ellen smiled and held her fingers out wide.

The child nodded and the other girls stepped closer, each stroking a nail in wonder.

"Stay here and I'll be right back." Gracefully she rose and headed for the transport truck as if on a mission. She climbed onto the back bumper and reached in to pull out a backpack. Looking through a side pocket, she removed a small bottle. After dropping the bag back into the truck, she returned to the girls. Ellen sat and the children gathered around her again. She patted the blanket and invited them to join her, then opened the bottle. Taking one of the girls' hands, Ellen placed it on her bent knee and applied polish to a nail. There was a unified sound of awe.

What the hell? The woman had brought fingernail polish into the jungle.

Bright smiles formed on dark faces. Small bodies shifted closer in an effort to have a turn. Ellen had their complete attention. Her blonde head contrasted against those around her. The girls giggled and admired their nails, showing them off to their friends before jumping up and running to display them for someone else. As one left another joined Ellen.

Her mirth mingled with the children's. The sound was unusual in the rain forest yet seemed to belong. Like the sweet song of birds in the trees.

Chance walked toward her. It was time to get started again or patients would go unseen and he couldn't let that happen. He stood over the little group. "You seem to have created a stir."

Ellen looked at him with a grin on her face and moved to stand. "Every female likes to do a little something special for herself."

She wobbled and Chance reached for her elbow, helping her to stand. A shot of awareness he'd not felt in years went through him. It was both exciting and disturbing.

To cover his reaction he said, "Even if they can't have it all the time."

Ellen glared at him. "Especially then. A moment of pleasure is better than none."

What would it be like to share pleasure with her? Whoa, had the noon sun gone to his head? That wasn't something he should be thinking about in regard to any of his staff and certainly not about this too young, too idealistic newcomer. Life had taught him that picking women wasn't his strong suit.

Chance released her arm as if it had turned into a hot coal. "I'll see you in the clinic. You'll be working with Michael this afternoon until I think you know the ropes well enough to handle cases on your own."

Ellen didn't know what had gotten into Chance but she was relieved that she didn't have to assist him. Working with Michael was easy and fun so why did it seem anticlimactic next to helping Chance? There was an intriguing intensity about him that tugged at her.

He had seemed so much larger than life when she'd heard him speak. The passion and compassion he felt for the people of Honduras had vibrated through her with each of his words. She'd been drawn to this place. But she'd fought too long and too hard to make her own decisions and Chance was too bossy for her taste. She didn't need another man overseeing her life.

One of the girls who'd had her nails done was Chance's patient at the next table. Despite having her back to them, Ellen overheard him say, "Your nails are so pretty."

She smiled. Mr. Gruff and Groan might have a heart after all.

During the rest of the afternoon and into the dimming light of evening came the continuing blur of people with open wounds, bug bites, sores, to serious birth defects.

Thunder rolled in the distance and the wind whipped the tent as the last of the patients were being seen.

"Get started on putting things away. We need to get on the road before this hits," Chance called to everyone as he finished cleaning a wound on the calf of his last patient, a middle-aged man.

Ellen began storing the supplies in the van. As she passed by Chance he said, "Ellen, would you get an antibiotic out of the med cabinet for me?" He held up a key attached to a ring.

"Sure." Her hand brushed his larger one as she took it. A tingle went through her. Why this reaction to him of all people? She wasn't looking for that. Hadn't come here expecting it. She hurried toward the van.

Entering the vehicle, she made her way down the small isle to where the med box was located. Constructed of metal and bolted to the floor for security, it was situated behind the bench seat. She went down on her knees in front of it. The light was so poor she fumbled with the key in the lock. Slipping her hand into the side leg pocket of her cargo pants, she pulled out her penlight. She balanced it on a nearby shelf, directing the beam toward the lock.

The screech of the driver's door opening drew her attention. She glanced over her shoulder. A thin young man held a knife in her direction. Fear made her heart pound. Her hand holding the lock shook. She opened her mouth to scream.

The man leaned over the seat bring the knife to her neck. *"Tranquillo."*

Ellen remained quiet as he'd asked. She glanced out the end of the van. What was she going to do? She couldn't give him the meds and she had to protect the others.

The tip of the knife was pushed against her skin. The man hovered over her. He smelled of sweat and wet clothes.

"What do you want?" she asked.

"The drugs," the man bit out. "Open the box."

The urgent demand in his voice told her he meant business. When she didn't immediately move he pressed the knife against her and growled, "Now."

Panic welled in her. She couldn't give him the drugs but the blade at her neck reminded her that she couldn't put him off long either.

With relief and renewed alarm she heard Chance call, "Ellen?"

"Say no word," the man whispered, slipping down behind the seat but still holding the knife to her neck.

She had to warn Chance.

Why hadn't Ellen returned? Chance headed toward the van.

He had finished applying the bandage around the man's leg. All he needed to do now was give him the antibiotics and they could get on the road. A commotion outside caught his attention. A young man who looked like he was in his twenties was being helped into the tent by another Honduran about the same age. There was a rag soaked in blood on his arm. Michael and Karen were aiding them. Marco and one of his men had started setting up the exam table they had just folded. They could handle the situation. He wanted to know what Ellen was doing.

He instructed his patient to remain where he was. The rear of the van had been driven under the back of the tent. The area was shadowy because the portable lamps were being used around the exam tables. With the dimming light of the day, compounded by the storm, it was hard to see.

As Chance neared the open doors he saw the small glow of what must be Ellen's penlight. "Hey, what's taking you so long?"

She was on her knees on the floor, facing the medicine box. Her head turned slowly toward him. Even in the disappearing light Chance could see the fear in her eyes. She looked as if she was imploring him to leave. There was a slight movement behind her. Ellen shook her head almost imperceptibly.

Chance kept eye contact and nodded. "Hurry up, I need those meds."

"Yes, sir."

Sir? She knew he didn't like being called sir. Something was definitely wrong.

He backed away from the van. The others were still busy with the injured patient. Rushing past them and outside, he started round the tent when he met Marco. In a low voice he told him that Ellen was in trouble and to give him to the count of ten then run inside the clinic, hollering for help. Marco nodded and Chance circled the outside of the tent until he could see the driver's side van door. It stood open. He could make out the outline of a man in the seat with his back to the door and one leg on the running board. Dread seized him. The man must have a weapon on Ellen.

Giving thanks for the storm brewing, which would cover any noise he made, Chance moved out to the edge of the clearing and followed it around until he was facing the front of the van. When the thunder rolled again Chance ran as fast as he could and slammed his body into the door. The man let out a startled yelp and twisted in the seat, reaching for his leg. Chance grabbed the door and swung it hard again. This time it hit the man in the head and he dropped to the ground, along with a knife.

"Ellen!" Chance barked. "Ellen, are you okay?"

"I'm fine." She sounded shaken.

Marco joined him. Chance left him to tie the vandal up while he climbed into the van. Looking over the seat, he saw Ellen still sitting on the floor, with her head in her hands. "Are you hurt?"

She said nothing.

He reached out and placed a hand on her shoulder. "Ellen, are you hurt? Did he cut you?"

Slowly she looked up. "No." She held up his keys. "And I didn't let him get any drugs. Do I get atta-girl points?"

"Hell, woman, I'd rather he'd had all the drugs than hurt you."

A stiff smile came to her lips. "Aw, you do care." She looked away and a loud sniff filled the air.

"What's going on?" Michael called from the end of the van.

"A guy was trying to steal drugs. Had Ellen at knife-point," Chance answered.

Michael climbed in, went to Ellen and gathered her into his arms. She buried her face in his chest. For some reason Chance wished he was the one she had turned to. He left the van and spoke to Marco, who'd already tied the man up, but his thoughts were still with Ellen. The trespasser admitted that he was with the injured man Michael had been caring for. The injury had been a small self-inflicted wound and used as a diversion.

The rest of the staff had to know what had happened in detail before they returned to packing up. Chance gave the short version on what he'd done before Ellen told her side. He was all too aware of Michael's arm around her shoulders the entire time. Why shouldn't she seek reassurance and comfort from him?

Marco would see to it that the Honduran authorities picked up the man they had captured and looked for the other two. Little would be done to them because Honduras had larger drug problems than these petty thieves.

Half an hour later it was dark and the trucks were loaded and ready to leave.

"Ellen, come on up here," Michael called from the cab of the truck. "I think you're still a little shaken up."

"I'm okay back here." She climbed in the rear with Karen and Peter.

She was tough. Chance admired her for that. After those few minutes of emotion with Michael she'd joined in and helped store the supplies, acting as if nothing had happened.

That evening at dinner Chance watched as Michael stood and tapped his fork against a glass.

"We have a few awards to give out tonight. First, to the great Dr. Freeman, for his heroic use of a van door to apprehend a drug dealer." Michael grinned. "Well done, Chance." He placed a second plate of dessert near him.

Chance smiled and nodded. Why did Michael have to make a big deal of what happen?

"And last but not least, to Dr. Ellen Cox, who held herself together under pressure and didn't give up the key to the drug cabinet." Michael held up his drink glass. The others joined him. A soft clinking of glass touching glass sounded around the room. "For you a flower." He bowed as he presented her with a large orange Bird of Paradise.

Ellen smiled but it didn't quiet reach her eyes. Had she been and was she still more scared than she let on?

"Chance deserves all the accolades. I did nothing." Ellen looked directly at him with sincerity in her eyes. "Thanks for saving me."

Examining the terror coursing through him when he'd realized Ellen was being threatened was something he didn't want to look at too closely. The emotion had been too strong, raw. Still he couldn't deny the relief that had replaced the terror when he'd known she was okay.

Satisfaction he'd not felt in a long time filled him. His look held hers as he nodded. Why did he suddenly feel like standing and thumping his chest?

Ellen rolled to the left and minutes later to the right. She'd been trying to sleep for hours. The sound of rain with the steady dripping off the hut roof would normally lull her to sleep but not tonight. At least the adrenalin rush she'd experienced today should have had her in a deep sleep but it didn't seem to come.

She rubbed the back of her neck. The feel of the man's breath on her skin and the prick of the tip of the knife remained. Even after a hot shower and neck massage the ache between her shoulders blades remained. Would it ever go away? Could she forget that feeling of helplessness? Fear for the others?

It had been that same feeling she'd had when she'd been trapped in the car with her mother. They had been making a simple trip to buy Ellen a dress. It had been a pretty day but the traffic had been heavy. Her mother had sped up to go through a traffic light that had turned yellow. The next thing Ellen had known they'd been upside down and her mother's blood had been everywhere.

Her mother had said, "Your father always says I take too many chances." Then the life had left her.

Slinging the covers away, Ellen slid out and grabbed the thin blanket off the end of the bed, wrapping it around her shoulders. She headed out the front door. Maybe if she watched the rain for a few minutes she could sleep.

She walked to the porch rail. The shower had eased and a full moon was making an appearance every now and then behind the clouds. When it did the soft glow made the raindrops on the ferns surrounding the hut glisten. She stood there, absorbing the peace.

"Can't sleep?"

She yelped and spun toward Chance's hut. He climbed out of the hammock wearing nothing but tan cargo shorts that rode low on his hips. She couldn't help but stare. "Have you been there since I came out?"

"Yep."

"Why didn't you say something?" she snapped.

"I thought you needed a few moments to yourself. What happened today can be hard to process."

He wiped all the times he'd been less than warm away with one compassionate comment. "Yeah, it got to me more than I wanted to admit at dinner."

He came down the steps and started toward her hut. "You wouldn't be human if it hadn't affected you. And you are very human."

She looked down at him. Her heart fluttered as she watched his half-naked body coming toward her. "What's that supposed to mean?"

He started up her steps. "That you're one of the most empathetic and naturally caring doctors I've ever worked with. You feel things more strongly than most. There's no way you wouldn't be upset about being held at knifepoint."

"Wouldn't anyone be?" How did he know so much about her when they'd only known each other such a short time?

He came to stand an arm's length. "Sure they would, but I have a feeling you were not only worried about yourself but the rest of us. Or what would happen to the local boy if you gave up the drugs. Your heart is too ten-der for this type of work."

"I thought caring was what it took to work here." She continued to watch a small stream of water flow over a large leaf and to the ground.

"Yeah, but it also makes for a great victim."

Ellen turned to face him, propping a hip against the rail. She was no victim. When her mother had died she'd proved that. "You know, there was a moment there that I thought you might be trying to cheer me up. I should have known better."

"Look, you did good today. Held it together. I don't know if anyone could have done better. How was that?"

The corner of her mouth lifted. "Better. But it lacked a ring of sincerity. By the way, I really do appreciate you saving me."

"That's what I do, save people."

Was he embarrassed by the praise? "You make it sound like it's no big deal but to them it is. And to me it was."

He bowed. "Then you're welcome. Let's just hope I don't have to do it again."

This time she had the idea that his words were to cover up his awkwardness at being thought a hero. "It would suit me just fine for it not to happen again as well."

Chance moved toward the steps. "We have another early morning so you best get to bed."

"I'm sorry if I woke you."

He looked up at her from the walk. "Not a problem. The view was well worth it."

"Uh..."

"A woman in the moonlight dressed in a sexy see-through gown is always worth being woken up for. Get some sleep. You'll need it tomorrow."

Yeah, as if she was going to sleep after that statement.

* * *

Two days later Ellen scanned the clinic area. Since the incident with the vandals, she looked over her shoulder any time she was alone. Being held at knifepoint had rattled her more than she wanted to show. She had been paralyzed by fear. No way was she going to let on how much what had happened in the van stayed with her. If she showed weakness around Chance, he would see to it that she was sent home. She was determined to stay and continue her work. Ellen was surprised to find that she'd drifted off to sleep after their conversation on her porch. He'd managed to make her think of something else besides what had happened. She wouldn't have thought that was possible. Had his last remark been to get the incident off her mind or had he meant what he'd said?

She glanced at him working at the next exam table. He was great with the patients and got along with the others in the group. Was even known to laugh on occasion. It was a wonderful full sound. He didn't treat her differently in an obvious way but she sensed something...perhaps that he was weary of her for some reason. Her assignments were almost always with Michael. That suited her. At least she didn't have to deal with Chance's moods or with her uncontrollable thirst to understand him better.

Chance never sat beside her if there was a choice of another open chair at dinner. They were never alone even if they were going to their huts at the same time. Apparently for him to approach her porch had been completely out of character. It was as if she had the plague and he was highly susceptible. Sometimes she thought about just forcing the issue and asking him what his problem was, but why should it matter? She had come to Honduras to work, not to get caught up in the great Dr. Chance Freeman's life.

And she was working. Hard. It was invigorating. The days were long but satisfying. It was as if she had been liberated from a cage. She belonged here. Her father may not like it but she wouldn't be returning to New York to work ever again.

Minutes later Karen was called to assist Michael with a patient while Ellen was still doing a wound cleaning. When she finished Karen and Michael were still involved with the patient so she was left with no choice but to help Chance.

"Ellen, would you mind calling the next patient?"

She did as he asked. A highly deformed man entered the tent with the help of a woman who Ellen guessed was his mother. The man had elephantiasis. His arms and legs were enlarged, as were areas of his head and neck. She couldn't prevent her intake of breath. The only case she'd ever seen had been in a medical textbook.

"We mustn't make him feel unwelcome," Chance said from close enough behind her that she felt the warmth of his body.

He spoke to the man in Spanish and he returned a lop-sided smile that appeared sincere.

"Ricardo is one of my regular patients."

"Hello, Ricardo," Ellen said, giving him her most genuine smile. "Nice to meet you."

Ricardo gave her the same smile he'd given Chance.

"We're going to need to get some blood work today, Ricardo." Chance said, pulling on gloves.

The man nodded and spoke but it came out as gibberish.

Ellen went to get a blood sample kit. She returned and Chance said, "Ricardo, do you mind if Ellen draws your blood?"

Ricardo nodded his head in agreement. As she pressed to find a good vein Ricardo said, "Pretty."

"Yes, she is," Chance answered as he continued to examine Ricardo.

She smiled at Ricardo. "Thank you. You are very sweet."

Even with his distorted face she could see his discomfort. This man was a gentle giant who'd been given a bad deal in life by contracting elephantiasis.

Chance finished his examination and gave Ricardo a supply of antibiotics before he left. With him gone Chance asked, "You've never seen someone with a major case of elephantiasis, have you?"

"No. I had no idea. I'm sorry I reacted poorly."

"Don't worry about it. It's hard not to."

There was that compassion she rarely saw but which pulled her to him. "What can you really do for him?"

"For right now he's getting the antibiotic diethylcarbamazine but that only really deals with the symptoms. He has lymphatic filariasis. It's from worms introduced by mosquitoes. It's common in the tropics. Ricardo is just one of many. If you stay around long enough you will see more. Ricardo's case is getting bad enough he'll need surgery to keep walking."

"Where will he go to have that?"

"I had hoped we would have a standing hospital built by now but we're still working on the funding. Right now he'll have to go to the city or hope a visiting group of orthopedists is able to come here."

"That's sad." Her heart hurt for Ricardo and the others like him. These people needed more help.

Their next patient entered and ended their conversation but the needs in the small tropical country remained on Ellen's mind. Chance was working hard to do what he could but it wasn't enough. What would happen if he didn't get the funding required and the clinic closed?

The rest of the afternoon was one more patient after another. Once again a storm built and seemed primed to dump water over them. As much as Ellen enjoyed rain, every day was a little much. Thirty minutes after the last patient was seen the clinic was dismantled and she, Karen and Peter were running for the truck as the first fat drops of water fell.

"You guys will be drenched. We're going to have to double up in the cabs," Michael yelled over the sound of thunder and wind. "Ellen, you go in the van. Karen and Peter, we'll just have to make do in the truck cab."

The rain started coming down in sheets. Ellen didn't hesitate before running to climb into the van. Marco was already in the driver's spot. Her bottom had hardly hit the seat before she was being pushed across it by Chance. His body leaned heavily against hers as he slammed the door. He moved off her but she was still sandwiched between him and Marco. The gearshift on the floor forced her legs into Chance's space. She shifted to an upright position but remained in too close contact with him.

"Maybe I should just ride in the back of the truck," she murmured.

Chance looked out the window shield. "Not in this storm. Scoot over."

"To where? I'm practically sitting in Marco's lap now." She shifted away from him but it made little difference. Her right side was sealed to his left from shoulder to knee.

Marco put the truck into gear and it launched forward. They hadn't gone far when the truck hit a bump that almost brought her down in Chance's lap. She squirmed away from him. Gritting her teeth, she did her best not to touch him any more than necessary. Her mind as well as her body were hyperaware of even his breathing. She'd be sore in the morning from her muscles being tense in her effort to put space between them.

The storm continued to rage around them as they traveled over the muddy roads. Finally, they reached the poorly maintained paved road. She was exhausted and the cab was warm and steamy. With the steady swish-swish of the wipers the only sound in the cab, Ellen's chin soon bobbed toward her chest. Sometime during the ride her head came to rest against a firm cushion.

A hand on her arm shook her. "We're home."

Ellen jerked straight. She'd been leaning against Chance's shoulder. "I'm sorry. I didn't mean to fall asleep on you."

He ignored her, reached for the door handle and said a little stiffly, "Since it's so late we won't be eating in the dining room tonight. A supper tray will be brought to your hut."

A light rain fell as she climbed down from the van. "I'm glad. I don't think I have the energy to walk up to the main building."

Karen joined them and handed Ellen her backpack. "I'm headed for a hot shower and bed."

"Me too," Ellen agreed. "I'll walk with you. Good night," she said to the group in general.

"We have another early morning tomorrow. Be here ready to go at six a.m.," Chance called after them.

Karen mumbled, "Slave driver."

Ellen giggled. "And a few other things."

Foliage dripped around them and the moon shone above as they walked along the path toward their huts.

"Chance is something else, isn't he?" Karen said with admiration in her voice.

"He's something all right," Ellen mumbled.

"Very good looking, and super smart. I can see why the women that come down here are known to get crushes on him."

Ellen huffed. "Where did you get that bit of info?"

"Michael told me."

"Well, I won't be developing one, that's for sure." Ellen pushed a strand of escaped hair out of her face. Wasn't she already headed that way? She stood in front of Karen's hut.

She'd stopped at the top of her steps and looked at Ellen. "What is it with the two of you anyway?"

"He doesn't like me for some reason."

Karen gave her a searching look. "Aren't you over-reacting?"

"I don't think so. I'm too tired to worry about what Dr. Freeman thinks of me tonight. See you in the morning." Ellen continued along the path.

"Well, you're blind if you don't see how attractive he is," Karen called after her.

Ellen was well aware of how handsome Chance was but it wasn't enough to overlook his controlling and sometimes overprotective attitude where she was concerned.

The shower water couldn't get hot enough for her. Ellen stood in it until it started to cool. She loved this shower. It was almost like she was skinny dipping. With a towel wrapped around her, she entered the back door of the hut just as a light came on in Chance's. She watched as he pulled his safari shirt off over his head and let it drop to the floor. From her vantage point she was a voyeur but she couldn't stop herself from looking.

Chance was older than any other men she had been attracted to but he still had a nice body. He flipped his belt out of the clasp then looked up. It was as if they were standing inches apart and he was reading her every thought. Heat flashed over her. She released the blind but it hadn't fallen between them before she saw a sexy grin cross his lips.

CHAPTER THREE

CHANCE LAY BACK in the lounger located in a recess surrounded by plants near the pool. Only a person who looked carefully or passed him could see him, while he had an open view of most of the water. He needed some down time, just like the others. Thank goodness Friday was the transition day for guests so this afternoon there were few around. The resort would be full for the week by the next evening.

He'd worked his staff hard over the last week. They had moved to five different areas in five days, with each day starting at four a.m. The team not only needed a break but deserved one. Michael had volunteered to show the others around Trujillo. Karen and Peter had taken him up on the suggestion but for some reason Ellen had declined to join them. Chance had paperwork to see to and a conference call to make so he'd remained behind as well. He'd not seen Ellen since that morning and assumed she was resting in her hut.

In the short time since the three new staff members had arrived, their clinic team had turned into a cohesive group that worked well together. Ellen had assisted him some but mostly he'd stationed her with Michael or given her triage duty. She and Michael had become regular buddies. When there weren't patients to see, they had lunch together, laughing over something that had happened. It reminded him too much of Alissa and his ex-colleague Jim.

Even Marco and his crew gave Ellen special attention. She shared her sunshine with everyone but him. It wasn't that she wasn't civil, it was just that he didn't receive the same warmth. The times she had worked with him they had said little outside the need-to-know arena. He shouldn't have cared but he felt left out. When she'd first arrived he'd wanted it that way but now he wasn't so sure. The more he was around her the more he admired her. She wasn't the pampered princess he'd wanted to believe she was.

Ellen was an excellent doctor. When she was working triage she recorded what was wrong and had everyone in order of need so that no time was wasted between patients. Maybe it was time to let her start handling patients on her own. They could see three times more patients if he did.

After the excruciating return ride to the resort, when she'd fallen asleep against him, and later, when he'd caught her watching him undress, he'd renewed his vow to stay clear of her as much as possible. He'd be lying if he said he hadn't enjoyed the feel of a soft body against him. But wouldn't he have reacted the same to any female contact?

There wasn't much opportunity for a sex life around here but when he'd found companionship he'd been discreet about it. After his wife had left he'd been the favorite subject of discussion and he hadn't enjoyed it. He preferred his private life to remain just that—private. A few times in Honduras he'd met a woman of interest and when he'd return to the States he had a few ladies he regularly stayed in contact with, so he had hardly been celibate. Still, there was something about Ellen that made his hormones stand up and take notice whenever she was near, as if he had been a monk and left the order.

If the ride home hadn't been painful enough, the fact that she'd been watching him undress while wearing nothing but a towel had made him even more sexually aware. Every time they were alone it was like she was teasing him, daring him to come closer. He was confident this was something she did unconsciously yet it was still there, pulling him to her. As his body heated with need he imagined stepping across the short space between their huts and taking her in his arms. That would have shown her not to be poking the bear. Instead, she'd let the blind down, shutting him out.

He understood that feeling. In this case, he was glad she had. Even a short moment of pleasure would turn into a bad idea in the long run. Despite how she might act about work here, she wasn't the type to stay with him. No woman was. His life was in Honduras. She would never be satisfied with him or living here for the long run. He wasn't her prince charming.

Chance opened one eye to a slit at the soft pad of feet along the bricks around the pool. Ellen stood there in a blue bikini, preparing to dive. He shifted uncomfortably in the chair as his body reacted to all the beautiful skin on display. Her hair was down around her shoulders. The woman was going to be his undoing. He'd been played for a fool before and if he wasn't careful he would give Ellen the opportunity to do the same again.

With a perfect arch, she dove into the pool and surfaced. As she swam to one end and back, he was fascinated by each smooth movement she made. What he wouldn't do to be the water flowing around her. He had to get some control but that wasn't going to happen right now. On her next pass he stood. Hopefully his baggy swim trunks would disguise most of his body's reaction to her.

A yelp of surprise came from her when he stepped into her view.

"Hey." He watched as all that long blonde hair swirled around her on the surface of the water.

"Hi. I didn't see you sitting there."

He stepped closer. "I thought you would've gone to town with the others."

"I thought about it. But I hate to admit that after the pace we've kept this week I needed a little extra rest. I can be a tourist on our next day off."

"Do you like being a tourist?"

"I do. I love to see new places. See how others live." She held on to the edge of the pool.

Her position gave him a tantalizing view of her breasts scantly covered in triangles of dark blue that reminded him of a sky just before a storm. "So what do you think of Honduras?"

"I like it. The people are wonderful. Every day is exciting."

"Some days, too much so." Like the day she had almost been stabbed. It still sent fear though him when he thought about it.

Ellen pushed away and floated toward the other side of the pool. Chance took a seat on the edge, letting his feet dangle in the water.

"So why aren't you off doing something exciting on your day off? Surely you get away from work sometimes," she asked.

"Not as much as I would like." He enjoyed watching her tread water. She had managed to put as much space as possible between them. For that he was grateful. He was far to attracted to her. "When I get a couple of days I like to spend them scuba diving. Hiking in the jungle."

She moved closer. "I would love to learn to scuba dive. My father said no when I was a kid. Never took the time to learn after I started college. And hiking? After all the lectures you've given me about safety, you hike in the jungle?"

"I stay on the touristy trails. More than one person has gotten into trouble, venturing off too far."

"Michael offered to take me to see a waterfall one day." With a kick, she swam away from him again.

"I wouldn't get too attached to Michael if I were you." Chance didn't like how that sounded. Like a jealous middle-schooler. "Hey, I shouldn't have said that. It's none of my business what you two do after hours."

She headed for deeper water. "I'm pretty sure Michael flirts with every woman in his age group who comes down here. I don't take anything he says seriously."

That's what his wife had said when he'd questioned her about her relationship with Jim. Still, coming from Ellen he wanted to believe her.

"Anyway, I'm down here to work, not play around." She started toward the shallow end.

"But it's always nice to have a friend."

Could they be friends? He wasn't so sure. This attraction would also be vibrating between them.

"Well, I think I'll get a nap in before dinner. See you later." Ellen took the steps out of the pool, giving him a tantalizing view of her backside that included a sexy swing of her hips.

Chance slipped into the water and began making strong, sure laps until he was exhausted.

Ellen paused in the doorway of the restaurant. Maybe she'd just eat in the main dining area tonight. She'd given thought to having her meal brought to her hut but she wasn't going stay in such a beautiful place and hole up in her room.

She'd made it halfway to the private dining room when her name was called. She recognized that voice.

Chance sat at a table overlooking a bubbling water fixture among ferns. A candle flickered in the lantern on the table. "We have to eat out here tonight. Not enough of us to prepare the extra room for. You're welcome to join me but I'm almost done."

She looked around the area at all the empty tables. Hating to cause any of the staff more work, she still wasn't sure she wanted to eat a meal with Chance in such a romantic setting. Maybe she should order her food then make an excuse to carry it back to her hut. "Okay."

Chance half stood as she took her seat cross from him.

After feeling vulnerable at the pool in nothing but her swimsuit, she wasn't sure she could handle more time between the two of them. Every nerve in her body had been aware of Chance watching her leave the pool. It had been exciting and terrifying at the same time.

Apparently she was worrying for no reason. Chance ate and shuffled papers he had spread out on the table without paying any notice to her. She finally asked, "So what are all these?"

"Med invoice forms. I'm expecting a shipment any day." He didn't look at her.

"You do work all the time."

He glanced up. "Someone has to do the paperwork."

"Can't someone else do that?"

He made an exaggerated scan of the room. "You see someone else volunteering?"

"I'll be glad to. It wouldn't hurt you to accept help sometimes."

He put down the paper he had been reviewing. "Do you always say what you're thinking?"

"Not always." She certainly didn't where her father was concerned and kept some of her thoughts about him to herself.

A waiter showed up with her meal. They fell into silence as they both ate. For some reason she didn't even think to ask to take her meal to the room. "You know, I could help with those. I'm a pretty good organizer. Maybe I can set up a system that'll make it easier for you."

"Don't you get enough work during the day not to want more?"

She shrugged. "I want to help. That's what I'm here for."

He looked at her. "And why is that? Here in Honduras?"

"Because of you." She wanted that passion and conviction she'd heard in his voice in her life.

"That's right, you said. Where was the fund-raiser?"

"In New York about six months ago." She'd spent the next few months trying to convince her father that her life's calling was in Honduras. He'd spent the time fighting the idea.

"That long ago."

"Yeah, it took me awhile but I made it."

Chance looked at her instead of the papers. "Why not sooner?"

"Well, mostly because of my father."

Chance lifted his chin in question. The man had a way of getting people to talk to him. He was practicing that bedside manner she'd seen him use on his patients. It was powerful when turned on someone. She was that person now. The feeling that if he turned up the charm she couldn't resist him anything filled her. Caution was what she needed to use.

"I'm an only child with an overprotective father. Make that way overprotective."

"I guess if I had a beautiful daughter and she wanted to come down here to work I'd be concerned also."

He'd said she was beautiful. Other men had but for some reason she especially liked hearing it from Chance.

"I love my father but after my mother died he just couldn't stand the thought of losing me too. He seemed to think that making all the decisions in my life was the answer to keeping me safe."

"He wouldn't be pleased to know what happened the other day, would he?"

"No, he wouldn't, and I don't plan to tell him. It would only worry him. He already thinks I take too many risks."

"Risks?"

"Yeah, like going into medicine, working in an inner-city clinic, or like coming down here."

"Then I'd better see that you get home safe."

Anger shot though her. "That's not your job. I can take care of myself. I don't need someone else watching over me."

"Whoa." He held up a hand. "I stepped on a tender spot. Sorry." He went back to looking at his papers.

Taking a deep breath, she focused on her meal again. She watched the candle flicker and listened to the tinkle of water in the fountain then glanced at Chance. He was a handsome man. One of those who drew a woman's attention naturally. There was an aura about him that just made her want to know him better. But what she didn't need was someone caging her after she'd finally found her freedom.

Done with her meal, she asked, "Of all the places in the world, why did you decide to start a clinic in Honduras?"

Chance looked up. "I came here to do summer work with one of my professors while in med school."

"That was it. You decided to start the Traveling Clinic?"

"Yeah, something like that. I saw the hardship and wanted to work here."

Something about his tone made her think there was more to it than that. "So you decided to make it your life's work."

"It sort of evolved into it." He took a bite of the fruit they'd been served for dessert.

"How's that?"

Chance put his fork down. "You're full of questions."

"No more than you were."

"Okay, so I had high hopes that I could make life better for the Hondurans. Make a real difference. But that, like everything else, costs money. Each year that has been harder to come by."

"So when you made fun of me for trying to save the world you weren't any different your first time in Honduras."

A sheepish look came over his face. "Yeah, I know that stars-in-the-eyes look. I've had it and seen it hundreds of times. I've also seen people go home defeated by the amount of need here."

"Is that why you're so tough on me, because you don't want me to be discouraged?"

He crossed his arms on the table. "I just want you to understand what you're getting into. This isn't a fairy-tale world."

"What makes you think I need that?"

"Look at you. Your polished nails. You don't belong here. This isn't a place for you."

She leaned toward him. "Who gave you such a narrow view of women and their abilities?"

"That would be my ex-wife, who came down here and stayed a few months before she left me for my colleague."

By the tone of his voice he was still terribly bitter. She couldn't keep the amazement in her voice from showing. "You were married?"

"Don't sound so surprised. Even I can make a mistake."

"Mistake? That's a sad view of marriage."

"But honest. Enough on that subject." Chance returned to the papers at his fingertips.

He had been hurt, deeply. Did he judge all women by his ex-wife's behavior? Even her? Maybe that's why he treated her so unfairly. A few minutes later, she pushed back from the table. "Thank you for the stimulating company but I think I'll call it an evening."

To her disbelief Chance gathered his work, stood and stuffed the forms in his back pocket. "I'll walk back with you."

She didn't question his motives; instead, she said thank you to the waiter and headed for the door. Chance caught up with her and they walked out of the main building.

She needed to apologize for spying on him but she couldn't bring herself to say anything. They continued walking.

At her hut Ellen said, "Uh, about the other night, the window and all. I'm sorry."

"Don't be. I was flattered."

She shifted from one foot to the other, not meeting his eyes. "Still, I shouldn't have been invading your privacy. It won't happen again."

"That's a shame. I found it flattering."

"Why am I not surprised?" Where she had been embarrassed now she was indigent. He was enjoying her discomfort.

"What man doesn't appreciate a lovely woman admiring him?"

"My, you have an ego."

He grinned. "I'm just teasing you."

"Since when do you tease?"

"Maybe I'm finding a new side to my life."

"Could another one be you getting over your issues with me?"

Suddenly the current of awareness between them went up three notches. The air almost sparked. He stepped into her personal space. "Sweetheart—" the word was more growl than endearment "—I don't think so. I have too many where you are concerned. The main one is wanting you."

Her heart quickened. She'd not anticipated that declaration. In fact, by the way he'd treated her she hadn't been sure he even liked her. Chance stepped closer. She refused to back away. His head lowered and an arm went around her waist. He drew her against him. His mouth found hers and she forgot to think. She hung on for dear life. It wasn't a simple meeting of lips. Too many emotions roiled in her and flowed between them. The kiss was a mixture of shock, amazement, taking, giving, and abrupt release.

Without a word Chance left her staring after him as he stalked off past his hut and up the path.

On weak legs Ellen slowly climbed the steps to her porch. What had brought that on?

For days he'd treated her as if she was an interloper in his world. Out of nowhere he'd kissed her like there was no tomorrow.

Then he'd abruptly let her go. Why? What had suddenly turned him against her? There had been something real between them and just as quickly he'd broken the connection as if it was something he wanted no part of. Her arms went around her waist and she squeezed. Being pushed away hurt.

She knew what she had been thinking. No one had kissed her like that in her life. The electric ripple had rolled through her, making her ultra-aware of her body and his. She'd come close to marrying other men who had never had that effect on her. What if she had never known those brief moments of passion with Chance?

How far would she have allowed Chance to go? By her reaction to his kiss, too far. She bit her lower lip. Even now her lips still tingled.

But could she afford to act on her feelings again? Coming to Honduras had been her way of finding her place in the world. A space she chose and to make hers. Not one that her father oversaw or controlled. Did she want to get involved in something that might hurt her chances of staying here?

It really wasn't an issue. Chance had walked way.

Chance hesitated at the bottom step to Ellen's hut. He had no choice but to knock on her door. Never having been an indecisive person, he couldn't understand why this time it was so difficult to do something so simple. Maybe because he was afraid she'd chew him out for the abrupt way he'd grabbed her, kissed her and walked off. He deserved her disdain even if he had done the right thing. Now he had a larger issue. A shipment of drugs was coming in and he needed to meet the plane. She'd offered to help with the paperwork and this was one of the times he needed her.

Needed her. Unfortunately, that seemed to be happening on a number of levels.

He prided himself on facing problems head on but the thought of approaching Ellen so soon after their kiss had him feeling uneasy. The kiss they'd shared had rattled his nerves and his convictions. He wanted more than a kiss and that shook him to the core. She shouldn't interest him, shouldn't affect him in any way, but she did, far too much. He'd spent the night vacillating between berating himself and wanting to crawl into Ellen's bed. The latter he wasn't going to do under any circumstances. He had to stop whatever was happening before it got out of hand.

He wouldn't kiss her again.

For him, controlling his emotions had been a lifetime thing. He done it when his mother had left, when his father had sent him to boarding school, separating him and his sister, and yet again when the headmaster had stated frankly he would never amount to anything. He would do so again where Ellen was concerned. It was necessary if he didn't want to lose his sanity, or, worse, hurt her.

She was a good doctor and he was as well. They were in Honduras to help people and that was what they would do. Their relationship would remain professional. He wasn't some teen whose body ruled his brain or some lovestruck young man who went after the first beautiful woman he'd seen in a while. As a mature man he could handle any fascination he might feel for her, especially a woman he wasn't sure he liked.

Chance gave the door a sharp, solid tap. There was no response. His knuckles rapped against the wood once more.

"Coming." The word had a groggy sound.

Ellen opened the slatted door and stood on the other side of the screen door.

"Did I oversleep?" Panic filled her voice.

Her mass of hair fell in disarray around her face. The temptation to open the door, take her in his arms and walk her backwards to the bed almost got the better of his control. How much was a man supposed to take? Chance sucked in a breath.

"No. Were you serious about helping with the paperwork?" He sounded gruff and formal even to his own ears.

She blinked twice. "Yes."

"Then I need you to come with me. We have a shipment. I want to show you how to handle it and what's involved." He was already making his way down the steps again.

"Okay. Give me ten minutes."

"I'll get us something to eat and meet you at the truck." He didn't wait for her to answer before heading along the path.

As good as her word, which he was coming to learn was ingrained in Ellen's makeup, she showed up at the Jeep dressed and ready to go right on time. He'd never known a woman as attractive as she who could be dressed on such short notice. His ex-wife would have certainly balked at his request, expecting at least an hour to prepare herself to go out in public, even in the wee hours of the morning.

Ellen climbed into the seat beside him and he handed her a cup of juice and a banana. "Breakfast of champions."

"Or the crazy," she mumbled.

Chance grinned. He found she had that effect on him more often than most. There was never a dull moment around Ellen. He was learning to like it. Putting the Jeep in gear, he headed toward the road that would take them to the nearby airstrip.

Ellen yawned. "Why so early? It's three a.m."

"This is when a plane was available to bring supplies in. We use volunteers and have to work around their schedule. This plane was making another delivery and just added us as an extra stop."

"Oh. You couldn't have told me about this last night? I would have been ready."

"I didn't know for sure and I had other things on my mind." Like kissing you, holding you, taking you to bed.

A soft sound of realization came from her side of the cabin.

"Uh, Ellen, about that kiss. Look, I'm sorry, I shouldn't have done that. You didn't come down here to have an affair and I certainly don't make it a habit of taking advantage of young women. It won't happen again." Out of the corner of his eye he saw her shift towards him in the seat.

"For starters, I'm old enough to take care of myself and I make my own choices about who I kiss, not you."

"But I took advantage of the situation…"

He felt her glare. "Chance, just shut up and drive."

Half an hour later they had reached the airfield. Marco and a couple of the others were helping set out lanterns along a dirt runway.

"This looks a little illegal to me," Ellen said as they waited on the plane circling the field.

"It would be by American standards but by Honduran ones it's the only way to get the drugs safely into our hands." Chance pointed toward a car sitting near the tree line. "That's one of the officials. We'll give him the papers, a little cash and he'll sign off on them."

"So it is illegal?"

"No, we just have to get our shipments in a less orthodox method so that we don't draw the drug traffickers' attention. This way we're not robbed on the road. Marco, Ricardo and Perez will ride as an armed escort back to the resort just to be sure."

"Is this how it's handled every time?" Ellen sounded excited by the whole idea.

"Pretty much, but we change up meeting points and times. Nothing's the same twice."

"Interesting. I kind of like this cloak-and-dagger stuff."

Chance grinned. He could see her as a femme fatale. "Rest assured, it's necessary and not something to take lightly."

The plane's wheels touched the runway, throwing up dust.

"Do you ever see the humor in something or do you always take everything seriously?"

"When it comes to my work it's serious."

And unfortunately where you are concerned it is serious as well.

Chance stepped on the gas and raced after the plane. They needed to have it unload and gone before anyone took notice. He pulled to a stop beside the plane. Thrusting some papers into Ellen's hand, he said, "As I call out the meds, you mark them off the list."

"Got it."

By the time he had the first box in his hands and was placing it in the trunk, Ellen was standing at the hood with a penlight in her mouth and the papers spread across it.

"Do you have a pen?"

"No."

She dug through her bag a second. "Never mind. I've got something."

"Amoxicillin."

"Okay," she called.

"Penicillin."

There was a pause. "Got it."

The government representative stood beside her as Chance named the medicine labeled on each of the boxes. The man didn't ask to see inside any of them. When it came time for him to sign the government form, Chance slipped him some bills and he went away smiling. The price of doing business. The process went on for another fifteen minutes.

Chance looked at Marco and his crew. "Okay, guys, are you ready to go?"

"*Sí.* We behind you."

Chance climbed into the Jeep. Ellen was already there, holding a paper by the corner as she flapped it. "What're you doing?"

"Making sure it's dry."

The paper must have sucked up moisture from the night air. Chance breathed a sigh of relief that they were loaded and headed back to the resort. He was always on edge when waiting in the open. Drug traffickers were everywhere and as far as he and they were concerned his cargo was gold. The antibiotics were not the most valuable of drugs for resale but they certainly were important to the work of the clinic.

He glanced at Ellen. She'd gathered the forms firmly in her hands. He started the Jeep and they were soon turning into the resort entrance and driving round to the staff parking lot. Chance pulled into a slot next to the van. He waved at Marco as he turned in behind them then back out again on his way home.

"Marco isn't staying?"

"No, we're safe here. Now we need to get these

counted and stored." Chance opened the back end of the van.

"How can I help?"

How like Ellen not to complain and join in. "As I bring you the boxes, open them, count the contents and store them in the lockbox."

"Will do."

Over the next half hour they worked together, getting the medicine into place. Ellen did everything he asked. With all the boxes in the van, he joined her inside it as well. Being in the tight area with her made him even more aware of his desire. Working shoulder to shoulder, with hands brushing on occasion, he questioned his judgment at having Ellen help him over asking Karen.

He'd chosen Ellen because she had offered and seemed good at this type of work. The other part of his reasoning had been to see how she reacted to the clandestine operation that was sometimes necessary. He was pleased, she'd come through like a champ.

With the medicine stored, Chance climbed out of the van and offered his hand to Ellen. She hesitated a second before she placed hers in his then jumped the short distance to the ground.

To his disappointment she let go of his hand. "Bedtime."

She yawned. "Past it."

"Tomorrow's clinic is in a village not far away. You and I will sleep in. The others will go ahead and we'll catch up with them before midmorning."

She pulled her bag out of the Jeep. "I can go earlier if I'm needed."

"No, you need your rest."

"But—"

What was the problem? The idea that she'd have to

ride out with him? Or she wanted to spend time with Michael? "No buts. Be here at nine ready to go."

"Okay, but before I go I need to ask you a question." It had been worrying her all night. Ellen had to get some kind of answer for his behavior in front of her hut.

He stopped and turned. She moved toward him. Looking him straight in the eyes, she asked, "Why did you kiss me?"

A stillness came over Chance then he wiped his hand over his face. "Let's not get into it again. I've already apologized. It won't happen again."

"You didn't answer my question." Ellen refused to back down until he gave a reason. She said softly, "Why?"

"What do you want me to say? Because I wanted to more than anything in the world."

Did he mean that? Joy swelled in her chest. She stepped closer. "If that's the truth, why not?"

"Come on, Ellen, this isn't a good idea."

"Probably not. But I still want to know." She continued to study his face in the dim light.

"Look, you deserve more than I can or am willing to give."

"I don't remember asking for anything. And if I was, you don't get to decide that for me. My father has done that all my life and I don't need you taking his place. I choose what I want." Since when did he think she wasn't capable of making her own decisions?

"The most that can be between us is an affair. You don't want that. Go to bed, Ellen. Forget about what happened."

"Just for the record, I asked about a kiss, you are the one that brought up an affair. Good night, Chance."

That would give him something to think about. She took the path leading to their huts.

* * *

After a few hours of sleep, which were not refreshing by any standard, Ellen was sitting in the truck, waiting for Chance. She'd decided after their discussion that she would do her job, be as much help as she could be to the clinic, and stay out of Chance's way. He'd made it clear where he stood regarding her and she would respect that. That was just as well for her, she didn't need to get involved with someone who thought they knew all the answers where her life was concerned.

Chance walked up looking as if he hadn't fared any better since they'd parted than she had. His hat was crammed on his head and his aviator sunglasses were in place.

"Good morning," she offered.

Chance climbed into the driver's seat. "Mornin'."

"It came around pretty quickly."

A grin covered his lips. The one she didn't see often. "Nights like last night remind me I'm not as young as I used to be."

"I can understand that," Ellen mumbled as he started the Jeep and pulled out of the lot.

She looked at Chance's large, capable hands on the steering wheel and then moved her eyes up to his face to settle on his mouth. She like his full lips that remained far too serious far too often. As he slowed, her attention went to his strong thigh muscles flexing and contracting as he pressed the gas pedal after shifting gears.

He intrigued her, made her want to know more about him, figure out what made him react to her as he did. It wasn't just his kisses, his air of authority but his devotion to the people he was trying to help that fascinated her. Yet the hurt from the night before wasn't easy to let go of. There was still an ache behind her heart. No one liked being rejected, especially when they were told it was for their own good.

Ellen peeled an orange that she had taken from the bowl in her hut. Breakfast had been delivered without her request. It was her guess that Chance had seen to it. "Want some?"

"No, thank you."

"You sure?" She offered a couple of slices, holding them out. "I bet you didn't eat much for breakfast."

After shifting gear again, he reached out and took the slices from her.

A shiver of warmth went through her. All it took was one innocent touch and her heart rate jumped. If she was going to keep her promise to herself, she would have to get a handle on her reaction to Chance.

Ellen pulled a slice off the orange and popped it into her mouth, making an effort not to let it show how rattled she was. What she needed to do was focus on something else. "Tell me what you need done to get the paperwork in order."

"I have to see that everything is turned in on time and in order to the foundation as well as to the government representative. I need help doing what we did last night and an inventory of supplies done regularly. I also need shipments set up. Have papers in order for customs."

For the next few minutes Chance continued to list different areas where he needed assistance.

"Where's the paperwork right now?" Ellen threw the orange peel out of the window.

"Most of it is on a table in my hut."

He was a control freak? Did he think he could do everything? "Have you been seeing to it since the clinic opened?"

"Pretty much, but lately it has been more difficult.

The foundation is now required to submit items it didn't have to in the past. I have to admit I hate doing it as well."

"But you didn't plan to ask for help, did you?"

He glanced at her. "I let you help last night, didn't I?"

Chance had, but she had a feeling that was a rarity. She suspected she should feel honored.

By the time she and Chance arrived at the clinic area there was a line of people waiting.

"I should have come on with the others," Ellen said as she hopped out of the car. "So many waiting."

"It doesn't do them any good if you're so tired that you don't know what you're doing. They'll be seen. We won't leave until we do." Chance grabbed his to-go bag off the backseat.

He sounded like he knew from experience what bone tired meant. As if he'd been there before.

"I just hate the never-ending need here."

A weary look came over Chance's face. "I know what you mean. I often wonder if we'll ever make headway."

The statement was like a thump to her chest. She would've never thought she'd hear that discouraged tone from Chance. The great man who had stood at the podium and proudly shared the work being done in Honduras on behalf of the people. The work the clinic was doing. His voice made him seem demoralized. As if he could give up the effort. Didn't he see that just being here, his caring was making a real difference in these people's lives? Marco and his crew were better off just by the pay.

She walked beside him. "But it's worth it. We do make a difference. I see it in every place we go."

"Yeah, but it doesn't appear any different when we return. These people need local permanent clinics."

Was he just tired? She'd never heard him talk like this. "Then why do you keep on doing it?"

"Because no one else is. Where would these people go for help if the clinic wasn't here? Where would I go?"

A cloud of sadness settled around her. Why did he think he had no other place to go? What had happened to him? Where was his family?

Ellen followed Chance into the tent where the clinic was already in full swing. He took his spot at a table where Karen was prepping a patient for an exam. Peter was doing triage. Ellen joined Michael and went to work.

In the middle of the afternoon a mother brought in a baby who had a cleft palate. He was thin but had bright eyes. Not only his looks suffered from his mouth deformity but his ability to eat had as well. Ellen's heart went out to the child like it had to no other. The mother also had a three-year-old with her.

Michael lifted the older child onto the table. As he did the mother watched intently. Michael examined the boy and then said to the mother, "You'll need to clean this area."

The baby in her arms began to squirm.

"May I hold him?" Ellen asked.

The mother looked unsure but she handed the boy to Ellen.

She looked into the baby's face. With the right funding and the right people, how many children with cleft palates could be given a better life? Maybe she could get some support from her father and his contacts. Her fear was that in return his demand would be that she return to New York.

Michael said to her, "Chance will see the baby. He handles all the cleft palates."

* * *

Chance looked up when Michael called his name.

"Can you see this little boy now or do you want them to wait?" Michael asked.

"I'll be ready for him in a second."

He looked at Ellen, who was speaking baby talk to the child. She was absorbed in the child's happy but distorted sounds. Motherhood would suit her. She would make a good wife to someone. The idea left a sour taste in his mouth.

His voice was gruff when he said, "Ellen, bring him here and let me have a look."

She did as he asked.

"Hold him while I check him out." Chance pulled his stethoscope from around his neck and put the earpieces in place. He leaned close, placing the disk on the child's chest. The soft smell filled his nostrils. *Ellen*. Would her scent always remind him of flowers? She'd stopped wearing perfume after he'd explained it wasn't a good idea but still he would know her aroma anywhere.

Chance glanced up to find her watching him. They were so close he could see the black flecks in her blue eyes. He had to count the baby's heartbeats twice. Returning his attention to the child's chest didn't help matters. One of Ellen's breasts, covered in a tight T-shirt, was only inches from his hand. He dreamed of touching. Just once...

He closed his eyes and opened them again. Only by focusing on a tree outside the tent door was he able to record the child's respirations accurately the first time. The fascination with Ellen had to stop. Someone was going to notice. Worse, he was going to act on his desires.

The boy baby looked well cared for but thin. He would need surgery to continue to grow, for his teeth to form correctly and for him not to develop ear problems. Chance had just finished his examination when the mother, along with the older child, joined him and Ellen.

"Please continue to hold the boy," he said to Ellen. She smiled and nodded, appearing glad to do so. "I need to take some pictures." He then spoke to the mother, telling her he could help the child but that he would need surgery. That he wanted to take some pictures of the boy's mouth for the doctors.

The mother gave her agreement but she continued to look concerned.

"Ellen, I need you to hold him in front of you so I can get some pictures from different angles. Just stand where you are and try to keep him happy."

"That's not a problem. He's precious."

Chance hurried to the van and brought back the high-resolution camera then began taking pictures. The boy remained happily in Ellen's arms.

He wasn't surprised people were content around her. If it wasn't for the fact he was fighting his attraction to her all the time, he'd feel the same way around her.

Minutes later Chance had all the pictures he needed. "Ellen, get Marco to help you get all the information you can about names and where she lives so that we can contact her when the team comes down here. Marco knows what to do."

"Okay." She placed a kiss on the child's cheek and handed the boy back to his mother.

Despite the pretty picture, Chance was aware of the price of becoming too emotionally involved. Ellen would get hurt if she rushed in and opened her heart too freely.

He made sure that didn't happen to him.

Fifteen minutes later Ellen returned. He was between

patients. "We got all the information you requested," she said.

"Good. The plastic surgery team should be here the week after next. We'll put the boy on the list. They'll have a full week of surgery."

"He's a cute little thing." She looked out the clinic door wistfully. "It's a shame he has to go through surgery."

"I could tell you liked him."

"How can you not?"

"Be careful, Ellen. Your bleeding heart is showing. Don't get too attached. You'll get hurt."

"You keep telling me that." She gave him a direct look. "Yeah, maybe. But if you never get attached you might miss out on something wonderful."

Pete asked her for some help and she left him. Chance had the idea that her remark had more to do with what was happening between them than dealing with their patients. He had closed himself off. Had meant to. How many times could he get kicked in the teeth and still survive? It had already happened twice. If he became involved with Ellen it would occur again. He was confident her kick would be the hardest of them all. He wouldn't give her up easily, but give her up he would.

CHAPTER FOUR

THE STAFF ATE supper together that night. Afterwards Ellen and Karen took a walk around the resort before heading for their huts. When Karen had said good-night and left, Ellen glanced at Chance's place. A light was on inside. She shrugged. Tonight would be as good a time as any to tackle those reports he was concerned about. Maybe he had time now to show her what needed doing.

A roll of thunder from the west arrived just as a soft rain began to fall. Ellen climbed the steps of Chance's hut. The main door was open. She knocked, at the same time looking through the screen.

"You looking for me?" The low rumble came from the hammock hanging near the edge of the porch.

Startled, she turned. "Are you spying on me again?"

"Hey, you're the one on my porch, looking into my hut."

The hammock swung slowly as he spoke. She stepped toward him, close enough to look down at him. Chance was stretched out with his hands behind his head and his legs crossed, wearing a T-shirt and cargo shorts. He appeared more relaxed than she'd ever seen him. Chance carried a heavy burden with all he did to make the clinic function. He deserved his down time.

"I came over to see if you wanted me to look at that

paperwork but I can see you're taking some time for yourself. We can do it tomorrow."

A streak of lightning flashed in the darkening sky seconds before thunder hit. Ellen yelped, jumped, and grabbed the rope supporting the end of the hammock where Chance's head lay. It swung. She tipped forward and down on top of him.

Strong arms circled her waist. "There's nothing to be afraid of."

With her palms she pushed against his chest. "I'm sorry. I didn't mean to fall on you."

Lightning flashed again. She shuddered.

"Don't worry, I have you."

There was security in those words. She looked into his eyes and found compassion there.

"It'll pass soon."

She relaxed into him. Found sanctuary. "Thanks. I've not been too fond of lightning since I was a child."

Chance continued to hold her but his body remained tense as if he was trying not to get too close, even though they were touching from shoulder to toes.

The lightning eased. She looked at him. "I think I'm good now. If you'll give me a little push, I can get off you."

Instead of doing as she requested, his lips found hers and her world exploded with pleasure. The hammock drifted to the side as he brought her up alongside him. She entwined her legs with his. He wore shorts and her bare legs brushed against his rougher ones. She stifled a moan.

Chance's hand slid down to cup her butt then squeezed it, lifting her against him. The knit tank top sundress she wore rode up her legs. He ran a hand along the back of a thigh, setting her skin tingling. She flexed into him.

The evidence of his desire stood long and ridged between them.

Ellen didn't question why Chance was kissing her after he'd made it clear earlier he didn't want her. She didn't care. He wanted her now. That was what mattered.

Chance's tongue demanded entrance and she gladly offered it. Her center throbbed. She was crazy for this man, had been since she'd heard him speak so passionately about the people he cared about. Even then she'd been half in love with him.

Vaguely aware of the rain falling around them as if curtaining them from the outside world, her hands shook as they pushed upward over his T-shirt and circled his neck, letting her fingers curl into his hair. His scalp was warm.

Chance's mouth left hers to nuzzle behind her ear. His fingers found her leg and the edge of her panties. Tracing the elastic, he teased her. His other hand splayed across her back, holding her close.

Ellen rolled her head to the side, giving Chance better access to her neck. He whispered, "Sweet, sweet El."

She slipped a hand under the hem of his shirt and found warm skin waiting there. His muscles rippled as her fingers brushed over them on her way around his waist to his back. It was heaven to touch Chance, to have him near.

His lips traveled over the line of her jaw and back to her mouth. He placed small hungry kisses on her mouth before he captured her lips completely in a hot kiss, full of need and question.

Ellen squeezed his neck and gripped his back, squirming against him.

"Woman, you're killing me."

"Good." Her lips found his and took command.

Abruptly Chance rolled forward, causing her to slide behind him, her face buried between his shoulder blades. The thump of steps on the boards of the porch stopped her complaint.

"Chance, I need to see you about your plans for the surgery team." At Michael's words Ellen went stone still.

"I'll meet you up by the reception area," Chance said.

"It'll just take a minute." Michael said.

Ellen grinned against Chance's back and brushed a fingertip over his waist. His hand captured hers and squeezed, holding it in place. Her body shook with a giggle.

Chance said tightly, "I'll see you up front."

There was silence for a second, then an "Oh…" from Michael. He added, with humor wrapping the word, "Gotcha."

As the sound of his footsteps disappeared, Ellen kissed the back of Chance's neck and ran her hands around his waist beneath his shirt. She snickered. "We almost got caught."

Chance's swung his feet to the floor and stood. He turned and offered her a hand. "I think you should go."

Really! She could kick Michael for showing up. Finally Chance was letting her in, showing his true feelings, and Michael barged in. Maybe she had been stepping over an edge that would end up hurting her but it would have been a wonderful trip down. Chance's touch sent her body into awareness overdrive.

As soon as Michael had left, Chance had turned cold. What was he afraid of? She wouldn't let him walk away as if nothing had happened. This time she wasn't going to stand for it.

Putting her hand in his, she let Chance pull her to a standing position. As soon as she had, he let her go and stepped back. She glared at him as she straightened her dress, then stepped close enough that her chest came into contact with his. His eyes widened but he didn't move. How much humiliation could she take?

"Dr. Freeman, I don't know what you're playing at but I'm tired of it. We're both adults. I'm old enough to know what I want and to be responsible for my decisions. I've made it clear I want you. I know you want me too. You made that obvious minutes ago. So give it a rest. It's not me you are protecting, it's yourself."

He said nothing but his jaw muscle jumped. She'd made her point. Shaking all over, she said, "I'll be going now."

Had he been gut punched? Chance stood there looking at the spot where Ellen had stood. He hadn't planned on what had happened. The second she'd fallen into his arms he'd been unable to let her go. If Michael hadn't walked up Chance had no doubt where it would have ended. His bed. Every fiber in his being wished it had.

Ellen was angry. She should be. He deserved every word she'd said. She felt used. What had he been thinking? That's just it, he didn't think around her. He'd wanted her to stay away. After tonight it looked like she would without him saying it again. Why didn't that make him feel better?

She been right about him protecting himself. He was afraid of her. Ellen had the capability of taking his heart and crushing it.

Inhaling a few deep breaths, he headed to the lobby area to meet Michael.

He was sprawled in a chair, flipping through a magazine as if he wasn't really interested in the material. When Chance approached, he sprang out of the chair with a wide grin on his face. "Sorry, man, I didn't mean to break something up. I had no idea."

Chance didn't want to talk about what had happened between him and Ellen. His nerves were too raw. The need still too intense. "What do you need to know?"

"Oh, yeah, yeah. You're in a hurry to get back to Ellen."

Michael had seen her. Chance had tried his best to protect her. What was or wasn't between them, he wanted it to remain theirs alone.

Michael was saying, "I think it's great and about time. Ellen's crazy about you. I've tried to get something going but she'll have none of it. But you, she can't seem to keep her eyes off. Even when we're working she knows where you are all the time."

She did? Chance hadn't been aware. Maybe he hadn't wanted to. Regardless, he didn't want to discuss Ellen with Michael. "What did you need from me?"

Michael looked at him a second then said, "I need the list of patients and their diagnoses to fax to the surgery team ASAP."

"I need to double-check the info. Can I get them to you first thing in the morning?"

Michael grinned. "I'm sure that'll be soon enough."

"Good. See you then." Chance started back toward his hut.

A few minutes later he shuffled through the papers on his desk, the same ones that Ellen had come over to work on before he had distracted her. He looked at the drug list from a few nights before. Beside each drug there was a pink dot. What the hell?

That damn fingernail polish. The same that had covered her nails as she'd raked them over his skin just a few minutes earlier. And the ones he wished were still pulling him close.

He had to figure out a way around this obsession with Ellen. All he need to do was endure a few more weeks and she would be gone. The bigger question would be how would he survive after that?

Despite Ellen's anger with Chance, she was still basking in the glow of his kisses days later. She didn't like it but couldn't seem to do anything about it.

What would have happened if Michael hadn't interrupted them? Would Chance have forgotten all the opposition he'd put up against her and taken her to bed? Would she have let him? Could she have resisted?

Even now she wished she could be alone with him again. But she had no intention of allowing that. She wanted someone who trusted her to make her own decisions.

She looked at him sitting at the head of the table as if he were the patriarch of a family. Forking another piece of the succulent fruit off her dinner plate, she scanned the table. The staff was sitting down together for the first time in over a week. She relished it when they ate in their dining area, almost like they were a family. It had been just her father and her for so long that she enjoyed a meal with the large, boisterous group.

Chance tapped his fork against his glass. "Okay, listen up. Here's the plan for the next couple of days."

Everyone quieted.

"We'll be going to two outlying villages that are farther away from here than we normally go. Because of this, we'll have more armed guards than usual. Security will be extra-tight. We'll be in drug-trafficker country.

They shouldn't bother us unless we give them a reason. And we'll be making every effort not to do that."

Ellen's newfound freedom shook a little. They were going to spend the night in the jungle? This was more than she'd expected when she'd decided to come to Honduras. She looked at Chance again. Everything was more than she'd expected.

"Is there a problem, Ellen?"

"No, sir."

His eyes narrowed at the use of *sir*. "You're welcome to stay here if you're not comfortable." His blue gaze bored into her. Daring her.

Was he trying get her to stay here? "No. I'm good. I wouldn't miss it."

His look moved to Peter and then Karen. They both nodded.

"Good. There has been some trouble with the local traders and we need to be very careful about every move we make. Don't ask any questions of the patients that aren't medical." He looked at her. "Don't leave the clinic area unescorted for any reason. My priority is everyone's safety. Take no chances. Pack for a two-night stay. Enjoy the comforts of home tonight because we'll be sleeping in the trucks or on the ground for the next couple of nights. Any questions?"

Ellen listened as the others talked and made comments about the plans. She couldn't decide if she was excited or terrified. Either way, this was the type of work she'd come to Honduras to do and she would do it without complaint.

"Pack light but be sure to have your long pants and long-sleeved shirts, hat and boots. Don't forget the bug spray and sunscreen." He looked at her. "This won't be a picnic. So be prepared."

He acted as if she had been complaining. Not once, to her knowledge, had she not risen to expectations. If she hadn't been sure she could do it she hadn't let on and had forged ahead. She was tired of trying to prove herself to him.

The next day consisted of a long drive into the interior of the country. Ellen had been told by Michael that the people they would be seeing had only seen a doctor a few times. She was looking forward to helping them.

She'd kept her distance from Chance whenever she could. Disgusted with him for not facing the fact that he cared for her, she was also furious at herself for letting it matter. She was slowly accepting he was right. If they had a relationship and it went bad, she didn't think she could continue to work here. She would have to look elsewhere for a clinic. But would she like the country and the people as much as she loved this one? It would be better if they just remained professionals. But could she face Chance every day without her feelings showing?

They arrived at the village where they were to work by midafternoon. Before they had finished setting up people were waiting. Again, Ellen worked primarily with Michael, only occasionally swapping to help Chance. At those times they were almost too formal in their interactions. A couple of times the others gave them strange looks or knowing smiles. Would it be worse if they were together?

As the day ended, Marco and his men set up a food table. There were double the number of helpers, with two of them stationed on the perimeter of the area with rifles. Folding chairs were placed at the table so that everyone could sit in comfort to eat.

Growing up in New York City, Ellen hadn't had a

chance to do any real camping. She'd attended summer camp but there had been beds with mattresses and running water. This was going to be rough camping and she was rather looking forward to the new adventure after the initial shock. The most interesting aspect so far was the tent structure with covered sides that had been set up as a bathroom area.

While they were eating Chance announced, "Ladies, you may have first turn in the bathroom. You'll find your sleeping bags in the back of the truck. Don't forget to pull the mosquito netting over you when you go to sleep. Marco's men will be keeping watch tonight. Don't get up and wander around. Get some sleep. We'll start early tomorrow."

Ellen and Karen headed straight to the bathing area after dinner. They were allowed nothing more than a sponge bath but that was better than nothing. They changed into clean work clothes, which they would sleep in. Ellen left her bra off for ease of sleeping and planned to slip it on before anyone noticed in the morning. When she and Karen stepped out of the tent the men were already lined up, waiting to get in. Ellen pulled her towel up against her chest to cover the fact she was braless.

Chance was at the end of the line but she didn't met his gaze as she passed him.

There was a lantern burning in the truck and her and Karen's sleeping bags were already rolled out on the benches across from each other, their nets hanging from the side rails of the truck.

"I've always loved camping out," Karen said as she slipped into her bag.

"This is a first for me."

"Really? And no complaints. I like that about you. Always a good sport."

"Thanks. I wish others thought that." Ellen helped Karen adjust her net around her.

Karen lay back. "You really have a thing for Chance."

"I've sure tried not to." Ellen opened her bag.

"I've worked with many doctors but I've never seen one more dedicated than Chance. Sometimes people can't see past their job."

"I think most of it has to do with him thinking he needs to protect me."

Karen harrumphed then murmured, "It's more like the fact he has the hots for you that's bothering him."

He might but Chance had made it clear he wasn't going to act on them.

Ellen settled into her bag, turned the lantern down and pulled the net around her. Lying back, she looked up at the stars. This was an amazing country. Even with the poverty, need and sometimes danger she'd be happy to live here forever.

Sometime during the night Ellen woke, needing to go to the restroom. After debating having to get out of the sleeping bag, climb down out of the truck and walk across the camping area to the bathroom tent, she decided she had no choice. Using her penlight and moving as quietly as possible, she made her way there.

She was returning to the truck when a figure loomed near her. A hand touched her arm. She jerked away.

"Shush. You'll wake the whole camp." Chance stood close enough that she could feel his breath against her cheek. "What're you doing out here, wandering around? I've told you it isn't safe."

Ellen clenched her teeth. "I had to go to the restroom. Why should it matter to you anyway? You've made it clear you don't care about me."

Chance's fingers wrapped around her forearm and he

pulled her behind the clinic tent, putting it between them and where the rest of the group slept. His arms crushed her against him and he growled, "You make me crazy. And the problem isn't that I don't want you but that I do." His mouth found hers.

Despite everything her brain told her about him hurting her again, her body told her to take what she could. She dropped her light and her hands clutched his waist. His tongue caressed the interior of her mouth and she join in the sweet battle. One of Chance's hands slipped under her shirt and slid over her ribs to cup her breast.

He groaned.

A flash of awareness went through her. Her flesh tingled. Reveled in Chance's touch. He took her nipple between two fingers and gently tugged.

Her womb contracted.

"Sweetheart," he murmured against her lips. He pushed the shirt higher. The moist night air touched her skin seconds before Chance leaned her over his arm. She held on as his wet, warm mouth covered her nipple and sucked. His tongue circled and teased her. Blood flowed hot and heavy to her center, feeding the throbbing there.

She moaned. Chance stood her up and his mouth covered hers. His hands went to her hips and brought them against his. With a hand behind his neck, she held his lips to hers.

"Mr. Chance, I heard a noise." Marco stood nearby.

Chance continued to hold her close as he said over his shoulder, "Everything is fine. Miss Ellen got lost. I'll see her back."

"*Sí.*" By the tone of Marco's answer he saw through that lie.

With Marco gone, Chance tugged Ellen's shirt back

into place. "Let's get you back to bed. We'll talk about this later."

Ellen's heart flew. At least this time he wasn't walking away mad, apologizing or denying that there was something between them.

He picked up her penlight then took her elbow, guiding her around the tent toward the truck. There he gave her a quick kiss and brushed her already sensitive breast with the knuckle of his index finger before he handed her the light and walked off into the darkness.

On shaky legs, Ellen climbed into the truck and into her sleeping bag. Her heart thumped as if she had been running and her center burned as she relived every second of the last few minutes before she finally drifted into a dream of Chance doing it all again.

Had he lost his mind? Chance walked the few paces to his tent. Ellen was driving him beyond reason. He'd always been a sensible adult, one who thought before he acted, yet when he was around Ellen he came unglued. She brushed against him and all he could think of was kissing her, having her. It had become worse when he'd discovered her bare breast. Heaven help him. He'd almost taken her behind the clinic tent. Worse, he still wanted to.

He had to get Ellen out of his system.

Chance slapped at his pants leg in frustration. They were both adults. She had more than proved that with her warm welcome when he'd kissed her. So why couldn't they have a short and satisfying affair while she was here? He would make it clear there would be no ties when the time came for her to leave.

Maybe it was time to stop protecting her. If he didn't do something soon, he wouldn't be able to concentrate on his work. One thing he did know was that he would not be able to push her away any longer. No matter the reason, he wanted her beyond sanity. He would have her.

Come morning, he assigned Ellen to work with Michael as usual. If he'd assigned her to assist him after all this time the others would notice, especially Michael. He wasn't ready to answer questions about his feelings for Ellen.

Throughout the day he would meet Ellen's gaze and she would smile. Once they grabbed for a bandage at the same time. Their hands touched. By his body's reaction he was reverting back to his youth. When they stopped for lunch he sat under a banana tree to eat and watched as Ellen and Karen walked to the truck that doubled as their bedroom. Even Ellen's walk had him turned on.

Michael squatted on his heels beside him. He looked off toward the two women as well. With humor hanging on each word, he said, "I never thought I would have seen it. The untouchable Chance Freeman has fallen hard."

Chance cut his eyes to him. "What does that mean?"

"You have it bad for Ellen."

"You're crazy." Chance picked up a tiny stick and threw it.

"So it's okay if I go after her?"

"You already said she wasn't interested."

"I haven't given her the full court press," Michael said with a smile.

"Leave it alone, Michael," Chance growled.

"Then I suggest you do something about it." Michael looked at the women again.

"You know, it's none of your damn business." Chance didn't need pushing toward something he had every intention of taking care of himself.

Michael chuckled. "No, I guess it isn't but it's nice to

see the cool, calm and collected Dr. Freeman squirm." His grin grew larger. "I'll see that the clinic is ready for this afternoon around two."

Michael had been a friend for a number of years and had often listened into the early morning hours to Chance's sad story of his poor choices where women were concerned. More than once they had handled issues having to do with the clinic together. If Michael wasn't such a friend, he would've never gotten away with those remarks about Ellen.

The afternoon work went every bit as well as the morning had. It was dusk when a couple of gunshots rang out in the distance.

"What's that?" Karen asked in alarm.

Michael, appearing unconcerned, continued to store equipment. "Drug dealers most likely. We've been lucky we haven't heard more shots."

Fifteen minutes later Chance stepped out of the clinic to see a boy of about twelve run into the clearing and stop. He gave the area a wide-eyed look as if searching for something. Ellen slowly approached him from the direction of the truck. She spoke to him.

Chance hurried toward them. As usual she wasn't considering the danger. The boy could be luring her into the jungle. Kidnappings happened often for ransom in this area. She didn't have to step beyond the clearing but a few paces before she wouldn't be seen. Not wanting to spook the boy, Chance slowed as he joined them.

As he came closer the boy said something about his father being shot and asking for her to come help. Chance's heart rate jumped. That had to have been the shots they'd heard. The boy's father must be working with the drug traffickers or had crossed their path.

"Must come," the boy cried. He stepped forward with his hand out as if he were going to take Ellen's.

Chance stepped closer to Ellen and told the child, "You'll need to bring him here."

"Can't. He no walk," the boy said as he looked back toward the opening in the foliage he'd just come out of. "Hurry. Lots blood."

"Then have someone carry him here." Chance made it a firm statement.

The boy looked around as if expecting someone to pop out of the jungle. "No one help. Afraid."

Chance shook his head. "Then I'm sorry."

Ellen gave him a pleading look. "Chance, we have to help."

"My first concern is the staff of this clinic, their safety. Leaving this area would not be safe. The drug traffickers have free rein. We don't even know the boy is telling the truth."

"He die. Please." The boy looked from Ellen to Chance and back again, tears forming in his eyes. "It not far. Promise."

"We have to help him," Ellen begged.

Chance was torn. If it was true he wanted to give the help. But what if it was a trap?

Ellen grabbed his arm and squeezed as she looked at him.

"How far?" Chance asked the boy.

He said a village name Chance wasn't familiar with.

By this time Marco had joined them. Chance looked at him, "How far?"

"Ten-minute walk," Marco said.

"Okay, I'll get supplies and you get my to-go bag." Ellen left before he could say more.

"Should be safe. I send Ricco with you." Marco waved Ricco over.

"Tell me what happened to your father and what part of his body has been hurt," Chance said in rapid Spanish to the boy. Heaven help them if they ran into trouble. He'd let his better judgment be overshadowed by Ellen's beautiful eyes. That unrestricted, forge-forward determination might get them all into trouble. Yet he felt the pull to go as well. There was a patient who needed his help regardless of the danger.

Ellen hurried into the clinic tent and snatched up Chance's bag then headed for the supply van. At first she'd been angry with him for hesitating to help the boy's father. As far as she was concerned, if a person was hurt you had to do whatever was needed to take care of them. Chance's hardline stance didn't impress her. As he spoke more to the boy she saw the sympathy in his eyes. It wasn't that Chance didn't want to go, it was more that he was responsible for everyone and couldn't make snap decisions. The fact they were going showed that Chance really did care.

Grabbing suture kits, she stuffed them in his bag. She took a couple of bottles of saline out of a storage basket. Finding a spare backpack by the shelf, Ellen dropped the bottles in. She added additional supplies that from her experience might be needed.

Chance entered the van. "I need to get some antibiotics. The boy says his father was shot in the leg."

Ellen stood, letting Chance come behind her. Their bodies bumped in the close quarters. Minutes later, they had what they thought they might need. She left the van first, with him right behind.

"Hand me that backpack," he ordered.

"I can carry it." Ellen offered him his to-go bag instead.

Chance glared at her. "You're not going. Ricco and I will handle this."

"Ricco has medical experience now? How's he supposed to handle a gun at the same time he's helping you? I'm going." Ellen watched his mouth form a tight line. He wasn't going to agree.

"Peter or Karen—"

Ellen huffed. "Karen couldn't keep up the pace and Peter is needed here. We can stand around and argue about this while a man is dying or we can get going." She turned to leave the tent.

He grabbed her under the arm, jerking her round to face him. "You can go *only if* you agree to follow my orders to the letter. No arguments. No going rogue. Either you agree or you stay here. This is still my clinic and my call."

She glared at him and said through her teeth, "I promise to do as you say."

Chance searched her face. "Okay, let's go take care of this patient."

Ellen had no doubt that he didn't like the idea of her going but he recognized he clearly needed her help. She adjusted the pack on her back as he slung the strap of his bag across his chest. At a lope he crossed the clearing and Ellen followed close behind.

"You ready?" Chance asked Ricco, who nodded. "Ellen, I want you between Ricco and me."

She moved into position.

To the boy Chance said, "Take us to your father."

The boy dipped his head under a large leaf and moved into the jungle. Chance followed with Ellen and seconds behind her Ricco. The path was little more than a foot wide. She wouldn't have even said there was one if she hadn't been behind Chance. As they walked he held leaves and vines back. She accepted them and did the same for Ricco.

"Stay close and don't speak unless necessary," Chance hissed over his shoulder.

Underfoot was dark packed dirt crisscrossed with roots. Her boots were so new they didn't make the best hiking wear. A couple of times she caught a toe on a root but righted herself before she tripped. Once Ricco caught her arm before she fell.

Another time Chance stopped and she bumped into his back. He cautiously looked around. The boy was standing a few feet in front of him, looking down the path. They waited then moved forward at a slower pace. Finally, they broke out of the jungle into an open space next to a creek with five small huts. The roofs were pieces of tin or plastic tarps peaked just enough for rain to roll off. The walls were little more than uneven boards wired together to form a square. The boy led them through knee-high grass to one of the stacks closest to the water.

He stepped through an opening into a hut that had no door. Chance and she followed. Ricco stayed on guard outside. The sun was almost over the horizon, making it dark inside. The boy told a woman there that he had brought the doctors.

Ellen could make out someone lying on an old mattress on the dirt floor across the room. Chance was already stepping that way and Ellen joined him.

"We have to have some light here." He sounded exasperated as he went down on his knees to speak to the barely conscious man.

Ellen pulled off the backpack, opened it and removed a flashlight. Clicking it on, she held it over Chance's head.

He glanced up. "Well done, Ellen. I should have known you'd consider the details."

She couldn't help but be pleased with his praise.

"Can you point the light toward the left some?"

Ellen did as he requested. From her vantage point she could see the dark-skinned man was maybe thirty, dressed in a torn shirt with baggy shorts. One leg of the pants was pulled high on his leg. Below that on his thigh were two dirty rags covered in blood. Even if they could help him, fighting infection would be the larger battle.

"Look at this," Chance said with revulsion in his words.

She understood his feelings. "Two shots. He really needs to be in a hospital."

"Agreed, but that would be in a perfect world and this isn't one. Nearest hospital is too far away and he would never make it, even if he would allow us to take him."

Ellen leaned closer for a better look. "He's lost a lot of blood. He needs a transfusion."

"I'm O. Have you ever done a transfusion outside a hospital?"

"No."

"Then I'll set that up and you can take care of the wounds while I'm giving blood. Ever removed a bullet?"

She gave him a wry smile. "I saw it done during emergency rotation."

"Can you handle it?"

"Sure I can. So if I understand this right, you're going to lie around while I do all the work?"

"Funny lady." Chance reached for his pack.

She came down on her knees beside him.

Chance called to the boy to come and hold the flashlight and asked the woman to get them some hot water. He then prepared a syringe of antibiotic and injected it into the man's arm. "It'll be too little, too late, but it's better than nothing."

Ellen could identify with his frustration. She pulled the saline bottles out of the backpack as Chance removed supplies from his bag. Slipping on gloves, she lifted the bandage off the upper hole in the man's leg. It was still oozing. She opened up some four-by-fours and placed them over it, then gave the same attention to the other one. As Ellen worked Chance was busy setting up an IV line. With efficiency and precision that she admired, he'd already inserted the needle into the man's arm.

Chance spoke to the boy again and he dashed out the door. The woman arrived with the water. Ellen continued to clean around the first wound. The boy returned with a wooden chair that had seen better days and a lantern. Chance placed the chair close to the mattress. Ellen took the lantern, situating it so she could get the most out of its light.

"I'm ready for you to finish this IV," Chance said.

"Let me change gloves." Ellen stripped off the ones she'd been wearing and pulled on clean ones. She moved close to Chance. Taking his arm under hers, she held his steady and began pressing on the bend in his elbow for a good vein. She was close enough to catch the natural scent of him.

"You know, you really are beautiful."

She glanced up then down again. "You're not already light-headed, are you?" With a firm, steady push she inserted the large IV needle into his arm. "Hand me one of those tape strips."

"No, just speaking the truth." He handed her a strip from the ones he'd placed on the backpack. "This isn't your first stick. Nicely done."

"Thank you. Yes, I've done a few in my time." She looked him straight in the eyes. "But I'm always open to a first time in other areas." His eyes widened slightly before he started pumping his fist and blood flowed to their patient.

"You'd better get busy on those holes or you'll be wasting my blood."

"I'm on it." She removed her gloves and replaced them with clean ones again. "I'll have them taken care of and get back to you in a minute."

Ellen carefully cleaned around the surface of the first wound. She was going to have to remove the bullet and not damage the nearby artery while doing it. Even in the best of situations that would still have a degree of difficulty. Under these conditions that was upped a hundred times. Ellen counted on her skill to save this man, if not her experience.

Locating large tweezers, she cleaned the blood away and went after the bullet. She pursed her lips tightly as she continued to search. Finding the bullet, she grabbed it and pulled it out. The wound bled anew. She dropped the bullet to the floor and snatched some four-by-fours and placed them over the hole.

"Nice job, Doctor."

"Thanks, but I have to stop this bleeding. Could you apply pressure while I get the sutures ready?"

"Sure. Now I'm assisting you."

She glanced at him. "Problem with that?"

"Not at all." After she'd helped him pull on a glove, he put two fingers in the center of the pads.

Minutes later Ellen had the wound sutured closed. She checked on Chance as she worked. She didn't need him passing out. He seemed comfortable. The entire time she worked she was conscious of him watching her.

As she applied the final piece of tape to the bandage Chance said, "You handled yourself well, Dr. Cox."

"Thank you. How're you doing?" She took the patient's vital signs. He was stable, but barely.

"I think I'm about at the end of my giving. Head's a little light."

"Well, let me try to stand and I'll see about you." She pushed up but her knees were stiff and didn't want to move.

"Give me your hand and I'll pull."

She took his hand. It was a struggle but she finally made it to her feet.

"Walk around a minute and get some feeling back into your legs."

Ellen took his suggestion and made a couple of circles around the shack.

Returning to Chance, she removed the needle and applied a pressure bandage. "Now, sit there for a while. I don't need two patients. I'll have to admit this is out of my usual wheelhouse. Even in a clinic in the middle of New York City, what we have done here is over the top."

"If it makes you feel any better, this is a little extreme for me as well."

"Thanks for that. I thought you might remind me again that I shouldn't be here."

"I only acted that way because I was afraid that you had bitten off more than you could chew. These conditions are harsh."

What he didn't say was that today was an example of that. She had a patient waiting and couldn't worry about that now. Going down on her knees again, she started caring for the last bullet wound. With the lower one, the bullet had gone clean through. Working as efficiently as

possible with the few supplies as she had left, she closed
the wounds Done, she started cleaning up.

In all the medical work she had ever done she'd never
felt better or more confident about herself than she did at
this moment. This work was what she had been born for.

She looked at him. "We're not all the hothouse flowers you think we are."

"I know that now. You've more than proved it." Chance
looked around the shack. "It seems we're here for the
night. We need to keep an eye on him." He nodded toward the injured man.

Ellen placed a hand on their patient's head. "Infection
is our enemy now. And you don't need to do any activity
for a while either."

Chance looked in the direction of the woman and boy,
who waited in the corner in what was nothing more than
a makeshift kitchen. There was a small table and a bench
with a shelf above it. A bucket sat on the bench. Chance
spoke to the boy, "Can you find us something to sleep
on? A blanket for your father? Something to eat?"

"Si." The boy left and the woman went out the door
behind him.

Chance stood and walked to the doorway. Ellen joined
him. Chance spoke to Ricco. He nodded and move to
the corner of the building, his gun at the ready. She and
Chance continued to stand there. The night sounds were
almost overwhelming as animals as well as bugs communicated.

"This is an amazing country," Ellen said. "I know why
you keep coming back."

"It is."

She looked at him. "You love it here, don't you?"

"If I said I didn't, you would call me a liar."

Ellen smiled. "That I would."

The boy returned carrying a rolled-up tarp. They followed him inside. He placed it on the floor. "Sleep." He pointed to it.

Chance chuckled. "All the comforts of home."

"Better than the dirt." Ellen sat on it with her legs crossed.

"Do you ever see the negative in anything?" Chance asked, taking the chair again.

"Sometimes but it's better to see the positive because the negative is usually far too obvious."

The woman came in holding two banana leaves. She handed one to her and the other to Chance. Ellen had never seen anything like it.

"Pulled pork and vegetables. It's cooked in the ground. You'll like it." Chance picked up a bite between his thumb and forefinger and put it in his mouth.

Ellen wasn't so eager. She looked at it more closely in the dim light then moved it around with a tip of a finger.

"This is the first time I've seen you squeamish about something. You need to eat."

"I'm just not sure about this. I usually have my food on a plate."

Chance chuckled. "Just pretend that you're at a baseball game and you're having a hotdog."

"My father has box seats for the Mets and a cook comes in."

Chance's fingers stopped halfway to his mouth. "Just who is your father?"

"Robert Cox." Even in the low light she could see Chance's eyes widen.

"As in Cox Media."

"Yes. That's my father's company."

"So why in the hell are you down here? You don't need the money or even to work."

She glowered at him. "I'm a doctor because I want to help people. And today shows that I'm needed. Even by you." In a show of defiance, she picked up a finger full of food and plopped it into her mouth. "That's good."

The boy came in again, this time with two bottled drinks. He gave them each one.

Chance said, "No matter how far out of civilization you get, soda companies are there. Thank goodness. We don't need to drink the water."

Ellen finished off her meal and stood. "Let me have those." Chance handed her his leaf and bottle. "I'll put this away and then check the patient. You need to sleep. Work on building new blood cells."

"Yes, ma'am."

"No argument?" Ellen looked at him.

"Nope."

"We really have gone into a different world." She placed the stuff she held on the bench then stepped over to her patient. He seemed comfortable enough. There was a low fever but that was expected. "We'll need to get him out of here and to a hospital tomorrow."

"Agreed," Chance said as he lay out on the tarp. "Come on, you need some rest as much as I do."

Ellen stretched out beside him, leaving as much space as possible between them. She put her arm under her head, trying to get comfortable.

"Come over here," Chance said. "You can use my shoulder for a pillow."

The tarp made a crinkling sound as she shifted closer. She laid her head on his broad shoulder. He moved his arm around her and his hand settled on her waist.

In a sleepy voice he said, "I've dreamed of sleeping with you but never in a shack in the middle of the jungle."

Ellen rolled toward him and her arm went across his waist. She didn't care where it was, just that she was near him.

CHAPTER FIVE

CHANCE ROSE A couple of times during the night to check on their patient. Each time Ellen curled into the warm spot he had left. When he returned she moaned her appreciation as he took her into his arms again. That kind of treatment he could get used to.

He looked out the doorway at the full moon. It was well after midnight. Their patient had spiked a fever. After giving him another dose of antibiotics, Chance used a four-by-four to bathe his head. Under these conditions there wasn't much more he could do. He joined Ellen again.

"How's he doing?" she murmured.

"Fever's down. Go back to sleep."

"Next time I'll get up."

He pulled her close again. "Deal."

The sky was still more dark than light when Chance was shaken awake. "Must go," the boy said in a low urgent whisper. "Now."

Chance was instantly alert.

The boy was already picking up Chance's to-go bag and putting things in it. "Bad men come. Must hide."

Chance stood and helped Ellen to her feet.

"They find you, they kill you." The boy didn't slow down.

His statement propelled Chance into action. "Ellen,

make sure we have everything picked up that might indicate who we are. Leave nothing behind." He grabbed her backpack and finished putting their things, even the paper covers, into the pack. Done, he zippered it up.

"What's going on?" Ellen looked around as if unsure what to do first.

"Drug traffickers. They're looking for our patient over there. If they find us they'll kill me and ransom you. If you're lucky."

"What about our patient?" She started toward the man.

"We've done all we can for him. Now we have to take care of ourselves." He thrust the backpack at her. "Put it on. Do exactly as I say. No more questions." He took his pack from the boy and pulled the strap over his shoulder. "Let's go."

"Ricco?" she asked.

The boy went to the door and stopped. "He leave when the men come close. Hide. Then warn doctors." The boy waved them on. Instead of heading across the grassy field, the boy led them to the edge of the jungle. There he went into a squat. Chance followed suit and pulled Ellen down beside him. The boy searched the area.

There was a stillness in the air as if nature was waiting for something to happen. No birds chattered in the trees or monkeys swung from limb to limb. Seconds later voices broke the silence. The boy put his finger across his mouth. They waited, waited. The sounds came no closer.

The boy, followed by Ellen and then Chance ran stooped over around the edge of the field for a time until they ducked into the foliage near a large banyan tree. At almost a run they headed down a path that was harder to follow than the one they had been on the day before. They had been moving at a fast pace for about ten minutes when Ellen tripped and went down on her hands. Chance grabbed her by the waist and pulled her to her feet.

"Are you all right?" he whispered close to her ear.

She nodded.

Chance looked at the boy, who had paused. He waved them forward.

"We have to move." Chance took Ellen's hand and started after the boy.

As they ran Chance tried to push the leaves back so they wouldn't slap Ellen in the face but wasn't always successful. She kept up despite the difference in their size and the fact she was wearing chunky boots. A few minutes later the boy pulled to a stop and squatted on his heels.

Ellen took a seat on a large root. Strands of hair hung around her face. Her cheeks were bright red. Her deep breathing filled the air along with his and the boy's.

Standing, the boy said quietly, "I must go to my father. You follow path to river, then go down river to Saba." The boy headed up the path the way they had come.

"He's leaving us?" Ellen whispered in disbelief.

"Yes. He'll be missed and we'll be in more danger."

"Won't they know we have been there when they see his father?"

"Maybe they won't look that closely or hopefully they don't even check the shack." Chance offered her his hand and she took it. "We need to put as much distance between us and them as we can."

He hurried down the path but not at a run and Ellen kept pace with him. As they went the birds started to call at each other and the animals scurried off. At least the jungle was accepting them. If the traffickers were close and they heard no noise they would know where he and Ellen were.

They had been walking for about an hour when Chance stopped and led Ellen off the path. Stepping through the vegetation about ten feet, he found a large fig tree that would give them plenty of cover.

"Why're we stopping?"

"You need to rest." He looked around. "Hell, I need to rest. Take a seat."

Ellen pulled off her pack and dropped it to the ground. Satisfied that they were out of sight of the path, Chance joined her on the ground.

"Any way you have some food in that bag?"

He grinned. "As a matter of fact I do. Two or three breakfast bars."

"That's what I love, a man who's prepared for a quick run through the jungle."

Chance chuckled and started searching though his bag. No one was prepared for this situation but he didn't want to scare her by saying that. He pulled out a bar. Tearing it open, he handed her half of it. "It's more like a man who has had to go a day without a meal."

"Do you know where we are?"

This was a conversation he wasn't looking forward to having. It would go one of two ways: she would panic or she would take it in her stride. So far Ellen had been a good sport but this was more than they both had bargained for when he'd agreed to go help the boy's father. "Three days is my best guess if we don't run into trouble."

"Three days!" Her voice rose. Birds squawked and flew away.

"Shush, we don't know who else is nearby."

Ellen's brows grew together and she looked around with concern. "Sorry."

"Just be careful from now on. We have to walk and it

won't be an easy one. Even following the river, we have to circle any villages we come to. We don't know who we can trust."

"We really are in a mess. I'm sorry I insisted that we help the father." She took a bite of the bar. "Now I've put us in danger."

"It didn't take much for me to agree. Let's not worry about it. We need to make plans. First, we have to conserve what food we have. Which consists of two and a half bars. We'll need water." He was now talking more to himself than her.

"We have the two saline bottles. We can fill them up at the river."

"No, we mustn't drink the water unless we have no other choice. The chance of getting a parasite is too great. We'll collect rain water. We'll just have to make do until it rains." Thankfully it did that almost daily.

By the deflated look on Ellen's face he suspected she was thirsty now but she didn't say anything.

"Do you have any idea where we are?"

"Some but we're far deeper in-country and north than I've ever been." Maybe he shouldn't be quite so truthful with her but he couldn't bring himself to lie either. He finished his half of the bar and put the paper in his bag. "We'd better get going."

They both stood. He gave her a hand signal to stay and stepped out to check the path then waved her to join him. Chance offered his hand. Ellen took it. She trusted him to get them out of this. He just hoped he'd earned her faith.

Ellen realized she was in over her head this time. She'd done what her had father worried would happen. Taken a risk. It was starting to take a great deal of effort to contain her fear. The pace Chance set had her feet aching and her body sweating. By the time the rush of the river could be heard the sun was high in the sky.

Her mouth was desert dry and her clothes stuck to her skin. She couldn't remember being more miserable but she refused to say anything or ask to slow down. There was no way she would be responsible for putting them in more danger. She'd already placed them in enough.

Chance stopped. "Stay here. I'll be right back."

She nodded but didn't like the idea of being left. By the sound of the water the river was around the next bend. Surely Chance wouldn't be gone long. When he was no longer in sight panic pushed its way into her chest. She looked up the path from the direction they had come. Then back to where Chance had gone. What if something happened to him and she was left out here alone? What if he got hurt and needed her? What if those men found him? Why didn't he hurry?

With a flow of relief that had to equal the river in size, she saw Chance coming back.

When he joined her again he gave her a searching look. "You okay? Hear something?"

She gave him a weak smile. "I'm fine. Everything is fine."

"That might be stretching the truth. River's right ahead. There's a path running beside it. We'll use it but we'll have to be careful not to run into anyone."

"You lead, I follow."

"When we get down a way we'll stop and cool off for a while."

"Gives me something to look forward to."

Chance started down the path. "I'll give you this, Ellen Cox, you're a trouper."

The path widened and she walked beside him. "You

might want to save that praise until you see how I do over the next few of days."

He took her hand and squeezed it. "We'll make it."

Ellen couldn't contain the "Aw" that came out at the sight of the river. It was breathtaking. The water flowing over the white rounded boulders whooshed and boiled as it made its way to the coast. The contrast of the vivid vegetation framing it and the blue of the sky above made for a perfect picture. If it hadn't been for the situation they were in she would have sworn she was in paradise.

Chance let go of her hand and stood beside her. "It's just one of the many things I love about this country, the beauty."

They started moving again. "Still, you've had a hard time dealing with all the needs you see and keeping the hospital going."

"I have to admit that the struggle to retain staff, find funding and most of all making a real difference here has started to eat away at me."

It was the first time she'd heard him really share his feelings about anything personal. "So your plan was to discourage help when it shows up?"

As they walked along the path beside the river he pointed down, "Watch the rocks. We don't need a twisted ankle to deal with."

A couple of minutes went by as they maneuvered over a narrow, difficult area. Back on a wider section, Ellen said, "You didn't answer my question."

"I don't discourage people from coming. In fact, I encourage them. We need the help down here."

"I didn't get that kind of welcome."

"Only because you reminded me of my ex-wife at first, then because you didn't. I wasn't sure you could handle this type of work. I was concerned for your safety. Still am." He took her hand and helped her down over a slippery area.

It was nice to have someone care but she was a survivor. She'd learned that when her mother had died and during those days in the hospital. "But there's more to it."

It took him a second to answer. "I was attracted to you and I didn't want to be."

"Why's that such a bad thing?"

"Because I have nothing real to offer you."

Before she could get him to clarify that statement he said, "Here's a good place to rest." The river slowed and created a pool. "I'll keep watch while you clean up. Just be sure not to swallow any water despite how temping it might be."

Ellen crouched beside the river. She must look a fright. Cupping her hands, she splashed water onto her face. She did it again, rubbing her hands down her cheeks, and was amazed at the dirt that came off. The water felt wonderful. Cool and refreshing. Cupping another handful of liquid, she ran her hand along the back of her neck. Now, if she could just have a drink.

She sat on a rock and started working with her bootlace. "I'm going to take my boots off and cool off my feet for a second."

"No. Don't." Chance's tone was sharp. "You won't be able to get them back on because your feet will be so swollen. Hopefully, we'll be somewhere tonight where you can remove them."

Ellen started re-lacing her boot. So much for the pleasure of having water run over her throbbing feet. Done, she stood. "Your turn."

Chance stepped to the river and began cleaning himself. As she expected, he poured and splashed the water into his hair. He slung his head back. His hair curled and dripped around the collar of his safari shirt. In an odd way he belonged to the wild uncertain world around them.

While he was doing that she checked up and down the path. Pulling her band from her hair, she let it fall then gathered it again, working to get all the loose strands back under control.

The shrill call of a bird had her jerking around to search the area behind them. She looked back at Chance. He was on guard as well.

Stepping away from the river, he picked up his bag and came to her. "Come on, we're both tired and jumpy. We need to rest. Get out of the heat. We'll start again in an hour or so." He pushed leaves of rhododendron the size of a man and vines out of the away, putting distance between them and the path. They soon came to a banyan tree.

"This should do. We have cover here." He bent over and weaved his way between the roots that grew almost head high in abundance around the tree.

Ellen followed.

Chance put his satchel on the ground, lay down and used the bag as a pillow. Ellen took the space beside him, doing the same with her backpack. After they were settled and still, the birds started talking again. She looked up into the tree, catching glimpses of sky through the thick canopy.

"Chance," she whispered.

"Mmm?"

"Tell me about your ex."

He rolled his head toward her and opened one eye. "Why do you want to know about her?"

There was a hint of pain in his voice. She must have destroyed him.

"Because I think she is part of the reason why you've been trying to stop anything from happening between us."

Chance looked away. She wasn't sure if his eyes were closed or if he was staring off into the distance.

He took a deep breath and let it out slowly. "I met her at a fund-raiser. She was all about looks, which worked because she had them. In spades. Blonde, blue-eyed, leggy."

Ellen's lips tightened. *Like her.*

"I fell for her right away. She liked the good things in life and she was more than glad to hitch a ride with me. What she didn't bargain on was living in Honduras. She came from a middle-class background where they camped on vacation and didn't have the comforts of high living so I thought she would do fine down here, especially staying at the resort. It didn't take her long to start complaining about the heat, the bugs, the rain and most of all having to spend the day by herself. She wanted nothing to do with the clinic. There wasn't enough to do and she was lonely."

Ellen could hear the disgust and disappointment in his voice.

"One of my buddies from med school came down to work for six weeks. She had been so unhappy that when she started spending time with Jim and smiling again I was glad. Suddenly she wanted to come out with us and help at the clinic. I thought it was a good idea. The more she saw maybe the more she'd want to help. Yeah, right. It turned out they were having an affair. He was from an old Boston family with the name and money to please her. When he left, she went with him." The last he all but spit out.

"I'm sorry that happened to you."

"It was a long time ago. I've moved on."

Ellen had never known a person more in denial. "You do know I'm nothing like her?"

"Yeah, I figured that out pretty quickly." There was a contrite note in his voice. "I was tough on you there at first."

"You think?"

He smiled slightly.

"So those question and comments about Michael and me was you being jealous?"

"I wouldn't say that."

She leaned over him and looked into his eyes. "I would."

Their gazes held for a long time before he said, "Lie back, Dr. Cox, and get some rest. You're going to need it."

Ellen did as he asked with a grin on her face. He cared far more than he let on. Could she have a relationship with Chance and still maintain the freedom she'd fought so hard to gain? From what she'd learned about him, he had a strong need to protect. Could she handle that?

The sounds of the birds as they took flight from the top of the trees woke her. Chance rolled over her and put a finger to her lips. His body remained rigid and still. Seconds later the voices of males speaking in Spanish reached her ears. They were on the path. She only caught a few words because the dialect was so different. Words like "find" and "American" she understood.

They were looking for them!

Chance saw the fear in Ellen's eyes. Her body trembled beneath him. She'd heard the men. They were in more danger than he'd believed. The drug traffickers were determined to find them. Ellen's eyes were wide with terror. She squirmed as if wanting to run.

He brushed his lips over hers as he shook his head. Bringing his hand to her cheek, he held her so that he could deepen the kiss. Ellen opened. Her tongue mated with his. Fingers weaved into the hair at the nape of his neck and her body softened. She kissed him with the passion of a person hanging on to life. An arm came down to his waist then pushed under his shirt and grasped his back.

Heaven help him, Chance wanted her. Here. In the jungle. On the ground. Beneath this tree. But he couldn't. He must keep her safe.

His lips remained on hers as he listened for the men. They had moved on but they were going the same way as them. They would have to wait here and let them get further down river then cross over. Find somewhere to hole up for the night. It would mean more time in the jungle but getting Ellen back in one piece would be worth it.

She quit kissing him. He opened his eyes. Hers were fixed on him. He put his finger to her lips. She kissed it. Thankfully the panic had cleared from her eyes. Passion and questions filled them now.

"Shh."

She nodded. He rolled off her and sat up. She did the same. They waited there, just listening, for what seemed like an eternity. The birds settled again. All he could make out was the usual jungle sounds.

Standing, he extended his hand and helped her to her feet. He put his finger to his lips again then gently pushed the undergrowth back as they made progress toward the river. Ellen was glued to his back as if they were one. He paused and carefully searched the area before they stepped out onto the path.

Using a low voice, he said, "We have to cross the river

and find somewhere to stay the night. Maybe they'll give up by tomorrow."

She nodded.

"We need to do it here. I'm afraid to go downstream any farther. We'll cross at those rocks." He pointed down the river just below the pool. "Guess what? You get to take those boots off after all. We don't want to get them wet or they'll be even harder to walk in. Tie the laces together and put them around your neck."

Ellen did as he instructed without question. Minutes later they were ready to go. Chance led her across some rocks and down into the water and up again. There was a section where the water was moving fast between two large rocks close to the bank. It was moving rapidly enough that Ellen wouldn't be strong enough to walk through it without assistance.

"I'll step over then help you though." Chance didn't wait for a response. They had to get out of the open. There was no way of knowing if the men would come back this way. He held on to the rock and put a foot into the gushing water. Secure, he took a long step, making it across the flow. He offered his arm to Ellen. She grasped his forearm and he hers. He swung her more than helped her over the divide. She now stood a little in front of him.

In his peripheral vision he saw a flash of color. He pushed Ellen into the deeper water surrounding a large rock. When he did so he slipped. He was headed down the river and right into the sight of the men looking for them.

His bag strap held him back. Seconds later he felt a tug across his chest.

"Help," Ellen whispered close to his ear.

Using a foot, Chance pushed against a rock beneath the water and back toward her. He did it once more. Now at least half of his body was behind the rock, lying over

Ellen's. She held tightly to the strap, pulling him against her chest. The water tugged at him as it flowed over his legs but Ellen held steady. They stayed in that position without daring to look to see where the men were for a long time. The shadows were long on their side of the river before Chance had the nerve to lean forward. Scanning the area, he saw no sign of human life.

He worked to find adequate footing then managed to get turned around and to the bank. Ellen took his hand and he brought her over to join him. They climbed out of the water and moved into the vegetation. Sitting, he said, "Thanks for saving my butt back there."

"Think nothing of it." She sounded exhausted.

"When did you see—?"

"About the same time you did. I couldn't think of anything to do but hold on."

"You did well." What he didn't want to tell her was that they had bigger problems now. Like it was getting dark and they had no safe place to stay for the night. "Let's get our boots on. We need to get moving. The good news is that they were headed upstream so the chances of us meeting them again is slim."

"So there'll be no more distraction kisses?"

"I hope not."

"Shame, I rather enjoyed it."

He grinned. "I did too. Get your shoes on. We need to get going."

"I'm afraid they're wet." Ellen dumped water out of one of hers.

"We'll have to wear them anyway."

They both had their boots on and were ready to go in a few minutes. Once again Chance led, pushing plants out of the way. It was rough walking but they made headway. He almost kissed the ground when they came to a path.

Keeping the sound of the river to his right, he could be sure they were still headed toward the coast.

Now to find a place for them to stay for the night. They were both soaking wet. He was starting to chap and Ellen must be also. But still no complaint. He shook his head. The woman with hot pink fingernails had just saved his life. Who would have thought?

Where did she find that fortitude? In his experience with women they would have broken down long ago. As the daughter of Robert Cox she'd grown up in a privileged home. He couldn't imagined her having done anything that would prepare her for this type of undertaking. It was nice to have someone he wasn't having to reassure all the time. A partner in the effort.

They walked about an hour without seeing any obvious good place for shelter. Under the tree canopy it was almost dark. He had to find something soon. As if in answer to his prayer, a giant kapok tree came into view. It was so large that its trunk and roots created a cave of sorts. They had just made it to the tree when rain started to fall. Ellen stood with her mouth open, letting the drops off a leaf fall into her mouth. He wished he could let her continue but they had to see to their needs first.

"Get the bottles and put them where they'll collect water. I'll make sure we don't have any company inside this tree. Then we need to get out of these clothes and shoes. We can't take a chance on a fire but we do need to give our bodies relief from the damp."

Chance left her to see about the drinking water while he checked out the tree. There was just enough room for them to both lie down. At least it was dry. He returned outside and found a banana tree and started stripping leaves from it. He would use them to clean out any ants or spiders that might want to share their room. They couldn't afford to be bitten.

He'd just finished and had their bags inside when Ellen joined him, soaking wet. She had one full bottle of water in her hand.

"I poured what I had in one. I'll go out after the other in a few minutes. Have some." She handed it to him like she was giving a Christmas present. "It's wonderful."

Chance gladly took a swallow. And another, before handing it back to her. "Drink all you can so we can fill it up again."

She did as he said and passed it to him once more.

"I think we're safe here so we need to get out of these clothes. There's a root we can hang them on. They won't dry completely but it's better than nothing." Chance started unbuttoning his shirt. He couldn't help but watch Ellen pull her T-shirt over her head. Why couldn't there be more light? Beneath she wore a sports bra.

"Please, don't look at me like that. I'm not used to undressing in front of a man."

Chance unbuckled his belt, bent over and removed his boots then dropped his pants. "You certainly have nothing to be ashamed of. You're amazing."

"From what I can see of you, you're not so bad yourself. So you're a briefs guy. And I would have said boxers."

She'd given thought to what type of underwear he wore? He rather liked that idea.

Ellen sat on a banana leaf and removed her boots then stood. The sound of a zipper drew Chance's attention away from hanging clothes. In the dim light he could see a strip of white bikini panties. Once again he had to remind himself to focus on keeping them alive instead of his baser desires.

"Hand me those," he said in a gruff voice.

She gave him her pants.

"We need to go through our packs and see what we have that we can use to gather food and attend to our feet. I don't know about you but mine feel like shriveled-up prunes." The job needed to be done but it would also keep his mind off the half-naked woman sharing a tree bedroom in the middle of nowhere with him. It should have been the stuff that dreams were made of. Instead they were in a nightmare.

He'd worked hard all day to sound upbeat and not to show his fear and concern. Gut-wrenching anxiety filled him any time he let himself think about their situation. People with guns were after them, they were dehydrated, had no real food, their feet were blistered, they were insect bitten, and exhausted. He just couldn't let on to Ellen how dire their situation was.

She sat on a banana leaf again and opened her backpack. She started laying things out. When she found the flashlight she start to turn it on.

"Wait until we have everything out so we don't waste the batteries."

"It's so wet it might not work."

"It's the kind sealed for water. It should be fine."

She went back to digging in the pack. "What's this?" She held a rag with its ends tied. She opened it carefully. It was food like the boy had bought them last night.

"The boy must have put it in there when he was packing things up."

"I don't care how it got here, I'm just grateful to have it. I'm starving." She handed one to him.

They stopped what they were doing and took a moment to eat. Neither said anything about saving some but they only ate a little. Chance gave his back to her and she put them both back into the rag and tied it.

"Okay, what else do we have?" she asked.

Most of what they had was medical supplies, which did them little good for food or drink.

"Let me see that light. I want to look at your feet."

"Why, Doctor, that's a kinky idea." Ellen brought her feet around in his direction.

"Funny. You keep that up and I might tickle them." Chance shined the light on her feet. He wanted to cry. They had blisters and were bleeding in some places. "I have some antibiotic ointment I'm going to put on these. Why didn't you say something?"

"We couldn't stop, could we?"

"No."

"Then what was the point? I'm sure yours are just as bad. Finish up with mine and then I'll see to yours."

He gently applied the ointment to her feet but it wouldn't really help much. The air and time out of her boots were the best healer. "Before you do mine, let me go out and see to the water." Chance picked up the bottle and headed outside. He soon returned to find her repacking their bags.

"It's your turn." Chance wiped as much dirt off his feet as possible and sat down to let her examine them. Her hands were gentle as she checked each angry spot and applied the cream. She was an above-average doctor.

"We're both in sad shape but we'll survive. My father will never believe this. I'll be lucky if he lets me out of town again."

Chance placed banana leaves so that they had a bed of sorts. He put his bag and her pack on it and lay back. Patting the area beside him, he said, "Join me."

Ellen did but didn't touch him.

He clicked off the flashlight. "Would you mind keeping me warm?"

She placed her head on his shoulder and wrapped an arm around his waist. Shifting, she got comfortable and he became uncomfortable. He could so easily roll over and make love to her but he was bone weary and she could only be just as tired. They needed their rest more than release.

"These banana leaves make you think a dirty tarp isn't so bad."

Chance chuckled and kissed her temple. "You never cease to amaze me."

The soft sound of her even breathing brought the only feeling of peace he'd found all day.

CHAPTER SIX

THEY HAD BEEN walking since sunrise and Ellen's feet were already screaming. Even with the attention Chance had given them they'd still had to go back into damp leather boots. It hadn't been a pleasant experience. To have a thick, dry pair of socks would have been wonderful. But that was only a fantasy.

Ellen had wanted to work in a developing country but this was more than she had planned on. Sleeping in a tree in only her underwear hadn't been a scenario she would have imagined. She had slept, though. Exhausted from hiking, swimming and raw fear, she'd been fast asleep as soon as her head had snuggled into Chance's shoulder. Despite her lack of clothing, she'd been warm the entire night nestled against Chance.

Sometime she had been jerked awake by the sound of a wild animal growling.

"Shush, sweetheart. He's a long way off. Go back to sleep." Chance's hand had caressed her hip and waist.

For once she'd appreciated his protection. She hadn't questioned further and had soon been asleep again. How did Chance do that? Make her feel secure by just being there? She'd been consumed by fear the day before. She'd run down a path in the jungle without question because

Chance had said that was what they needed to do, and had been confident he would take care of her.

He'd distracted her by kissing her when she'd been so sure the bad men just feet away would find them. The kiss had started out as something to help her keep quiet but had turned into a passionate meeting of lips, as all of her and Chance's kisses had. Her distress had disappeared with only a touch from him.

The pinnacle of her terror had been those seconds before she'd wrapped her hands around his bag strap and pulled him back against her. It had taken all her strength but she'd managed by sheer determination. Her heart had been in her throat and there had been a roaring sound in her ears. Losing him hadn't been something she would even consider. If he had been washed away and the drug traffickers had seen him they would have shot at him. She couldn't let that happen. After they'd climbed out of the river the look on Chance's face had aid he was proud of her. She'd wanted to dance a gig in happiness that they'd been alive but she'd been afraid they'd be seen or heard.

Ellen watched Chance walking ahead of her a few paces. He was confident and watchful at the same time. He had to move a leaf or push away a vine more often than she because he was taller. His clothes clung to his body in the tropical dampness. Occasionally he pushed his hair back with a hand when he glanced over his shoulder to check on her.

She and Chance had become a true partnership through this ordeal. He was no longer pushing her away. Last night he'd trusted her to see to something as important as the water. He saw her as a competent person, something that her father would never open his eyes to. Someone who could take care of herself. For that alone she adored Chance. She looked at his broad shoulders and the back of his handsome head. Her heart was full.

Sometime later Chance called for a rest stop. They shared a bottle of water. There was little better than the feel of the liquid going down her parched throat.

"I'd like half a bar, if that's okay?" Ellen said.

"Sure. I'll join you." Chance pulled a food bar out of a side pocket of his bag. Opening and breaking it, he gave her a piece.

Ellen found a seat on a nearby root. "So how long should it take us to get to Saba?"

"Maybe tomorrow evening if we're lucky. If we can keep the same pace as we have been. How are your feet?"

"Much like yours, I imagine."

His chuckle was a dry one. "My boots are more broken in than yours. I'm sure your feet are dying to get out and dry out."

"It may be a long time before I can wear open-toed shoes again. I'm pretty sure I'm going to lose some skin."

Chance sat beside her and took one of her hands in his. He stroked a fingertip much like the Honduran girls had. Her nails were no longer neatly polished. A number of them were broken and chipped. Dirt circled the cuticles. Under any other circumstances she wouldn't have let him look at them. Now she was just too tired to argue.

"I'm sorry." He sounded sad.

"For what?"

"Your nails."

"I thought you hated them. Thought they were…frivolous."

"No. They're one of the nicest things about you."

"Really? You could have fooled me. You acted like I had committed a crime when I brought out my polish."

He kissed a knuckle. "Yeah, but you made those girls'

day." He kissed another. "I couldn't fault you for that."
He touched his lips to a different knuckle. "When we get
out of this I'll see that you get a day of pampering at the
resort. Including a manicure and pedicure."

"What about you? You'll deserve something."

"I'll get to enjoy you." He gave her a quick kiss.

Warmth seeped through her that had nothing to do
with the steamy weather or the sun beaming down on
them. They still hadn't had that talk he had promised but
she was going to see to it that they did.

"Come on, it's time for some more walking." Chance
stood and helped her up.

It was around noon when the sound of the river grew
louder.

"We're getting closer to the river," Ellen said.

"Yes. I think this path leads to a ford. It's time we
crossed back over," Chance said. "Wait here and I'll
check it out."

Her chest tightened. "I'm going with you. I don't like
it when you leave."

He regarded her a moment. "You know, that's the first
complaint you've made since we started this trek."

"Complaining does no good. I learned that a long
time ago." That lesson had been clear when she'd been
trapped in a car with her mother and later in the hospital. Even with her father she'd found out that she didn't
make headway by complaining. It hadn't been until she'd
forced the issue by coming here that she'd made a step
away from him.

Chance took one of her hands in his. "Why now?"

"Because I'm afraid that something will happen and
you won't come back." Was that how her father felt? This
was the fear he knew when he thought of losing her?

"I won't be out of your sight two minutes. Promise."

She tapped her wristwatch. "I'm going to time you."

"I expected nothing less. While I'm gone think about what you want to do when we get back to the resort. I want to hear every detail." He hurried off.

She was so busy making plans for their return, she forgot to check her watch. As good as his word, Chance was soon back.

"Did you miss me?" he asked with a grin.

"Always." But at least this time she hadn't been a big bundle of nerves thanks to him giving her something else to ponder. Maybe that's what her father needed— something else to focus on besides her. He'd not dated since they had lost her mother. It was time for him to move on. Past time.

Maybe it was time for her to embrace life more as well. She'd taken a major step by coming to Honduras but not in her personal life. Working so hard to earn her independence, she'd put her love life on hold. Was it time for her to open up? Let someone in? Should that person be Chance? If she did, would he accept her?

"This is a good place to cross. The river is wide but not running fast."

Ellen picked up her pack. "At least I don't have to worry about saving your butt."

"Did I say thank you for that?"

She smiled. "I think you did but feel free to do so again."

"Thanks. Let's get moving."

She hurried to catch up with him. There was the old Chance. Focused.

The river was much wider than it had been where they had crossed before. The rocks were not nearly as large and were spaced so that one large step or jump could get her from one to another. There was a real possibility they could cross without getting wet.

"I want to lead this time." Ellen wasn't sure what had gotten into her when she said that.

Chance looked surprised. "Okay."

Ellen chose her path carefully, managing to get out into the middle of the river without any mishaps. There the water was moving faster and the gap between the rocks was wider. She hitched up her pack, preparing to jump. Pushing off hard, she jumped over the water and landed on her hands and knees on top of the next rock. Chance stepped up beside her. He took her forearm and helped her up.

"You're the most determined woman I know."

"Thanks." Ellen moved on across the river. When she reached the other side she waited for Chance to join her, which he soon did. "Come on. We need to get going." She headed down the path.

"So are you usurping my authority now?"

"I just thought I'd like to lead for a while. You know the saying: if you aren't the lead dog, the view never changes."

He released a bark of laughter. The birds reacted by screaming and flying away.

"Shush," she said.

Chance looked contrite then searched the area. His gaze came back to her. "No more smart remarks from you."

"You can't blame me for that. You were the one being loud."

They didn't walk long before the sound of civilization could be heard over the flow of water. Chance took the lead again, making his way into the greenery under a large tree. From their location they could see women doing laundry at the riverbank. There was an open field of high grass between the women and a group of huts sitting back against the jungle.

Chance put his mouth close to her ear. "We'll have to stay here until they leave. We might as well rest."

They slowly and as quietly as possible removed their packs. He leaned his back against the tree and she scooted up next to him. The women's chatter lulled her to sleep.

"Ow!" Ellen woke, slapping at her pants leg. She'd been bitten. Shaking out the material, she saw nothing.

Something was wrong. *Chance was gone.* Going up on her hands and knees, she searched the river area where the women had been. There was no one in sight.

Chance knew how she felt about being left alone. How could he disappear? Terror threatened to fill her chest but she pushed it down.

He would be back. He had to come back.

Off in the distance, downriver, clothes were hanging over a rope strung between two trees. There was a movement. One of the items disappeared from the line. *Chance.* She watched another piece of clothing being snatched away.

He would have to cross the field and come upriver again to get her. It would be safer if she met him. Quickly pulling on her pack and putting his bag across her chest, she carefully left her hiding place. With her body as low to the ground as possible she worked her way across the field. A dog barked. She crouched down. Her calf burned. She couldn't worry about that now.

Waiting for further noise and hearing none, she hurried to the jungle edge and along it to where she'd last seen Chance. There he was, pulling another item from the lie. She moved again to where she'd seen him duck out of the trees.

Chance's eyes went wide when he saw her. He handed her a couple of articles of clothing and nodded his head downriver. He didn't give her a chance to respond before he took his bag from her and quickly moved to the river and down the path. They walked at a rapid pace for a good while before he stepped off the trail.

Out of sight he turned to her. "You scared me to death, showing up like that."

"And you left me."

"I planned to be back before you woke."

She glared at him. "Don't do that to me again."

Chance studied her a second then said, "I won't. I promise."

She believed him. "I saw you and knew you'd have to double back for me so I decided to meet you."

"Smart girl."

"So what did you get us?" She rubbed her calf. It was still stinging. What had bitten her?

"Something for us to sleep on and a couple of clean shirts."

Ellen grinned. "I look forward to high-style living tonight. Shouldn't we get moving?"

"You're starting to sound like me." Chance smiled back and headed down the trail. Ellen had almost scared the life out of him when she'd shown up near the clothesline. He had really misjudged her when he'd first met her. Ellen had a backbone of iron.

When she'd announced that she was going to take the lead he couldn't help but be proud. If he had been in her place he would have been tired of following as well. The woman was full of surprises. His mother and ex-wife would have given up before they'd even got started. He wasn't used to having such a resilient woman in his life. *Life?* Could he really have her in his life? Would she stay with him?

He set a steady pace and Ellen kept up. A couple of times he checked behind him to see how she was doing. There was a determined look on her face, but occasionally her face was twisted as if she were in pain. Her feet must really be bothering her.

It was drawing close to evening and he had started to look for a place to stay for the night when the sounded of rushing water reached his ears.

"Is that a waterfall?" Ellen asked with enthusiasm.

"Sounds like one." If luck was with them they might have a good safe place to sleep and an opportunity for a fire. Even a bath.

They made a turn in the path and the water disappeared over the edge of a cliff.

He called back. "Are you up for a little climbing?"

Ellen shrugged. "Do I have a choice?"

"Not really. But if all goes well it'll be worth it."

"Lead on, then."

Over the next half an hour they made their way around and down to the pool of water at the bottom of the falls.

"It's amazing," Ellen said.

"It is. Honduras has incredible falls. I'd leave you here but I know you'd have none of that so come on and let's see if we can find a room for the night."

"Here?"

"Sure." Chance led the way around the pool toward the falls. He made a few maneuvers across rocks until they had worked their way behind it. There was the small cave he was looking for. It was large enough for them to remain dry and still have a small fire.

Pulling his bag off, he dropped the clothes on top.

Speaking loudly, he worked at being heard over the roar of the water. "Your hotel room for the evening."

Ellen looked around. "It's wonderful."

"I need to look for something dry enough to burn before it gets too dark. Are you going to be okay here by yourself or do you want to come with me?"

"Aren't you worried about the smoke being seen?"

He smiled and pointed to the falls. "It'll blend in with the mist. We're safe. Hopefully we can have dry clothes."

She looked unsure a moment then straightened her shoulders. "No, I'll be fine here."

"I won't be long. Why don't you get that trash we have in our packs out to use as starter?"

It took Chance longer than he'd expected to find something in a tropical rain forest dry enough to burn. The entire time he was gone he worried about Ellen being frightened. He did manage to locate some dry leaves and small sticks. He and Ellen wouldn't have a bonfire but it would be something to dry clothes by.

With arms full, he made his way back to the river. He started to take his first step on the rocks when he saw her. Ellen stood naked beneath the falls. Her arms were raised as she held her hair out to let the water reach each strand. He'd never seen anything more breathtakingly beautiful or more uninhibited.

He should leave. Let her know he was there. But he couldn't.

Ellen turned, giving him a profile view of her delicious curves. His body hardened. Her breasts were high and her stomach flat. There was an arc to her behind that made his hands itch to hold her. He stood mesmerized by her splendor, unable to put a thought together beyond the acknowledgement of the desire building in him. Waiting and watching, he didn't want to disturb her or break the spell.

Ellen did it for him. She stepped out of the water. The gold of the evening sun caressed her skin as she walked to a nearby rock and gathered her clothes. She pulled on her shirt and pants and ducked behind the falls.

Chance remained where he was until he had control of his breathing. By the time he'd made it back to their hiding place some of his libido had eased but at the sight of Ellen it climbed again. He had to regain some perspective. It didn't help that Ellen's underwear lay in a small pile nearby.

The tension was thick between them. She wouldn't meet his gaze. Was she feeding off his emotion? Had she known that he'd been watching? It was as if the easiness between them over the last two days had disappeared and been replaced by the disquiet of heightened awareness of the weeks before. As alluring as Ellen had been as a water nymph minutes ago, he had to focus on them surviving. They needed to have a fire, eat and tend their feet. Those needs took precedence over his sexual cravings.

But those carnal needs pulled at him with each look he gave her.

He squatted and let the pile of brush fall from his arms. "Ellen, look in the side pocket of my bag and you'll find a round silver tube. Would you hand it to me?"

She did as he asked and included the trash as well.

He placed the paper under the brush and opened the watertight container, removing two matches.

"I should've known you'd have something up your sleeve to start a fire with."

"I keep them in case I have to go old school with sterilizing a needle. You just never know."

"Like this time."

He gave her a tight smile. "This was more than I planned for." Striking one match against the other, he quickly placed them on the paper. He slowly added some of the material he'd gathered until they had a small fire. "Bring your clothes over here and spread them out to dry. I wish this was going to be large enough for you to get your pants dry after a wash but I don't think they'll dry by morning. At least our underwear and shirts will be cleaner."

"Are you hungry?" she asked.

"Yes. I could eat."

"That was sort of a dumb question." Ellen picked up what little food they had and joined him beside the fire.

She gave him half of the food from the rag and ate the other. "That leaves us with one food bar."

"Hopefully we'll be in Saba by tomorrow night."

"As much as I've enjoyed this walk through the jungle, I have to admit I'm looking forward to seeing the resort again." She put the rag back in the backpack.

"Not New York? I would think after this you'd want to go home."

"No. Most of all I'd just like a good shower."

Chance looked at her. "I thought that's what you were having a few minutes ago." Even in the glow of the fire he could see her blush.

"You weren't supposed to see me."

He stood. "How was it?"

"Wonderful."

"If you'll keep the fire going I think I'll give the falls a try as well."

Ellen watched Chance leave. She wasn't sure why she had suddenly turned bashful around him. It was as if they had been fighting for their lives every hour of the last two days and she now felt safe enough to think of living. The intimate space they would share for the night only added to that awareness. She still tingled all over with the knowledge he had watched her bathe. For how long?

The waterfall had looked so inviting. She hadn't felt nastier in her entire life. Dirt mixed with sweat, her clothes sticking to her, pants less black than tan. Her hair had been a mass of tangles with bits of leaf and twigs. No one at home would have recognized her. The rush of the water had called to her. She had planned it to be a quick bath but she'd become caught up in the heavenly feeling of the water flowing over her and had stayed longer than she'd intended.

Ellen looked at the falls. She couldn't see Chance through the rush of water but she could picture him beneath it as water washed over his shoulders and ran down his chest. What if they didn't make it home the next day? Were caught? Never had a chance to be together?

What would it be like to really spend a night in his arms? Life was too short not to have that pleasure.

She spread the blanket out near the fire and stored their packs. Her leg let her know it was there as she moved. Sitting down, she pulled her pants leg up and twisted so she could see the back of her calf. There was a red welt just above where the top of her boot came. She had been bitten. It was tender and warm. There wasn't much she could do about it now. She'd check it again in the morning.

Pulling Chance's pack to her, she found the ointment and gave her feet some much-needed attention. Her blisters now had blisters. She dreaded putting her boots on in the morning. At least her socks had been rinsed, which would help cut down on infection. She would lose one of her big toenails, if not both.

Chance joined her. His hair was wet. He'd pushed it away from his forehead. A lock of it hadn't stayed in place. Bare-chested and with his pants low on his hips, he strolled toward her. The fire reflected off his still-damp skin. Every nerve in her body was alert to him.

He laid his clothing beside hers. There was something oddly intimate about their undergarments drying next to each other.

"You need to get some sleep. We have another day of walking ahead of us." He put another piece of brush on the fire.

He continued to stand as if he wasn't going to join her on the blanket. "You aren't going to sleep?"

"I think I'll sit up for a while."

"Then I'll keep you company unless you've had enough of it."

"I don't think that's possible." A stricken look covered his features as if he'd said something he hadn't meant to.

"We haven't had that talk yet," she said just loud enough that she could be heard over the falls.

"Ellen, I don't think—"

"You're right. I don't want to talk." She stood. "I've spent the last two days worrying about dying."

"Ellen..."

She stepped around the fire. "There might not be another day, another time and I want to celebrate being alive. With you." Placing her hands on his shoulders, she went up on her toes and kissed him.

Chance grabbed her around the waist. Pulling her against his chest, he brought her feet off the ground. His mouth devoured hers as if he was hungry and a banquet was being served.

CHAPTER SEVEN

How like Ellen to take the initiative. Chance wasn't going to turn her away again. The gentleman in him he'd left in that hovel days before. He was going to accept what was offered. All of Ellen.

He would inhale her, touch her, have her. Totally take what he'd desired for weeks.

His body was tense with anticipation. With one hot kiss his manhood stood ready. He craved everything about her.

With her still in his arms he walked around the fire to the blanket. She wrapped her arms around his neck as they went. Cupping the back of his head, she held his mouth to hers. Her tongue caressed, twirled and mated with his, mimicking the very things he wanted to do to her.

Chance hadn't planned this. But he wanted it. Needed her.

She was right. They had spent the last few days fighting for their lives. He didn't want to battle himself or her about the attraction between them. Now it was time to feel her against him for the pleasure of her, not for the need to survive. Chance eased her down his body and brought his hands up under her shirt tracing the lines of her body. Stepping away, he pulled her shirt over her head and dropped it to the stone floor.

She was stunning, standing before him. The flickering firelight touched her in places he had every intention of savoring. He cupped one of her breasts. Slowly, he pulled his hand away, caressing the breast from beneath. Ellen shivered, adding to his delight. He reveled in her soft sound of pleasure.

The pads of her fingers drifted over his chest then downward to the edge of his pants and around to his side. She slipped a finger beneath his waistband and moved it across his skin.

His manhood tightened. Strained against the front of his pants.

She grabbed a handful of material and pulled him to her.

Chance took her mouth again. This time she brought a leg up his, circling it with hers. He broke the kiss and looked into her eyes. "I desperately want you but I can't make any promises."

"Tonight isn't about promises. It's about being alive. Enjoying life."

She hadn't said it but he knew her too well not to know she cared deeply for people and that meant she didn't take relationships lightly. Should he let this continue? For his sake? Hers?

A hint of a smile came to Ellen's lips. "Remember what I said that day when I was polishing the girl's nails? A moment of pleasure is better than none. If something happens to you, I'd always regret not having you like this."

That brick wall Chance had built around his heart had just taken a battering. He couldn't let her get hurt. "This isn't some storybook adventure that's going to end in a happily-ever-after."

"Have I ever said that's what I want?"

She hadn't, and for some reason it stung that she didn't expect it.

Her hands ran up his ribs and down his arms. "What I'm saying is that I want you. I know you want me. I feel it." She flexed forward. "There might not be another time. We may not get out of this. I don't want any regrets. Not being with you would be a great regret."

Chance knew about regrets and disappointment. He'd experienced both a number of times in his life. With his mother. His sister. His ex-wife. Ellen wouldn't be one of those. He would see to that right now.

Cupping her face with his hands, he gave her a gentle kiss. "You deserve a big comfortable bed and someplace clean."

"I don't care as long as you are there."

Bam. There went another chip in the wall.

Pulling her against him, Chance savored the feel of her bare breasts against his chest. His mouth found hers again then moved over her cheek to kiss the hollow behind her ear. She tilted her head as if asking for more.

He found her waistband and unfastened the button. Deliberately, he pulled the zipper down. Her pants fell to her feet and she pushed them away. His mouth left her ear to travel over the ridge of her shoulder and down to the tip of one breast.

His mouth took it, sucked. Running his tongue around the nipple, he teased.

A soft, sensual sigh filled the air as Ellen combed her fingers through his hair.

Chance pulled away and blew over the damp mound he was giving attention to. Ellen's moan turned to a groan.

His length twitched. How much longer could he stand not having her? What would she sound like when she found release?

Cupping the other breast, he took it into his mouth, giving it the same attention as he'd lavished on the first. She held his head, encouraging him. Chance's mouth left her breast to kiss his way up her neck and capture her lips. The meeting of mouths was wild and hot.

Her hands went to his pants and released them, pushing them over his hips to the ground. She didn't hesitate before she wrapped her hand around his staff and gently stroked. If she kept that up he would combust before they made it to the blanket.

Chance moved back and she released him. "I'll lose control if you touch me."

"I don't care." Her voice was husky, which did nothing to ease his need.

"But I do. You deserve more." He kissed her deeply. One of his hands followed the curve of her shoulder, skimmed her breast to brush the line of her hip. The palm of his hand skimmed over her stomach before his fingers teased the curls between her legs.

She tensed in his arms.

He slid a finger between her folds and pulled away.

Ellen shook, making a delicious sound of protest.

Chance cupped her center then slowly pulled a finger between her folds. Her stance widened as her tongue entered his mouth. She clung to his shoulders. Using one finger, he went deeper, finding the wet, hot opening of her desire. He dipped the tip of his finger inside. Ellen hissed close to his ear. Bringing her leg up around his, she offered him clear passage. He took it, pushing his finger completely into her. She bucked, going up on her toes.

He removed his finger and pushed into her again. Her

hips flexed against him. She clawed at his back. Retreating, he thrust again. This time Ellen pushed down on his hand. Pulling his finger away, he entered her again. Her head fell back. Her hair was wild around her shoulders as she cried her pleasure and withered against him.

It took all Chance had within him not to throw Ellen to the ground and hammer into her.

Instead he held her, watching the soft look settle over her face as she eased to earth once more. The experience was something he'd never had with a woman before. It left a feeling of satisfaction he wasn't familiar with but desperately wanted again.

Was that another brick being knock away?

Ellen relaxed against him. He removed his finger and grasped her waist. Their gazes met. Hers was dewy. She gave him the tiny smile of a woman who'd found something special. He stood on top of the world because he was the one who'd given it to her.

That was an awesome responsibility. Did he want to carry that? Could he take that gamble?

Ellen placed a hand in one of his, went down on the blanket and pulled him to her.

Chance didn't resist. He couldn't.

"You deserve some attention." Her voice was deeper and even sexier than before.

"It's not necessary."

There was a look of concern in her eyes for a second then her lips turned upward. "Oh, but I think it is."

Ellen wanted to give Chance some of the pleasure he'd given her. She wasn't inexperienced but nothing she had felt before compared to what Chance's touch had done to her.

When he'd said it wasn't necessary she'd feared he was running away again. She wasn't going to let that happen.

Lying on her side, she faced him. His masculinity was almost more than she could comprehend. Holding his gaze, she reached out and placed her hand on the pectoral muscles of his chest then ran her index finger over his skin. Slowly she traced his ribs, dipping and rising as she moved downward.

She glanced up to see that Chance's pupils had dilated. They burned with desire. Her actions were having the effect she desired. Circling his belly button, she enjoyed the inhalation of his breath as she watched his skin react to her touch. It was exciting to see this strong, masterful man respond to her. Her hand followed a line of hair downward until she reached the head of his manhood. She ran the tip of her finger over him and watched the length twitch.

Chance growled and pulled her hand away.

Grinning, Ellen shifted so that she could push his shoulders to the blanket. That done, she straddled him. She kissed his jaw and moved down to the valley of his neck and onto his chest. As she went one of Chance's hands glided over her hip. When her tongue slid across his breastbone, he cupped a butt cheek and gently squeezed.

She rose above him. Looking into his eyes, Ellen slowly came down to kiss him. It was a kiss of not only passion but of heartfelt longing and caring.

Chance took control and rolled her to her back. One of his legs came to rest over hers. "I can't last much longer. I promise you slow next time."

Her heart swelled. He thought there would be a next time.

Ellen lifted her hips, pushing her center against his leg. She throbbed for him. Blood rushed in her ears. She needed him as well.

Chance settled between her legs, his manhood coming to rest at her entrance. He supported himself on his elbows as he looked down at her.

A stricken look crossed his face. "We have no protection."

Ellen's hands found his hips and pulled him to her as she lifted upward. "Don't worry. I have it taken care of." She reached up and kissed him with everything in her. She refused to let him leave her again.

Chance slipped into her until she held all of him. Ellen gripped his forearms and wrapped her legs around his waist, bringing him closer. He pulled back and pushed forward then did it again. Each time tension coiled tighter in her. She wiggled, begging to have more. Chance gifted her with a hard thrust.

Ellen squeezed her legs tighter around him, bowed her back as he pressed into her. Squeezing her eyes shut, she reached, searched and grabbed for what she needed. Finding the pinnacle, she came apart. She remained rigid, taking all Chance had to offer, until she started the blissful float downward.

Her legs fell away from his hips. Before she could think straight again Chance drove into her. Slowly at first, then faster he stoked. Her hands tightened around his neck. He grasped her hips and held her firmly against him. His mouth took hers and whatever else he wanted. Heat flared in her. She grasped his shoulders. It couldn't be happening again. Chance gained speed. Her scream of pleasure mixed with his groan of release as he sent her to the stars once more.

Chance held Ellen close as they lay on the too-small blanket. Her head lay against his shoulder and her arm rested across his chest with her hand buried under his hair. One of her legs wrapped around his and her foot was cupped in the arch of his.

She fit like she belonged. Perfectly. What would it be like to have her like this all the time?

He'd never been more satisfied in his life. She was everything he'd never thought to have in a woman. Beauty, intelligence, strength, passion, perseverance and most of all an easy smile. He shouldn't think like that but having Ellen in his arms made him want to dream again. She'd brought that back to his life.

Her hand moved over his shoulder and teased his earlobe.

He looked at her. "Hey, there. I thought you were asleep."

"Mmm… Just resting." She stretched against him, running her fingers across his belly.

"You keep that up and I'll have to retaliate."

"I don't have a problem with that." She kissed his neck. "Didn't you promise me slow next time?"

Chance kissed the top of her head as his hand caressed the under-curve of one of her breasts. "I can go slow. But the question is can you stand it?"

Ellen's hand drifted to his hip. "As long as you can."

He took the challenge and they both won.

They were still basking in a cloud of satisfaction while in each other's arms when Ellen said, "Tell me about your childhood."

Chance couldn't help but flinch. Why did Ellen want to know about that? He'd rather talk about anything else but that and his ex-wife. She'd already heard that sordid story.

"I was a baby, then a child and now a man. Pretty typical stuff."

She gave him a playful swat on the chest. "I know

well that you are a man. But what I want to know about is Chance the little boy."

Ellen wasn't going to back off from this. That wasn't who she was. He might as well tell her and then she'd quit asking. "I was raised in upstate New York. My father was a world-famous surgeon even when I was a young boy. He traveled and spoke a lot. We had everything money could buy but he was never around. My mother adored him." Chance had worshiped his mother. "But my father was so wrapped up in his life that he barely saw her. He liked the jet-setting, being the big shot, and he like the women that went with that recognition. I'm not sure why they ever married."

The same question had occurred to him when Alissa had left him. Had he, like his father, been so wrapped up in his work that he hadn't been taking care of what he'd needed to do at home? Had it been fair to ask a woman to live his lifestyle? The question still nagged at him.

He looked at Ellen. Her golden hair was spread out over his chest and shoulder. Her fingers ran along the center of his chest as if she couldn't get enough of him.

"How sad. Your mother must have been so lonely."

"She was."

"What happened?"

His chest tightened. "How did you know something happened?"

"By the tone of your voice."

Had he become that transparent? Or was she just that in tune with him? He wasn't sure which idea disturbed him more. "She left. Later I was told she joined a commune-type place. As far as I know, she's still there. I went to see her once when I was in college but she said she didn't want to see me. I never tried again."

Ellen's arm went to his waist and she gave him a tight hug. "Oh, Chance, I'm so sorry."

She'd lost her mother as well. If anyone could empathize it was her. "You understand too well, don't you?"

Her head nodded against him. "Mothers are important." She didn't say anything for a few minutes. Her voice wobbled as she said, "I watched my mother die."

Even during this ordeal she'd never sounded so close to tears. They shared a huge loss but hers had been far more traumatizing. He pulled her close. If only he could take her pain away. "Sweetheart, I'm so sorry."

Chance understood her agony. Knew the need of a child for comfort that only a mother could give. Or the smell of perfume that was hers alone. A whisper of a kiss on the cheek as she went by or that safe feeling when being tucked in at night.

Yet despite their similarities in background, Ellen saw the world as a sparkling place while he saw it as tarnished. She seemed to bubble even in the situation they were in now. He wanted that in his life.

Moisture touched his skin. Strong, resilient Ellen was crying for two children who had lost their mothers. Chance's chest tightened. His father not caring was painful but his mother's defection was devastating. At least Ellen hadn't felt unloved. He squeezed her close as she cried. "I'm sorry about your mother too."

Minutes later she composed herself again then said, "Who would have thought we'd share something so awful?"

He kissed the top of her head. "I, for one, would prefer to remember something else we've shared."

Ellen moved to look up at him with eyes that were still misty. "Why, Dr. Freeman, I believe there might be a romantic under all that gruff and bluster."

He smiled. "Don't get that rumor started."

At least they had moved past that emotional moment but they continued to hold each for some time.

Finally Ellen asked, "Will you tell me the rest of the story now? Did your father come home then?"

"Yeah, just long enough to put me and my sister into boarding schools."

"You have a sister?"

"I do."

Ellen grabbed a shirt and pulled it on. "But you've never said anything about her."

He shrugged. "I don't really know her."

"How can you not know your sister?"

"Pretty easy when I only saw her once a year at Christmas."

"What? That's horrible."

"Maybe so, but that's the way it was."

"Still is, I gather." Ellen sounded as if she was accusing him of doing something appalling in a court of law.

He sat up and faced her. "We're just in two different worlds. She has her life and I have mine."

"So you didn't even have each other to lean on when your mother left. No wonder you have issues with women. Pushed me away," she murmured.

Chance stiffened. "Don't start analyzing me."

"It was more of an observation."

He didn't like that much better. Had Ellen seen something about him that not even he was aware of?

"Where's your father?"

"He died a couple of years ago."

"I don't know what I would have done without my father. He's been there for me all the way."

"That must be nice."

"It is, most of the time."

Chance was relieved they had moved past the subject of him. "Most of the time?"

"I told you, he tends to watch over me too much."

"I can understand a father wanting to protect you."

She chuckled. "I guess you can. You act like him sometimes."

"Is that so bad?"

"What, that you act like him? Or that he is overprotective?"

"The overprotective part." He studied her. Her hands were clasped in her lap in a ball.

"It is when you want to do more than work on the upper east side and in a hospital for women having their faces and breasts done."

He ran his palm lightly over one of her nipples. "Which you need neither of."

Ellen caught his hand and held it. "Thank you. But I wanted to work where people needed me. Where others weren't as willing to go."

"So what made you want to do that?"

"I don't know really. I guess it was because of what my doctors and nurses meant to me."

She waited as if she were in deep thought. He knew her well enough to know she would tell all if he just had the patience to wait.

"I still stay in touch with them."

"Who?"

"My doctor and nurses. I was in the car with my mother. I was in the hospital for weeks afterwards."

"That's why you balked the first day."

"Yeah. I've not done much emergency care and it takes me a second but I come around."

"And you did. And did great."

"Thanks. But that's not what you thought then. I saw it in your eyes."

"Guilty. But tell me about your father."

"He was devastated after my mother's death. He was at the hospital with me but he was so broken he wasn't much good around me. It was the doctors and nurses who looked after me. Brought me fast food. Talked and played with a scared little girl. I decided then that I wanted to be like them.

"It took a while but my father found his way out of his grief to see me again and then all he could think about was not losing me. I understand that but it can be stifling. When I went to work at an inner-city clinic he pitched a fit and hired a bodyguard to watch over me. Let's just say there was a large discussion over that. I didn't tell him until the night before I left to come down here that I was coming. Even then I didn't tell him where. I'm sure by now he knows about the resort."

Chance was sure her father didn't know the exact spot they were in now or they would have been rescued. If he ever met her father Chance was sure there would be hell to pay. A father who worried over his daughter that deeply wouldn't like her running for her life in the jungle or sleeping with the man who was responsible for the situation. It was just as well this thing between he and Ellen would end when she left Honduras. Why did the thought gnaw at him so much?

"At least your father cares. Mine hardly knew I was alive."

"That shouldn't have happened to you. I'm surprised you became a doctor like him."

"I was good at science and math. Medicine was—is— in my DNA. But I wanted to be a very different type of person from my father. From the beginning I wanted to help the less privileged."

"You are different. I can't see you not watching over the people you love and showing you care. Look what you're doing for the people of this country."

Her conviction had Chance wanting to believe her. He gave her a kiss that had nothing to do with wanting her sexually and everything to do with appreciating her large heart and loyalty. He needed both in his life.

Chance stood. "Enough talking or you'll have me telling stories of how I misbehaved in school."

"You were a troublemaker?"

"Only until the headmaster sat me down and said a few pointed words that made me think." He reached out his hand. "How about a moonlight trip to the falls?"

"Aren't you afraid we might be seen?"

"We won't stay long. I just keep thinking about you bathing and how much I wished I'd joined you."

"With an invitation like that, how can I refuse?" She took his hand.

Ellen couldn't remember ever being this uninhibited with a man before. She let Chance remove the shirt she'd pulled on and then held his hand as they carefully stepped over the rocks and into the falls under the full moon.

The ache in her leg had been forgotten as Chance had turned her mind toward what he'd been doing to her body. Then her entire attention had been focused on what he'd been saying. She was surprised by how open he'd been that she'd hung on each of his words.

Now there was an aching throb in her calf but as Chance pulled her under the falls it was eclipsed by the touch of his hands running over her waist and hips. She threw her head back and let the water wash through her hair as he kissed her shoulder and cupped her breasts.

There was something wanton, liberating, almost wicked about standing out in the middle of the world with no clothes on as a man loved her body. A tingle in her center grew to a pounding as blood flowed hot within her. She was a siren calling to her mate.

Her hands skimmed over Chance's wet arms and down his back as he kissed the outside of one breast. As he stood there she pushed his hair away from his face. His manhood, thick and tall, found the V of her legs as his mouth came to hers. His hands cupped her butt and lifted. She circled his hips with her legs. Chance shoved once and completely entered her. She held tightly to his shoulders. He eased away and pushed forward. She shuttered. He plunged deeper and joined her in the pleasure.

Chance released her, letting her slid down his wet body. He kissed her deeply then led her out of the falls and over the rocks. "As much as I'm enjoying your body, we need to get some sleep. We still have a day of walking tomorrow. We aren't out of danger yet."

"Boy, you have a way of putting a damper on the afterglow."

He gave her a quick kiss as they returned to their hiding place. "I'll do better next time but I want us to make it to the next time." Picking up a few sticks, he put them on the fire, which had turned to coals. "We need to dry off and get some sleep. As much as I hate to say this, we should sleep in our clothes in case we need to make a quick getaway."

Ellen picked up her underwear and began putting them on. "Is that your way of telling me you've seen all of my body you want to?"

Chance stepped to her and tipped her chin up with a finger. "I could never get enough of looking at your body."

Warmth went through her, settling in her heart. She wanted this moment, this feeling between them, always.

CHAPTER EIGHT

CHANCE WOKE. HE was hot. Too hot. On the side where Ellen rested. She was running a fever.

She groaned and sat up. Her eyes were red and face flushed. Little beads of sweat lined her upper lip.

Chance touched her cheek and confirmed what he already knew. This wasn't good. They already had a day's worth of travel ahead but with her sick it would slow them down.

"I don't feel well."

"I'm not surprised. You're running a pretty high fever. I'll check it in a minute. Do you hurt somewhere?" If they were lucky it was an intestinal problem from the food or lack of it.

"My leg."

He searched her face. "Your leg?"

"Something bit me yesterday when you were stealing clothes."

"Why didn't you say something?" She should have told him, especially after the number of bite cases they'd seen at the clinic. She knew better than to let something like that wait. Panic started to clench his gut.

"Show me."

"Can I have a drink of water first?" She lay back on the blanket.

Ellen was already too weak to sit up for any length of time. Chance picked up a bottle. Going down on one knee, he put an arm around her shoulders and supported her. Slowly she drank.

"Can I sleep a little longer?"

"Sure, sweetheart. Sleep while I look at your leg. Which one is it?"

Ellen stretched out her right leg. "Calf."

Chance pushed up the leg of her pants to reveal a large angry place that covered her calf from the back of her knee to her ankle. In the center there was a boil surrounded by deep purple. His heart constricted. Ellen should be in a hospital. Even if he lanced it the risk of infection was too great and she truly couldn't walk then.

"I wish you had said something." He wanted to shake her and hug her at the same time. They had little water, no food, and now Ellen was seriously sick. His concern for them getting out of this mess today had escalated a hundred percent.

"I was going to, but I was busy doing other things last night." There was humor in her voice.

"We were both thinking of other things last night."

Now he carried that burden of guilt. He should have stayed focused on their problem; instead he had been satisfying his need for her. That was another issue. He wasn't satisfied. Not by a long shot. But he wouldn't be misdirected by his desire again. It could mean Ellen's life and he couldn't abide anything more happening to her. He had to get them out of this new situation and Ellen safely home.

She started to rise.

"Stay put. I'm going to give you a quick exam. Then we'll need to get moving." Chance pulled his bag closer and removed his stethoscope then the thermometer.

"Let's see how high your fever is while I'm giving you a good listen."

Her grin was weak as she said, "I like the good things you give me."

How like Ellen to speak frankly, even about a night of passion. He kissed her forehead. "I enjoyed it too. Now stop distracting me and let me see how you're doing."

"I'm distracting you?"

"Sweetheart, you've been distracting me for weeks." Chance placed the stethoscope on her chest. Her heartbeat was steady, which was encouraging. He checked her pulse and blood pressure. They were up a little bit. Removing the thermometer, he wasn't pleased. He searched his med bag and found a bottle of aspirin. It wouldn't do much for the fever but it was better than nothing.

"Do you think you're up for some walking?" He was sure she wasn't but they really had no choice but to get moving. She wouldn't last another day in the heat and rain with that leg.

"Sure."

He didn't expect her to say anything different.

"Could I have that half of a bar now instead of later?"

"That's a great idea. We'll share it for breakfast. I also want you to take a couple of aspirin for me." He handed her the bar, medicine and set a bottle of water down beside her.

They ate in silence.

Done with her bar, Ellen said, "I'm sorry, but I'm going to need your help with my boot."

Chance assisted her with getting the boot on her foot but could only lace it up loosely around her calf. He was afraid that before the day was over she would be in real pain.

When they were done, he packed the bags except for

the rag the boy had placed the food in. He pulled the strap of his bag over his chest and shrugged into the backpack.

"What're you doing?" Ellen stood beside him. "I'll carry the backpack. That's my job."

"Today you get a day off. Come on, let's get going."

They headed out from behind the falls. Chance stopped a few times to make sure no one else was around.

When they came to the pool, he dipped the rag into the water, wetting it thoroughly, then wrung it out. "Ellen, come here." She stepped closer to him. He wrapped the rag around her head. "This'll help keep you cooler."

Her gaze found his. "Thank you. You're a good person, Chance Freeman."

Coming from her, the simple compliment sounded like he was receiving a great honor in front of thousands. He brushed her lips with his. "You're quite a woman yourself, Ellen Cox."

Chance set a slower pace than he had the days before but even then Ellen was lagging behind. What had at first been a slow walk had now turned into one that included a limp. They stopped often to rest but that didn't seem to give her any more energy. With each stop he wet the rag and retied it across her forehead.

Her fever eased at one point but by midmorning it had returned with a vengeance. He was going to have to find another way to get them to Saba sooner rather than later. Ellen couldn't continue the way she was going. During one of their rests he'd looked at her leg. It was more inflamed than before. Walking hadn't helped.

It hurt him to see her in pain. Yet she still didn't complain.

"Chance, I'm sorry I got us into this and now I'm holding us up."

"For starters, you didn't get us into this. I agreed to

see the boy's father. I knew the risks. That's all on me. As for your leg, yes, you should have told me sooner but there isn't much more we could have done. You didn't get bitten on purpose. So enough of that kind of talk."

"My, you are being all noble. But, then, that's who you are."

She made the statement sound as if she knew few people who were noble and admired him for it. He liked having Ellen think he was someone special.

By noon, he had to walk beside her while she leaned on him in order for her to move. Each time her injured leg touched the ground she winced. They had stopped again to rest when Chance said, "I'm going to have to carry you."

Thankfully the land had flattened out. The river was wider and slower, letting him know that were getting close to the coast.

Ellen shook her head. "How long would you last, doing that in this heat? Leave me and go for help."

"What?" She'd been terrified when he been gone for only minutes. He couldn't leave her with a dangerously high fever out in the jungle alone. "No way. We're in this together."

"I could never forgive myself if something happened to you because of me."

Chance cupped her face. "I think that's my line. Now, let's not talk about it any more. We're going to try you riding on my back for a while."

"Okay, but you let me have the packs."

He removed them and helped her on with them.

"Okay, you ready?" He squatted so she could reach around his neck.

She did so. Her heat seeped through his shirt. He wrapped his arms under her thighs and lifted her on his

back as he stood. Chance started down the path. It wasn't
an easy trek but it was far better than seeing Ellen's misery. They made it further than Chance had thought they
would before he had to rest. Ellen could hardly keep her
eyes open she was so consumed by fever. He had to find
help soon or she would be in real danger of having last-
ing side effects.

"It's time to go again." She offered little help getting
on his back. The fever was taking her energy.

Again Chance trudged down the path. There wasn't a
dry stitch of clothes on either one of them. Sweat poured
from where their bodies met. He leaned forward so that
Ellen rested on his back more than held on. She'd long
ago become heavier and her arms more relaxed. Had
she passed out?

The river now stretched out more like a placid lake.
High grass grew on each side of the path. The jungle was
far off to the sides, affording them little protection. The
only plan Chance had for them finding cover was to go
into the grass and lie down, hoping they weren't seen.
He'd reached the point that he needed someone to see
them. It would be an opportunity to get help for Ellen.

With an amount of relief he hadn't known it was possible to feel, he heard the sounds of life carried over the
water. There must be a village close by. He took Ellen to a
spot far enough off the path that he believed she would be
safe. He then eased her from his back and to the ground.
There was no argument. She was unconscious. At least
she wasn't feeling any pain.

He removed the packs and placed his under her head.
Checking her pulse, he was glad to find that it was strong
but she burned with fever. He pulled a bottle out and
poured a few drops of water into her mouth. Watching

her swallow, he gave her some more. He then drank a mouthful, leaving the bottle beside her in case she woke.

Kissing her on the forehead, he headed back to the path at almost a run. He hated leaving Ellen by herself but at least she was unaware he was doing so. That way she wouldn't fear being left alone.

When he reached the river he continued his pace along the path. After a couple of turns he came to a village of stilted homes built out over the water. These were much nicer dwellings constructed of finer material than those he had seen before. Still small, they appeared as if they might have more than one room.

Boats were tied below a number of them. Maybe he could find someone to take him and Ellen downriver. He continued running. A couple of children played in a bare spot at the bottom of a ladder to one of the huts. They chattered when they saw him and a woman stepped out onto the porch. Raising a hand to her forehead as if blocking the sun, she watched him approach.

Chance slowed his pace to a jog. He didn't want to scare away any aid he might find. "I need help," he called in Spanish. "A woman is sick."

A couple of other villagers exited their huts.

"I'm a doctor. I need to borrow a boat."

A young man joined the children as if in protective mode.

Chance stopped before he got too close to the first hut. "I have a sick woman with me. We need to get to Saba. I can pay for the boat. I'm Dr. Chance Freeman. I work with the Traveling Clinic out of La Ceiba."

Hopefully they had heard of the clinic. Maybe someone they knew had come to it.

The young man spoke up. "I know of it."

"Can you help me?" There was desperation in every

word. Chance would get down on his knees and beg if he had to. All his fear was for Ellen. Her life. Had she woken? Found herself alone? He'd promised not to leave her again, yet he had. "Will you take me downriver to Saba?"

The young man looked around at the women then back at Chance. "I have no boat."

"What about these?" Chance waved his hand in the direction of the boats under the huts.

"Not mine."

The woman standing above them said, "Take my husband's. But you better return it."

"Come," the young man said, and headed toward the boat under the hut.

He didn't have to ask Chance twice. The man untied the boat and held it. The craft reminded Chance of a canoe with a flat bottom. There were no benches to sit on so he took a seat on the planks. The vessel seemed water-worthy enough but at this point it didn't matter. He needed to get back to Ellen. The man pushed away from shore, using a long-handled narrow paddle.

"We must go upstream, two bends in the path." Chance pointed in the direction he wanted them to go.

The man nodded and pushed against the bottom of the shallow riverbed, turning the boat so that Chance sat in the front. They headed upstream. Keeping the boat close to the shore, the man maneuvered them toward Ellen's hiding place. Even with the regular flap-flap of the water against the hull, they weren't moving fast enough for Chance. Worry circled like a wild animal in him.

"Here." Chance pointed to the shore. "Stop here."

The man directed the boat to land and it had hardly hit when Chance stepped out. He didn't wait on the man before he found the path along the river and backtracked to where Ellen waited. Running through the grass, he found her where he had left her. She looked as if she hadn't moved.

He went down beside her and lifted her head to his thigh. "Sweetheart. Wake up."

"You left me."

Great. If he didn't already feel horrible.

"I did but I'm back now. I found a boat and someone to take us to Saba."

"Good. I'm looking forward to sleeping in a bed with you."

"That sounds wonderful to me too but right now we need to get you to a hospital."

The young man arrived and looked down on them with curiosity.

Chance scooped Ellen into his arms. Her head rested against his chest. Even in the tropical weather he could tell her fever was still running high. "Please get the packs," he said to the man. Chance didn't wait to see if he did as he had asked. His concern was for getting Ellen to medical care as soon as possible, even if he had to steal the boat.

It wasn't an issue. The man passed him and Ellen on the path and was waiting at the boat when they arrived. Chance laid Ellen in the bottom then climbed in and sat behind her, situating her head against his thigh.

She sighed and closed her eyes. The man pushed the boat out into the river. Soon they were in the main channel.

"How long to Saba?" Chance asked over his shoulder.

"Dark. Maybe sooner."

Chance wasn't pleased with the answer. That was three or four hours away. He brushed Ellen's hair back from her forehead. She mumbled something unintelligible. Her soft skin was damaged from the sun, her lips parched and swollen. She was dehydrated. The list could go on and on.

Her hand found his and held it against her cheek. "I'll be fine."

Chance kissed the top of her head. "Sure you will." He wouldn't allow himself to think otherwise.

What in her made her so tough? It had to have been when she had been trapped in the wreck with her mother. She'd known pain on a physical and emotional level that most people never experienced. How long had they waited for help? What had the pain been like as she'd healed? For her, this bug bite wasn't unendurable. She'd learned early in life what she could withstand.

He'd been playing her protector when Ellen was already a survivor.

Chance looked down into her beautiful face. She had the strength that it took to live and work here. Ellen didn't give up, she persevered. She wasn't a quitter. When she made a commitment it was forever. Could he open his heart enough to accept that?

If Ellen died Chance was afraid he would too. Despite what he had already lost in the world, his family, his wife, Ellen would be the greatest loss. When had she cracked through that wall and stepped into his heart? Had it been when she'd pulled out that hot pink nail polish, or stood up to him about his feelings for her, or her determination to care for a patient? Whenever it had been, she'd done it. He'd fallen for her.

The knowledge didn't make him feel better. He looked down at Ellen again. She just couldn't die now that he'd found someone who he knew with all his heart would stand by him the rest of his life.

Over the next few hours he bathed her head, neck and chest with the wet cloth, hoping he could keep the fever at bay. He did manage to get some water down her. But she needed so much care that he didn't have available. Even unconscious most of the time, she clutched his hand.

The sun was low in the sky when the man said, "Saba."

Relief washed through Chance. They were finally back in civilization.

"Help's not far away, sweetheart." He brushed a damp strand of hair away from Ellen's face. "We'll have you in a hospital soon."

Ahead Chance saw a high, modern bridge spanning the river. He'd heard of it but had never seen it. It was a major thoroughfare over the river and to the coast. And an answer to his prayers.

"I stop," the young man said as he pulled over to a pier. "Water too low past here."

Chance stepped out of the boat with Ellen in his arms and with the help of the man. "Thank you. I hope I'm able to repay you one day," Chance said, then hurried toward land.

He searched the area. Now he had to find a phone to call for help or someone to take them to the hospital. Determination and anxiety mixed, becoming a lump in his chest.

Chance hurried up a wide path with low green vegetation on each side toward houses. The path turned into a hard-packed dirt road wide enough for two cars. The houses lining the road were square and made of cinder block and plaster with only man-sized alleys between them. Chairs sat outside many of them.

Wasn't someone around?

The boy of about ten played in the street up ahead. "Help. Hospital."

Eyes going wide, the boy looked at him then ran into a nearby house.

He had to look like someone straight out of the child's bad dreams. With three days of growth on his face, his clothes dirty and smelly, and holding a woman burning with fever in his arms, he must look horrible.

A heavy woman appeared in the door of the house the child had run into.

Hope swelled. "Please help me. I have a sick woman. I need a phone or a way to the hospital."

"No phone. The boy will take you to someone who can help."

The boy was already headed up the street. Chance lifted Ellen more securely against his chest and followed. They walked a block and the boy ran up to a man talking to a group of other men. He pulled on the man's arm. The boy pointed to them. The man stepped away from the group and came toward Chance.

"I need a hospital. Do you have a phone? A car?"

"Car. Come this way." The man directed Chance toward a rusty and dented old sedan. Chance had never been so glad to see anything in his life. Opening the back door, the man then moved away so that Chance could place Ellen inside.

She opened her eyes for a second. "Where are we?"

"In Saba and on our way to the hospital, sweetheart."

"I like sweetheart."

Chance couldn't help but smile. "Good. I like calling you that."

As ill and in pain as Ellen must be, she still had a positive attitude. She'd told him she was tougher than she looked and she was right. Her life hadn't always been easy but she'd managed to find humor and wonder in it.

Convinced by his first impression and his past prejudice that she was weak and needy, he'd learned through this ordeal she was actually the stronger one of the two of them. He'd not been pushing her away for her good but his. What if he pursued a relationship and she rejected him? Would he survive the loss? Would he regret it more if he didn't try?

"No hospital close by," the man said.

Chance was afraid of that. "Where?"

"San Pedro Sula." The man glanced at Ellen. "I take there."

That hope started to build again. Chance had never been there before but that didn't matter. Ellen needed care.

They bounced over rocks and through ditches as the car rattled up the unpaved street. The going was excruciatingly slow for Chance but they were moving toward help for Ellen. He was sitting in the back, with her head resting in his lap. Checking her vitals for the second time since they had left the boat, he was terrified by what he found. Her heart rate was becoming irregular. Her blood pressure was very high as well as her fever.

He looked up when the tires of the car hit pavement and his teeth quit knocking together. The car picked up speed and they were soon rolling over the high bridge that Chance had seen from the river.

"How far?"

"Thirty minutes," the man called back over his shoulder.

Did Ellen have that kind of time? Ellen started mumbling, throwing her head back and forth. She was delirious.

Guilt flooded him. Chance had never felt more helpless in his life. Here he was a doctor and he couldn't even help Ellen. He should have put her on a plane straight home the minute he'd seen her. This country and the type of work the clinic did was too dangerous. She should be someplace less demanding.

They left the city and drove along the highway into a less populated area. The hot wind coming through the open windows did nothing to make him feel more comfortable. They sped down the road but it wasn't fast enough for Chance. Houses started showing up again as they approached what he desperately hoped was San Pedro Sula.

The man pulled off the highway and made a few turns until he entered the drive of a pink sprawling building with a flat roof. Instead of stopping in front of it, he drove under the awning with the word *Emergencia* on the sign.

As the car came to a stop, Chance opened the door. He lifted Ellen into his arms and headed for the glass doors. As he came to a desk he said, "I'm Dr. Freeman. This woman needs medical attention now."

A nurse in a white dress came toward him with concern on her face. "This way."

Chance followed her down a hallway to an exam room that looked like something out of the nineteen-fifties, but it appeared clean and adequate. Beggars couldn't be choosers and he was glad to have anything that would offer Ellen a chance to live.

He placed Ellen on the examination table. "I need a suture kit. An IV set up. Any penicillin-based medicine you have. *Stat.*" He started unlacing Ellen's boot.

The nurse stood there stunned.

A man in a white lab coat came into the room. "Who are you and what are you doing in my ER?"

"Dr. Freeman, of the Traveling Clinic. My friend needs medical attention. She has been bitten by a spider. Her fever is high. Blood pressure up and her heart rate irregular. She is dehydrated, hasn't eaten in three days and sunburned."

The doctor said something to the nurse but Chance paid no attention to their conversation.

Chance was done explaining himself. He had Ellen to see about and no one was going to prevent him from doing so. After removing her boot and sock, he asked the nurse for scissors and she handed them to him. Without hesitating, Chance started cutting away Ellen's pants leg. His lips tightened when he saw her wound. There was no way she wasn't in extreme pain.

"Help me roll her to her stomach." He didn't speak to anyone in particular but the doctor came forward to assist him. Together they settled Ellen so that Chance could see the wound clearly.

What he needed to clean the wound showed up on the table beside Ellen. It wasn't the sterilized plastic covered prepackaged set-up he normally used but he was glad to see the instruments. Over the next hour he opened and cleaned the wound. While he was busy the nurse took care of starting an IV. As he worked, he checked to make sure it was done to his satisfaction.

Chance began preparing to bandage the wound when the Honduran doctor said, "The nurse will take care of that. It's time you tell me what's been going on and for you to be examined."

The idea of arguing with the doctor crossed Chance's mind but by the determined look on the man's face it wouldn't make a difference. "Agreed. But I need to make a phone call first."

Ellen's eyes flickered open. For once her leg wasn't screaming with pain, taking her to the point of tears.

The last thing she remembered was Chance carrying her piggyback.

She looked around the room. It was a simple one with white walls and very few furnishings. A hospital room? It reminded her of the black and white pictures on the history wall of the hospital where she'd done her fellowship. Her gaze came to rest on a sleeping Chance leaning back in a chair far too small for him. Clean-shaven and dressed in clothes that were probably borrowed, he looked wonderful.

When he woke would he gather her in his arms? She wanted that. Desperately.

They were out of the jungle. Safe. He hadn't been hurt. She was alive. They had shared something special. Did he feel the same way? By all his actions he must. He had cared for her tenderly. She remembered him brushing her hair back. Speaking to her encouragingly. Begging her to hang in there until he found help.

But wouldn't he have done that for anyone? Chance was a dedicated doctor.

He'd said no promises. Had never spoken of tomorrow other than when they were going to get out of the jungle.

Chance stirred. He blinked.

"Hey." Her voice was little more than a whisper.

He sat forward. Urgency filled his voice as he asked, "How're you feeling?"

No sweetheart. She wanted to hear him say sweetheart. "Better. Thanks for saving my life."

He shrugged. "I'm just sorry you had to go through that."

Fear built, swirling around her. Why didn't he touch her? Kiss her? Had something changed? She fiddled with the hem of the bedsheet. "I think we both went through it."

"You got the worse end of things." He stood.

Why didn't he come closer? Chance walked across the small space. He looked at her.

"It couldn't have been great fun carrying me around on your back." She paused. "Tell me what happened after I passed out."

He relayed what she was sure were the highlights and little of the drama that had gone into getting her to safety. "Where are we?"

"San Pedro Sula for now." He turned and paced the other direction.

They were interrupted by a nurse entering. She spoke to Chance. "We are ready."

"Ready for what?" Ellen asked.

Now he looked at her. "I called your father. He has sent a plane for you."

Ellen sat up in bed. "You what? You had no right to make that kind of decision for me." Her head swam and she leaned back.

"You need attention that can't be given here. It's my responsibly to see about you. You should be in a hospital in the US and checked out completely. Your body has been through a major ordeal. You need to be seen by a cardiologist."

"I don't need you to see about me. I'm a grown woman who can make her own decisions."

"Yeah, and see where that got you." He moved across the room again.

"It could have been you instead of me who was bitten."

He gave her a pointed look. "But it wasn't."

"What about you? Are you coming? You went through the same ordeal."

"The doctor here checked me out."

"But I'm feeling better." She was weak but she wouldn't admit how much.

"You've been out of your head for most of two days. You need to go home and get healthy."

"When will I see you again?" Ellen reached out a hand. She saw the hesitation in his face before he walked over and took it. His hand was large, warm and safe. She never wanted to let it go.

"I don't know for sure."

"You're running now. Just like you did when you came down here."

"What're you talking about? I'm not running any-where."

"You're running away from me. You can't hide here forever, you know. One day you're going to have to face the fact that you have to take a gamble on someone again. We aren't all like your mother and your ex-wife. Some of us can be loyal."

He pulled his hand away. "This is not the time or the place to be having this conversation. You don't need to get upset."

Ellen wanted to snatch his hand back but he'd crammed both in his pockets. She didn't care about anything but him. This was her heart on the line. "Okay, if we don't talk about it now, then when?"

He looked toward the wall instead of at her. "I don't know."

"See, there it is. You're shutting me out."

Chance's look met hers. He growled, "I'm not! I'm thinking about your safety. You could have been killed out there."

"I'm a big girl. I make my own decisions. Can take what comes my way."

"And down here those decisions can get people killed. Get you hurt."

"What're you trying to say?"

"That in your fight for freedom you can be reckless. Can get people hurt. Get yourself hurt. Sometimes you need to think before you act. You go all in, heart leading. No wonder your father feels the need to shelter you."

If she didn't feel so awful she'd climb out of the bed and stomp her foot. "That's not fair."

Two men that looked like orderlies entered with a squeaking gurney. She and Chance said no more as the men settled her on it. They wheeled her from the room and down the hall. Chance walked at her feet.

As they lifted her into the ambulance Chance said, "It's for your own good."

Her gaze remained locked with his as the attendants pushed the doors together. "I don't need you to protect me, I need you to love me."

The doors clicked closed. Ellen held a sob threatening to escape.

The nurse that was riding with her patted her shoulder. "The doctor must care a great deal to sit by your bed for two days and nights."

If only he would admit it.

CHAPTER NINE

CHANCE HAD BEEN miserable before. But never on this
level. He missed Ellen with a vengeance. Everything that
happened at the clinic reminded him of her. Each child
they saw he imagined Ellen teasing a smile out of him
or her. Anytime an unusual case came in he wanted to
discuss it with her.

The nights were the worst. He wanted Ellen in his
arms. All he had to do was look at his hammock on his
porch and think of those moments they had spent there.
Taking a shower became something to dread instead of
something to look forward to at the end of a long hot
day. It reminded him too much of standing in the falls
with Ellen.

How had she managed to fill all the cracks in his life
to the point he almost needed her to breathe?

His staff had taken to not asking him anything unless
it was medically related. He'd given the bare minimum
of information about Ellen's and his time on the run. But
beyond that he didn't want to talk about the fear, guilt and
relief he'd suffered through over the three days they had
been in the jungle and, worse, those when she had been
so sick. He certainly didn't want to discuss those intense
life-changing moments when he and Ellen had made love.

Love. That had been such an elusive emotion in his life

he would have sworn he had no idea what it was. Then in had waltzed Dr. Ellen Cox. Bright smile, infallible attitude, and fortitude that could withstand the worst situation. And it had. He needed someone in his life like that, but did she need someone in hers like him?

A guy who felt he had nothing to offer her. One who chose to work in a developing country. A dangerous one. With Ellen's background, would she really be content to live and work here with him? She had seemed to love it when she was here as much as he did. Would she feel the same way after she fully recovered?

Anticipation and insecurity hit him at the same time. He'd given up on having a wife, really caring for someone, long ago. But Ellen had him thinking *Can I?* again.

She deserved someone who could sustain an ongoing relationship. He'd not ever managed to do so. Was it possible for him? History said no. Could he learn? The real question was that if he wanted Ellen, was he willing to try?

She'd been disappointed in him when she'd found out he had a sister that he didn't stay in contact with. Maybe he should start there. Would Abigail be interested in seeing him? Could they be a family after all these years? Did they even have anything in common outside being from the same dysfunctional family? Every fiber in his being said Ellen would be pleased to know he'd tried. That alone was enough reason to make an effort. But something deep inside him was screaming for him to do it for himself as well. See if he could handle a relationship.

Ellen wiped her cheek and declared she'd shed her last tear over Chance Freeman. She'd not heard anything from him in the six weeks since she had been home. Not a word.

She was cycling though the steps of grief and she was firmly on anger. As far as she was concerned, she could stay on that emotion for a long time. If she saw him now it might be dangerous for him.

Michael had called and invited her out to lunch the Saturday after Thanksgiving. She had been tickled to see him. He'd filled her in on what had been going on with the clinic and had told her a few funny stories about the patients but that was about it. She was hungry for information about Chance but the only thing Michael had said was that he would be home during the Christmas holidays.

How could Chance act this way after what they had shared in the jungle? After she had exposed her heart? Had she misjudged the type of person Chance was? Keeping the resentment at bay was difficult. Even when her mother had died she hadn't felt this abandoned. She hadn't had a choice. Chance did. If anyone should know how she was feeling it should be him. So why didn't he care enough to do something about it?

When he did come to the States, would he call her? Ask to see her? How could a man be so smart yet so dense? She clenched her teeth, almost as angry with herself for caring as she was with Chance.

That went for her father as well. He'd been harping on at her for weeks to take a job at the big teaching hospital in the city. He'd even had one of his buddies call and put in a good word for her. Today was the day that they had the talk that was long overdue.

She had given her apartment up when she'd left for Honduras so her father had insisted that she stay with him until she figured out what she was going to do next. That wasn't a question. She already knew what she was going to do. Return to Honduras, and if not there then someplace that really needed her.

Her father had had a fit when she had announced the week before that she was on the schedule at the clinic where she had worked in the city. The conversation had gone something like, you could have been killed, you are lucky to be alive, you should be grateful, you need to think about what you are doing. She didn't expect today's discussion to go much better but what she had to say needed to be said.

Chance had accused her of being reckless. She'd never thought of herself that way. Her father had put her in a box of protection that she had wanted to get out of but which had made her take chances. When her mother had died she'd learned at a young age that life was short, but had she really become irresponsible with her decisions?

The last thing she wanted to do was put anyone in danger. She knew from her and her mother's accident that poor decisions could cause horrible outcomes. Did she get so caught up in what she wanted that she didn't think about others? Had she been reckless where Chance was concerned?

She'd made reservations at her and her father's favorite café and arrived early enough that she had gotten them a table in the back. Despite the hustle and bustle of Christmas shoppers stopping for a break, they would have a quiet place to talk.

"How're you feeling?" her father asked, after he'd kissed her and taken his seat.

He was a large, burly man who looked out of place in a suit despite having worn one most of his life. Ellen liked nothing better than being pulled into one of his bear hugs. They had never had a real disagreement until she had informed him she was going to Honduras. She had not left on good terms and had returned to him telling her he'd told her so. Today's conversation wouldn't be an easy one.

"Much better. I'm not having to sit down as often at work as I did the first few days."

"You went through some ordeal. Dr. Freeman didn't tell me a lot but from the look of you when you got to the plane you had been close to death."

Her father had come for her himself. Had even brought their private doctor with him.

The waitress came to their table for their order.

"I'll have afternoon tea," Ellen told her.

"I'll have the same," her father said. As the waitress moved away he continued, "I don't know what I would've done if I had lost you. It isn't fair to put me through something like that. Sometimes you're so like your mother."

There it was. The guilt. Had her mother really been reckless or just enjoying life? Even if Ellen was like her mother, her feelings and desires had merit. She deserved to live her own life.

"I'm sorry. Maybe I do need to be more careful but that doesn't mean I need to give up my dreams just to make you happy."

She had to make it clear she wasn't going to live in a bubble just for him. That she needed his love and support but not at the cost of what she wanted. She'd learned life was too short for that. More recently, and in the past.

"Dad, it didn't happen to you. I was the one who had the reaction to the spider bite."

"Yes, but I was the one scared to death that I might lose you."

What little she could remember about Chance after she'd become sick, he had been scared too but he had still praised her for her strength, encouraged her to keep going. He'd been concerned about her but had never wanted to hold her back. Her father wanted to do just that.

"Yeah, it was pretty frightening in parts. But I'm here."

"And that's where I want you to stay."

"That's what I want to talk to you about."

His bushy brows rose.

"Daddy, I'm going back to Honduras if the clinic will have me. If not, then I'll go to another Central American country to work."

Her father's palm slapped on the table, rattling the silverware. "Haven't you had enough? After what happened to you?"

"Daddy, I know you love me. I know I'm all you have. But this is something I'm compelled to do. I'm grown, heaven's sake I'm a doctor. I'm needed there. I wished you would understand but if you don't, that is fine. I have to go anyway."

Her father studied her. "Does this have something to do with Dr. Freeman?"

She looked away. "Some, but not all."

"That's what I thought. I had him checked out. He's known for having women falling for him."

Her chest tightened. She could understand why. She certainly had. "That may be so but that doesn't mean he doesn't do good work. That the Traveling Clinic doesn't have value."

"There's plenty of work you can do here. Of value. Did you even talk to the hospital about the job?"

"Daddy, I'm not going to. That's not where I belong."

The waitress returned with their tea. They sat quietly until she had finished placing the tea stand in front of them and left.

"I love you, Daddy. I do, but I have to be true to myself. I know you have lost. I have too. I miss Mother every day. I know you worry about me. You've worked to protect me. But you can't do that forever. I'll get hurt. Bad things will happen to me. That's life. What I need is your support. Encouragement."

Her father ate without saying anything. He finally looked at her. His eyes glistened. The last time she'd seen him close to tears had been when he'd sat beside her bed in the hospital and had had to tell her that her mother had died.

"I love you dearly. The only thing I've ever wanted to do was keep you safe. See that you were cared for."

"You have."

"I do support you. Want the best for you, but you can't stop me from worrying about you."

She placed her hand on his arm. "I know and I love you for it."

For the rest of their time together they talked about their plans for Christmas and what gifts they might like to receive. They were pulling on their coats to go out into the snowy weather when Ellen asked, "Dad, have you ever thought about dating? You're still a young man."

Those brows of his rose again. "What brought that on?"

She tugged at his lapel, lifting in around his neck. "I just think that everyone should share their life with someone who cares about them. You've concentrated on me long enough. It's time for you to live."

"Have you found someone you want to share your life with?"

"I thought I had."

Her father kissed her forehead and tucked her arm

though his. "One thing I've learned in this life is that anything can happen."

Did she dare hope?

She returned to her father's penthouse to prepare for her shift at the clinic that evening. An envelope lay waiting on the table in the hall with her name on it. Inside was an invitation to a gala event to benefit the Honduras Traveling Clinic.

Would Chance attend? Did she care if he did?

Chance had been in the States a week. There had been meetings at the foundation and a couple of speaking engagements. Ellen constantly called to him. If he went to her would she even speak to him after so much time had passed? She had to be mad. He couldn't blame her.

He'd kept tabs on how she was doing. Once he had called and spoken to her father. Not known for being easily intimidated, Chance's conversation with Mr. Cox had been an uneasy one. He was a man who loved his daughter deeply and Chance had put her in danger. It wasn't something her father was going to forgive quickly. Their discussion had been to the point but Chance had learned what his heart so desperately wanted to know. Ellen was doing well. Had recovered. For that Chance would be forever grateful.

He also checked up on her through Michael. He had seen her at Thanksgiving and Chance was jealous. What he wouldn't give to just see her for a second. Make sure for himself she was fine.

When Michael had returned he'd had enough compassion for Chance that he hadn't made him ask about Ellen. Michael had offered right off that he'd had lunch with Ellen.

"She's back at work at the same inner-city clinic she

was at before she came down here." Michael had spoken to everyone at the dinner table but had given Chance a pointed look. "Says she coming back here or another Central American country as soon as the doctor gives her a complete release. Which should be soon."

Karen spoke up. "We sure could use her here."

In more ways than one. Chance ached with the need to touch her, hold her. See her smile.

"You should talk to her when we you go to the States next week, Chance. Get her to consider coming back here," Pete added.

"Yes, you should speak to her," Michael stated. "She asked how everyone is doing."

Michael looked at him again. There was a deeper meaning to his words, he was sure.

Would Ellen really want to see him? He'd done the one thing that could destroy her trust.

Called her father. She'd said she wanted his love. Could he give it? Take a chance on her leaving him? Maybe she had changed her mind. After all, their relationship had been during a fight for life. They'd been emotionally strung out. Had what she'd said about wanting love been in the heat of the moment?

What Ellen had done was make him determined to contact his sister. See if he could repair that bridge. He'd put off seeing her long enough. Gripping the phone with a knot in his throat, he remembered what they'd said to each other at their father's funeral. She'd invited him to their father's house for the will reading. Chance had had no interest in ever going there again. He'd told her she could have the house and everything else, that he only wanted the cabin. It was about two hours away and gave him a home base when he was in country.

"But you'll keep in touch, won't you? I would like to know how you are doing."

Chance had just nodded, making no commitment. She'd called him a few times but when he'd not returned them the calls had become fewer then died away. His sister had left him too. Or was it more like he'd pushed her way? Had he done the same with Ellen?

The phone rang almost long enough that Chance thought he had a reprieve. Just as he was preparing to hang up a woman answered.

"May I speak to Abigail? Tell her it's Chance."

"Chance?" The sound of disbelief had him regretting so many things he'd left undone and unsaid.

"Abigail?"

"Yes."

"I'm in town until after the Christmas holidays and I was wondering if you would like to have lunch?"

The pause was so long that he was afraid she might have hung up. Then there was a sniffle on the other end of the line. "Why don't you come here for dinner? Tomorrow night at six."

"Okay, I'll be there."

Chance drove up the drive to the large Tudor-style home built among the trees in an affluent neighborhood. This was his childhood home. There were few happy memories here for him.

He stood outside the front door for a minute before he knocked. As if she was standing behind it, waiting for him, the door opened and Abigail reached out and took him in her arms. "It's about time, Chance-man."

That had been her nickname for him growing up. He forgotten about it.

"It's about time." Now she was using that big-sister reprimand voice.

"I know. I should have come before."

She pulled him into the house and closed the door. Her husband and children waited in the hall. The excitement in her voice couldn't be denied. "Stan, Chance is here. Wendy and Jonathan."

Chance was caught up in a whirlwind of hugs and hellos. What had he missed all these years?

Dinner was served in the same room where dinner had been served when his father had come home but this time it wasn't a meeting of a family that was unsure of each other but of one glad to see each other. Chance hadn't enjoyed a meal more since Ellen had left.

To his great surprise, his sister knew about his work and the family had numerous questions about the Travelling Clinic and Honduras. The discussion was open and frank, with none of the tension he'd expected.

As the kitchen help began clearing the table, Abigail suggested they have coffee in the other room. The living room was the same place but the furniture had been replaced with a more modern version. What really held Chance's attention were the pictures. They were of the smiling and happy group of people who now lived in the house. There were even a couple of pictures of him and Abigail as children. Here he had been part of a family and hadn't even known it. Abigail had not abandoned him.

Her husband and children joined them for a while but slowly drifted away as if they were giving him and Abigail a chance to talk.

"Chance, I'm so glad you are here. I have missed you."

"I've missed you too." To his amazement he meant it.

"I'm sorry we've been so distant for so long. I wished it had been different."

He did too, but couldn't admit it out loud.

"I should have done better as the older sister in keeping in touch. I shouldn't have given up. You are my family."

She had cared. Abigail had carried a burden as well. "There wasn't anything you could have done. That was on me."

"When you came home from school at Christmas you were so different. I couldn't seem to reach you any more. After Daddy died you just never came around again. It was like you blamed me as well as Dad for sending you away."

He had. His mother had been gone. His father hadn't wanted him and his sister had said she couldn't take him. There had been nothing secure in his life and he'd wanted nothing to do with her betrayal.

"I wish I could have made it different for you. Fixed it so you could stay with me, but Daddy would have none of it. He said I was too young to see about you and that you were going to learn to behave. That sending you off to school was the way to do it. I fought for you but he wouldn't let you stay."

All this time Chance had believed she hadn't wanted him around. Had blamed her.

"Those weren't happy years for me either and I know they weren't for you. I hated that we were separated. I hated more that you wanted nothing to do with me. After a while I didn't know how to bridge the gap. Then you wouldn't let me and I stopped trying."

"Part of that is my fault."

"Then let's just start here and go forward. Promise me we'll see each other often. After all, we are family."

Family. That sounded good. "You have my word."

"We'll see you at Christmas." It wasn't a question but a statement.

"I'll be here."

"Chance, you may not want to talk about this but I just want to let you know that I saved your half of the inheritance for you. It's been in the bank, waiting on you."

He would never have thought he would be interested in the money but he knew where he could put it to good use. "Thank you."

"You're welcome. I would've never felt right about keeping it."

After his evening with Abigail and her family Chance saw his past and his sister in a different light. Had he been unjust in his view of Ellen too?

Could he humble himself and beg enough to convince her he loved her and would never let her go again? He could if that was what it took to rid himself of the unceasing ache for her.

CHAPTER TEN

CHANCE PULLED AT his tux jacket. He didn't make a habit of dressing up in one and he knew why. They were uncomfortable. Here it was a week before Christmas and he was going to some fancy party. He much preferred a T-shirt and cargo shorts.

He wasn't fond of a dog-and-pony show but he'd participate in the gala if that was what it took to raise money for the clinic. Tonight's event in the great hall of the Metropolitan Museum of Art, if successful, should raise enough money to supply the clinic for the next year and give him start-up funds for a permanent building.

What he really wanted to do was find Ellen and beg her to forgive him for being such an idiot. If his sister could welcome him back, maybe Ellen could too. He had a feeling he would have to work harder where Ellen was concerned.

From wealthy and socially known families on both sides, maiden and married, his sister was well connected. To Chance's shock she'd been on a committee that helped fundraise for the clinic for years. Abby's group had already had this event planned before he'd called her. She'd asked him to attend and say a few words about his work in Honduras.

The great hall of the Met was already crowded with

guests and more were arriving by the time Chance made it there.

"Doesn't the place look beautiful with all the twinkling lights and the Christmas tree?" his sister said beside him after they had left her wrap and the men's overcoats at the cloakroom.

Chance was sure he would have been overwhelmed by the event if it hadn't been for his social training during boarding school. He certainly didn't attend anything like this in Honduras.

Was Ellen here? If she wasn't, he would leave to find her.

Chance didn't see her in the crush of people. He'd had his sister send her and her father an invitation. It wouldn't be like Ellen not to show up. Despite how she might feel about him, she would be supportive of the clinic. In this environment, he hoped she might be more favorable to listening to him plead for her forgiveness.

A woman who Abigail whispered to him was the head of the fund-raising committee took the stage and asked for the crowd's attention. She thanked everyone for coming and introduced him, requesting he come forward.

As he spoke he scanned the room. *Was she there?* Once he thought he saw Ellen but if it was her she'd moved out of sight. He gave his prepared speech, which included sharing about how a visiting doctor had communicated with young girls over fingernail polish, pointing out that the smallest things could make a big difference. Ellen had taught him that. That the work wasn't just about the grand scale but the small everyday efforts and relationships the clinic was building.

When he had finished, the committee chair returned to the stage. "We have a little something different planned for this evening. We're going to have the men make a pledge of support in order to dance the first dance with a woman of their choice. Would anyone like to start the pledging?"

There was a soft murmur around the room then a man in the middle of the crowd raised his hand. "I bid a thousand dollars for a dance with my wife."

"Come on, is that all Margaret is worth?" the committee chair said with a smile. "You can do better than that, Henry."

"Make it five, then," the man called.

"That's better. Please come up and sign your pledge card and escort your partner to the dance floor. Anyone else? Come on, gentlemen, what's a dance worth to you?"

"I bid five thousand dollars for a dance with Miss Jena Marshall," called a young man.

"I bid six for the same lady," another man said.

"Make that seven," the first man came back.

The chairwoman looked at the other man but he shook his head. With a smile she said, "Miss Marshall, I believe you have your partner."

From Chance's vantage point beside the stage he could see the smile on the girl's face. While the committee chair was encouraging another bid, he caught a glimpse of Ellen. A joy so large filled him to the point he didn't know if his chest could contain it.

"I bid ten thousand dollars for a dance with Ellen Cox," said a man Chance couldn't see.

Without hesitation Chance lifted his hand. "I bid fifty thousand dollars for a dance with Dr. Cox."

Heat swept over Ellen. Her heart did a fast tap dance and she stood stock still. A hush had fallen over the crowd and everyone looked toward her.

She knew that voice. It called to her in her dreams. The voice she hadn't heard in weeks until tonight.

Her body had jerked and flushed when Chance's name had been called to come to the stage just half an hour earlier. Her traitorous heart had flipped. *He's here!*

Why hadn't Chance gotten in touch with her? *Because he doesn't care.* After so many weeks of not hearing from him that could only be the answer. Despite that, his informative speech, which was filled with knowledge and passion for what he did, had her falling in love with Honduras and him all over again.

She stood glued to the floor until someone nudged her forward. The crowd separated as she moved to meet him on shaky legs. Chance's bid made her feel dizzy. Why did he want to dance with her? He could have given the money to the clinic without involving her. Where had he gotten that kind of money?

Ellen had smiled when the interesting pledge twist had been announced. It could either be a flop or a hit. Ellen had been interested to see which. She had watched as her father had made his way to the front of the room. His amazing bid had blown her away. He knew how important the clinic was to her, even if he didn't support her working there.

Now Chance stood in front of her. He was so handsome in his tux it almost hurt to look at him.

A flutter of excitement filled her midsection. She had to remind herself of how angry she was. So why was she so pleased to see him?

The band played the first notes of a waltz.

Chance offered his hand. "May I have this dance?"

She said in a low voice, "I don't want to."

There was a surprised gasp from a few people around them.

He met and held her gaze. "Sweetheart, I'm sorry."

"Don't call me that," she hissed. "It's been almost two months since I've spoken to you."

His smile never wavered. "Let's not fight about it here. We can find someplace private to talk after our dance."

Ellen heard the pleading in his voice and took his hand. It was like coming home to touch him again. He led her to the dance floor and there his arm came to rest at her waist. She could hardly breathe. Her hands shook. She worked to push the pure happiness down, to stop it from overflowing and washing her anger away. They moved across the floor. Chance was an excellent dancer. But even if he hadn't been, she was in heaven by just being in his arms again.

You are mad at him. Remember that.

"I've missed you."

Could she trust him? Was he playing at something? She'd already spent two months in misery. Her feet quit moving. "You think you can literally waltz in here after not speaking to me for weeks and I'm going to fall at your feet?"

"No, that's the last thing I thought. With you I was fully anticipating I'd have to fight my way back into your good graces." He pulled her closer.

Ellen pushed against his shoulder, putting some space between them. "Just where did you get fifty thousand dollars?"

"Let's just say I came into some money. By the way, you look beautiful. That green is gorgeous on you."

She couldn't help but warm at his praise.

"How're you feeling? How's your leg doing?"

"Now you're showing interest?" She wasn't going to give him the chance to hurt her further.

He didn't ease his hold as he whispered close to her ear, "I've always been interested."

"You have a funny way of showing it. No phone calls. No handwritten letter. Not even an email or text."

He twirled her away from him and then brought her back to his chest. "I deserve that. And more. But I have checked on you."

She glared at him. "When?"

"I spoke to your father after you'd been back in the States a couple of days. And Michael gave me a report."

"At least *he* cared enough to see me when he was here."

"I'm sorry. I should have called you. I have no excuse but that I was a coward. I screwed up."

"Well, you're right about that."

He lowered his voice and searched her face. "How are you?"

"Do you really want to know?"

"Yes, I want to know everything about you. I've missed you."

"I'm fine. I've been back to work for a number of weeks. The leg is healing nicely." She purposely filled her voice with sarcasm. "I had a good doctor."

"Yeah, but not much of a human being."

"You expect me to disagree with that?"

"I really am sorry. If you'll forgive me I'll spend the rest of my life trying to make it up to you."

Hope soared within her. What did he mean by the rest of his life?

The number ended and Chance released her from his arms but continued to hold her hand. "I'd like you to meet my sister and her husband."

"What?" So he had contacted his sister. She was so surprised she didn't stop him from leading her off the dance floor.

He grinned. "You sure are using that word a lot. I've never known you to be at a loss for words."

Leading her to a group of people standing near the refreshment table, he waited until a couple broke away.

"Abigail and Stan, I'd like you to meet Dr. Ellen Cox," Chance said. "She worked at the clinic for a while. I'm hoping to convince her to return."

Ellen's eyes widened. She stared at him. Chance wanted her to return?

"It's so nice to meet you, Ellen. We appreciate all the work you have done. I know Chance will be glad to have you join him again." His sister's smile was sincere.

Ellen's head was spinning with all that Chance had said. She hoped she made all the proper responses to Chance's sister's remarks. Had she walked into a third dimension where everyone understood what was happening but her?

Chance broke in on the conversation and said to his sister, "If it's okay with Ellen, I'm going to take her somewhere so we can talk privately. I'll see you at the hotel tomorrow."

Abigail nodded.

He kept a hand on Ellen's waist as they sidestepped their way toward the cloakroom.

"Why do you think I want to talk to you?" Ellen asked.

"Don't you?" He kept her moving, not giving her time to argue.

A number of times people stopped them to ask him a question or make a comment. Keeping a hand on Ellen, he smiled and gave a short answer then made an excuse to move on.

"I think what you haven't said in the last few weeks speaks loudly enough."

He handed their tickets to the attendant and collected their coats.

"Please, let me explain."

The clerk handed him Ellen's full-length hooded cape, with white fur inside and the same green as her dress on the outside, edged with fluffy fur. He placed it over her shoulders.

"You look like a Christmas fairy." Chance was mesmerized. "I thought you were beautiful before but you take my breath away."

"Not too over the top?" She made a half-twirl.

It was the first really civil thing she had said to him all night. She was coming around slowly. "You're amazing."

She smiled at him. His heart flipped. He was headed in the right direction. Pulling on his overcoat, he beamed back at her. "I have missed you."

Bundled up, they stepped through the outside doors into a snowy night.

"It's beautiful." Ellen looked up into the sky illuminated by the lights of the skyscrapers. "I love this city at Christmastime."

Chance offered his elbow as they made their way down the numerous steps to the street. "It's completely different from Honduras."

"Which is equally beautiful in its own way." She took his arm but he was sure it was more out of the need for help than her having forgiven him. Ellen wouldn't go easy on him. He had hurt her deeply. They continued downward. "Where're we going?" she asked.

"How about a carriage ride?"

"Now you're turning into Mr. Romance?"

"That's my Ellen. Give no quarter."

"I'm not yours."

He needed to slow down. Give her time to think. Stopping, he looked at her a second. "Maybe not, but I'm hoping you will be. Just hear me out, please."

She nodded and he led her to a horse-drawn carriage parked on the street. It was decked out in white lights and bells for the season. He spoke to the driver and then helped Ellen into the carriage. With her settled in the seat, Chance joined her and pulled the heavy blanket waiting there across their waists and legs, tucking it around them.

"Warm?" he asked.

"Mmm…"

The horse started off at a slow clop-clop and continued as they turned into Central Park. The jingle of the bells on the horse's rig only added to the perfect winter dream feel of the moment.

"It's been forever since I've taken a ride through the park. I've never done it in the dark while it's snowing." She raised her face to the sky. "I love the sound of the bells. It's magical."

"Sort of like standing under a waterfall," he said softly.

"Yeah. Just like that." Wonder filled her voice.

She was softening. He took her hand under the blanket.

Her eyes came around to pierce him with a look. This was the Ellen he knew so well. "Why haven't you called?"

There it was. The hurt. Raw and deep.

"Because I didn't want to face what I feel."

She continued to glare at him. "I like that answer."

He brushed a snowflake from her cheek. "I thought you might. I'm sorry, Ellen. I was an idiot. There hasn't been a moment I haven't thought of you."

"You had a fine way of showing it."

"I know. You made me think about caring for someone again. But that brought the fear of rejection. I had to face my past before I could ask you about a future."

"So you reached out to your sister?"

Chance nodded. Ellen squeezed his hand. It was as if that one action had shown her that he meant what he was saying.

"I'm so proud of you. That couldn't have been easy."

"You know that if you had died it would have killed me."

Ellen pulled her hand from his and cupped his cheek. Her hand was warm against his cold skin. "I'm made of tougher stuff than you give me credit for."

He covered her hand with his. "I know that now. You have more than proved it. I love you, sweetheart."

A smile spread across her face. "That's all I've ever wanted. I love you too."

He held her close and kissed her. Her lips were cold against his but they soon warmed.

"I told my father I was returning to Honduras or another developing country," Ellen said, with her head against his shoulder.

"How did he take that?"

"Better than I thought he would. He still wants to protect me but he is also starting to understand my need for independence. This time he knows I'm not rushing into a decision."

"No more being reckless?" Chance asked.

"I promise to think twice before I react."

"And I promise to let you be who you are without holding you back."

She gifted him with a bright smile. "I love you, Chance Freeman. I also promise to never leave you."

His hands cupped her cheeks and kissed her softly

with all the love in his heart. "If you tried, I would come and find you. I love you."

Chance had found what had been missing in his life. It was all right here in his arms.

* * * * *

If you enjoyed this story, check out these other great reads from Susan Carlisle

MARRIED FOR THE BOSS'S BABY
ONE NIGHT BEFORE CHRISTMAS
HIS BEST FRIEND'S BABY
THE DOCTOR'S REDEMPTION

All available now!

CHRISTMAS WITH THE SINGLE DAD

BY
LOUISA HEATON

Published in Great Britain 2016
By Mills & Boon, an imprint of HarperCollins*Publishers*
1 London Bridge Street, London, SE1 9GF

© 2016 Louisa Heaton

ISBN: 978-0-263-91531-0

Printed and bound in Spain
by CPI, Barcelona

Dear Reader,

Parenthood is not an easy thing. None of us is really experienced when we go home with that newborn baby in our arms, no matter how many nieces, nephews, cousins or younger siblings we might have cared for. Looking after your *own* child is completely different, and we can only hope we'll muddle through and know what we're doing.

Sydney Harper, my veterinary surgeon heroine, is a mother *without* a child, desperately trying to get through the days, and my hero doctor, Nathan Jones, is having to be both mother *and* father to his daughter, whilst fighting the knowledge that he has a medical condition that could possibly make their lives even harder.

Being a parent with a chronic medical condition is hard. I know this from personal experience. But the reserves of strength you draw on, knowing that you have to get through each day for the sake of your children, is as strong as your intense love for them, and you'll do anything not to let them down. We see this in Nathan, and it's the kind of strength that Sydney needs in her life. She is pulled to Nathan like a moth to a sea of flame.

I hope you'll enjoy their story, and that if you have children you'll give them an extra-big hug before they go to sleep.

Happy reading!

Louisa xxx

For Mrs Duff, my first English teacher,
for telling me I had a wonderful imagination
and that I was never to stop writing.

Books by Louisa Heaton

Mills & Boon Medical Romance

The Baby That Changed Her Life
His Perfect Bride?
A Father This Christmas?
One Life-Changing Night
Seven Nights with Her Ex

Visit the Author Profile page
at millsandboon.co.uk for more titles.

Praise for
Louisa Heaton

'An emotional rollercoaster ride… *One Life-Changing Night* is medical drama at its best.'

—*Goodreads*

'*The Baby That Changed Her Life* moved me to tears many times. It is a full-on emotional drama. Louisa Heaton brought this tale shimmering with emotions.'

—*Goodreads*

CHAPTER ONE

SYDNEY HARPER CONFIRMED her appointment details on the surgery's check-in touchscreen and headed into the waiting room.

It was full. Much too full. Eleven of the twelve available chairs were filled with faces she recognised. People she saw every day in the village. One or two of her own clients from the veterinary practice she ran. Were they *all* before her? Would she be sitting in this waiting room all morning to see Dr Preston? She had patients of her own waiting—it was a busy time of year. Close to Christmas. No doubt everyone was trying to see their doctor before the festive season.

With a sigh at the thought of the inevitable wait she strode in, looking for the book she always kept in her bag for situations such as this.

At the empty seat she sat down and opened the book, slipping her bookmark into her fingers. She tried to focus on the words upon the page, but her eyes were tired and she kept reading the same sentence over and over again. The words were refusing to go in and make sense.

It was happening again. Every year when it started to get close to *that date* her body rebelled and she couldn't sleep. The date would be hanging heavy in the near future, along with the dread of having to get through

Christmas again, reliving what had happened before, every moment as clear as if it had just occurred. The shock. The fear. The *guilt*.

The difficulty getting to sleep. Then the difficulty *staying* asleep. She'd keep waking, staring at the clock, staring at those bright red digits, watching them tick over, minute to minute, hour to hour. Feeling *alone*. So alone in the dark! With no one to talk to. No one to go to, to reassure herself that everyone was fine.

That first year—the first anniversary of when it had happened—she'd got up and stood in the doorway of Olivia's old room, staring at her daughter's empty bed. She'd stood there almost all night. Trying to remember what it had looked like when it had been filled with life and laughter and joy.

The second year after it had happened she'd got up again and, determined not to stand in the doorway for another night, gawking at nothing, she'd decided to make herself useful. She'd cleaned. Scrubbing the oven in the middle of the night until it shone like a new pin was perfect therapy as far as she was concerned. She could get angry with the burnt-on bits. Curse at them. Moan about the ache in her back from all the bending over. But it felt better to be focused on a real physical pain than a mental one.

Last year, when the anniversary of Olivia's death had come around, she'd decided to visit Dr Preston and he'd given her a prescription for some sleeping pills and told her to come and see him if it happened again.

This year, though her oven could no doubt do with another clean, the idea of being up all night again—alone again—just wasn't an option. She hated losing all this sleep. And it wasn't just the one night any more. She was losing sleep earlier and earlier, up to a month or more before the anniversary.

So here she was.

All she needed was a quick prescription. She could be in and out in seconds. Get back to her own patients—Fletcher the Great Dane, who needed his paw checked after a grass seed had become embedded under his pad, a health check on two new ferrets and the first set of jabs for Sara's new kitten. There were others, she knew, but they were her first three and they would be waiting. Even now. Patiently watching the clock in *her* waiting room.

The screen on the wall in front of her gave a beep and she looked up to see if she was being called in. It wasn't, but the person next to her got up out of her chair and left. Sydney was glad for the space, but it didn't last long, Mrs Courtauld, owner of a retired greyhound, settled into the newly vacant seat.

'Hello, Sydney. How nice to see you. How are you doing?'

'Mrs C! I'm fine. How are you?'

'Oh, you know. The usual aches and pains. That's why I'm here. My knees are giving me a bit of gyp. They have been ever since Prince knocked me over in the park and broke my wrist.'

'You did get quite a knock, didn't you?'

'I did! But at my age you expect a bit of wear and tear in the old joints. I'm no spring chicken now, you know. I get out and about each day if I can. It's good to keep mobile.'

Sydney nodded, smiling. 'But you're still looking great, Mrs C.'

'You're too kind, young Sydney. I do have mirrors in the house—I know how old I look. The skin on my neck is that red and saggy I'm amazed a farmer hasn't shot me, thinking I'm an escaped turkey.'

Sydney laughed. 'Ridiculous! I'd be happy to look like you if I ever make it to pensionable age.'

Mrs Courtauld snorted. 'Of course you'll make it to my age! What are you now? Thirty-three? Thirty-four?'

'Thirty-five.'

'You see? Loads of years left in you.' She thought for a moment, her eyes darkening, and she looked hard at Sydney in concern. 'Unless, of course, you're here because there's something wrong? Oh, Sydney, you're not dreadfully ill, are you?'

Mrs Courtauld's face filled with motherly concern and she laid a liver-spotted wrinkly hand on Sydney's arm.

'Just not sleeping very well.'

Mrs Courtauld nodded, looking serious. 'No. 'Course not. The anniversary is coming up again, isn't it? Little Olivia?'

Sydney swallowed hard, touched that Mrs Courtauld had realised the date was near. How many in the village had forgotten? *Don't cry.*

'Yes. It is,' she answered, her voice low. She wasn't keen on anyone else in the waiting room listening in.

Mrs Courtauld gripped Sydney's hand and squeezed it. 'Of course. Understandable. I'm the same each year when it comes round to my Alfred's birthday. Ten years since I lost him.' She paused as she looked off, as if into the distance. But then she perked up again. 'I laid some flowers at Alfred's grave the other day and I thought of you. Your little Olivia's plot is so close. I hope you don't mind, but I put an amaryllis against her headstone.'

Oh.

Sydney wasn't sure how to respond. That was sweet. It was nice to think that Olivia had a bright, beautiful

flower to brighten up her plot. Nice for her to be remembered in that way.

She hadn't been to the graveyard for a while. It was
just so impossibly bleak and devastating to stand there
and look down at the headstone, knowing her daughter
was...

She swallowed hard.

Don't even think it.

It hurt too much. Going to the grave just kept prov-
ing that she was dead, making Sydney feel helpless and
lost—a feeling she couldn't bear. She'd found that by
staying away, by existing in her dreams and her memories, she could still see her daughter alive and well
and she never had to stare at that cold, hard, depressing
ground any more.

Blinking back the tears, she was about to thank Mrs
Courtauld when the computer screen that announced pa-
tient's names beeped into life and there was her name.
Ms Sydney Harper. Dr Jones's room.

She got up quickly, then did a double-take, looking at
the screen again. Dr *Jones?*

But she'd booked in with Dr Preston. *He* was her doctor, not this Jones person! And who was it? A locum?
A new partner? If it was, and she'd been passed on to
someone else...

She shoved her book back into her bag, wondering
briefly if she ought to go and check with Reception and
see what had happened, but the doctor was probably waiting. If she faffed around at Reception she might lose her
appointment altogether—and she needed those tablets!

Clearing her throat, she pushed through the door and
headed down the corridor. To the left, Dr Preston's room.
To the right, Dr Jones's.

Sydney hesitated outside the door, her hand gripping the handle, afraid to go in. What if this new doctor wanted to *ask questions?* She wasn't sure she was ready to tell the story *again*. Not to a stranger. Dr Preston knew everything. There was no need to explain, no need for her to sit in front of him and embarrass herself by bursting into tears, because he *knew*. Knew what she'd gone through and was *still* going through. He often saw her in the village and would call out with a cheery wave, ask her how she was doing. She appreciated that.

A newcomer might not understand. A locum might be loath to hand out a prescription as easily.

Please don't ask me any probing questions!

She sucked in a breath and opened the door, not knowing what or who to expect. Was Dr Jones a woman? A man? Young? Old?

She strode in, her jaw set, determined to be as brief as possible so she could get her prescription and get out again but she stopped as her gaze fell upon the extremely handsome man seated behind the doctor's desk.

Her breath caught in her throat and somehow paralysed it. He was a complete shock to her system. Totally unexpected. It was like walking into a room expecting to see a normal person—some old guy in a boring shirt and tie…maybe someone bald, with old-fashioned glasses and drab brown trousers—but instead laying eyes upon a movie star in all his airbrushed glory.

The man was dressed in a well-fitting dark suit, with the brightest, bluest eyes she'd ever seen. There was a gorgeous smile of greeting upon his face. The type that stopped your heart. That stopped you breathing for a moment.

Oh, my!

Sydney had not noticed a good-looking man since Alastair had left. There was no point. Men were not on her radar. She wasn't looking for another relationship. What was the use? She'd only end up getting blamed for everything.

She was sure those men were out there. Somewhere. Even though Silverdale Village wasn't exactly overrun with hot guys. The type who ought to star in Hollywood movies or get their kits off for a charity calendar. She'd just never noticed. Living too much in her own head.

But *this* guy? Dr Jones?

I'm staring at him! Like a goldfish with my mouth hanging open! Speak, Sydney. Say something. Anything! So he knows he's not dealing with a mute.

She turned away from him to close the door, shutting her eyes to compose herself and take in a steadying breath. Hoping her cheeks had stopped flushing, hoping he hadn't noticed the effect he'd had on her.

He's just a guy.

Just.

A.

Guy.

She blew her breath out slowly before she turned around, telling herself to try and sound haughty and distant, whilst simultaneously feeling her cheeks flame hot enough to sizzle bacon. 'I…um… I don't mean to be rude, but I made an appointment to see Dr Preston…?'

An angel had walked into his consulting room.

An angel with long, luscious waves of chocolate-coloured hair and sad grey eyes. Big, sad eyes, tinged with red, in the fresh face of an English rose.

Startled, he dropped his pen, fumbling for it when it fell from his fingers and smiling in apology. What the hell had just happened? Why was he reacting like this? She was just a patient!

He'd not expected to feel suddenly...*nervous*. As if he'd never treated a patient before. Tongue-tied. Blindsided by his physical response to this woman. He could feel his normal greeting—*Morning, take a seat, how can I help?*—stifled in his throat and he had to turn to his computer, glancing at the screen briefly to gather his thoughts before he could speak.

Sydney Harper.

Beautiful. Enchanting.

A patient!

Reel your thoughts back in and show that you know what you're doing.

He cleared his throat. 'Er...yes, you did... But he... er...got overbooked.' He paused briefly, noticing the way she hovered uncertainly at the door. The way her long cardigan covered her almost to mid-thigh, the shapeless garment hiding any figure she might have. The way her heavy tartan skirt covered her legs down to her boots. The way her fingers twisted around each other.

Curious... Why is she so frightened? Why do I get the feeling that she tries her best not to be noticed?

He could see her gaze darting about the room, as if she were looking for means of escape, and suddenly curiosity about this woman overrode any previous nervousness.

'Is that okay?'

'I'd prefer to see Dr Preston. He knows me. I'm *his* patient.'

Nathan glanced back at the computer, so that he wouldn't stare at her and make her feel even more uncomfortable. Did Dr Preston *really* know her? The last time she'd been into the surgery had been—he checked the screen—a year ago. A lot could change in a year.

He should know.

Forget that. Concentrate on your work.

He was itching to know what ailed her. What he could help her with. How to keep her in the room and not have her bolt like a skittish horse.

Purely on a professional basis, of course. I'm not interested in her in that *way.*

What had brought her to the surgery today? She looked anxious. A bit stressed. Not entirely comfortable with this change.

He gave her his best friendly smile. 'Why don't you take a seat? You never know, I might be able to help. Doctors do that.' He tried to reassure her, but she approached the chair opposite him as if she were a gazelle trying to sidle past a ravenous lion.

He waited for her to sit and then he looked her over. A little pale, though her cheeks were flushed. Her pulse was probably elevated. Her blood pressure rising. What had made her so anxious? He was intrigued. But he'd learnt a valuable trick as a doctor. Silence was a wonderful tool. People would feel compelled to fill it. They'd start talking. Eventually.

So he waited, noting how white her knuckles were as they clutched the bag upon her lap.

And he waited.

She was looking at anything *but* him. Checking out the room as if it were new to her before she finally allowed herself to glance at his face. Her cheeks reddened in the most delightful way, and she was biting her bottom lip as she finally made eye contact.

'I need some sleeping pills. Dr Preston told me to come again if I needed a repeat.'

Ah. There we go!

'You're not sleeping well?'

Her cheeks reddened some more, and again she averted her eyes. 'Not really. Look, I'm needed back at work, so if you could just write me a prescription? I don't want to keep my clients waiting.'

Nathan Jones sat back in his swivel chair and appraised her. He was curious as to why she needed them. 'Sleeping pills are really a last resort. I'll need a few details from you first of all.'

The flash of alarm in her eyes was startling to observe. And if she twisted the strap of her handbag any more it would soon snap.

Sydney shook her head. 'I don't have long.'

'Neither do I. So let's crack on, shall we? Eight minutes per patient can go by in the blink of an eye.' He was trying to keep it loose. Casual. Non-threatening. This woman was as taut as a whip.

She let out an impatient breath. 'What do you need to know?'

'Tell me about your sleep routine.'

Does your husband snore? Does he toss and turn all night, keeping you awake? Wait... What the...?

Why was he worrying about whether she had a husband or not? He wasn't looking to go *out* with this woman. She was a patient! At least for now. He had no doubt that the second she bolted from his consulting room she would make sure she never had to see him again!

'What about it?'

'Is it regular?'

'I work long days at the veterinary surgery across the road from here. I'm the only vet there, so I'm on call most nights, and since the new homes got built I've been busier than ever.'

'So you get called out a lot?'

'I do.'

He nodded and scribbled a note. 'And are you finding it difficult to drop off to sleep?'

'Yes.'

'Worried about your beeper going off? Or is it something else?'

She looked at him directly now. 'Look, Dr Preston has given me the pills before. I'm sure he won't mind if you give me some more.'

She didn't like him prying. He glanced at her records, his eyes scanning the previous note. Yes, she was correct. She'd been given sleeping pills by Dr Preston this time last year...

'*...due to the sudden death of the patient's daughter three years ago, patient requested tranquillisers...*'

He felt a lump of cold dread settle in his stomach as he read the notes fully.

She'd lost her *child*. Sydney Harper had lost her daughter and she couldn't sleep when the anniversary of her death got close. It happened every year. *Oh, heavens.*

He closed his eyes and gritted his teeth, mentally apologising.

'I...er...yes. I can see that in your notes.'

How terrible. The most awful thing that could ever happen to a parent. And it had happened to her and he was trying to poke around in her despair when it was clear in her notes why she needed the pills. But would he be being a good doctor just to give them to her? Or would he be a *better* doctor if he tried to stop her needing them? They could be addictive...

'I'm sure he won't mind if you give me some more tablets.'

Nathan had a daughter. Anna. She was six years old and she was all he had in this world. He couldn't imagine losing her. She was everything to him right now. What this poor woman had been through...! No wonder she looked the way she did.

'I can write you a prescription, but...' He paused. 'Have you ever been offered counselling?'

She looked directly at him, her demeanour suggesting she was about to explain something to a child. 'I was. And I did go to start with. But it didn't help me so I stopped going.'

'Perhaps you weren't ready for it then. Would you be interested in trying it again now? It might help you with this sleeping issue. I could arrange it for you.'

The computer whirred out the prescription and he grabbed it from the printer and passed it over to her.

'Counselling is not for me. I don't...talk...about what happened.'

'Maybe that's the problem?' The words were out before he could censor them. He bit his lip with annoyance. Too late to take the words back. He needed to cover their crassness. And quickly. 'Have you tried a different night-time routine? Warm milk? A bath? That kind of thing?'

But she'd stood up, was staring down at him, barely controlling the anger he could see brewing behind her eyes. 'Are you a father, Dr Jones?'

He nodded solemnly, picturing his daughter's happy, smiling face. 'I am.'

'Have you ever experienced the loss of a child?'

He could see where she was going with this, and felt horrible inside. He looked away. 'No. Thankfully.'

'Then don't tell me that *warm milk*—' she almost spat the words '—will make me better.' She spun on her heel and when she got to the door, her hand on the handle, she paused, her head low, then glanced over her shoulder, her teeth gritted. 'Thank you for my prescription.'

Then she left.

He felt as if a hurricane had blown through the room. He felt winded. Stunned. He had to get up and pace, sucking in a lungful of air, running both hands through his hair before he stood and stared out of the window at the sparrows and starlings trying to take food from the frozen feeders hanging outside. The smaller birds were carefully picking at the peanuts, whereas the starlings were tossing white breadcrumbs everywhere, making a mess.

No, he had *not* experienced the same pain that Sydney had gone through. He would never want to. But he *did* know what it felt like to realise that your life had changed for evermore.

People dealt with tragedies in different ways. Some found comfort in food. Some in drink or drugs. Some kept it all inside. Others found it easy to talk out their feelings and frustrations. A few would blindly choose to ignore it and pretend it had never happened.

He felt deflated now that she'd left his room. Sydney Harper was intense—yes—and hurting—definitely— but there was something about her. He couldn't quite put a finger on it.

It bothered him all day. Through seeing all his patients. The chest infection, the sprained ankle, a case of chicken pox, talking someone through using his asthma medication. His thoughts kept returning to his first patient at his new job.

Sydney Harper.

Beautiful. Elegant.

Fragile.

And then it came to him. The reason why he couldn't forget her. The reason he kept going over and over their interaction that morning.

I'm attracted to her.

The thought stopped him in his tracks. No. He

couldn't—*wouldn't*—be. He had nothing to offer her. Besides, he had a child to take care of. Clearly!

No. That way danger lay.

He doubted he would ever see her again. Not as his *patient*. She had clearly wanted to see Dr Preston, and the way she'd stormed from the room had left him feeling a little bit stunned. He'd *never* had a patient walk out on him like that.

A fiancée, yes.

The mother of his child, yes.

But never a patient.

Sydney strode from the room feeling mightily irritated with Dr Jones, but not knowing why. Because she had the prescription she needed. She'd obtained what she'd wanted when she'd made the appointment. But now that she was out from under Dr Jones's interested, *unsettling* gaze she felt restless and antsy. Almost angry. As if she needed to go running for a few miles to get all of that uncomfortable adrenaline out of her system. As if she needed to burn off some of the inner turmoil she was feeling. As if she needed to let out a giant enraged scream.

Averting her gaze from the people in the waiting room, she went straight back to Reception and leant over the counter towards Beattie the recetptionist—the owner of a moggy called Snuggles.

'Beattie, I've just been seen by Dr Jones. Could you make a note on my records that when I make an appointment to see Dr Preston—my *actual* doctor—that I should, indeed, *see* Dr Preston?'

Beattie looked up at her in surprise. 'You didn't *like* Dr Jones?'

Her jaw almost hit the floor.

'*Like* him? Liking him has nothing to do with it. Dr

Preston is my GP and that is who I want to see when I phone to make an appointment!'

Beattie gave an apologetic smile. 'Sorry, Syd. Dr Jones offered to see you as Dr Preston was overrun and he knew you were in a rush to get back to work.'

Oh. Right. She hadn't thought of that. 'Well, that was very kind of him, but...'

It *had* been very kind of him, hadn't it? And what was she doing out here complaining? Even though she'd got what she needed.

Deflating slightly, she relaxed her tensed shoulders. 'Next time just book me in with Richard.'

'Will do. Anything else I can help you with?'

Not really. Though a niggling thought had entered her head... 'This Dr Jones that I saw today... Just a locum, is he? Just here for the day?'

She tried to make it sound casual. But it would be nice to know that she wouldn't be bumping into him in the village unless she had to. Not after she'd stormed out like that. That wasn't her normal behaviour. But something about the man had irritated her, and then he'd made that crass suggestion about warm milk...

'No, no. He's permanent.' Beattie's face filled with a huge grin. 'He moved to the village a week ago with his daughter. Into one of the homes on the new estate.'

'Oh. Right. Thank you.'

Permanent. Dr Jones would be living here. In Silverdale.

'Please don't tell me he's got an aging pet dog or anything?'

'I don't think so. But you'll run into him at the committee meetings for the Christmas market and the village nativity.'

What? She'd only just decided to return to those meetings. Had been looking forward to them!

'Why?'

Beattie looked at her oddly. 'Dr Preston is cutting down on his commitments now that he's nearly retired. He's asked Nathan to take over. You didn't like him? We all think he's gorgeous! Have you seen him smile? I tell you, that man's a heartbreaker!'

A heartbreaker? Not if *she* had anything to do with it.

Sydney grimaced, but thanked Beattie once again and left the surgery, pausing to wait for traffic to rush by so she could cross the road over to her own practice.

The new doctor was going to be on the Christmas committee. And she'd just agreed to go back. To help. She'd told them she would *be there*. Her heart sank at the thought of it as she neared her place of work.

Silverdale Veterinary Surgery was a relatively small building, comprised of two old cottages that had been knocked through inside and transformed from homes into a business.

Sydney loved it. It was clinical and businesslike, but still retained its old-world charm with white walls and large exposed oak beams and, outside, a thatched roof. There were even window boxes, which she'd learnt to tend. They overflowed with primulas and pansies in the spring, but right now were hung with dark green ivy and indigo lobelia. And *no* fairy lights. Even if everyone else seemed to think it was okay to start decorating for Christmas in *November!*

She'd never been a green-fingered person. Not before she'd got married. But when Olivia came along the little girl had loved being in the garden and growing pretty things. Although Sydney had managed to kill the first few plants they'd got, they'd eventually learned together and their flowers had begun to thrive. There'd been nothing she'd liked better than to watch Olivia use her pink tin watering can to water them each evening, when it was cool. And Syd's talent with flowers had not gone unnoticed around the village either. She'd often been in charge of the flower stalls at the Christmas market each year.

When she'd been involved, anyway.

She pushed through the door and saw that her waiting room was pleasingly busy. There was Mr Shepherd, as expected, with his Great Dane, Sara with her new kitten, and no doubt in the box by Janet's feet were her two ferrets, Apollo and Zeus.

'Morning, everyone! Sorry to keep you waiting.'

Her anxiety was gone here. This was her home turf. Her safe haven. The place that *she* controlled. Was in charge of. Where there were no surprises. Well, nothing life-changing, anyway. Not to her. Here she could cure illnesses. Make things better. As much as she could.

Her clients waved and smiled and said good morning, too. They weren't too bothered about waiting for her. And she appreciated them for that.

In the staff room, she put on her green veterinary top and prepared to start work.

This was better.

This she could do.

This she was in control of.

Nathan stood in the playground, surrounded mostly by mothers waiting for their children to come out of infant school. As always, he felt like a complete fish out of water here. All the mothers stood in little groups, chatting and laughing. They all *knew* each other. And him…? He was the lone male, feeling awkward. Sure that he was standing out like a sore thumb.

He could feel their eyes on him. Judging him. Assessing him. Were they talking about him? Could they see his awkward gait? His limp? Could they see what was wrong with him? *It feels like they can.* He almost felt as if he was carrying a huge sign naming his condition around his neck.

Silverdale Infants had seemed the perfect place for Anna when he'd first come to the village for his job interview. He'd scouted the place out and asked the headteacher to give him a tour. He'd walked through the school with her, looking in the classrooms, seeing the happy children and their paintings, listening to them singing in assembly and watching as they'd sat for storytime in their impossibly small chairs. He'd genuinely felt his daughter would be happy there. It had a good vibe. The head was a nice woman and Miss Howarth, Anna's teacher-to-be, seemed really lovely and welcoming.

Nathan had just had his first day in his new job and this had been Anna's first day at her new school. He could only hope that it had gone as well as his own day, and that she would come running out with a big smile on her face. Then, perhaps, the lump of anxiety in his stomach would disappear and they'd be able to go home and he'd cook dinner.

Nathan hated being away from Anna. Giving her into the care of someone else. But he had to work and she had to learn—and weren't schools considered *in loco parentis?*

He was grateful for the flexible hours his new job afforded him. Since Gwyneth had left them he'd had to become both father *and* mother to Anna. And he didn't think he was doing too badly. Anna seemed happy enough, only occasionally asking why she didn't have a mummy, like other children. Those days were hard.

When he could see the hurt in his daughter's eyes. And when it happened he would curse Gwyneth inwardly, whilst outwardly he would throw everything he had at making his daughter happy.

He just couldn't give her the mother that she wanted. He wasn't ready to be with someone new. To open himself up to possible hurt and betrayal. To being left again. And why put Anna through the hope of getting to know someone when they might walk away and break her heart, too?

He didn't bad-mouth Gwyneth to Anna. It wasn't up to him to tell Anna how to feel about her mother. Anna might want to find her one day and see her. Talk to her. Ask her things. Did he want Anna to grow up resentful and hating her mother? No. Even if it was hard for him. Because Gwyneth had abandoned them both. And that hurt. Not so much now, but it still caused pain whenever he thought about his and Anna's future.

He sighed as he thought about his mistake in getting involved with Gwyneth. She'd been so much fun to begin with, but—as was sometimes the way with relationships—they'd both realised something was missing. And then they'd discovered she was pregnant...

Life was short. And he would not have Anna spending hers moping about for a mother who had no interest in her whatsoever. He was only sorry that he hadn't noticed Gwyneth's shallowness earlier on. Before he'd got in too deep.

The school bell rang and he braced himself. Now he'd know. Had it gone well?

Crossing his fingers in his jacket pockets, trying not to shiver in the late November cold, he looked for her familiar face amongst the mass of children pouring out through the door, all of them almost identical in their little green jumpers and grey skirts or trousers.

Then he saw her and his heart lifted.

'Daddy!'

She was *smiling*. Beaming at him as she ran to his open arms, clutching a painting that was still slightly wet. Nathan scooped her up, hefting her onto his hip, trying not to grimace at the pain in his shoulder.

'What do we have here?' He glanced at the painting. There were daubs of brown and green that he guessed was a tree, and to one side was a large black blob with ears. 'Is that Lottie?'

Anna nodded, grinning, showing the gap where her two front teeth were missing. 'Yes!'

Lottie was their pet rabbit and his one concession to Anna's demands to fill their house with pets of all shapes and sizes. Anna *adored* animals, and ever since she'd started at nursery had plagued him with requests for cats or dogs or parrots or anything that had fur, feathers or a cute face.

Knowing that they would both be out all day—him at work, she at school—he'd not thought a dog or a cat was appropriate, but he'd given in and allowed her a rabbit. It had the added bonus of living outdoors and its presence had stopped Anna from 'rescuing' injured insects and bringing them in to be 'nursed'.

'It looks just like her.' He squinted as he saw a small daub of bright orange. 'Is that a carrot?'

'No, Daddy. Silly! That's a worm.'

'Oh, right.' He gently placed his daughter back on the ground, being careful not to grimace or wrench himself further. 'So how did it go? Was it good? Did you make friends?'

She nodded. 'Lots and lots.'

She proceeded to list them as they walked back to the car. There seemed an *awful* lot, and to his ears it sounded as if she'd just memorised the register, but he nodded and smiled at her as she told him about Hattie with the bright pink glasses, and George who had held her hand as they'd walked to assembly.

They were soon home. Nathan still had half their life packed away in boxes after the move, but he knew they'd get there eventually. All the important stuff was unpacked. And Anna's room had everything. He'd done that first. Everything else could wait for when he had the time. He just had to decide where he wanted it all to go.

The house was brand-new, so had none of that old-world character the rest of the cottages in the village had. He had tiles on his roof, not thatch. A modern fake fireplace rather than an old rustic one with real flames. Flat, smooth walls rather than whitewashed ones with crooked oak beams.

Still, the place would get its character eventually.

'I'm going to see if Lottie missed me.' Anna ran through the house towards the back door, so she could go into the garden.

'Not yet, young lady,' he called after her. 'Go upstairs and get out of your uniform first.'

'Daddy, please!'

'It was raining this morning, Anna. I'm not having you getting your uniform covered in mud and straw. Please go and get changed.'

She pouted, but only briefly, and then she ran back past him, clambering up the stairs as he took their bags through to the kitchen, pinned her painting to the fridge with a magnet that was shaped like a banana. He'd picked up some vegetables from a farm shop, so he popped those in the fridge, then switched on the kettle for a drink.

Upstairs, he heard a small *thunk* as Anna kicked off her shoes and soon enough she was trotting back down the stairs, wearing a weird combination of purple corduroy skirt, green tee shirt and a rather loud orange and yellow cardigan.

'Nice... I'm liking your style.' He was keen to encourage her to wear what she wanted and to pick her own clothes. He'd learned that it was important—it helped Anna to develop her independence and allowed her to express herself. And he needed Anna to be a strong character. He wanted to encourage her at all times to feel happy about herself and her own decisions. To feel valued and beautiful. Because she *was* beautiful. With her mother's good looks but thankfully none of her character.

'Will you do me a juice, Daddy?'

'Sure thing, poppet.' He watched her twist the back door key and trot out into the garden. It wasn't huge out there, and as theirs was one of the original show houses it was just plain grass, with one side border of bushes. Nothing too impressive. Nothing that needed that much work. Something he figured he'd get to later. Maybe in the New Year.

But it had the rabbit hutch. The main reason for Anna to go and play outside. He was hoping to get her a trampoline, or a bike, or something. Maybe for Christmas.

He was just diluting orange juice with some water when he heard his daughter let out a blood-curdling scream.

'Daddy!'

'Anna?' His body froze, his heart stopped beating just for a millisecond, and then he was dropping the glass into the sink and bolting for the back door. What on earth had happened? Why had she screamed? Was she hurt?

Oh, please don't let her be hurt!

'Daddy!'

She ran into his arms, crying, and he held her, puzzled. What was it? Had she fallen over? What?

'Let me look at you.' He held her out at arm's length to check her over, but she looked fine. No scuffed knees, no grazes, no cuts. Just a face flooded with tears. What the...?

'Lottie's *bleeding*!' She pointed at the hutch before burying her face in his shirt.

He looked over the top of her head and could now see that the hutch had a broken latch and poor Lottie the rabbit sat hunched within, breathing heavily and audibly, with blood all over her and in the straw around her, as if she'd been involved in some sort of weird rabbit horror movie.

'Oh...' He stood up and led Anna away and back into the kitchen, sitting her down on one of the chairs by the table. 'Stay here.'

'She's bleeding, Daddy.'

'I know, honey. We'll need to take her to the vet.'

He didn't know if the poor thing might have to be put to sleep. There was a lot of blood, and Lottie looked like she might be in shock. He dashed for the cupboard under the stairs, where they'd put Lottie's carrier and got it out. Then he grabbed some latex gloves from under the sink and headed for the garden.

'I'll get Lottie. Can you get your shoes on for me? And your coat?'

'Where are we going?'

'The vet. The animal doctor. She'll need to check her over.'

'What if she dies, Daddy?' Anna sobbed, almost hiccupping her words.

He hadn't imagined this. He'd agreed to have Lottie knowing that rabbits lived for around ten years, hoping that they wouldn't have to face this day until Anna was in her teens. But not this early. Not *now*. He wasn't sure how she'd handle a pet's death at this age.

'Let's cross that bridge when we come to it. Get your shoes on. We need to get her there quickly.'

Nathan headed into the garden, slipped on the gloves and picked up the poor, shocked rabbit and placed her in the box. Normally she fought going in the carrier. But there was no fight today. His heart sank at the thought of having to tell his daughter her rabbit might die. Had Anna not been through enough?

He pulled off the bloodied gloves and quickly discarded them in the bin.

He could only hope that the veterinary surgery was still open.

CHAPTER TWO

IT HAD BEEN a long, tiring day. After her doctor's appointment Sydney had come back to the surgery and seen her first ten patients, and then she'd got round to her surgeries—a dental clean, two spays on cats, a dog to be neutered. Lunch had been quick, and then there had been more appointments: kitten visits, puppy checks, suture removals, an elderly dog that had had to be euthanised. Then she'd returned phone calls, given owners blood test results and now she was finishing off her paperwork. Filling in records. There were three animals being kept in overnight, but Lucy, her veterinary nurse, was giving them their final check before they left for the evening.

'I'll be ready to put my feet up tonight. Have you seen my ankles?' said Lucy.

Sydney smiled sympathetically. Lucy did seem to be suffering lately.

Almost all the lights were off, except for in her office and at the surgery entrance, and Sydney was just debating whether to have a cup of tea here or go home and have it there when she heard a loud banging on the surgery's front door.

A last-minute emergency?

She hurried through, switching on the lights as she

went, and stopped when she saw who was on the other side of the door.

Dr Jones.

Oh.

Her pause was barely noticeable. At least she hoped so. Then she was rushing to the door, her cheeks flaming at having to let in the dishy doc. Though, judging by the look of worry on his face, he wasn't here to continue his conversation about warm milk.

She opened the door and Dr Jones came in, carrying a pet carrier. Behind him, a little uncertainly, followed a little girl with chestnut-brown hair in two ponytails held by pink bobbles, her face tearstained, pale and stunned. Seeing the little girl, so like Olivia—*no, so like her father*—startled her and her stomach twisted painfully. As if she'd been punched in the gut.

She dragged her gaze away from the little girl and looked over at the doctor. 'Dr Jones? Can I help?'

Am I stammering? I feel like I'm stammering.

'My daughter's rabbit. I think it's been attacked.'

He lifted up the carrier, so she could see through the barred door, but it was impossible to gauge the extent of the animal's injuries.

Sydney glanced quickly at the little girl. She looked around Olivia's age. Maybe a bit older. She wasn't sure. But she was young, and she didn't need to see Sydney examining the rabbit if it was in a bad way. There were a lot of foxes out here in Silverdale Village. It was a very rural area, surrounded by farms and woodlands. Occasionally they even saw deer. The likelihood that there were animal predators around was very high.

All business now, she took the carrier from the doctor. 'Maybe your daughter should sit in the waiting room whilst I take a look?'

The little girl slipped her tiny hand into her father's. 'Don't leave me, Daddy.'

Dr Jones looked torn, but then he nodded. 'I'll sit with you.' He looked up at Sydney. 'Is that okay? If I sit out here with Anna?'

Anna. A lovely name.

'Of course. I'll just take a quick look.'

She hurried the rabbit through to the surgery, closing the door behind her and leaning back against it for a moment whilst she gathered herself.

That's Anna. Anna! Not Olivia.

The table where she usually examined pets had already been cleaned down, so she laid the carrier upon it and opened it up.

Inside was a very scared, very shocked black rabbit. From what she could see at this stage it had injuries to the top of its head, its left eye looked damaged, and there were other fine puncture marks across its back and legs. Sydney held it gently whilst she checked it over. The ears looked okay, as did its throat, and it seemed to be breathing fine, if a little loudly. She listened to its chest through her stethoscope and tried to get a better look at the eye, but she couldn't tell if it was ruptured or not.

Poor thing.

She suspected it might die of shock. She felt for its pulse. It was slow and faint, but that was typical for an animal like this in such a situation. Its gums were pale, too and its ears cool.

There wasn't much she could do at this point. Technically, she couldn't see any *fatal* injuries. The shock itself might be the killer here. All she could do at the moment was give the rabbit a painkilling injection and some antibiotics. But she'd need to check with Dr Jones first, in case they requested euthanasia.

Sydney put the rabbit back into the carrier and secured it, then headed to the waiting room, her own heart thumping rapidly at the thought of returning to speak to him.

'Dr Jones?'

He looked up when she called his name and then patted his daughter's hand and told her to stay in her seat before he came over to her and whispered in a low voice, 'How is she?'

Sydney also kept her voice low, not wanting to upset Anna. 'She's in a great deal of shock. Can you tell me what happened?'

He shrugged. 'We're not sure. I'd been at work all day and then went to pick Anna up from school. She found Lottie like that when we got back.'

She nodded. 'She has sustained a great deal of damage to her left eye, but it's hard to see at the moment whether the eyeball itself has been ruptured. If it has, we might have to remove it, but at this stage I think we need to see if she'll survive the night.'

Dr Jones let out a heavy sigh and glanced at his daughter. 'Do you think Lottie might die?'

'It's fifty-fifty. I can give her a painkiller and some antibiotics if you wish. The bite marks are quite small and thin, possibly caused by a cat or a fox. Their mouths are filled with bacteria, so the chance of infection is high. There aren't any fatal injuries, but shock can kill an animal like this. It's up to you what measures you'd like me to take.'

She left the implication hanging. Did he want to see if the rabbit survived? Or did he want her to put the rabbit to sleep?

Dr Jones thought for a moment. 'Lottie is Anna's world. She loves animals. If there aren't any fatal injuries I think I owe it to her to see if Lottie makes it through the night. She won't be in any pain?'

'There'll be some discomfort, but the painkillers should help her an awful lot. I'll give her the injections, but if you can take her home, keep her somewhere warm and safe where she won't be disturbed. Do you have an indoor cage?'

He shook his head. 'I don't.'

'A bathroom, then. It's the safest place—somewhere there aren't any cables or wires to chew.'

'Will she want to eat?'

'You must get her to try. When a rabbit goes into shock it sometimes stops eating, and it will just lead to further complications if her digestive system shuts down. Offer her all her favourites and try to get her to drink, too. I'll need to see her first thing in the morning. Can you bring her in then?'

'Before surgery, yes. About eight?'

She nodded. 'I'll be here.'

Sydney slipped back inside her room and administered the injections. She really hoped on their behalf that Lottie would survive, but the poor thing had been through a terrible ordeal.

Back in the waiting room, she handed the carrier to Dr Jones and then, hesitantly, after thinking twice about doing so, she knelt in front of Anna. She tried not to notice the way the little girl's eyes looked into hers with so much hope. The way tears had welled in her eyes.

'Stay nice and quiet for her. No loud noises. Lottie needs to rest. Can you help her do that?'

Anna nodded. 'Yes.'

'Good.' She stood up again, frighteningly taken in by the little girl's big blue eyes. So similar to Olivia's it was unsettling. How was it possible that this little girl should remind her so strongly of her own?

Backing away, she held open the door for them, eager for them to go. So she could breathe again.

'What do I owe you?' Dr Jones glanced over at the till.

'We'll sort it in the morning. Don't worry. And good luck.'

She watched them go and backed away from the door. They were a nice family, little Anna and her father. Was there a wife at home, waiting for news? It hadn't sounded like it. *He'd* been at work, *he'd* picked his daughter up from school. No mention of anyone else.

It doesn't matter. You're not interested in him anyway. Dr Jones is off limits!

So why was she thinking about him? Just because he was handsome? No. She wasn't that shallow. It must be because of the way she'd walked out on him that morning after her consultation. She'd been rude and had not apologised for it, either. She'd been defensive. Abrupt. Even though he had suggested the most ridiculous thing. And now she'd helped with their rabbit; that was all. They'd all had a shock and she knew how that felt. She wanted it to be easier for them.

Poor rabbit.

She hoped it was still alive in the morning.

Nathan had a sleepless night. It wasn't just because of the rabbit. Though he *was* worrying about getting up in the morning and finding her dead on the floor of the bathroom. If that happened then he wanted to deal with everything before Anna saw any of it. She shouldn't have to see that.

But, no. It was his own body that had kept him from sleeping.

Yesterday he'd tried to give advice on getting a good

night's sleep to Sydney and he felt a bit hypocritical. Yes, there were tried and tested methods—relaxation, a milky drink, a warm bath, checking you had a comfortable bed—but they didn't work for him, either.

The spasticity he suffered from his multiple sclerosis kept *him* awake at night.

It wasn't as bad as it was for some people, and he knew he was lucky that no one just looking at him could guess his condition. He liked it that way. Fought to keep it so. But that didn't stop the damned stiffness that never seemed to go away. Sometimes he would lie there, trying to relax, and he would feel his muscles tightening so hard it almost felt like a vice. Then he would have to rub at his arm or his leg and hope that it would go away. It never did. And he knew it wouldn't. But that didn't stop him from trying.

So he'd spent the night alternately staring at the ceiling and getting up to check that the rabbit was still breathing.

At five a.m. he crawled out of bed, ready for a cup of tea, and checked on Lottie once more.

She's still alive. Thank goodness!

He gave her some dandelion leaves from the back garden and happily watched as she chewed them down, Her appetite was still good. Then he tried to pipette some water into her mouth—which she didn't like—so he decided to leave her a small bowl to drink from instead.

Anna was thrilled when she woke to find Lottie moving about in the bathroom. The rabbit's left eye still looked pretty mangled, though, and Anna was keen for the time to pass so she could go to the vet with her dad before school.

'You won't be at the vet, Anna. I'm dropping you at breakfast club, as normal.'

'But, Daddy, I want to go! Please?'

'No, Anna. I'm sorry.'

It was important that she kept to her routine. He hated changing things in Anna's life. And, though the incident with Lottie was out of the ordinary, it didn't mean that Anna's life had to be disturbed. It had changed enough already. Her mother had walked out on them both, not to mention that he had his diagnosis to deal with. Life for Anna would change dramatically at some point, if his condition worsened. Best to keep things as normal as he could, for however long he could. He would not have her upset unnecessarily.

Anna pouted for a bit, but got in the car happily and whispered good things to Lottie through the carrier door as he drove. 'You'll be okay, Lottie. The vet will take good care of you.'

With his daughter at breakfast club, Nathan drove to work, parked, and then walked across the road to the veterinary surgery with Lottie in her carrier once more. He was kind of proud of his daughter's little rabbit. Getting through a severe trauma and surviving. It was like finding a kindred spirit, and after getting up all night to check on her he felt he was bonding with her. And though last night he'd almost expected to have to tell Sydney to put Lottie to sleep, the fact that she'd lived... Well, he was kind of rooting for her now.

He was looking forward to seeing Sydney's reaction. She was an intriguing woman, and he was keen for her to see that the rabbit was still alive and find out her plan of action. But picturing the look of surprise on her face, or even trying to imagine what her smile might be like, was doing surprising and disturbing things to his insides. Things he didn't want to examine too closely for fear of what they might mean.

The bell above the door rang as he walked through,

clutching the carrier, and he headed over to the reception desk, where a veterinary nurse sat.

'Lottie Jones to see Sydney, please.'

'Ah, yes. Please take a seat—you'll be called through in a moment.'

He sat and waited, his nerves strangely on edge. For the rabbit? For himself? For seeing Sydney again? Last night when he'd lain awake he'd thought about her a great deal. She was very beautiful, and totally out of his league, but...she intrigued him. For all that she'd been through—the loss of her daughter—she seemed surprisingly together. A little terse, maybe, but professional and she clearly cared for her animal charges.

What made her tick? What kept her going? Her bravery in the face of immense tragedy was a very positive force, and he liked to surround himself with positive people. He needed that; he tried to stay positive himself. Perhaps just by knowing her a little bit better he might learn her secret? If she ever forgave him for what he'd said. She was a strong woman. Determined. He could see that. The complete antithesis of Gwyneth.

He shook his head as he thought of his thoughtless advice to her. *Warm milk?*

So busy was he, feeling embarrassed for what he'd said, that he wasn't ready when she opened her surgery door and called his name. 'Dr Jones?'

He looked up, startled. Today, her long brown hair was taken up into a messy ponytail. There were little wavy bits hanging free around her face, and even without make-up she looked amazing. He quickly cursed himself for noticing.

He got up, loudly cleared his throat and took the carrier through to her consulting room, determined to be distant and professional.

'She's still with us. Lottie survived the night.'

He placed the carrier onto her examination table and stood quite far back, as if the physical distance would somehow stop him stealing glances at her.

Her eyebrows rose in surprise. 'Okay. Let's have a look at her.'

He watched as Sydney's very fine hands opened the carrier and she gave Lottie a thorough assessment, listening to her chest and abdomen with her stethoscope, taking the rabbit's temperature, checking the bites and scratches and finally examining the wounded eye.

He tried not to take notice of the small beauty mark on Sydney's bared neck, her delicate cheekbones, or the way she bit her bottom lip as she concentrated. She had a very fine mouth. With full, soft-looking lips.

Dragging his eyes away from her mouth, he stared hard at Lottie. *Focus on the rabbit!*

'It's impossible for me to see if the eyeball itself has ruptured. The damage is too extensive. But until the swelling goes down I don't think we should assume that it has. I'm going to prescribe antibiotic drops for her eye, more painkillers, and a drug to keep her digestive system working which is an oral medicine. Rabbits don't like receiving oral meds, so if you can put the medicine in a food that you know she will eat you can get it into her that way.'

He nodded, keeping his gaze fixed firmly on Lottie's thick black fur so that he didn't accidentally start staring into Sydney's soft grey eyes. 'Okay. How often does she need the meds?'

'The eye drops three times a day, the oral meds four times a day. Will you be able to do that?'

He thought about his work schedule. It would be tough.

But manageable. Perhaps if he kept Lottie in her carrier at work? In an unused room?

'I'll find a way.'

'I'll need to see her in about four days' time. The swelling should have gone down by then, we'll know if the antibiotics have worked, and I'll be able to see if the eye needs to be removed.'

He risked a glance at her wide almond-shaped eyes. 'She'd cope with that?'

'Not all rabbits do well with surgery, and if we do have to remove the eye then she could be susceptible to further infection. Keep it clean. Bathe it with cooled boiled water when you can—three or four times a day.'

'Like a proper patient.' He smiled and closed the door on the carrier once again. 'Thank you, Sydney, for seeing us last night. I appreciate that you were probably closed and your staff were ready to go home.'

She glanced away, her cheeks glowing slightly, before she began typing notes into her computer. 'It was no problem.'

He watched her where she stood by the computer. It was better with her further away and not looking at him. He could think more clearly. And he wanted to make things right between them. He hated it that she'd left his consulting room feeling stressed and angry. Hated it that he'd insulted her daughter's memory with a crass piece of advice.

'I'd like to thank you properly, if I may? We got off to a bad start the other day and… Well, we both live in this village. It'd be nice to know I've not upset the first person I got to properly meet. Would you join me for a coffee some time? I'd really appreciate the chance to apologise.'

What on *earth are you doing?*

The invitation had just come out. He cursed himself

silently, knowing she would refuse him, but, hell, he kind
of wanted her to say *yes*. He couldn't just see her about
rabbits and sleeping tablets. Part of him wanted to know
more about her. About that strong side of her that kept
her going in the cruel world that had taken her daughter.
That inner strength of hers...

But he also got the feeling that if they were given the
chance the two of them might become friends. It had been
a long time since he'd sat down and just chatted with a
woman who wasn't a patient, or some cashier in a shop,
someone with whom he could pass the time of day.

'Oh, I don't know. I—' She tucked a stray strand of
hair behind her ear and continued typing, her fingers
tripping over one another on the keyboard, so that he
could see she had to tap 'delete' a few times and go back,
cursing silently.

He focused on her stumbling fingers. Tried not to
imagine himself reaching for her hands and stilling them.
'Just coffee. I don't have an evil plan to try and seduce
you, or anything.'

Shut up, you idiot. You're making it worse!

Now she looked at him, her hands frozen over the
keys. Her cheeks red. Her pause was an agonising silence
before her fingers leapt into life once more, finishing her
notes before she turned to him and spoke.

'That's kind of you, but—'

'Just a chat. Anna and I don't really know anyone
here, and—well, I'd really like to know you.' He smiled.
'As a friend.'

It could never be anything else. Despite the fact that
she was the most beautiful creature he had ever seen.
Despite the fact that he could see her pulse hammering
away in her throat. That her skin looked so creamy and

soft. That he wanted to lift that stray strand of hair from her face and...

'I—'

'No pressure. Not a date. Just...coffee.'

He realised he was rambling, but he was confused. *She* confused him. Made him feel like he was tripping over his own words even though he wasn't. Made him surprised at what came out of his own mouth.

He'd not reached out to a woman like this since Gwyneth had left. He'd tried to become accustomed to the fact that he would spend the rest of his life alone. That he would not parade a stream of women past Anna. That he would not endanger his heart once again because on the one occasion he had given it to a woman she had ripped it apart.

The only female who would have his undying love was his daughter.

Which was as it should be.

Anna didn't need the huge change that a woman in their lives would bring. He was lucky that Gwyneth had left before Anna knew who she was or formed a bond.

But he missed being able just to sit with a woman and chat about everyday things. He missed asking about another person's day. He missed having adult company that didn't involve talks about unusual rashes, or a cough that wouldn't go away, or *could you just take a look at my boil?* And he imagined that Sydney would be interesting. Would have intelligent things to say and be the complete opposite of his ex-fiancée.

That was all he wanted.

All he *told* himself he wanted.

He waited for her to answer. Knowing she would turn him down, knowing it would hurt for some reason, but knowing that he'd had to ask because... Well, because he'd said something stupid to her the other day and he needed to apologise in the only way he knew how.

He waited.

Just a coffee?

Was there really such a thing as 'just a coffee' when a guy asked you out?

Because that was what he was doing. Asking her out. Like on a date. Right? And though he said there was no pressure, there was *always* pressure. Wasn't there?

Besides, why would she want to meet him for a drink? For a chat? This was the man who had got her so riled up yesterday, what with his probing questions and his damned twinkling eyes.

Did he not know how attractive he was? Because he seemed oblivious to it. Either that or he was a great actor. With great hair, and an irresistible charm about him, and the way he was looking at her right now... It was doing unbelievable things to her insides. Churning her up, making her stomach seem all giddy, causing her heart to thump and her mouth to go dry. She hadn't felt this way since her schoolgirl crush had asked her to the local disco. And her hands were trembling. *Trembling!*

Why had he asked her out? Why did he want to go for coffee? She had nothing to talk to him about. She didn't know this guy. Except that he was a hot doctor with effortlessly cool hair and eyes that melted her insides every time he smiled at her. Oh, and that he had a daughter. A beautiful little girl who seemed very lovely indeed, but who made her feel uncomfortable because she reminded her too much of Olivia.

If he wanted to apologise to her then why didn't he just do it? It wouldn't take a moment. No need for them to go to a coffee shop. He could say it here. Now. Then she could thank him, and then he could go, and it would all be over.

Why would she get any kind of involved with this man? He was dangerous in so many ways. Intelligent, good-looking, attractive. Not to mention his adorable daughter… She pushed the thought away. *No.*

She wanted to say, *We have nothing to talk about.* She wanted to say, *But there's no point.* She wanted to yell, *You're so perfect you look airbrushed. And I can't have coffee with you because you make me feel things that I don't want to feel and think of things I sure as hell don't want to think about!*

But she said none of those things. Instead she found herself mumbling, 'That'd be great.' Her voice almost gave out on that last word. Squeaking out of her closed throat so tightly she wondered if only dogs would have been able to hear it.

Oh, no, did I just agree to meet him?

The goofy smile he gave her in return made her temperature rise by a significant amount of degrees, and when he said goodbye and left the room she had to stand for a minute and fan her face with a piece of paper. She berated herself inwardly for having accepted. She would have to turn him down. Maybe call the surgery and leave a message for him.

This was a mistake.

A big mistake.

Nathan waited for his computer system to load up, and whilst he did he sat in his chair, staring into space and wondering just what the hell he had done.

Sydney Harper had said yes to his coffee invitation. *Yes!*

It was unbelievable. There must have been some

spike, some surge in the impulse centre of his brain that had caused his mind to short circuit or something. His leg muscles would sometimes spasm and kick out suddenly—the same must have happened with his head. And his mouth.

He had no doubt that they would get on okay. She would show up—a little late, maybe—pretend that she couldn't stay for long, have some excuse to leave sooner than she'd expected. Maybe even get a friend to call her away on an invented emergency. But…they'd get on okay. He'd apologise right away for what he'd said. Be polite as could be.

Surely it was a good thing to try and make friends when you moved to a new area? That was all he was doing.

And how many guys have you invited for coffee?

The only people he really knew in Silverdale were Dr Preston, some of the staff at the medical centre and his daughter's teacher at school, and they were more colleagues than actual friends. He'd left all his old friends behind when he'd moved from the city to this remote village. They kept in touch online. With the odd phone call and promises to meet up.

Sydney could be a *new* friend. A female friend. That was possible. How could it *not* be in today's modern age? And once he got past her prickly demeanour, made her realise he was sorry and showed her that he was no threat to her romantically, then they could both relax and they would get on like a house on fire.

He had no doubt of that.

So why, when he thought of spending time with Sydney, did he picture them kissing? Think of himself reaching for her hand across the table and lifting it to his lips while he stared deeply into her eyes. Inhaling the scent of her perfume upon her wrist...

And why did that vision remind him of Gwyneth's twisted face and her harsh words?

'I can't be with you! Why would anyone *want to be with you? You're broken. Faulty. The only thing you can offer is a lifetime of pain and despair and I didn't sign up for that!'*

Determined not to be haunted by his ex-fiancée's words, he angrily punched the keys on his keyboard, brought up his files and called in his first patient of the day.

Sam Carter was a thirty-two-year-old man who had just received a diagnosis of Huntington's Disease. His own father had died from it quite young, in his fifties, and the diagnosis had been a terrible shock to the whole family after Sam had decided to have genetic testing. Now he sat in front of Nathan, looking pale and washed out.

'What can I do for you, Sam?'

His patient let out a heavy sigh. 'I dunno. I just... need to talk to someone, I guess. Things are bad. At home. Suddenly everything in my life is about my diagnosis, and Jenny, my wife... Well...we'd been thinking about starting a family and now we don't know what to do and...'

Nathan could see Sam's eyes reddening as he fought back tears. Could hear the tremor in his patient's voice. He understood. Receiving a diagnosis for something such as Huntington's was very stressful. It changed everything. The present. The future. His own diagnosis of multiple sclerosis had changed *his* life. And Anna's. It had been the final axe to fall on his farce of a relationship.

'What did your consultant say?'

Sam sniffed. 'I can't remember. Once he said the

words—that I had Huntington's—I didn't really hear
the rest. I was in shock… He gave us leaflets to take
home and read. Gave us some websites and telephone
numbers of people who could help, but…' He looked up
at Nathan and met his eyes. 'We wanted to start a *family!* We wanted babies! And now… Now we don't know
if we should. Huntington's is a terrible disease, and I'm
not sure I want to pass that on to my children.'

Nathan nodded. It was a difficult thing to advise upon
as a general practitioner. He didn't have a Huntington's
specialty. He didn't want to give Sam the wrong advice.

'I hear what you're saying, Sam. It's a difficult situation and one that you and your wife must come to an
agreement about together. I'm sure your consultant could
discuss giving you two genetic counselling. A counsellor would be able to advise you better about the possibility of passing Huntington's to your children and what
your options might be in terms of family planning. Have
you got another appointment scheduled with your consultant soon?'

'In a month.'

'Good. Maybe use the time in between then and now
to think of what questions you want to ask him. Just because you have Huntington's, and your father did too, it
does not mean that any children you and Jenny have, will
develop it. It's a fifty per cent chance.'

'They could be carriers, though.'

'That's a possibility, yes. Your consultant will be much
better placed to talk this over with you, but if I'm right
CVS—chorionic villus sampling—can be used to gain
some foetal genetic material and test for the disease. And
I believe there's also a blood test that can be performed on
Jenny to check the cell-free foetal DNA, and that would

carry no risk of miscarriage. How are you coping on a day-to-day level?'

'Fine, I guess. I have a chorea in my hand sometimes.' A chorea was a hand spasm. 'But that's all, so far.'

Nathan nodded. 'Okay. What about sleeping? Are you doing all right?'

'Not bad. I've lost some sleep, but I guess that's down to stress. My mind won't rest when I go to bed.'

'That's understandable. If it gets difficult then come and see me again and we'll look at what we can do.'

'How long do you think I've got, Dr Jones? My dad died young from this; I need to know.'

Nathan wanted to reassure him. Wanted to tell him that he would live a long life and that it would all be fine. But he couldn't know that. He had no idea how Sam's Huntington's would affect him. It affected each sufferer differently. Just like multiple sclerosis did.

'It's impossible to say. You've just got to take each day as it comes and live it the best you can. Then, when-ever the end does arrive, you'll know you lived your life to the fullest.'

Sam smiled. 'Is that *your* plan, Doc?'

Nathan smiled back. It certainly was. Living his life and trying to be happy was his number one aim. And he wanted the people around him to be happy too. The fact that he'd upset Sydney the way he had... Perhaps that was why he had asked her to coffee.

'It is.'

Sydney stared at her reflection in the mirror. 'What on earth am I doing?' she asked herself.

Her make-up was done to perfection. Her eyeliner gave a perfect sweep to the gentle curve of her eyelid. The blusher on her cheeks highlighted her cheekbones and her lipstick added a splash of colour, emphasising the fullness of her lips. Her eyelashes looked thicker and darker with a coating of mascara, making her grey eyes lighter and clearer. Her normally wavy hair had been tamed with the help of some styling spray, and the earrings in her ears dangled with the blue gems that had once belonged to her grandmother.

She looked completely different. Done up. Like a girl getting ready for a date. Like a girl who was hoping that something might happen with a special guy.

It's just coffee! Why have you put in this much effort? Is it for him?

Grabbing her facial wipes, she rubbed her face clean, angry at herself, until her skin was bare and slightly reddened by the force she'd used upon it. She stared back at her new reflection. Her normal reflection. The one she saw every day. The one bare of pretence, bare of cosmetics. Mask-free.

This is me.

She was *not* getting ready for a date! This was coffee. Just coffee. No strings attached. They were just two people meeting. Associates. She did *not* have to get all dressed up for a drink at The Tea-Total Café.

So she pulled the dress off over her head and put on her old jeans—the ones with the ripped knees—slipped on a white tee and then an oversized black fisherman's jumper and scooped her hair up into a scruffy bun, deliberately pulling bits out to give a casual effect. Then she grabbed her bag, thick coat and scarf and headed out, figuring that she'd walk there. It wasn't far. The wind might blow her hair around a bit more. She would *not* make any effort for Dr Jones.

Striding through the village, she hoped she looked confident, because she wasn't feeling it. She had more nerves in her stomach now than she'd had taking her driving test or her final exams. Her legs were weak and her nerves felt as taut as piano strings.

It was all Dr Jones's fault—that charming smile, those glinting blue eyes, that dark chestnut hair, perfectly tousled, just messy enough to make it look as if he hadn't touched it since rolling out of bed.

She swallowed hard, trying *not* to think of Dr Jones in bed. But Sydney could picture him perfectly...a white sheet just covering his modesty, his naked body, toned and virile as he gazed at her with a daring smile...beckoning her back beneath the sheets...

Stop. It.

She checked her mobile phone. Had the surgery been in touch? A last-minute patient? An emergency surgery, maybe? Something that would force her to attend work so she didn't have to go? But, no. Her phone was annoyingly clear of any recent messages or texts. She was almost tempted to call the surgery and just check that things were okay—make sure no cows on the nearby farms were about to calve. Right now she'd be much happier standing in a swamp of mud or manure with her arm in a cow's insides. Instead she was *here*.

She stood for a moment before she entered, psyching herself up.

The bell above the door rang as she went inside and she was met by a wall of heat and the aroma of freshly brewed coffee and pastries. Praying he wouldn't be there, she glanced around, ready to flash a smile of apology to the staff behind the counter before she ducked straight out again—but there he was. Dashing and handsome and tieless, dressed in a smart grey suit, the whiteness of his shirt showing the gentle tan of his skin.

He stood up, smiling, and raised a hand in greeting. 'Sydney. You made it.'

Nervous, she smiled back.

Dr Jones pulled a chair out for her and waited for her to sit before he spoke again. 'I wasn't sure what you'd like. What can I get you?'

He seemed nervous.

'Er...just tea will be fine.'

'Milk and sugar?'

She nodded, and watched as he made his way over to the counter to place her order. He looked good standing there. Tall, broad-shouldered. Sydney noticed the other women in the café checking him out. Checking *her* out and wondering why she might be with him.

You can have him, ladies, don't worry. There's nothing going on here.

He came back moments later with a tray that held their drinks and a plate of millionaire's shortbread.

She was surprised. 'Oh. They're one of my favourites.'

He looked pleased. 'Mine too. Help yourself.'

She focused on making her tea for a moment. Stirring the pot. Pouring the tea. Adding sugar. Adding milk. Stirring for a while longer. Stopping her hand from shaking. Then she took a sip, not sure what she was supposed to be talking about. She'd been quite rude to this man. Angry with him. Abrupt. Although, to be fair, she felt she'd had reason to be that way.

'So, how long have you lived in Silverdale?' he asked.

I can answer that.

'All my life. I grew up here. Went to the local schools. I left to go to university, but came back after I was qualified.'

She kept her answer short. Brief. To the point. She

wasn't going to expand this. She just wanted to hear what he had to say and then she would be gone.

'And you now run your own business? Did you start it from scratch?'

'It was my father's business. He was a vet, too.'

'Does he still live locally?'

'No. My parents moved away to be closer to the coast. They always wanted to live by the sea when they retired.'

She paused to take another sip of tea, then realised it would be even more rude of her if she didn't ask *him* a question.

'What made you come to live in Silverdale?'

'I grew up in a village. Loved it. Like you, I left for university, to do my medical training, and then after Anna was born I decided to look for a country posting, so that Anna could have the same sort of childhood I had.'

She nodded, but knew he was glossing over a lot. Where was Anna's mother? What had happened? Anna wasn't a baby any more. She was five years old, maybe six. Was this his first country posting?

Who am I kidding? I don't need to know.

Sydney gave him a polite smile and nibbled at one of the shortbreads.

'My name's Nathan, by the way.'

Nathan. A good name. Kind. She looked him up and down, from his tousled hair to his dark clean shoes. 'It suits you.'

'Thanks. I like *your* name, too.'

The compliment coupled with the eye contact was suddenly very intense and she looked away, feeling heat in her cheeks. Was it embarrassment? Was it the heat from the café's ovens and the hot tea? She wasn't sure. Her heart was beginning to pound, and she had a desperate desire to start running, but she couldn't do that.

Nor could she pretend that she was relaxed. She didn't want to be here. She'd said yes because he'd put her on the spot. Because she hadn't been able to say no. Best just to let him know and then she could go.

She leaned forward, planting her elbows on the desk and crossing her arms in a defensive posture.

'You know…this isn't right. *This*. Meeting in a coffee shop. With you. I've been through a lot and you…' she laughed nervously '…you make me *extremely* uncomfortable. When I met you yesterday, in your surgery, I was already on edge. You might have noticed that. What with your doctor's degree and your—' she looked up '—your incredible blue eyes which, quite frankly, are ridiculously much too twinkly and charming.'

She stood, grabbing her bag and slinging it over her shoulder.

'I'm happy to help you with your daughter's rabbit, and I'll be the consummate professional where that poor animal is concerned, but *this*?' She shook her head. 'This I cannot do!'

She searched in her bag to find her purse. To lay some money on the table to pay for her tea and biscuit. Then she could get out of this place and back to work. To where she felt comfortable and in control. But before she could find her purse she became aware that Nathan had stood up next to her and leaned in, enveloping her in his gorgeous scent.

'I'm sorry.'

Standing this close, with his face so near to hers, his understanding tone, his non-threatening manner, his apology… There was nothing else she could do but look into his eyes, which were a breathtaking blue up close, flecked with tones of green.

She took a step back from his gorgeous proximity. 'For what?'

'For what I said to you. In our consultation. My remark was not intended to insult you, or the memory of your daughter, by suggesting that you could get over it with the help of...' he swallowed '...warm milk. But you were my first patient, and I knew you were in a rush, and I got flustered and...' His voice trailed off as he stared into her eyes.

Sydney quickly looked away, aware that the other customers in the café might be watching them, sensing the tension, wondering what was going on.

'Sydney?'

She bit her lip, her cheeks flushing, before she turned back to meet his gaze. 'Yes?'

'I promised this was just coffee. We've had tea and shortbread which may have changed things slightly, but not greatly. So please don't go. We're just drinking tea and chomping on shortbread. Please relax. I'm not going to jump your bones.'

'Right.' She stared at him uncertainly, imagining him *actually* jumping her bones, but that was too intense an image so, giving in, she sank back into her seat and broke off a piece of shortbread and ate it.

Her cheeks were on fire. This was embarrassing. She'd reacted oddly when all he'd expected was a drink with a normal, sane adult.

She glanced up. He was smiling at her. She hadn't blown it with her crazy moment. By releasing the steam from the pressure cooker that had been her brain. He was still okay with her. It was all still okay. He wasn't about to commit her to an asylum.

'I'm out of practice with this,' she added, trying to explain her odd behaviour. 'Could you please pretend that you're having tea with a woman who behaves normally?'

He picked up his drink and smiled, his eyes twinkling with amusement. 'I'll try.'

She stared back, uncertain, and then she smiled too. She hadn't scared him off with her mini-rant—although she supposed that was because he was a doctor, and doctors knew how to listen when people ranted, or nervously skirted around the main issue they wanted to talk about. Nathan seemed like a good guy. One who deserved a good friend. And good friends admitted when they were wrong.

'I'm sorry for walking out on you like that yesterday.'

'It's not a problem.'

'It is. I was rude to you because I was unsettled. I thought you were going to ask questions that I wasn't ready to answer and I just wanted to get out of there.'

'Why?'

'Because you made me nervous.'

'Doctors make a lot of people nervous. It's called White Coat Syndrome.'

She managed a weak smile. 'It wasn't your white coat. You didn't have one.'

'No.'

'It was you. *You* made me nervous.'

He simply looked at her and smiled. He was understanding. Sympathetic. Kind. All the qualities she'd look for in a friend.

But he was also drop-dead gorgeous.

And she wasn't sure she could handle *that*.

CHAPTER THREE

HE WAS SITTING there trying to listen to Sydney, hearing her telling stories of veterinary school and some of the cases she'd worked on, but all he could think about as he sat opposite her was that she was so very beautiful and seemed completely unaware of it.

It was there even in the way she sat. The way she held her teacup—not using the handle but wrapping her hands around the whole cup, as if it was keeping her warm. The way her whole face lit up when she laughed, which he was beginning to understand was rare. He'd wondered what she would look like when she smiled and now he knew. It was so worth waiting for. Her whole face became animated, unburdened by her past. It was lighter. Purer. Joyous. And infectious. Dangerously so.

And those eyes of hers! The softest of greys, like ash.

He was unnerved. He really had just wanted to meet her for this drink and clear the air after yesterday's abrupt meeting in his surgery. And to thank her for helping Lottie after her attack. But something else was happening. He was being sucked in. Hypnotised by her. Listening to her stories, listening to her talk. He liked the sound of her voice. Her gentle tone.

He was trying—*so hard*—to keep reminding himself that this woman was just going to be a friend.

Sydney worked hard. Very hard. All her tales were of work. Of animals. Of surgeries. She'd not mentioned her daughter once and he knew *he* couldn't. Not unless she brought up the subject first. If she wanted to share that with him then it had to be *her* choice.

He understood that right now Sydney needed to keep the conversation light. This was a new thing for her. This blossoming friendship. She was like a tiny bird that was trying its hardest not to be frightened off by the large tom cat sitting watching it.

'Sounds as if you work very hard.'

She smiled, and once again his blood stirred. 'Thank you. I do. But I enjoy it. Animals give you so much. Without agenda. Unconditionally.'

'Do you have pets yourself? It must be hard not to take home all the cases that pull at your heart strings.'

'I have a cat. Just one. She's ten now. But she's very independent—like me. Magic does her own thing, and when we both get home after a long day she either curls up on my lap or in my bed.'

Her face lit up as she spoke of Magic, but she blushed as she realised she'd referenced her bed to him.

A vision crossed his mind. That long dark hair of hers spread out over a pillow. Those almond-shaped smoky eyes looking at him, relaxed and inviting, as she lay tangled in a pure white sheet...

But he pushed the thought away. As lovely as Sydney was, he couldn't go there. This was friendship. Nothing else. He had Anna to think about. And his health.

He had no idea for how long he would stay relatively unscathed by his condition. His MS had been classified as 'relapsing remitting multiple sclerosis'. Which meant that he would have clear attacks of his symptoms, which would slowly get better and go away completely—until the next attack. But he knew that as the disease progressed his symptoms might not go away at all. They would linger. Stay. Get worse with each new attack, possibly leaving him disabled. But he was holding on to the thought that it wouldn't happen soon. That he would stay in relative good health for a long time.

But he could not, in any good conscience, put anyone else through that. Who deserved that?

And he had a child to think about. A child who had already lost her mother because of him. Who did not know what it was like to have that kind of female influence in her life. Bringing someone home would be a shock to Anna. It might upset her. It might bring up all those questions about having a mother again.

Sydney Harper was just going to be his *friend*.

That was all.

He smiled as she talked, trying not to focus all of his attention on her mouth, and pushed thoughts of what it would be like to kiss her completely out of his head.

Later, he offered to walk her back to work.

'Oh, that's not necessary. You don't have to do that,' she protested.

'I might as well. I'm heading that way to pick up my pager as I'm on call tonight.'

She nodded her reluctant acceptance and swung her bag over her shoulder. Together they exited into the street.

It was a cold November day. With blue skies, just a few wispy white clouds and a chill in the air when they moved into the shade and lost the sun.

They walked along together, respectfully a few inches apart. But she was *so* aware of him and trying her hardest not to be.

Nathan Jones was delicious. Of course she was physically attracted to him. Who wouldn't be? Aside from his good looks, this man was intelligent. A good listener. Not at all judgemental. He'd seemed really interested in her. He'd asked questions without being too probing and really paid attention to her answers.

She was very much aware that although they had just spent an hour in each other's company she still didn't know much about him. They'd both edged around serious subjects. They'd both avoided talk of past traumas and upsets. And they'd both kept everything light. Unthreatening. No mention of the baggage that each of them had to be carrying.

She liked that about him. It was as if he knew what she needed.

She frowned, spotting someone from the local council up a ladder, arranging the Christmas lights. 'It gets earlier and earlier each year.'

Nathan nodded. 'I love Christmas.'

She certainly didn't want to talk to him about *that*!

She changed the subject. 'Do you know your way around Silverdale yet?' she asked him, aware that the village had many tiny roads, closes and cul-de-sacs. And now, with the new build of over two hundred new homes on the edge of Silverdale, a lot of new roads had popped up that even *she* was unfamiliar with.

'Not really. But the GPS system in the car helps.'

'If you ever need help finding your way I could help you out. I know most places. Just pop in and ask at the desk.'

He looked at her. 'Thanks. If I ever get a call-out to the middle of nowhere I'll be sure to call in and pick you up first.'

Sydney glanced at him quickly, then looked away. That

was a joke, surely? She'd meant that he could call in to her *work* and ask whoever was on Reception.

She felt his gaze upon her then, and she flushed with heat as they came to a stop outside her veterinary practice.

'Well, thank you for the tea. And the shortbread.'

'It was my pleasure.'

'I'll see you at the end of the week? When you bring in Lottie again?' she added.

The rabbit was due another check-up, so she could look at its eye and see if it needed removing or not.

'Hopefully I'll see you before that.'

Her heart pounded in her chest. What did he mean?

'Why?'

'Because we're friends now, and friends see each other any time—not just at preordained appointments.' He smiled and held out his hand.

She blushed. 'Of course.'

She took his hand in hers and tried to give him a firm handshake, but she couldn't. All she could think of was that he was touching her. And she him! And that his hand felt warm and strong. Protective. It felt good, and she briefly imagined what it might feel like if he pulled her into his arms and pressed her against his chest.

He let go, and when he did she felt an odd sense of disappointment.

Now, why am I feeling that?

She stared back at him, unsure of how to say goodbye to this new friend. Should she give a small wave and go inside? Should they just say goodbye and walk away? Or should there be some sort of kiss on the cheek?

But if I kissed him and liked it...

'Well...maybe I'll see you later, then?'

He nodded. 'Yes.'

'Right. Bye.'

'Goodbye, Sydney.'

And then, with some hesitation, he leaned in and kissed the side of her face.

She sucked in a breath. His lips had only brushed her cheek, and were gone again before she could truly appreciate it, but for the millisecond he'd made contact her body had almost imploded. Her heart had threatened to jump out of her chest. Her face must have looked as red as a stop sign.

She watched him turn and walk across the road to his place of work and she stood there, breathing heavily, her fingers pressed to her face where his lips had been, and wondered what the hell she was doing.

With this *friendship* with Dr Nathan Jones.

Technically, they hadn't done *anything*. Just shared a pot of tea. A plate of shortbread. A quick chat and a walk to work.

But all she could think of was how he'd looked when he'd smiled at her. His beautiful blue eyes. The way he'd listened, the way he'd filled the space of the cafeteria chair, all relaxed and male and virile. How attracted she was to him physically. How his lips had felt…and how frightened that made her feel.

Sydney turned and went into her own place of work.

She needed to cool down.

In more ways than one.

And she needed to stay away from Dr Nathan Jones. He was going to be trouble.

The kiss had been an impulse. To fill an awkward pause. It was just what he did when he left female friends or relatives. He kissed them goodbye.

It didn't *mean* anything. The fact that he'd breathed in

her scent as he'd leaned in…the fact that his lips had felt scorched the second they'd touched her soft cheek…the fact that he'd got a shot of adrenaline powerful enough to launch an armada meant nothing.

Did it?

It was just that it was something new. A new friendship. The fact that she was the most stunningly beautiful woman he'd met in a long time had nothing to do with it. He felt for her. She'd been through a trauma. The loss of a daughter was something he simply couldn't imagine. The fact that she was still standing, smiling and talking to people was a miracle, quite frankly. He couldn't picture going through that and having the power or strength to carry on afterwards. And she was so nice! Easy to talk to. Friendly once you got past that prickly exterior she'd erected. But he could understand why that was there.

What he felt for her was protective. That was all. And didn't friends look out for one another?

Crossing the road, he called in to the surgery and picked up his pager for the evening, along with a list of house calls that needed to be completed before he had to pick up Anna at three-thirty. He had a good few hours' worth of work ahead of him, but he was distracted.

A simple coffee had been something else.

And he was afraid to admit to himself just what it had been.

Sydney sat hunched up on her couch, clutching a mug of cold tea and worrying at a loose bit of skin on her lip. Behind her head lay Magic the cat, asleep on the back of the couch, her long black tail twitching with dreams. The house was silent except for the ticking of the clock in the hallway, and Sydney's gaze was upon the picture of her daughter in the centre of the mantelpiece.

In the picture Olivia was laughing, smiling, her little hands reaching up to catch all the bubbles that her mum was blowing through a bubble wand.

She could remember that day perfectly. It had been during the summer holiday before Olivia was due to start school and it had been a Sunday. Alastair—Sydney's husband and Olivia's father—had gone to the supermarket to do a food-shop and Sydney and Olivia had been playing in the back garden. Her daughter had been so happy. Chasing bubbles, giggling. Gasping when Sydney made a particularly large one that had floated up higher and higher until it had popped, spraying them with wetness. She'd been chasing down and splatting the smaller ones that she could reach.

'Mummy, look!' she'd said when she'd found a bubble or two resting on her clothes.

Sydney remembered the awe and excitement in her daughter's eyes. They'd been happy times. When they'd all believed that life for them was perfect. That nothing could spoil it. Olivia had been about to start infant school; Sydney had been going back to work full-time. It had been their last summer together. The last summer they'd enjoyed.

Before it had all changed. Before it had all gone dreadfully wrong.

Why did I not listen when she told me she had a headache?

She tried to keep on remembering that summer day. The sound of her daughter's deep-throated chuckles, the smile on her face. But she couldn't.

Every time she allowed herself to think of Olivia her thoughts kept dragging her back to that morning when she'd found her unconscious in her bed. To the deadly silence of the room except for her daughter's soft, yet ragged breaths. To the dread and the sickness in her stomach as she'd realised that something was desperately, deeply wrong. That her daughter wouldn't wake up no matter how much Sydney called her name. To the moment when she'd unzipped her onesie to see *that rash*.

If Olivia had lived—if meningitis had not got its sneaky grasp on her beautiful, precious child—then she would have been nine years old now. In junior school. There'd be school pictures on the mantel. Pictures that showed progress. Life. But her pictures had been frozen in time. There would be no more pictures of Olivia appearing on the walls. No more videos on her phone. No paintings on her fridge.

And I could have prevented it all if only I'd paid more attention. Alastair was right. It was all my fault.

Sydney put down her mug and hugged her knees. The anniversary of Olivia's death was getting closer. It was a day she dreaded, that relentlessly came round every year, torturing her with thoughts of what she might have done differently. Tonight she would not be able to sleep. At all.

I can't just sit here and go through that insomnia again!

She got up off the couch and looked about her for something to do. Maybe declutter a cupboard or something? Deep-clean the kitchen? Go through her books and choose some for the bookstall at the Christmas market? Something... Anything but sit there and dwell on *what ifs*!

The doorbell rang, interrupting her agonising.

She froze, then felt a rush of relief.

Thank goodness! I don't care who you are, but I'm going to talk to you. Anything to get my mind off where it's going!

She opened the door.

Nathan!

'Oh. Hi.' She'd never expected him to turn up at her door. How did he know where she lived?

Nathan looked a little uncomfortable. Uncertain. 'I… er…apologise for just turning up at your house like this.'

'Is it Lottie?'

He shook his head and scratched at his chin, looking up and down the road. 'No. I've…er…got a call-out. Nothing urgent, but…'

She'd thought that what he'd said previously about calling in on her had been a joke. Had he actually meant it?

Spending more time with the delicious Nathan since that kiss on her cheek had seemed a bad idea. She'd made a firm decision to avoid him. And now here he was!

As if in answer to her unspoken question he looked sheepish as he said, 'I looked up your home address at work. Sorry. It's just… I tried to use my GPS, but it hasn't been updated for a while and it led me to a field, so… I need your help.'

He needed to find an address! She *had* offered to help him with that, and though she'd told herself—harshly— not to spend time alone with Nathan Jones again, she was now reconsidering it. After hours of feeling herself being pulled down a dark tunnel towards all those thoughts that tortured her on a nightly basis—well, right now she welcomed his interruption. What else would she be doing anyway?

Not sleeping. That was what. The damn pills he'd given her just didn't seem to be having the desired effect. Were they different from last year's? She couldn't remember.

Nathan though was the king of light and fluffy, and that was what she needed. Plus it would be interesting to see what he did at work. And she would be helping by telling him the way to go. Anything was better than sitting in this house for another night, staring at the walls, waiting for sleep to claim her.

'Sure. I'll just get my keys.'

She tried not to be amused by the look of shock on his face when she agreed. Instead she just grabbed her coat, locked up and headed out to his car—a beat-up four-wheel drive that, quite frankly, looked as if it deserved to be in a wrecker's yard. There were dents, one panel of the car was a completely different colour from the rest of it, and where it wasn't covered in rust it was covered in mud. Even the number-plate was half hanging off, looking as if it wanted to escape.

She looked at the vehicle uncertainly. 'Does that actually work?'

He smiled fondly at it. 'She's old, but she always starts. I promise it's clean on the inside.' He rubbed the back of his neck.

Sydney almost laughed. 'Don't worry. I've got a matching one over there.' She pointed at her own vehicle and saw him notice the dried sprays of mud—not just up the bodywork, but over the back windows too.

He smiled, relaxing a little. 'That makes me feel much better.'

Sydney smiled and got into his car. 'Where are we going?'

'Long Wood Road?'

She nodded. 'I know it. It's a couple of miles from here. Take this road out of the village and when you get to the junction at the end turn right.'

'Thanks.' He gunned the engine and began to drive.

Strangely, she felt lighter. More in control. And it felt great not to be sitting in her cottage, staring at those pictures.

'Who are you going to see?'

'Eleanor Briggs?'

'I know her. She has a Russian Blue cat called Misty.'

'I'm not seeing her about Misty. I'm afraid I can't say why. Patient confidentiality prohibits me sharing that with you.'

'That's okay.' She smiled as he began heading to the outskirts of Silverdale.

It felt good next to him. Comfortable. Was that because this was business? And because he was working?

The focus isn't on me. Or us. This is just one professional helping out another.

She'd never been comfortable with being the focus of people's attention. Even as a child she'd tried to hide when she was in the school choir, or a school play. Trying her hardest not to be given a main role, trying not to be noticed. At university, when she'd had to give a solo presentation on the dangers of diabetes in dogs, she'd almost passed out from having to stand at the front of the lecture hall and present to her lecturers and tutor. The *pressure!*

But here they were, stuck in a car together, music on the radio, and she was much more relaxed. This was much better than being stuck at home, staring at old pictures that broke her heart.

Glancing at him driving, she noticed he'd rolled up his sleeves and that his forearms were lightly tanned, and filled with muscle as he changed gear. A chunky sports watch enveloped his wrist. He had good arms. *Attractive* arms. She glanced away.

A song came on that she knew and quietly she began singing and bobbing her head to the music.

Nathan looked over at her. 'You like this?'

Sydney nodded and he turned up the sound. She began to sing louder as it got to the chorus, laughing suddenly as Nathan joined in. Out of tune and clearly tone deaf.

They began to drive down a country road.

Silverdale was Sydney's whole life. A small pocket of English countryside that she felt was all hers. The place where she'd hoped to raise her daughter. In its community atmosphere where everyone looked out for one another.

Pushing the thought to one side, she turned back to Nathan. He was concentrating on the road now that the song was over and the DJ was babbling, his brow slightly furrowed, both hands gripping the wheel.

'You need to take the next left. Long Woods Road.'

Nathan indicated, following the twists and turns of her directions, and soon she was pointing out Eleanor's small cottage. They turned into the driveway and parked in front of the house. Killing the engine, he turned to her. 'Thank you. I wouldn't have got here without you.'

'And I wouldn't have had my eardrums assaulted.'

He raised an eyebrow.

'Your singing.'

'I have a lovely voice. I'll have you know that when I was in my school choir I was the only child not selected to sing a solo.'

She smirked. 'You should be proud.'

'I am.'

Then he grinned and reached for his bag, which was down by her feet. She moved slightly, out of his way, as he lifted it up and past her.

He was smiling still. Looking at her. She watched as his gaze dropped to her mouth and instantly the atmosphere changed.

Sydney looked away, pretending that something out of the window had caught her eye.

'Will you be okay for a while? I can leave the radio on.'

She didn't look at him, but dug her phone from her

pocket. 'I've got my phone. I'm playing a word game against my veterinary nurse.'

Nathan said nothing, but got out of the car. Once he was gone, she suddenly felt *alone*. His presence had filled the car, and now that he was gone it seemed so empty. The only reminder a very faint aroma of cologne. She would never have thought that spending time with Nathan would be so easy, after their coffee together. But he'd been just what she needed tonight. Bad singing included.

In the sky above stars were beginning to filter through the dark, twinkling and shining. She looked for the biggest and brightest. Olivia's star. The one she had once pointed out to her daughter as her very own special light. Just remembering that night with her daughter made her eyes sting with unshed tears, but she blinked them away.

I can't keep crying. I've got to be stronger than this!

She switched on her phone and stared at the game she no longer wanted to play.

It was pitch-black along the country roads as they followed behind another four-wheel drive that was towing a horsebox. In the back, Sydney could see a large black horse, easily fifteen hands high. Was it the Daltons? They had a horse like that. Though she guessed it could be the Webbers' horse. They had one like it too. Or maybe it wasn't anyone she knew. She didn't get called out to *all* the horses in the Silverdale area. There was a specialised equine veterinary service in Norton Town. Sometimes she worked alongside it.

As they drove back along Long Wood Road, Sydney realised she was feeling more relaxed and happy than she had for a few weeks. It was strange. Perhaps it was a good thing not to be wallowing in her memories tonight.

Perhaps getting out and about and doing something was the right thing to do.

I need a hobby. An evening class. Something. Maybe it'll be better when we start those meetings for the Christmas market and fête.

What she knew for sure was that she had felt better when she'd seen Nathan returning to the car. Seen his smile. Felt his warmth. Knowing that he wasn't the type to pry into her past. He made her feel weirdly comfortable, despite the physical response she felt. It was something she hadn't felt for a long time, and she was really glad she'd agreed to come out with him and spend some more time with him.

She was just about to say something about it—thank him for earlier—when she spotted something, off to Nathan's right, illuminated by the lights of the vehicles. It was a small herd of deer, running across the field at full pelt.

'Nathan, look!' She pointed.

There had to be seven or eight. Mostly fully grown and running hard. The lead deer had full antlers, like tree branches.

And they were heading straight for the road.

'I think I'm going to slow down.'

But as Nathan slowed their vehicle it became clear that the vehicle in front, with the horse trailer, had continued on at a normal speed.

Sydney leaned forward. 'Have they not seen them? What can we do?'

Nathan hit his horn, hoping it would make the driver ahead pay attention, or at least startle the deer into heading in another direction, but neither happened.

The biggest deer burst through the undergrowth, leaping over the ditch and straight out onto the road—right in front of the other vehicle.

Sydney watched, horrified, and brake lights lit up her face as the car in front tried to swerve at the last minute, but failed. The horsebox at the back wobbled, bouncing from left to right with the weight of the horse inside, before it tipped over and pulled the car straight into the ditch. The rest of the deer leapt by, over the road and into the next field.

Nathan hit the brakes, stopping the car. 'Call for help.'

Her heart was pounding madly in her chest. 'What are you going to do?'

'I'm going to check for casualties. After you've contacted emergency services go into the boot of the car and find the reflective triangle and put it in the road. We're on a bend here, and we need to warn other traffic. We're sitting ducks.'

Then he grabbed his bag and was gone.

She watched him run over to the car through the light of the headlamps as she dialled 999 with shaking fingers. As she watched Nathan trying to talk to someone she saw the driver fall from the driver's side. Then her gaze fell upon the horse in the horsebox. It was moving. Alive.

I have to get out there!

But she had no equipment. No bag. No medicines. She felt helpless. Useless! She'd felt this way just once before.

I'll be damned if I feel that way again!

'Which service do you require?' A voice spoke down the phone.

'*All of them.* We need them all.'

CHAPTER FOUR

S<small>YDNEY DASHED TO</small> the boot of Nathan's car and panicked as she struggled to open it. At first she couldn't see the reflective triangle he'd mentioned—his boot was full of *stuff.* But she rummaged through, tossing things to one side, until she found it. Then she dashed to the bend in the road and placed it down, hoping that it would be enough of a warning to stop any other vehicles that came that way from running into them.

She ran over to the ditched car and horsebox, glancing quickly at the horse in the back. It was neighing and huffing, making an awful lot of noise, stamping its hooves, struggling to find a way to stand in a box that was on its side. She couldn't see if it had any injuries. She hoped not. But there wasn't much she could do for the horse anyhow. She needed to help Nathan and the people in the car.

She'd already seen the driver was out of the vehicle. He was sitting in the road, groaning and clutching at his head. He had a bleeding laceration across his brow, causing blood to dribble down his face and eyes.

Nathan was in the ditched vehicle, assessing whoever was in the front seat.

Sydney knelt down, saw the head wound was quite deep and pulled the scarf from around her neck and tied it around the guy's scalp. 'You need to come with me. Off the road. Come and sit over here.'

She pointed at the grass verge.

'I didn't see... I didn't notice... We were arguing...' the man mumbled.

He was in shock. Sydney grabbed the man under his armpits and hauled him to his feet. Normally she wouldn't move anyone after a car accident. She knew that much. But this man had already hauled himself out of the vehicle and dropped onto the road before Nathan got there. If he'd done any damage to himself, then it was already done. The least she could do was get him out of the middle of the road and to a safer zone.

The man was heavy and dazed, but he got to his feet and staggered with her to the roadside, where she lowered him down and told him to stay. 'Don't move. Try and stay still until the ambulance gets here. I've called for help—they're on their way.'

The man looked up at her. 'My wife...*my son*!'

He tried to get up again, but Sydney held him firmly in place. 'I'll go and help them, but you *must* stay here!'

The man looked helpless and nodded, trembling as he realised there was blood all over his hands.

Sydney ran back over to the ditched car, heard a child crying and noticed that Nathan was now in the back seat. He called to her over his shoulder.

'There's a baby. In a car seat. He looks okay, but I need to get him out of the vehicle so I can sit in the back and maintain C-spine for the mother.'

Sydney nodded and glanced at the woman in the front seat. She was unconscious, and her air bag had deployed and lay crumpled and used before her. There was no bleeding that she could see, but that didn't mean a serious injury had not occurred. If a casualty was unconscious, that usually meant shock or a head injury. She hoped it was just the former.

'I'm unclipping the seatbelt.'

Sydney heard a clunk, then Nathan was backing out, holding a car seat with an indignant, crying infant inside it, bawling away.

The baby couldn't be more than nine months old, and had beautiful fluffy blond hair. But his face was red with rage and tears, and his little feet in his sleep suit were kicking in time with his crying.

'Shh... It's okay. It's okay... I've got you.' Sydney took the heavy seat with care, cooing calming words as she walked back across the road to take him to his father.

In the distance she heard the faint, reassuring sound of sirens.

'Here. Your little boy. What's his name?' she asked the man, who smiled with great relief that his son seemed physically okay.

'Brandon.'

That was good. The man's bump to the head hadn't caused amnesia or anything like that. 'And your name...?'

'Paul.'

'Okay, Paul. You're safe. And Brandon's safe—he doesn't look injured—and that man helping your wife is a doctor. She's in good hands. He knows what he's doing.'

'Is she hurt? Is Helen hurt?'

Sydney debated about how much she should reveal—should she say that Helen was unconscious? Or stay optimistic and just tell him she was doing okay? The truth won out.

'I don't know. She's unconscious, but Nathan—that's Dr Jones—is with her in the car and he's looking after her. Do you hear those sirens? More help will be with us soon.'

The sirens were much louder now, and Sydney knew she was breathing faster. Hearing them get closer and closer just reminded her of that morning when she'd had to call an ambulance for Olivia. Wishing they'd get to her faster. Feeling that they were taking for ever. Praying that they would help her daughter. She could see the same look in Paul's eyes now. The distress. The *fear*.

But this was an occasion where she actually had her wits about her and could do something.

'I need to go and help Nathan.'

She ran back across the road. The car's radiator or something must have burst, because she could hear hissing and see steam rising up through the bonnet of the vehicle. She ducked into the open door.

Nathan was in the back seat, his hands clutching Helen's head, keeping it upright and still. His face was twisted, as if *he* was in pain.

'Is she breathing still?' he managed to ask her.

Is she *breathing?* Sydney wasn't sure she wanted to check—her own shock at what had happened was starting to take effect. What if Helen wasn't breathing? What if Helen's heart had stopped?

'I—'

'Watch her chest. Is there rise and fall?'

She checked. There was movement. 'Yes, there is!'

'Count how many breaths she takes in ten seconds.'

She looked back, counting. 'Two.'

'Okay. That's good.'

She saw Nathan wince. Perhaps he had cramp, or something? There was some broken glass in the car. Perhaps he'd knelt on it? She pushed the thought to the back of her mind as vehicles flashing red and blue lights appeared. An ambulance. A fire engine, and further behind them she could see a police car.

Thank you!

Sydney got out of the car and waved them down, feeling relief flood her.

A paramedic jumped out of the ambulance and came over to her, pulling on some purple gloves. 'Can you tell me what happened?'

She gave a brief rundown of the incident, and pointed out Paul and baby Brandon, then filled him in on the woman in the car.

'Okay, let's see to her first.' The paramedic called out to his partner to look after the driver and his son whilst he checked out Helen, still in the car with Nathan.

Sydney ran back over to Paul. 'Help's here! It's okay. We're okay.' She beamed, glad that the onus of responsibility was now being shouldered by lots of other people rather than just her and Nathan.

As she stood back and watched the rescue operation she realised there were tears on her face. She wiped them away with a sleeve, aware of how frightened she'd been, and waited for Nathan to join her, shivering. She wanted to be held. To feel safe. She wanted to be comforted.

The morning she'd found Olivia she'd been on her own. Alastair had already left for work. So there'd been no one to hold her and let her know it was okay. She'd needed arms around her then and she needed them now. But Alastair had never held her again.

If she asked him, Nathan would hold her for a moment. She just knew it. Sensed it. What they'd just experienced had been traumatic. But she remained silent, clutching her coat to her. She just stood and watched the emergency services get everything sorted.

And waited.

Nathan was needed by the paramedics, and then by

the police, and by the time he was free she was not. The horse needed her—needed checking over.

She told herself a hug wasn't important and focused on the practical.

Paul and Brandon had been taken to hospital in one ambulance; Helen had been extricated and taken away in another, finally conscious. The horsebox had been righted and the horse had been led out to be checked by Sydney. It had some knocks and scrapes to its legs, mostly around its fetlocks—which, in humans, was comparable to injuries to an ankle joint—but apart from that it just seemed startled more than anything.

They'd all been very lucky, and Sydney now stood, calming the horse, whilst they waited for an animal transporter to arrive.

Nathan stood watching her. 'That horse really feels safe with you.'

She smiled. 'Makes a change. Normally horses see me coming with my vet bag and start playing up. It's nice to be able to comfort one and calm it down.'

'You're doing brilliantly.'

She looked at him. He looked a little worn out. Wearied. As if attending to the patients in the crash had physically exhausted him. Perhaps he'd had a really long day. Just like being a vet, being a doctor had to be stressful at times. Seeing endless streams of people, each with their own problems. Having to break bad news. She knew how stressful it was for her to have to tell a customer that their beloved pet was dying, or had to be put to sleep. And when she *did* euthanise a beloved pet she often found herself shedding silent tears along with the owner. She couldn't help it.

Perhaps it was the same for Nathan. Did seeing people in distress upset him? Wear him out?

'*You* did brilliantly. Knowing what to do…who to treat. How to look after Helen. I wouldn't have thought to do that.' She stroked the horse's muzzle.

'It's nothing.'

'But it is. You probably saved her life, keeping her airway open like that. She could have died.'

'At least they're in safe hands now.'

She looked at him and met his gaze. 'They were *already* in safe hands.'

She needed to let him know that what he'd done today had *mattered*. Paul still had a wife. Brandon still had a mother. Because of *him*. A while ago she'd almost lost her faith in doctors. She'd depended on them to save Olivia, and when they'd told her there was nothing they could do…

At first she hadn't wanted to believe them. Had *raged* at them. Demanded they do *something*! When they hadn't she had collapsed in a heap, hating them—and everyone—with a passion she had never known was inside her. Today, Nathan had proved to her that doctors did help.

'How do you think the horse is doing?'

Sydney could feel the animal was calmer. It had stopped stamping its hooves and snorting as they'd stood there on the side of the road, watching the clean-up operation. It had stopped tossing its head. Its breathing had become steadier.

'She's doing great.'

'Paul and Helen aren't the only ones in safe hands.' He smiled and sat down on the bank beside her, letting out a breath and rolling his shoulders.

She stared at him for a moment, shocked to realise that she wanted to sit next to him, maybe to massage his shoulders or just lean her head against his shoulder. She wanted that physical contact.

Feeling that yearning to touch him surprised her and she turned away from him, focussing on the horse. She shouldn't be feeling that for him. What was the point? It was best to focus on the horse. She knew what she was doing there.

It didn't take long for the accident to be cleared. The police took pictures, measured the road, measured the skid marks and collected debris. The car was pulled from the ditch and lifted onto a lorry to be taken away, and just as Sydney was beginning to doubt that a new horse-box would ever arrive a truck came ambling around the corner and they loaded the mare onto it to take her back to her stable.

Sydney gave the truck driver her details and told her to let Paul know that she'd be happy to come out and check on the horse, and that he was to give her a call if she was needed urgently.

Eventually she and Nathan got back into his car and she noticed that it was nearly midnight. Normally she would be lying in bed at this time, staring at the ceiling and worrying over every little thought. Wide awake.

But tonight she felt tired. Ready for her bed even without a sleeping pill. It surprised her.

Nathan started the engine. 'Let's take you home. Our little trip out lasted longer than either of us expected.'

'That's okay. I'd only have been awake anyway. At least this way I was put to good use.'

'You've not been sleeping for some time?'

She shook her head and looked away from him, out of the window. 'No.'

He seemed to ruminate on this for a while, but then he

changed the subject. 'Good thing I didn't get any more house calls.'

That was true. What would he have done if he'd got a page to say that someone was having chest pains whilst he'd been helping Helen? They'd been lucky. All of them.

It was nice and warm in Nathan's car as he drove them steadily back to Silverdale. For the first time Sydney felt the silence between them was comfortable. She didn't need to fill the silence with words. Or to feel awkward. The circumstances of the emergency had thrown them together and something intangible had changed.

It felt nice to be sitting with someone like that. Even if it *was* with a man she had at first disliked immensely.

A jolt in the road startled her, and she realised she'd almost nodded off. She sucked in a breath, shocked that she'd felt comfortable enough to fall asleep.

She glanced at Nathan just as he glanced at her, and they both quickly looked away.

Sydney smiled.

It was beginning to feel more than nice.

It was beginning to feel *good*.

Nathan pulled up outside Sydney's cottage and killed the engine. He looked out at the dark, empty street, lit only by one or two streetlamps, and watched as a cat sneaked across the road and disappeared under a hedge after being startled by his engine.

Despite the accident he'd had a good time tonight. It had felt really good to spend time with Sydney, and he felt they'd cleared the air after their misunderstandings at their first meeting and the awkward coffee.

Turning up at her door to ask for help with directions had almost been a step too far for him. He'd joked about asking her for her help, but when he'd tried to find

Eleanor's cottage on his own his stupid GPS had made him turn down a very narrow farming lane and asked him to drive through a muddy field! He'd got out and checked that there wasn't a farmhouse or something near, where he might ask for help, but there'd been nothing. Just fields. And mud. Plenty of mud!

He'd argued with himself about going to her house. Almost not gone there at all. He knew her address. He'd seen it on his computer at work and for some reason it had burnt itself into his brain. She didn't live far from her place of work, so it had been easy to find her, but he hadn't known what sort of reception he'd get. She might have slammed the door in his face.

He'd felt awkward asking for help, but thankfully she'd agreed to go with him, and it had been nice to have her with him in his car, just chatting. It had been a very long time since he'd done that with anyone. The last time had been with Gwyneth. She'd always talked when they were driving—pointing things out, forming opinions on people or places that they passed. Her judgemental approach had made him realise just how insecure she'd been, and he'd done his best to try and make her feel good about herself.

Tonight, Sydney had been invaluable at the accident site—something he knew Gwyneth would never have been. She'd not been great with blood.

Sydney had been brilliant, looking after the driver and the baby, and then she'd managed to calm the horse and check it over. He wouldn't have known how to handle such a large animal. He barely coped with looking after a rabbit, never mind a terrified horse that had been thrown around in a tin box.

Now they were back to that moment again. The one where he normally kissed people goodbye. And suddenly there was that tension again. He wasn't sure whether he should lean over and just do it. Just kiss her.

'Thanks for everything tonight. I couldn't have done it without you,' he said honestly.

She'd grabbed her handbag from the footwell on her side and sat with it on her knee. 'No problem. I couldn't have done it without you either.'

Though half her face was in shadow, he could still see her smile.

'Well…goodnight, Sydney.'

'Goodnight, Nathan.'

She stared at him for a moment, and then turned away and grabbed the latch to open the door. It wouldn't budge and she struggled with it for a moment or two.

'Sorry…sometimes it catches.'

He leant over her for the handle and she flinched as he reached past her and undid the door for her. He sat back, worried that he'd made her start.

She hurried from the vehicle without saying a word, throwing the strap of her bag over her shoulder and delving into her coat pocket for her house keys.

Disappointment filled his soul. He didn't want her to walk away feeling awkward. That flinch, it had been… He wanted…

What do I want?

'Sydney?' He was out of his car before he could even think about what he was doing. He stood there, looking over the top of his car, surprising even himself. The night air had turned chill and he could feel goosebumps trembling up his spine.

She'd turned, curious. 'Yes?'

'Um…' He couldn't think of anything to say! What was he even doing, anyway? He couldn't turn this friendship with Sydney into anything more. Neither of them was ready for that. And there was Anna to think of too. He was sure Sydney would not want to take on someone with a little girl—not after losing her own. And surely she wouldn't want to take on someone who was ill?

Gwyneth had made it quite clear that he wasn't worth *her* time and affection. That he had somehow ruined her life with his presence. Did he want to put someone else through that? Someone like Sydney? Who'd already been through so much? He'd end up needing her more than she needed him, and he'd hate that imbalance. He knew the state of his health. His condition would make him a burden. And Anna had to be his top priority. And yet...

And yet something about her *pulled* at him. Her energy. Her presence. Those grey eyes that looked so studious and wise, yet at the same time contained a hurt and a loss that even he couldn't fully understand. He'd lost his fiancée, yes, but that had been through separation. It wasn't the same as losing a child. Nowhere near it. He and Gwyneth had hardly been the love story of the century.

Even though he'd only known Sydney for a couple of days, there was something in her nature that...

'Remember to take your sleeping pill.'

Remember to take your sleeping pill? Really? That's what you come up with?

Her face filled with relief. 'Oh. Yes, I will. Thank you.'

Relief. *See?* She was being polite. She was probably desperate to get inside and away from him, because he clearly had no idea how to talk to women, having spent the last few years of his life just being a father and—

Being a father is more important than your ability to chat up women!

'You get a good night's sleep yourself. You've earned it.'

He opened his mouth to utter a reply, but she'd already slipped her key into the lock. She raised her hand in a brief goodbye and then was inside, her door closing with a shocking finality, and he was left standing in the street, staring at a closed door.

Nathan watched as Sydney switched on the lights. He ducked inside his car as she came to her window and closed the curtains. He stared for a few minutes, then tore his gaze away, worried about what her neighbours might think. He started the engine, turned up the heater and slowly drove away. Berating himself for not saying something more inspiring, something witty—something that would have had her...*what?*

That wasn't who he was. Those clever, witty guys, who always had the perfect line for every occasion, lived elsewhere. He didn't have a scriptwriter to think up clever things for him to say that would charm her and make her like him more. He wasn't suave, or sophisticated, or one of those charming types who could have women at their beck and call with a click of their fingers.

And he didn't *want* to be a man like that. He was a single dad, with a gorgeous, clever daughter who any-one would be lucky to know. He led an uncomplicated life. He worked hard.

What did he want to achieve with Sydney? And why was he getting involved anyway? His own fiancée—the woman he'd been willing to pledge his entire life to—had walked away from him, and if someone who'd once said they loved him could do that, then a relative stranger like Sydney might do the same thing. She didn't strike him as someone looking to settle down again, to start a relationship in a ready-made family. Especially not with another little girl after losing her own.

Did she?

No.

So why on earth could he not get her out of his head?

* * *

Nathan was fighting fatigue. Over the last few days he'd been having a small relapse in his symptoms, and he'd been suffering with painful muscle spasms, cramps, and an overwhelming tiredness that just wouldn't go away. That accident had aggravated it. It was probably stress.

As he downed some painkillers he knew he'd have to hide his discomfort from his daughter. She mustn't see him weaken. Not yet. It was still early days. He didn't want her to suspect that there was something wrong. He had to keep going for her. Had to keep being strong. Normally he could hide it. And he needed his energy for today. Anna was still too young to understand about his condition. How did you explain multiple sclerosis to a six-year-old?

Today Lottie was due for her next check-up, and he was feeling some anticipation at seeing Sydney. At work, during breaks, he often found himself itching to cross the road on some pretext, just to see if she was there, but for the life of him he couldn't think of anything to say. His inner critic kept reminding him that seeing her was probably a bad idea. The woman practically had 'Keep Out' signs hanging around her neck, and she'd certainly not divulged anything too personal to him. She hadn't even mentioned her daughter to him.

And yet...

'Anna! Come on, it's time to go.'

'Are we taking Lottie now?'

'We are. But we're walking because...' he reached for a plausible excuse '...it's a nice day.' He smiled, reaching out for the counter as a small wave of dizziness affected his balance briefly. Of all his symptoms, dizziness and feeling off-balance were the worst. He couldn't drive like this. It would be dangerous. And at least the crisp, fresh winter air would make him feel better.

'Yay!' Anna skipped off to fetch Lottie's carrier.

He managed to stop the world spinning and stood up straight, sucking in a deep breath.

The rabbit was doing quite well, Nathan thought. She was eating and drinking as normal, had come off the medication and was settled back outside. The bite wounds had healed cleanly and Lottie's eye had escaped surgery, much to both his and Anna's delight. They were hopeful for a full recovery.

With Lottie in her box, Nathan locked up and they headed to the veterinary practice. He still wasn't feeling great—quite tired and light-headed—but he tried to keep up a level of bright chatter as they walked along the village roads.

His daughter hopped alongside him, pointing out robins and magpies and on one particular occasion a rather large snail.

The walk took a while. They lived a good couple of miles from the practice and his arms ached from carrying Lottie, who seemed to get weightier with every step, but eventually they got there, and Nathan settled into a waiting room seat with much relief.

He didn't get to enjoy it for too long, though.

Sydney had opened her door. 'Do you want to bring Lottie in?'

Sydney looked well, though there were still faint dark circles beneath her eyes. It felt good to see her again. He carried Lottie through and put her onto the examination table.

'How's she doing?'

He nodded, but that upset his balance and he had to grip the examination table to centre himself.

Had Sydney noticed?

He swallowed, suppressing his nausea. 'Er...good. Eating and drinking. The eye's clean and she seems okay.' He decided to focus on Sydney's face. When he got dizzy like this it helped to focus on something close to him. She wasn't moving that much, and he needed a steady point to remain fixed on.

'Let's take a look.'

Sydney frowned, concern etched across her normally soft features as she concentrated on the examination. She was very thorough, reminding him of her capability and passion. She checked Lottie's eye, her bite wounds, her temperature and gave her a thorough going-over.

'I agree with you. She seems to have recovered well. I think we can discharge this patient.' She stood up straight again and smiled.

'That's great.'

He realised she was looking at him questioningly.

'Are you okay?'

Nathan felt another wave of nausea sweep over him as dizziness assailed him again. 'Er...not really...'

Had the walk been too much? Was he dehydrated?

Sydney glanced at Anna uncertainly, then came around the desk and took Nathan's arm and guided him over to a small stool in the corner. 'I'll get you some water.'

He sank his head into his hands as the dizziness passed, and was just starting to feel it clear a bit when she returned with a glass. He tried not to look at Anna until he was sure he could send her a reassuring smile to say everything was okay.

He took a sip of the drink. 'Thanks.'

'Missed breakfast?'

He gratefully accepted the excuse. 'Yes. Yes, I did. Must have got a bit light-headed, that's all.'

'Daddy, you had toast with jam for breakfast.' Anna contradicted.

He smiled. 'But not enough, obviously.'

'You had three slices.'

He smiled at his daughter, who was blowing his cover story quite innocently. He was afraid to look at Sydney, but she was making sure Lottie was secure in her cage.

Then she turned to look at him, staring intently, her brow lined. 'Are you safe to get home, Dr Jones?'

He stood up. 'We walked here. And I'm fine.' He didn't want to let her see how ill he felt.

'You don't look it. You look very pale.'

'Right…' He glanced at Anna. 'Perhaps I just need some more fresh air.' He took another sip of water.

Sydney stood in front of him, arms crossed. 'You don't seem in a fit state to walk home yet. Or to take care of Anna.'

'I am!' he protested.

'You had nystagmus. I know your world is spinning.'

Nystagmus was a rapid movement of the eyes in response to the semi-circular canals being stimulated. In effect, if the balance centre told you your world was spinning, your eyes tried to play catch-up in order to focus.

'Look, let me tell my next client I'll be ten minutes and I'll drive you both back.'

'No—no, it's fine! I can't disrupt your workday, that's ridiculous. I'm okay now. Besides, that would annoy your patient. I'm fine.'

He stood up to prove it, but swayed slightly, and she had to reach for him, grabbing his waist to steady him.

'Honestly. I just need to get some air for a moment. I could go and sit down across the road at the surgery, maybe. Check my blood pressure. Have a cup of sweet tea. It'll pass—it always does.' He smiled broadly, to show her he was feeling better, even though he wasn't.

She let go of him. 'You're sure?'

No.

'Absolutely.'

He saw her face fill with doubt and hesitation. 'Maybe Anna could stay here with me. She could look after the animals in the back. Give them cuddles, or something.'

Anna gasped, her smile broad. '*Could* I, Daddy?'

He didn't want to impose on Sydney. He could see it had been tough for her to offer that, and she was working. Anna should be *his* responsibility, not someone else's.

'Er… I don't know, honey. Sydney's very busy.'

'It's no problem. Olivia used to do it all the time.' She blushed and looked away.

Her daughter.

'Are you sure?'

'I'm sure. You're clearly unwell today. She can stay with me for the day and I'll drive you both home when I finish. Around four.'

Anna was jumping up and down with joy, clapping her hands together in absolute glee at this amazing turn of events.

He really didn't want to do this, but what choice did he have? Sydney was right. And hadn't he wanted to move to a village to experience this very support?

'Fine. Thank you.' He knelt to speak to his excited daughter. 'You be good for Sydney. Do what you're told and behave—yes?'

She nodded.

Standing up, he felt a little head rush. Maybe Sydney was right. Perhaps he *did* need a break.

He was just having a difficult time letting someone

help him. It irked him, gnawing away at him like a particularly persistent rodent. How could he look after his
daughter if he was going to let a little dizziness affect
him? And this was just the *start* of his condition. These
were mild symptoms. It would get worse. And already
he was relying on other people to look after his daughter—Sydney, of all people!

'Perhaps she ought to stay with—'

Sydney grabbed his arm and started to guide him towards her exit. 'Go and lie down, Dr Jones.'

Nathan grimaced hard, then kissed the top of his
daughter's head and left.

It had been a delight to have Anna with her for the day.
The invitation to look after Nathan's little girl had just
popped out. She'd not carefully considered exactly what
it would mean to look after the little girl before she'd said
it, and once she had she'd felt a small amount of alarm
at her offer.

But Anna had been wonderful. She was sweet, calm
with the animals, with a natural affection and understanding of them that those in her care gravitated towards, allowing her to stroke them. The cats had purred.
Dogs had wagged their tails or showed their bellies to be
rubbed. And Anna had asked loads of questions about
them, showing a real interest. She'd even told Sydney
that she wanted to be a vet when she was older! That
had been sweet.

Olivia had liked being with the animals, but she'd only
liked the cuddling part. The oohing and aahing over cute,
furry faces. Anna was different. She wanted to know
what breed they were. What they were at the vet's for.
How Sydney might make them better. It had been good

to share her knowledge with Nathan's daughter. Good to see the differences between the two little girls.

Once they were done for the day, and the last of the records had been completed, she smiled as Lucy complained about her sore back after cleaning cages all afternoon, but then sat down to eat not one but two chocolate bars, because she felt ravenous.

They sat together, chatting about animal care, and Anna listened quietly, not interrupting, and not getting in the way.

When she'd gathered her things, Sydney told Anna it was time to go.

'Thank you for having me, Sydney.'

She eyed the little girl holding her hand as they crossed the road to collect Nathan. 'Not a problem, Anna. It was lovely to have you. Let's hope your daddy is feeling better soon, hmm?'

'Daddy always gets sick and tired. He pretends he's not, but I know when he is.'

'Perhaps he *is* just tired? He does a very important job, looking after everyone.' But something niggled at her. The way Nathan had been, and the nonchalant way Anna had mentioned that *'Daddy always gets sick and tired...'*

Was Nathan ill? And, if so, what could it be? Just a virus? Was he generally run-down? Or could it be something else? Something serious?

They quickly crossed to the surgery and collected a rather pale-looking Nathan. He insisted he was feeling much better. Suspecting he wasn't quite being truthful, she got him into the car and started the engine, glancing at Anna on the back seat through the rearview mirror.

Anna smiled, and the sight went straight to Sydney's heart. To distract herself, she rummaged in the glovebox to see if she had any of Olivia's old CDs. She found one and slid it into the CD player, and soon they were singing along with a cartoon meerkat and a warthog.

Driving through the village, she found herself smiling, amazed that she still remembered the words, and laughing at Anna singing in the back. It felt *great* to be driving along, singing together. She and Olivia had always used to do it. It was even putting a smile on Nathan's face.

Much too soon she found herself at Nathan's house, and she walked them both up to their front door, finally handing them Lottie's carrier.

Nathan smiled broadly. 'Thanks, Sydney. I really appreciate it. I got a lot of rest and I feel much better.'

'Glad to hear it. Anna was brilliant. The animals adored her.'

'They all do. Thanks again.'

'No problem. See you around.'

She began to walk away, turning to give a half wave, feeling embarrassed at doing so. She got in her car and drove away as fast as she could—before she was tempted to linger and revel in the feeling of family once again.

It felt odd to be back in the car, alone again after that short while she'd been with Anna and Nathan. The car seemed empty. The music had been silenced and returned to the glovebox.

By the time she got home her heart physically ached.

And she sat in her daughter's old room for a very long time, just staring at the empty walls.

CHAPTER FIVE

Somehow it had become December, and November had passed in a moment. A moment when natural sleep had continued to elude her, but her strange, mixed feelings for the new village doctor had not.

She'd listened as her own clients had chatted with her about the new doctor, smiled when they'd joked about how gorgeous he was, how heroic he was. Had she heard that he'd saved lives already? One woman in the village, who really ought to have known better, had even joked and blushed about Dr Jones giving her the kiss of life! Sydney had smiled politely, but inside her heart had been thundering.

She'd seen him fleetingly, here and there. A couple of times he'd waved at her. Once she'd bumped into him in the sandwich shop, just as a large dollop of coleslaw had squeezed itself from her crusty cob and splatted onto her top.

'Oh!' He'd laughed, rummaging in his pockets and pulling out a fresh white handkerchief. 'Here—take this.'

She'd blushed madly, accepted his hankie, and then had stood there wiping furiously at her clothes, knowing that he was standing there, staring at her. When she'd looked up to thank him *he'd* blushed, and she'd wondered what he had been thinking about.

Then they'd both gone on their way, and she'd looked over her shoulder at him at the exact moment when he'd done the same.

She felt that strange undercurrent whenever they met, or whenever she saw him. She kept trying to ignore it. Trying to ignore *him*. But it was difficult. Her head and her heart had differing reactions. Her head told her to stay away and keep her distance. But her heart and her body sang whenever he was near, as if it was saying, *Look, there he is! Give him a wave! Go and say hello! Touch him!*

Today frost covered the ground like a smattering of icing sugar, and the village itself looked very picturesque. Sydney was desperate to get out and go for a walk around the old bridleways, maybe take a few pictures with her camera, but she couldn't. There was far too much to do and she was running late for a committee meeting.

The Silverdale Christmas market and nativity was an annual festive occasion that was always held the week before Christmas. People came from all around the county, sometimes further from afield, and it was a huge financial boost to local businesses during the typically slower winter months. Unfortunately this year it was scheduled to fall on the one day that she dreaded. The anniversary of Olivia's death.

Sydney had previously been one of the organisers, but after what had happened with Olivia she hadn't been involved much. Barely at all. This year she'd decided to get back into it. She'd always been needed, especially where the animals were concerned. She'd used to judge the Best Pet show, and maintain the welfare of all the animals that got involved in the very real nativity—donkeys, sheep, cows, goats, even chickens and geese! But she'd also been in charge of the flower stalls and the food market.

It was a huge commitment, but one she had enjoyed in the past. And this year it would keep her busy. Would stop her thinking of another Christmas without her daughter. Stop her from wallowing in the fact that, yet again, she would not be buying her child any gifts to put under a non-existent tree.

She sat at the table with the rest of the committee, waiting for the last member to arrive. Dr Jones was late. Considerably so. And the more they waited, the more restless she got.

'Perhaps we should just make a start and then fill Dr Jones in if he ever gets here?' Sydney suggested.

Everyone else was about to agree when the door burst open and in he came, cheeks red from the cold outside, apologising profusely. 'Sorry, everyone, I got called out to some stomach pains—which, surprisingly, turned out to be a bouncing baby boy.'

There were surprised gasps and cheers from the others.

'Who's had a baby?' asked Malcolm, the chairman.

Nathan tucked his coat over the back of his chair. 'Lucy Carter.'

Sydney sat forward, startled. '*My* Lucy Carter? My veterinary nurse?'

His gaze met hers and he beamed a smile at her which went straight to her heart. 'The very same.'

'B-but...she wasn't pregnant!' she spluttered with indignation.

'The baby in her arms would beg to differ!'

'But...'

She couldn't believe it! Okay, Lucy had put some weight on recently, but they'd put that down to those extra chocolate bars she'd been eating... *Pregnant? That's amazing!* She felt the need to go and see her straight away. To give her a hug and maybe get a cuddle with the newborn.

'It was a shock for everyone involved. But they're both doing well and everyone's happy. She told me to let you know.'

A baby. For Lucy. That was great news. And such a surprise!

It meant more work for Sydney for a bit, of course, but she'd cope. She could get an agency member of staff in. It would be weird, not seeing Lucy at work for a while. They'd always worked together. They knew each other's ways and foibles.

She sighed. Everyone else seemed to be moving on. Lucy and her new baby. Alastair and his new bride, with a baby on the way. Everyone was getting on with their lives. And she…? She was still here. In the village she's been born in. With no child. No husband. No family of her own except her elderly parents, who lived too far away anyway.

She looked across at Nathan as he settled into his seat and felt a sudden burst of irritation towards him. She'd been looking forward to getting involved in these meetings again, getting back out there into the community, and yet now her feelings towards him were making her feel uncomfortable. Was it because he'd brought news that meant her life was going to change again?

'Let's get started, shall we?' suggested Malcolm. 'First off, I'd like to welcome Dr Nathan Jones to the committee. He has taken over the role from its previous incumbent, Dr Richard Preston.'

The group clapped, smiled and nodded a welcome for their new member. Sydney stared at him, her face impassive. He looked ridiculously attractive today. Fresh-faced. Happy. She focused on his hands. Hands that had just recently delivered a baby. And she felt guilty for having allowed herself to succumb to that brief, petty jealousy. She looked up at his face and caught him looking at her, and she looked away, embarrassed.

'I'd also like to welcome Sydney back to the committee! Sydney, as I'm sure most of you know, took a little… sabbatical, if you will, from the organisation of this annual event, and I'm most pleased to have her back in full fighting form!'

She smiled as she felt all eyes turn to her, and nodded hellos to the group members she knew well and hadn't worked with for so long. It did feel good to be back here and doing something for the community again. The Christmas market and nativity was something she hadn't been able to find any pleasure in for some time, but now she was ready.

At least she hoped she was.

'The market is going to be held in the same place as always—the centre of the village square—and I believe we've already got lots of things in place from last year. Miriam?'

Miriam, the secretary, filled them in on all the recent developments. Lots of the same stalls that came every year had rebooked. Music was going to be covered by the same brass band, and the school was going to provide a choir as well.

Sydney listened, scribbling things down on her pad that she'd need to remember, and thought of past activities. There was a lot to take in—she'd forgotten how much organising there was!—and as her list got longer and longer she almost wished she could write with both hands.

She'd also forgotten how soothing these meetings could be sometimes. The hum of voices, the opinions of everyone on how things should be done, the ebb and flow of ideas... She truly appreciated the need for all this planning and preparation. Even though sometimes the older members of the committee enjoyed their dedication to picking over details a little too much.

Briefly, she allowed her mind to wander, and the memory that sprang to her mind was of a happier year, when Olivia had played the part of Mary in the nativity. In the weeks beforehand Sydney had taught her how to ride the donkey, shown her how to behave around the other animals. She remembered holding her daughter's hand as they walked through the market stalls, making sure she didn't eat too many sweets or pieces of cake, and listening to her singing carols in the choir.

She smiled, feeling a little sad. She had those memories on camera. Alastair had videoed Olivia riding the donkey in the nativity, with her fake pregnancy bump. Olivia had loved that belly, rubbing her hands over it like a real pregnant mother soothing away imaginary kicks.

'And that brings us back to our star players for the nativity,' Malcolm continued. 'I have been reliably informed by Miss Howarth of Silverdale Infants School that our Mary this year will be played by Anna Jones, and Joseph will be Barney Brooks...'

Sydney was pulled from her reverie. *Anna? Dr Jones's Anna? She was going to play Mary?* Visions flashed through her mind. Anna wearing Olivia's costume... Anna riding Olivia's donkey... Anna being the star of the show...?

It simply hadn't occurred to her when she came back that someone else would be playing Olivia's part. But of course. There had already been new Marys in the years that she'd stayed away. She'd just not seen them, hiding away in her house every year, longing to clap her hands over her ears to blot out the sound of all those Christmas revellers. It had been torture!

It hurt to hear it. It was as if Olivia had been replaced. Had been *forgotten*...

Her chair scraped loudly on the floor as she stood, grabbing her notepad and pen, her bag and coat, and muttering apologies before rushing from the room, feeling sick.

She thought she was on her own. She thought she would get to her own car in peace. But just as she was inserting her key into the lock of her car she heard her name being called.

'Sydney!'

She didn't want to turn around. She didn't want to be polite and make small talk with whoever it was. She just wanted to go. Surely they wouldn't mind? Surely they'd understand?

She got into her seat and was about to close the door when Nathan appeared at her side, holding the car door so she couldn't close it.

'Hey! Are you okay?'

Why was he here? Why was he even bothering to ask? Why had he come after her?

'I just want to go, Nathan.'

'Something's upset you?'

'No, honestly. I just want to get home, that's all.'

'Is it Lucy? Are you worried about work?'

'No.' She slipped on her seatbelt and stared resolutely out through the windshield rather than looking at him. Her voice softened. 'I'm thrilled for Lucy. Of course I am!'

'Is it me?'

Now she looked at him, her eyes narrowing. 'Why would it be you?'

He shrugged. 'I don't know. Things haven't exactly been...straightforward. There's a...a tension, between us. We didn't exactly get off to the best start, did we?'

'It's not you,' she lied.

'Well, that's good, because they've asked me to work closely with you, seeing as I'm new and you're an established committee member.'

What? When did I miss that bit?

'Oh.'

'That's quite good, really, because—as you heard— Anna came home from school today and told me she's been picked to play the part of Mary. Apparently that means riding a donkey, and she's never done that before, so...'

'So?'

Push the memory away. Don't think about it.

'So we'll need your help.'

He smiled at her. In that way he had. Disarming her and making her feel as if she ought to oblige him with her assistance. His charming eyes twinkling.

'Know any good donkeys? Preferably something that isn't going to buck and break her neck?'

There was someone in the village who kept donkeys. They were used every year for the nativity. And she trusted the animals implicitly.

'Do you know the Bradleys? At Wicklegate Farm?'

He pretended to search his memory. 'Erm...no.'

'Do you know where Wicklegate Farm even *is*?'

He shook his head, smiling. 'No.'

Feeling some of her inner struggle fade, she smiled back. Of course he didn't. 'I suppose I'd better help you, then. Are you free next Saturday?'

'Saturday? All day.'

She nodded and started her engine. 'I'll pick you up

at ten in the morning. I know your address. Does Anna have any riding clothes?'

'Er...'

'Anything she doesn't mind getting dirty?'

'My daughter is always happy to wallow in some mud.'

'Good. Tell her I'm going to teach her how to ride a donkey.'

'Thanks.'

He stood back at last, so she could finally close her car door. She was about to drive off, eager to get home, when Nathan rapped his knuckles on her glass.

She pressed the button to wind the window down, letting in the cold evening air. 'What?'

'Lucy's at home. And waiting for your visit.'

She nodded, imagining Lucy in her small cottage, tucked up in bed, looking as proud as Punch with a big smile on her face.

'Has she picked a name for him?'

'I believe she has.'

'What is it?'

He paused, clearly considering whether to say it or not. 'She's named him Oliver.'

Oliver. So close to...

A lump filled her throat and she blinked away tears. Had Lucy chosen that name in honour of her own daughter? If she had, then...

Sydney glanced up at Nathan. 'I'll see you on Saturday.' And she quickly drove away, before he could see her cry.

Nathan had driven round to Paul and Helen's to check up on them after the accident. They lived on the outskirts of Silverdale and were pretty easy to locate, and he pulled into their driveway feeling optimistic about what he would find. Helen had been released from hospital a while ago and he only needed to remove Paul's stitches from the head laceration.

As he drove in he saw the horse grazing in a field, a blanket wrapped around its body, and smiled. They'd all been very lucky to escape as easily as they had. The accident could have been a lot worse.

But as he pulled up to the house, he spotted another vehicle.

Sydney's.

Why was she here? To check on the horse? It had to be that. It was odd that she was here at the exact same time as him, though.

Just lately she'd been in his thoughts a lot. The universe seemed to be conspiring to throw the two of them together, and whilst he didn't mind that part—she was, after all, a beautiful woman—she did tend to remind him of all his faults and of how he could never be enough for her.

His confidence had taken a knock after Gwyneth's departure. Okay, they'd only been staying in their struggling relationship because she'd learnt she was expecting a baby and Nathan had wanted to be there for her. He'd always had his doubts, and she'd been incredibly high-maintenance, but he'd honestly believed she might change the closer she got to delivering. That they both would.

She hadn't. It had still been, *Me, me, me!*

'Look at all the weight I'm putting on!'

'This pregnancy's giving me acne!'

'I'm getting varicose veins!'

'You do realise after the birth I'm going straight back to work?'

Nathan had reassured her. Had promised her it would be amazing. But it had been *his* dream. Not hers.

It had only been when she'd left him for someone else

that he'd realised how much relief he felt. It had stung that she'd left him for someone better. Someone unencumbered by ill health. Someone rich, who could give her the lifestyle she craved. But he'd felt more sorry for his baby girl, who would grow up with a mother who only had enough love for herself.

In the weeks afterwards, when he'd spent hours walking his baby daughter up and down as he tried to get her off to sleep, he'd begun to see how one-sided their relationship had always been.

Gwyneth had always been about appearances. Worrying about whether her hair extensions were the best. Whether her nails needed redoing. How much weight she was carrying. Whether she was getting promoted above someone else. She'd been a social climber—a girl who had been given everything she'd ever wanted by her parents and had come to expect the same in adulthood.

He'd fallen for her glamorous looks and the fact that in the beginning she'd seemed really sweet. But it had all been a snare. A trap. And he'd only begun to see the real Gwyneth when he'd got his diagnosis. Multiple sclerosis had scared her. The idea that she might become nursemaid to a man who wasn't strong, the way she'd pictured him, had *terrified* her.

When Nathan had discovered his illness, and Gwyneth had learned that their perfect life was not so perfect after all, her outlook had changed and she'd said some pretty harsh things. Things he'd taken to heart. That he'd believed.

He didn't want to burden Sydney with any of that.

She'd looked after his daughter for a few hours, she'd looked after and cured their rabbit, she was kind and strong...

She's the sort of woman I would go out with if I could...

But he couldn't.

She'd lost her only daughter. And where was the child's father? From what he'd heard around the village, the father had left them just a couple of months after Olivia had passed away. Shocking them all.

It seemed the whole village had thought the Harpers were strong enough to get through anything. But of course no one could know how such a tragic death would affect them.

Hadn't Sydney been through enough? He had a positive mind-set—even if he did sometimes take the things that Gwyneth had yelled at him to heart. He tried to remain upbeat. But just sometimes his mind would play tricks with him and say, *Yeah, but what if she was right?*

Besides, he wasn't sure he could trust his own judgement about those kinds of things any more. Affairs of the heart. He'd felt so sure about Gwyneth once! In the beginning, anyway. And he'd wanted to do everything for her and the baby. Had wanted the family life that had been right there in front of him. Ready and waiting.

How wrong could he have been?

He'd been floored when she'd left. She'd been high-maintenance, but not once had he suspected that she would react that way to his diagnosis. To having a baby, even. She'd been horrified at what her life had become and had been desperate to escape the drudgery she'd foreseen.

And Nathan had *known* Gwyneth. Or thought he had.

He didn't *know* Sydney. As much as he'd like to.

And he sure as hell didn't want his heart—or Anna's—broken again.

Getting out of the car, he looked up and saw Paul, Helen and Sydney coming out of the house. Helen was standing further back, her arms crossed.

'Dr Jones! Good of you to call round! You've arrived just in time. Your wife was just about to leave.'

He instantly looked at Sydney. My *wife?*

Sydney blushed madly. 'We're not married!'

Paul looked between the two of them. 'Oh, but we thought... Partners, then?'

'No. Just...friends. Associates. We just happened to be in the car together, that's all...' he explained, feeling his voice tail off when he glanced at Sydney's hot face.

'Really? You two look perfect for each other.' Paul smiled.

Nathan was a little embarrassed, but amused at the couple's mistake. 'Hello, Sydney. We seem to keep bumping into each other.'

She shook his hand in greeting. 'We do.'

'Did you get to see Lucy?'

'I did. The baby is gorgeous.'

'He is.' He was still holding her hand. Still looking at her. Someone seemed to have pressed 'pause', because for a moment he lost himself, staring into her grey eyes. It was as if the rest of the world had gone away.

Paul and Helen looked at each other and cleared their throats and Nathan dropped Sydney's hand.

'You're leaving?'

'I just came to check on the horse. No after-effects from the accident.'

'That's good. How about you, Paul? Any headaches? Anything I should be worried about?'

'No, Doc. All well and good, considering.'

'How about you, Helen?'

'I'm fine. Physically.'

'That's good.'

Sydney pulled her car keys from her pocket. 'Well, I must dash. Good to see you all so well. Paul. Helen.' She looked over at Nathan, her gaze lingering longer than it should. 'Dr Jones.'

He watched her go. Watched as she started her engine, reversed, turned and drove out of the driveway. He even watched as her car disappeared out of sight, up the lane.

Suddenly remembering that he was there to see Paul and Helen, he turned back to them, feeling embarrassed. 'Shall we go in? Get those stitches seen to?'

Paul nodded, draping his arm around Nathan's shoulder conspiratorially. 'Just friends, huh?'

He felt his cheeks colour. They'd caught him watching her. Seen how distracted she made him.

'Just friends.'

Inside the house, Helen disappeared into the kitchen to make a cup of tea.

'So, Paul… How are you?' He noted the stitches in his scalp. He'd certainly got a nasty laceration there, but apart from that obvious injury he seemed quite well.

'I'm good, Doc, thanks.' Paul settled into the chair opposite.

They had a lovely home. It was a real country cottage, with lots of character and tons of original features. There was a nice fire crackling away in the fireplace. It looked as if they were in the process of putting some Christmas decorations up.

'So I need to remove your stitches. How many days have they been in?'

'Too long! I'm really grateful for you coming out like this. I was going to make an appointment to come and say thanks to you. For saving me and Helen. And Brandon, too, of course.'

'It wasn't a problem. We were just in the right place at the right time.'

'You were in the perfect place.' He looked down at

the floor and then got his next words out in a quiet rush, after he'd turned to check that Helen wasn't listening. 'Helen and I didn't see that deer coming across the field because we were arguing.'

'Oh?' Nathan sensed a confession coming.

'I...er...hadn't reacted very well to the fact that... well...' He looked uncomfortable. 'Helen had had a miscarriage. Two weeks earlier. The hospital said they'd send you a letter... We hadn't even known she was pregnant, but she had this bleed that wouldn't stop, and we ended up at A&E one night, and they found out it was an incomplete miscarriage. She needed a D&C.'

Nathan felt a lurch in his stomach. 'I'm very sorry to hear that.'

'Yeah, well...apparently *I* wasn't sorry enough. Helen got mad with me because I wasn't upset about losing the baby. But neither of us had even *known* about the pregnancy! How could I get upset over a baby I didn't know about?' Paul let out a heavy breath. 'She thought I didn't care. We were arguing about that. Yelling...screaming at each other—so much so that Brandon started too. We didn't notice the deer because I wasn't paying attention.' He sounded guilty. 'And now, because I didn't notice the deer running in front of us, and because I didn't notice my wife was pregnant, *I'm* the bad guy who nearly got us all killed.'

How awful for them! To lose a baby like that and then to have a serious accident on top of it. They were both very lucky to have got out alive. Brandon, too. It could all have gone so terribly wrong.

'Well, I can sort your stitches for you. And I'm not so sure I would *want* to stop Helen being mad. She's had a terrible loss, Paul. You both have. And she needs to work through it.'

'I know, but...'

'There are support groups. Ones specifically for women who have suffered miscarriage. I can give you some information if you drop by the surgery. Or maybe I could ask Helen if she wants to come in and have a chat with me? You may not have known about the pregnancy, but she still lost a baby. A D&C can be a traumatic event in itself, when you think about what it is, and it can help some women to talk about things. She's had a loss and she needs to work her way through it. And I'm sure, in time, so will you.'

Paul rubbed at his bristly jaw. 'But even *she* didn't know.'

'It doesn't matter. It was still a baby, Paul. Still a loss. A terrible one. And she knows *now*. She probably feels a lot of guilt, and the easiest person to take that out on is you.'

'Does she think *I've* not been hurt too? To not even know she was pregnant and then to see her so scared when she wouldn't stop bleeding? And then to learn the reason why?' He shook his head, tears welling in his eyes. '*Why* didn't I know?'

'You're not to blame. It's difficult in those early weeks.'

'I keep thinking there must have something else I could have done for her. Something I could have said. To see that pain in her eyes... It broke my heart.'

Nathan laid a hand on Paul's shoulder.

'It *has* hurt me. I *am* upset. And I feel guilty at trying to make her get over something when she's just not ready to. Guilty that I won't get to hold that baby in my arms...'

'Grief takes time to heal. For both of you.'

Paul glanced at his hands. 'But she won't talk to me. She doesn't talk to me about any of the deep stuff because she thinks I don't care. She never shares what she's feeling. How are you supposed to be in a relationship with someone who won't tell you what's really going on?'

With great difficulty.

He looked at Paul. 'You wait. Until she's ready. And when she is...you listen.'

Nathan was so glad he'd never had to go through something like this with Gwyneth. They'd come close, when she'd thought there might still be time for an abortion, but the thought of losing his child...? It was too terrible even to think about.

Sydney would understand.

Just thinking about her now made him realise just how strong she was to have got through her daughter's death. And on her own, too.

'So I've just got to take her anger, then?'

'Be there for her. Be ready to talk when she is. She's grieving.'

Was Sydney still grieving? Was that why she wasn't able to talk to him about what had happened? Should he even *expect* her to open up to him?

He opened his doctor's bag and pulled out a small kit to remove Paul's stitches. There were ten of them, and he used a stitch-cutter and tweezers to hold the knots each time he removed them. The wound had healed well, but Paul would be left with a significant scar for a while.

'That's you done.'

'Thanks. So I've just got to wait it out, then?'

'Or you could raise the subject if *you* feel the need. I can see that you're upset at the loss, too. Let her know she can talk to you. That you're ready to talk whenever she is.'

Paul nodded and touched the spot where his stitches

had been. 'Maybe I will. I know I've lost a baby, but I'm even more scared of losing my wife.'

Nathan just stared back at him.

Sydney felt odd. She had to call round to Nathan's house in a minute, so she could take them to Wicklegate Farm and teach Anna how to ride the donkey. But for some reason she was standing in front of her wardrobe, wondering what to wear?

It shouldn't matter!

Deliberately she grabbed at a pair of old jeans, an old rugby shirt that was slightly too big for her and thick woolly socks to wear inside her boots.

I have no reason to dress up for Dr Jones.

However, once dressed, she found herself staring at her reflection in the mirror, messing with her hair. Up? Down?

She decided to leave her hair down and then added a touch of make-up. A bit of blush. Some mascara.

Her reflection stared back at her in question.

What are you doing?

Her mirror image gave no response. Obviously. But that still didn't stop her waiting for one, hoping she would see something in the mirror that would tell her the right thing to do.

She even looked at Magic. 'Am I being stupid about this?'

Magic blinked slowly at her.

She *liked* Nathan, and that was the problem. She liked it that he was comfortable to be with. She liked it that he was great to talk to. That he was very easy on the eye.

There was some small security in the fact that his little girl would be there, so it was hardly going to be a seduction, but… But a part of her—a small part, admittedly—

wondered what it would be like if something were to happen with them spending time together. What, though? A kiss? On the cheek? *The lips?* That small part of her wanted to know what it would feel like to close her eyes and feel his lips press against hers. To inhale his scent, to feel his hands upon her. To sink into his strong caress.

Alastair, in those last few months, made me feel like I had the plague. That I was disgusting to him. It would be nice to know that a man could still find me desirable.

She missed that physical connection with someone. She missed having someone in her bed in the morning. Someone to read the papers with. To talk to over a meal. She missed the comfort of sitting in the same room as another person and not even having to talk. Of sharing a good book recommendation, of watching a movie together snuggled under an old quilt and feeding each other popcorn. Coming home and not finding the house empty.

But so what? Just because she missed it, it didn't mean she had to make it happen. No matter how much she fantasised about it. Nathan was a man. And in her experience men let you down. Especially when you needed them the most. She'd already been rejected once, when she was at her lowest, and she didn't want to go through that again.

It was too hard.

So no matter how nice Nathan was—no matter how attractive, no matter how much she missed being *held*—nothing was going to happen. Today was about Anna. About donkeys and learning how to ride.

She remembered teaching Olivia. It had taken her ages to get her balance, and she'd needed a few goes at it before she'd felt confident. She hadn't liked pulling at the reins, had been worried in case it hurt the donkey.

Thinking about the past made her think of the present. Her ex-husband, Alastair, had moved on. He'd found someone new. Was making a new family. How had he moved on so quickly? It was almost insulting. Had she meant nothing to him? Had the family they'd had meant less to him than she'd realised? Perhaps that was why he'd walked away so easily?

Everyone in the village had been shocked. *Everyone*. Well, she'd make sure that everyone knew *she* wasn't moving on. Keeping Nathan and Anna at arm's length was the right thing to do, despite what she was feeling inside.

She considered cancelling. Calling him and apologising. Telling him that an emergency had cropped up. But then she'd realised that if she did she would still have to meet him again at some point. It was best to get it over and done with straight away. Less dilly-dallying. Besides, she didn't want to let Anna down. She was a good kid.

She held her house keys in her hand for a moment longer, debating with her inner conscience, and her gaze naturally strayed to a photograph of Olivia. She was standing with her head back, looking up to the sun, her eyes closed, smiling at the feel of warmth on her face. It was one of Sydney's favourite pictures: Olivia embracing the warmth of the sun.

She always enjoyed life. Even the small things.

Sydney stepped outside and locked up the cottage. She needed to drive to Nathan's house. The new estate and the road he lived on was about two miles away.

It was interesting to drive through the new builds. The houses were very modern, in bright brick, with cool grey slate tiles on their roofs and shiny white UPVC windows. They were uniformly identical, but she could see Nathan's muddy jalopy parked on his driveway and she pulled in behind it, letting out a breath. Releasing her nerves.

I can do this!

She strode up to the front door, trying to look businesslike, hoping that no one could see how nervous she suddenly felt inside. She rang the bell and let out a huge breath, trying to calm her scattered nerves.

The door opened and Nathan stood there. Smiling. 'Sydney—hi. Come on in.' he stepped back.

Reluctant to enter his home, and therefore create feelings of intimacy, she stepped back. 'Erm...shouldn't we just be off? I told the owners we'd be there in about ten minutes.'

'I'm just waiting for Anna to finish getting ready. You know what young girls are like.'

She watched his cheeks colour as he realised what he'd said, and to let him off the hook decided to step in, but keeping herself as far away from him physically as she could.

'I do...yes. Anna?' she called up the stairs.

Sydney heard some thumps and bumps and then Anna was at the top of the stairs. 'Hi, Sydney! I can't decide what to wear. Could you help me? *Please?*'

Anna wheedled out the last word, giving the cutest face that she could.

The look was so reminiscent of Olivia that Sydney had to catch her breath.

'Erm...' she glanced at Nathan, who shrugged.

'By all means...'

'Right.'

Sydney ascended the stairs, feeling sweat break out down her spine. She turned at the top and went into Anna's room. Her breath was taken away by how *girly* it was. A palace of pink. A pink feather boa hung over the mirror on a dresser, there were fairy lights around the headboard, bubblegum-coloured beanbags, a blush-pink carpet and curtains, a hammock in the corner filled with all manner of soft, cuddly toys and a patchwork quilt upon the bed.

And in front of a large pink wardrobe that had a crenelated top, like a castle, Anna stood, one hand on one hip, the other tapping her finger against her lips.

'I've never ridden a donkey. Or a horse! I don't know what would be best.'

Sydney swallowed hard as she eyed the plethora of clothes in every colour under the sun. 'Erm...something you don't mind getting dirty. Trousers or jeans. And a tee shirt? Maybe a jumper?'

Anna pulled out a mulberry-coloured jumper that was quite a thick knit, with cabling down the front. 'Like this?'

Syd nodded. 'Perfect. Trousers?'

'I have these.' Anna pulled a pair of jeans from a pile. They had some diamanté sequins sewn around the pockets. 'And this?' She pointed at the tee shirt she was already wearing.

'Those will be great. I'll go downstairs whilst you're getting dressed.'

'Could you help me, Sydney? I can never do the buttons.'

Sydney stood awkwardly whilst Anna changed her clothes, and then knelt in front of the little girl to help her do up her clothes. It had been ages since she'd had to do this. Olivia had always struggled with buttons. These two girls might almost have been made out of the same mould. Of course there were so differences between the girls, but sometimes the similarities were disturbing. Painful.

She stood up again. 'Ready?'

Anna nodded and dashed by her to run downstairs. 'I'll get my boots on!'

She sat at the bottom of the stairs and pulled on bright green wellington boots that had comical frog eyes poking out over the toes.

Sydney stood behind her, looking awkwardly at Nathan.

'Will I need boots, too?' he asked.

She nodded. 'It's a working farm...so, yes.'

She watched as they both got ready, and it was so reminiscent of standing waiting for Olivia and Alastair to get ready so they could go out that she physically felt an ache in her chest.

They had been good together. Once. When she and Alastair had married she'd truly believed they would be in each other's arms until their last days. Shuffling along together. One of those old couples you could see in parks, still holding hands.

But then it had all gone wrong.

Alastair hadn't been able to cope with losing his little girl and he'd blamed her. For not noticing that Olivia was truly ill. For not acting sooner. The way he'd blanked her, directed his anger towards her, had hurt incredibly. The one time she'd needed her husband the most had been the one time he'd failed her completely.

When Nathan and Anna were both ready she hurried them out of the door and got them into her car.

'Can you do your seatbelt, Anna?'

'Yes!' the little girl answered, beaming. 'I can't wait to ride the donkey! Did Daddy tell you I'm going to be Mary? That's the most important part in the play. Well... except for baby Jesus...but that's just going to be a doll, so...' She trailed off.

Sydney smiled into the rearview mirror. How many times had she driven her car with Olivia babbling away in the back seat? Too many times. So often, in fact, that she would usually be thinking about all the things she had to do, tuning her daughter out, saying *hmm*...or *right*...in all the right places, whenever her daughter paused for breath.

And now...? With Anna chatting away...? She wanted to listen. Wanted to show Nathan's little girl that she heard her.

I can't believe I ignored my daughter! Even for a second!

How many times had she not truly listened? How many times had she not paid attention? Thinking that she had all the time in the world to talk to her whenever she wanted? To chat about things that hadn't meant much to her but had meant the world to her daughter?

'All eyes will be on you, Anna. I'm sure you'll do a great job.'

Nathan glanced over at her. 'I appreciate you arranging this. I don't suppose you're a dab hand with a sewing machine, are you?'

She was, actually. 'Why?'

'The costume for Mary is looking a bit old. The last incumbent seems to have dragged it through a dump before storing it away and now it looks awful. Miriam has suggested that I make another one.'

She glanced over at him. 'And you said...?'

'I said yes! But that was when I thought a bedsheet and a blue teacloth over the head was all that was needed.'

'You know... I might still have Olivia's old outfit. She played Mary one year.'

'She did?' Nathan was looking at her closely.

'I still have some of her stuff in boxes in the attic. Couldn't bear to part with it. Give me a day or two and I'll check.'

'That's very kind of you.'

She kept her eyes on the road, trying not to think too

hard about going up into the attic to open those boxes. Would the clothes still have Olivia's scent? Would seeing them, touching them, be too painful? There was a reason they were still in the attic. Unsorted.

She'd boxed everything up one day, after a therapist at one of her grief counselling sessions had told her it might be a good thing to do. That it might be cathartic, or something.

It hadn't been.

She'd felt that in boxing up her daughter's clothes and putting them somewhere they couldn't be seen she was also been getting rid of all traces of her daughter. That she was hiding Olivia's memory away. And she'd not been ready. She'd drunk an awful lot of wine that night, and had staggered up into the attic to drag all the boxes back downstairs, but Alastair had stopped her. Yelled at her that it was a *good* thing, and that if she touched those boxes one more time then he would walk out the door.

She'd sobered up and the next morning had left the boxes up there—even though she'd felt bereft and distraught. And dreadfully hungover.

Alastair had left eventually, of course. Just not then. It had taken a few more weeks. By then it had been too late to drag the boxes back down. Too scary.

'What was she like?'

'Hmm?' She was pulled back to the present by his question. 'What?'

'What was Olivia like?' he asked again.

She glanced over at him quickly. He sounded as if he really wanted to know, and no one had asked her that question for years. All this time she'd stayed away from people, not making connections or getting close because she hadn't wanted to talk about Olivia. It had been too painful. But now she *wanted* to talk about her.

Was thrilled that he'd asked, because she was *ready* to talk about her. He'd made it easy to do so.

'She was…amazing.'

'Who's Olivia?' asked Anna from the back seat.

Sydney glanced in the rearview mirror once again and smiled.

The donkey was called Bert and he had a beautiful dark brown coat. The farmer had already got him saddled before their arrival and he stood waiting patiently, nibbling at some hay, as Sydney gave Anna instructions.

'Okay, it's quite simple, Anna. You don't need Bert to go fast, so you don't need to nudge him with your feet or kick at his sides. A slow plod is what we want, and Bert here is an expert at the slow plod and the Christmas nativity.'

'Will he bite me?'

She shook her head. 'No. He's very gentle and he is used to children riding him. Shall I lift you into the saddle?'

Anna nodded.

Sydney hefted Anna up. 'Put your hands here, on the pommel. I'll lead him with the reins—the way we'll get the boy playing Joseph to do it.'

'Okay.'

'Verbal commands work best, and Bert responds to *Go on* when you want him to start walking and *Stop* when you want him to stand still. Got that?'

Anna nodded again.

'Why don't you give that a try?'

Anna smiled. 'Go on, Bert!'

Bert started moving.

'He's doing it, Sydney! He's *doing* it! Look, Daddy—I'm riding!'

'That's brilliant, sweetheart.'

Sydney led Bert down the short side of the field. She turned to check on Anna. 'That's it. Keep your back straight...don't slouch.'

They walked up and down. Up and down. Until Sydney thought Anna was ready to try and do it on her own. She'd certainly picked it up a lot more quickly than Olivia had!

'Okay, Anna. Try it on your own. Head to the end of the field and use the reins to turn him and make him come back. Talk to him. Encourage him. Okay?'

She knew Anna could do it. The little girl had connected with the donkey in a way no other had, and the animal responded brilliantly to her. Sydney really didn't think Anna would have a problem on the night of the nativity. Bert was putty in her hands.

They both stood and watched as Anna led Bert confidently away from them and down the field. Sydney almost felt proud. In fact, she *was* proud.

She became aware that Nathan was staring at her, and then suddenly, almost in a blink, she felt his fingers sliding around hers.

'Thank you, Sydney.'

She turned to him and looked into his eyes. The intensity of the moment grew. It felt as if her heart had sped up but her breathing had got really slow. Her fingers in his felt protected and safe, and he stroked the back of her hand with his thumb in slow, sweeping strokes that were doing strange, chaotic things to her insides, turning her legs to jelly.

'What for?' she managed to say.

'For helping me when it's difficult for you. I appreciate the time you're giving me and my daughter. I...'

He stopped talking as he took a step closer to her, and

as he drew near her breathing stopped completely and she looked up into his handsome blue eyes.

He's going to kiss me!

Hadn't she thought about this? Hadn't she wondered what it might be like? Hadn't she missed the physical contact that came with being in a relationship? And now here was this man—this incredibly *attractive* man—holding her hand and making her stomach do twirls and swirls as his lips neared hers, as he leaned in for a kiss...

Sydney closed her eyes, awaiting the press of his lips against hers.

Only there was no kiss.

She felt him pull his hand free from hers and heard him clearing his throat and apologising before he called out, 'You're doing brilliantly, Anna! Turn him round now—come on. We need to go home.'

Sydney blinked. What had happened? He'd been about to kiss her, hadn't he? And she'd stood there, like an idiot, waiting for him to do it.

How embarrassing!

Anna brought Bert to a halt beside them, beaming widely.

'I think that's enough for today. You've done really well, Anna.'

Anna beamed as her father helped her off the donkey, and then she ran straight to Sydney and wrapped her arms around her. 'Thanks, Sydney! You're the best!'

Sydney froze at the unexpected hug, but then she relaxed and hugged the little girl back, swallowing back her surprise and...for some reason...her tears. 'So are you.'

The farmer took Bert back to his field with the other donkeys, once he'd removed the saddle and tack, and Sydney and Anna said goodbye. Then they all got back into Sydney's car and she started to drive them home.

'Thank you for...er...what you've done for Anna today,' said Nathan.

She took a breath and bit back the retort she wanted to give. 'No problem.'

'You know...taking time out of your weekend...'

'Sydney could stay for dinner, couldn't she Daddy? We're having fajitas!' Anna invited from the back.

She would have loved nothing more than to stay. Her time spent with Anna had been wonderful, and the times when she'd looked across at Nathan and caught him looking at her had been weirdly wonderful and exciting too.

But after what had just happened—the almost-kiss... He'd been going to do it. She knew it! But something had stopped him. Had got in the way.

Was it because he'd suddenly remembered Anna was there? Had he not wanted to risk his daughter seeing them kissing? Or was it something else?

She was afraid of getting carried away and reading too much into this situation. She'd helped out. That was all. She'd felt a connection that Nathan hadn't. Getting too involved with this single dad was perhaps a step too far. Where would it end? If she spent too much time with them, where would she be?

She shivered, even though the car heater was pumping out plenty of hot air. 'I'm sorry, I can't. I've got a...a thing later.'

'Maybe another time?' Nathan suggested, looking embarrassed.

As well you might!

'Sure.'

There can't ever be another time, no.

She watched them clamber from her car when she dropped them off. Nathan lingered at the open window of the car, as if he had something else to say, but then he looked away and simply said goodbye, before following his daughter up the path.

Sydney drove off before he could turn around and say anything else.

I really like them. Both of them.

But was it what they represented that she liked? This dad. This little girl. They were a ready-made family. Being with them might give her back some of what she'd lost. They offered a chance of starting again. So was it the *situation* that she liked? Or *them* as individuals?

Nathan was great. Gorgeous, charming, someone she enjoyed being around. And Anna was cute as a button, with her sing-song voice and happy-go-lucky personality.

Was it wrong to envy them? To envy them because they still had each other?

Was it wrong to have wanted—to have *craved*—Nathan's kiss?

Feeling guilty, she drove home, and she was just about to park up when she got a text. A cat was having difficulties giving birth and she needed to get to the surgery immediately to prep for a Caesarean section.

Suddenly all business—which was easy because she knew what she was doing—she turned the car around and drove to the surgery.

Nathan sent Anna upstairs to get changed into some clean clothes that didn't smell of donkey and farm. Then he headed into the kitchen, switching on the kettle and sinking into a chair as he waited for it to boil.

What the hell had he done?

Something crazy—something not *him*—had somehow slipped through his defences and he'd found himself taking hold of Sydney's hand, staring into her sad grey eyes. And he had been about to *kiss her*!

Okay, so he'd been fighting that urge for a while, and it was hardly a strange impulse, but he *had* thought that he'd got those impulses under control.

Standing there, looking down into her face, at her smooth skin, her slightly rosy cheeks, those soft, inviting lips, he'd wanted to so badly! And she'd wanted him to do it. He'd wanted to, but...

But Anna hadn't been far away, and he'd suddenly heard that horrid voice in his head that still sounded remarkably like Gwyneth, telling him that no one, and especially not Sydney, would want him. Not with his faulty, failing body. Not with his bad genes. Not with a child who wasn't hers...

How could he ask her to take on that burden—especially with the threat of his MS always present? He knew the chances of the MS killing him were practically zero. Okay, there would be difficulties, and there would be complications—there might even be comorbidities such as thyroid disease, autoimmune conditions or a meningioma. But the MS on its own...? It was unlikely.

But it had been enough to make him hesitate. To think twice. And once he'd paused too long he'd known it was too late to kiss her so he'd stepped away. Had called out to Anna...said they needed to go.

Sydney deserved a strong man. A man who would look out for her and care for her and protect her. What if he couldn't do that?

Fear. That was what it had been. Fear of putting himself out there. Of getting involved. Of exposing himself to the hurt and pain that Gwyneth had caused once. How could he go through again? How could he expose Anna to that now that she was older? She would be aware now if she grew to love someone and then that someone decided it was all too much and wanted out.

Anna being a baby had protected her from the pain of losing her mother. And today he had saved himself from finding out if he could be enough for someone like Sydney. Gwyneth had made him doubt what he had to offer. She had probably been right in what she'd said. He didn't know what his future would be like. He couldn't be certain, despite trying his best to remain positive. But it was hard sometimes. Dealing with a chronic illness… sometimes it could get to you.

The kettle boiled and he slowly made himself a cup of tea. He heard Anna come trotting back down the stairs and she came into the kitchen.

'Can I have a biscuit, Daddy?'

'Just one.'

She reached into the biscuit barrel and took out a plain biscuit. 'I loved riding Bert. He was so cute! I love donkeys. Do *you* love donkeys, Daddy?'

He thought for a moment. 'I do. Especially Bert.'

She smiled at him, crumbs dropping onto the floor. 'And do you love Sydney?'

His gaze swung straight round to his daughter's face. 'What?'

'I think you like her.'

'What makes you say that?' he asked in a strangled voice.

'Your eyes go all funny.' She giggled. 'Joshua in my class—he looks at Gemma like that and he *loves* her. They're boyfriend and girlfriend.'

Nathan cleared his throat. 'Aren't they a little young to be boyfriend and girlfriend?'

Anna shrugged, and then skipped off into the other room. He heard the television go on.

She noticed quite a lot, did Anna.

Curious, he followed her through to the lounge and

stood and watched her for a moment as she chose a channel to watch.

'Anna?'

'Yes?'

'If I did like Sydney...how would you feel about that?'

Anna tilted her head to one side and smiled, before turning back to the television. 'Fine. Then you wouldn't be all alone.'

Nathan stared at his daughter. And smiled.

CHAPTER SIX

IT HAD BEEN a long time since Sydney had had to play 'mother', and now she had the pleasure once again. The cat she'd raced to had recovered from its surgery, but had disowned her kittens afterwards. It happened sometimes with animals, when they missed giving birth in the traditional way and there just wasn't that bond there for them.

The four kittens—three black females and a black and white male—were kicking off their December in a small cat carrier at her home and she was on round-the-clock feeding every two hours.

Sydney was quite enjoying it. It gave her purpose. It gave her a routine. But mostly it gave her something to do during the long hours of the lonely nights. Even if she *was* still torturing herself with what might have happened between her and Nathan.

I wanted him to kiss me and I made that perfectly clear!

She'd hardly fought it, had she? Standing there all still, eyes closed, awaiting his kiss like some stupid girl in a fairytale. He must have thought she was a right sap. Perhaps that was what had put him off...

Disturbed from her reverie by the sound of her doorbell, she glanced at the clock—it was nearly eight in the morning—and went to answer the door.

It didn't cross her mind that she'd been up all night, hadn't combed her hair or washed her face, or that she was still wearing yesterday's clothes and smelt slightly of antiseptic and donkey at the same time.

She opened the door to see Nathan and Anna standing there. 'Er... Hi... Sorry, had we arranged to meet?' She felt confused by their being there. And so early, too.

'We were out getting breakfast,' Nathan explained. 'Anna wanted croissants and jam. We didn't have any and...' He blinked, squirming slightly. 'I thought you might like to share some with us.'

He raised a brown paper bag that was starting to show grease spots and she suddenly realised how hungry she was.

Her mouth watered and her stomach ached for the food and nourishment. Warm, buttery croissants sounded delicious!

Even though she still felt embarrassed after yesterday, the lure of the food overpowered the feeling.

'Sure. Come on in.' She stepped back, biting her lip as they passed, wondering if she was making a huge mistake in accepting. Hadn't this man humiliated her just yesterday? Unintentionally, perhaps, but still... And today she was letting him in to her house? She had no idea where her boundaries were with them any more.

Following the scent of food to her kitchen, she washed her hands and got out some plates, then butter from the fridge.

'I don't have any jam...'

'We do!' Anna chirruped. 'Blackberry, apricot and strawberry!' She put a small bag holding the jars onto the kitchen counter.

Sydney nodded. 'Wow! You *do* come prepared, don't

you? There can't be many people wandering around with a full condiments selection.'

Nathan grinned. 'We weren't sure which one you liked, so...'

He was trying to say sorry. She could see that. The croissants, the jam, the sudden breakfast—these were all part of his white flag. His olive branch. His truce. She would be cruel to reject it. Especially as it was going to be so nice. When had she last had a breakfast like this?

'I like apricot, so thank you for getting it for me.'

She smiled and mussed Anna's hair, and then indicated they should all sit at the table. Sydney filled the kettle, and poured some juice for Anna, and then they all settled down to eat.

Her home was filled with laughter, flaky pastries and the wonderful sound of happiness. It was as if her kitchen had been waiting for this family to fill it, and suddenly it no longer seemed the cold empty room she knew, but a room full of life and purpose and identity.

For an hour she forgot her grief. She let down her barriers and her walls and allowed them in. Despite her uncertainty, they were good for her. Anna was wonderfully bright and cheerful and giggly. And those differences between her and Olivia were growing starker by the minute. Anna liked looking at flowers, but had no interest in growing them. She knew what she wanted to be when she was grown up. She liked building things and being hands-on. She was such a sweet little girl, and so endearing, and Nathan

They just got on well together. It was easy for them all.

Sydney was licking the last of the croissant crumbs from her fingers when Nathan said, 'How come you don't have any Christmas decorations?'

His question was like a bucket of ice-cold water being

thrown over her. It was a reality check. It pulled her back to her *actual* life and not the temporarily happy one she'd been enjoying.

'I don't do Christmas.'

He held her gaze, trying to see beyond her words. Trying to learn her reasons.

Anna looked at her in shock. 'Don't you believe in Santa Claus?'

Sydney smiled at her. If only it were that simple. 'Of course I do. Santa is a very good reason to enjoy Christmas.' She thought for a moment. 'Anna, why don't you go and take a look at what's in the blue cat carrier in my lounge? Be gentle, though.'

Anna gasped and ran into the other room, and Sydney turned back to face Nathan. She sucked in a breath to speak but nothing came out. Thankfully he didn't judge or say anything. He just waited for her to speak. And suddenly she could.

'Olivia died just before Christmas. It seems wrong to celebrate it.'

He swallowed. 'Do you want to talk about it?'

She did...but after the way he'd been with her yesterday... Did she want to share the innermost pain in her heart with a man who could blow so hot and cold? What would be the point in telling him if he wasn't going to stick around? If he wasn't going to be the kind of person she needed in her life? Because she was beginning to think that maybe there *could* be someone. One day. Maybe.

Could the person be Nathan?

She didn't want to feel vulnerable again, or helpless. But sitting in her home night after night, *alone*, was making her feel more vulnerable than she'd ever realised. Yet still she wasn't sure whether to tell him everything.

He stared at her intently, focusing on her eyes, her lips, then on her eyes again. What was he trying to see? What was he trying to decide?

He soon let her know, by confiding something of his own.

'I have MS—multiple sclerosis. To be exact, I have relapsing remitting multiple sclerosis. I have attacks of symptoms that come on suddenly and then go away again.'

She leaned forward, concerned. Intrigued. Was this what had been wrong with him the other day? When he'd been all dizzy at the veterinary surgery? And that time at the accident site?

'MS...?'

'I was diagnosed the week before Anna was born. It was a huge shock—nothing compared to losing a child, but it had tremendous repercussions. Not only my life, but Anna's too. Anna's mother walked out on us both during a time in which I was already reeling. Only a couple of weeks after we'd had Anna, Gwyneth left us...but it doesn't stop us from celebrating Anna's birthday each year. She gets presents, a cake, a party, balloons. You *should* enjoy Christmas. You *should* celebrate. There aren't many times in our lives where we can really enjoy ourselves, but Christmas is one of them.'

Sydney stood up and began to clear away the breakfast things. She'd heard what he'd said, but his story hardly touched hers. 'That's completely different.'

He got up and followed her into the kitchen, grabbed her arm. 'No, it isn't.'

She yanked her arm free. 'Yes, it is! My child *died*. Your girlfriend walked out. There's a *big* difference.'

'Sydney—'

'Do you think I can *enjoy* being reminded every year

that my daughter is dead? Every time Christmas begins—and it seems to get earlier every year—everywhere I look people are putting up decorations and trees and lights, buying presents for each other, and they're all in a happy mood. All I can see is my daughter, lying in a hospital bed with tubes coming out of her, and myself being told that I need to say goodbye! Do you have *any* idea of how that feels? To know that everybody else is *happy* because it's that time of year again?'

He shook his head. 'No. I couldn't possibly know.'

'No.' She bit back her tears and slumped against the kitchen units, lost in memories of that hospital once again. Feeling the old, familiar pain and grief. 'I became the saddest I could ever be at this time of year—when everyone else is at their happiest. I can't sleep. It's hard for me. I could *never* celebrate.'

Nathan stood in front of her and took one of her hands in his, looking down at their interlocked fingers. 'Perhaps you need to stop focusing on the day that she died and instead start focusing on all the days that she lived...'

His words stunned her. A swell of anger like a giant wave washed over her and she had to reach out to steady herself. It was that powerful.

How *dared* he tell her how she ought to grieve? How she ought to remember her daughter! He had no idea of how she felt and here he was—another *doctor*—telling her what she needed to do, handing out advice.

She inhaled a deep breath through her nose, feeling her shoulders rise up and her chin jut out in defiance as she stared at him, feeling her fury seethe out from her every pore.

'*Get out.*'

'Sydney—'

He tried to reach for her arm, but seeing his hand

stretched out towards her, without her permission, made her feel even more fury and she batted him away.

'You don't get to tell me how to deal with my grief. You don't get to tell me how I should be thinking. You don't get to tell me anything!'

She stormed away from him—out of her kitchen, down the hallway, towards her front door, which she wrenched open. Then she stood there, arms folded, as tears began to break and her bottom lip began to wobble with the force of her anger and upset.

She felt as if she could tackle anything with the strength of feeling she had inside her right now. Wrestle a lion? *Bring it on.* Take down a giant? *Bring it on.* Chuck someone out of her home? *Bring. It. On!*

Nathan followed her, apology written all over his features. 'Look, Syd, I'm sorry. I—'

She held up a finger, ignoring the fact that it was shaking and trembling with her rage. 'Don't. Don't you *dare.* I don't want to hear any of it. Not from you. You with your *"drink warm milk"* advice and your *"why not try grief counselling?"* and your *"focus on the days she lived"* advice. You couldn't *possibly* understand what I am going through! You couldn't even kiss me, Dr Nathan Jones, so you don't get to tell me how to live.'

He stared back at her, his Adam's apple bobbing up and down as he swallowed hard. Then he sighed and called out for his daughter. 'Anna? We need to go.'

They both heard Anna make a protest at having to leave. She was obviously having far too much fun with the orphaned kittens.

But she showed up in the doorway and looked at both her father and Sydney. 'Are we leaving?'

''Fraid so.' Nathan nodded and gave her a rueful smile. 'We need to head back now. Sydney's got things to do.'

'Not fair, Daddy! I want to stay with the kittens. Sydney, can I stay for a little bit—*pleeeeeease*?' She added a sickly sweet smile and clutched her hands before her like she was begging for a chance of life before a judge.

Nathan steered her out through the front door. 'Another time, honey.' As he moved out of the door he turned briefly to Sydney. 'I'm sorry I've upset you. I didn't mean anything by it.'

She closed the door, and as it slammed, as she shut out the sight of Nathan and Anna walking away down her front path, she sank to the floor and put her head in her hands and sobbed. Huge, gulping sobs. Sobs that caused her to hiccup. Sobs that took ages to fade away, leaving her crouched in the hallway just breathing in a silence broken only by the ticking clock.

Finally she was able to get to her feet, and listlessly she headed back to the kitchen to clear away the breakfast things.

Sydney had felt numb for a few hours. It was a strange feeling. Having got that angry, that upset, it was as if she'd used up a year's worth of emotions all in a few minutes, and now her body and her mind had become completely exhausted, unable to feel anything.

Now she sat in her empty home, looking at the pictures of her daughter, and felt...*nothing*. No sadness. No joy. She couldn't even bring herself to try and remember the days on which they'd been taken, and when she tried to remember the sound of her daughter's chuckles she couldn't conjure it up.

It was like being frozen. Or as if she could move, breathe, live, exist, but the rest of the world was seen through a filter somehow. It was as if her memories were gone—as if her feelings had been taken away and in their place a giant nothingness remained.

She didn't like it. It made her feel even more isolated than she had been before. Lonely. She didn't even have her daughter's memories to accompany her in the silence.

She wasn't ready to forget her daughter. To lose her. She needed to remind herself again. To reconnect.

Sydney looked up. Olivia's things were in the attic. Her clothes. Her toys. Her books. Everything. She hadn't been able to go up in the loft for years because of them, but perhaps she needed to at this moment.

So, despite the tiredness and the lethargy taking over every limb, muscle and bone, she headed up the stairs and opened up the attic, sliding down the metal ladder and taking a deep breath before she headed up the steps.

There was a stillness in the attic. As if she'd entered a sacred, holy space. But instead of vaulted ceilings with regal columns and priceless holy relics gleaming in soft sunlight there was loft insulation, piles of boxes and a single bulb that was lit by pulling a hanging chain.

She let out a long, slow breath as some of her numbness began to dissipate, and in its place she felt a nervous anxiety begin to build.

Was she right to be doing this? She hadn't looked through these things for so long!

Am I strong enough? What if it's too much?

But then there was another voice in her head. A logical voice.

It's only clothes. Books. Toys. Nothing here can hurt you.

Doubt told her that something might. But she edged towards the first box, labelled *'Costumes'*, and began to unfold the top, not realising that she was biting into her bottom lip until she felt a small pain.

The contents of the box were topped with taffeta. A dress of some sort. Sydney lifted it out to look at it, to try and force a memory. And this time it came.

Olivia had wanted a 'princess dress' for a party. They'd gone shopping into Norton town centre together, her daughter holding on to her hand as she'd skipped alongside her. They'd gone from shop to shop, looking for the perfect dress, and she'd spotted this one. With a beautiful purple velvet bodice and reams upon reams of lilac taffeta billowing out from the waist.

Olivia had looked perfect in it! Twirling in front of the mirror, this way and that, swishing the skirt, making it go this way, then that way around her legs.

'Look, Mummy! It's so pretty! Can I have it?'

Sydney smiled as she pulled out outfit after outfit. A mermaid tail, another princess dress, this time in pink, a Halloween costume festooned with layers and layers of black and orange netting. Sydney hesitated as she dipped into the box and pulled out a onesie made of brown fur. It had a long tail, and ears on the hood. Sydney pressed it to her nose and inhaled, closing her eyes as tears leaked from the corners of them.

Olivia had loved this onesie. She'd used to sleep in it. She'd been wearing it when… The memory came bursting to the fore.

The morning I found you.

She smiled bravely as she inhaled the scent of the onesie once again. It had been washed, but she was convinced it still had her daughter's scent.

An image of that awful morning filled her head. The day before Olivia had said she had a headache. She hadn't wanted to go to school. But Sydney had had a long day of surgeries, and Alastair had had work, so they'd needed their daughter to go in.

At the end of the day, when Sydney had gone to pick her up, Olivia had seemed in a very low mood—not her normal self. When they'd got home she'd said she was tired and that her head still hurt, so Sydney had given her some medicine and a drink and told her she could go to bed. She'd kept checking on her, but her daughter had been sleeping, so she'd just put it down to some virus.

When Alastair had got home he'd been celebrating a success at work, and that night they'd gone to bed and made love. The next morning Alastair had left early. Sydney had called for Olivia to come down for breakfast but she hadn't answered. So she'd gone up to get her and instantly known something was wrong. The second she'd walked into her daughter's bedroom.

She'd not been able to wake her. She'd called her name, shaken her shoulders—nothing. Olivia had been hot, and Sydney had gone to unzip the onesie, and that was when she'd seen the rash and called 999.

Sydney laid the onesie down. This was the last thing that Olivia had worn. It was too sad to focus on. Too painful.

She dug further into the box and pulled out a pirate costume.

Now, this has a happier memory!

There'd been a World Book Day and all the school's children had been asked to come in as one of their favourite characters. At the time Olivia had been into pirate stories, but none of the characters had been girl pirates, so she'd decided that she would be a pirate anyway. Sydney had rolled up a pair of blue jeans to Olivia's calves, bought a red and white striped tee shirt and a tricorne hat, and used an eye patch that they'd been gifted in an old party bag.

Olivia had spent all day answering every question Sydney had asked her with, *'Arr!'* and, *'Aye, Captain!'*

Sydney laughed at the memory, her heart swelling with warmth and feeling once again. Seeing her daughter happy in her mind's eye, hearing that chuckle, seeing her smile, feeling her—

She stopped.

Oh... Could Nathan be right? That I need to focus on the days she lived?

No. No, he couldn't be right. He hadn't experienced grief like this—he didn't know what he was talking about.

But I do feel good when I remember the good times...

Perhaps holding on to the grief, on to the day she died, on to the *pain* was the thing that anchored Sydney in the past? Maybe she was holding herself back? Isolating herself so that she could wallow in her daughter's memory. Was that why Alastair had moved on? Had he been able to let go of the misery and instead chosen to remember his daughter's vibrant life, not just her death?

Stunned, she sat there for a moment, holding the pirate tee shirt and wondering. Her gaze travelled to the other boxes. Books. Toys. Clothes. Was holding on to her daughter like this the thing that was keeping her from moving on? Perhaps keeping her daughter's things in the attic had kept Olivia trapped in a place that tortured them both.

I know I have to try to move on...but by letting go of my past will I lose my daughter?

The thought that maybe she ought to donate some of Olivia's stuff to a charity shop entered her head, and she immediately stood up straight and stared down at the open box.

Give her things away?

No. Surely not. If she gave Olivia's things away, how on earth would she remember her?

You've remembered her just fine with all this stuff packed away in the attic for four years...

She let out a breath. Then another. Steadier. It calmed her racing heart. What if she didn't do it all in one go? What if she just gave away a few pieces? Bit by bit? It might be easier that way. She'd keep the stuff that mattered, though. The onesie. Olivia's favourite toys—her doll and her teddy bear Baxter. Maybe one or two of her daughter's favourite books. The last one they'd been reading, for sure.

Maybe...

She saw the look on Nathan's face as he'd left. *'I'm sorry I upset you...'*

I need to apologise.

Guilt filled her and she suddenly felt sick. Gripping her stomach, she sat down and clutched the onesie for strength. For inspiration.

She would have to apologise. Make it up to him. Explain.

If he even wants to listen.

But then she thought, *He will listen.* He was a doctor. He was good at that. And she needed to let him know that she cared.

As she thought of how she could make it up to him she saw some other boxes, further towards the back of the attic. She frowned, wondering what they were, and, crouching, she shuffled over to them, tore off the tape and opened them up.

Christmas decorations.

Perhaps she could show Nathan in more than one way that she was trying to make things right...

She'd used to love Christmas. Olivia had *adored* it.

What child didn't? It was a season of great fun and great food, rounded off with a day full of presents.

She particularly remembered the Christmas before Olivia had died. She'd asked for a bike and Sydney and Alastair had found her a sparkly pink one, with tassels on the handlebars and a basket on the front adorned with plastic flowers.

Olivia had spent all that Christmas Day peddling up and down on the pathways and around the back garden, her little knees going up and down, biting her bottom lip as she concentrated on her coordination. And then later that day, after they'd all eaten their dinner, pulled crackers, told each other bad jokes and were sitting curled up on the sofa together, Olivia had asked if next Christmas she could have a little brother or sister.

Sydney's gaze alighted on the bike, covered by an old brown blanket...

She swallowed the lump in her throat. Olivia would have loved a sibling. A little baby to play with. What would she have made of Anna? No doubt the girls would have been best friends.

Thinking of Anna made her think of Nathan. She was so very grateful for him coming over today. Offering his olive branch. He had given her a new way of thinking. And how had she reacted? Badly! She'd seen it as an attack on her rather than seeing the kind and caring motivation behind it.

She could see now what he'd been trying to say. And she had missed it completely. It was true. She had been focusing so much on her daughter's death that she had forgotten to focus on her daughter's life.

And Nathan had also told her about his MS. It had been so brave of him to share that with her, and it must have been troubling him for some time. It must have been why he'd been so ill that day she'd looked after Anna. And hadn't Anna said her daddy was always sick and tired?

Poor Nathan. But at least he knew what he was fighting. It had a name. It had a treatment plan. She would have to look it up online and see what relapsing remitting multiple sclerosis really was. Especially if—as she was starting to hope—they were going to be involved with each other. It would be good to know what to expect and how to help.

Nathan had given her a gift. A way to try and lift the burden that she'd been feeling all this time. The guilt. The grief. He'd given her something else to think about. Told her to try and remember Olivia in a different way. A less heartbreaking way.

Could she do it?

Maybe she could start by honouring the season...

Sydney lifted up a box of decorations and began to make her way back down the ladder.

CHAPTER SEVEN

MRS COURTAULD HAD arrived for her appointment. She was there for a blood pressure check, and though she could have made an appointment to see the practice nurse to get it done she'd deliberately made a doctor's appointment to see Nathan.

She came into his room, shuffling her feet, and settled down into a chair with a small groan.

He forced a smile. 'Mrs Courtauld...how are you?'

'Oh, I'm good, Doctor, thank you. I must say *you* look a bit glum. I've been round the block enough times to know when someone's *pretending* to be okay.'

He laughed. 'I'm sorry. I'll try to do better. Are you ready for Christmas?'

Sydney's rejection of him had hurt terribly. Although he didn't think she'd rejected him because of his health—unlike Gwyneth—the way she'd thrown him out still stung.

'Of course I am! Not that there's much preparation for me to do...not with my Alfred gone, God rest his soul. But my son is going to pick me up on Christmas Eve and I'm going to his house to spend the season.'

'Sounds great. Let someone else look after you and do all the work. Why not?'

'I've brought those things that you asked for.' She

reached down into her shopping trolley and pulled out a small packet wrapped in a brown paper bag and passed it across the table to him. 'I asked around and so many people wanted to help. I hope it's the kind of thing you were after. Surprisingly, there was quite a bit that people had.'

He peeked inside and smiled. It *was* rather a lot. More than he could have hoped for. But would it be any good now?

'Perfect. Thank you, Mrs C. I appreciate all the trouble you went to to coordinate this. Now, shall we check your blood pressure?'

She began to remove her coat. 'Anything for our Sydney.' She looked at him slyly. 'Will you be spending Christmas together, then?'

He felt his face colour, but smiled anyway, even though he suspected that the chance of his spending Christmas with Sydney had about the same odds as his MS disappearing without trace. Choosing not to answer, he wheeled his chair over to his patient.

Mrs Courtauld couldn't know that they'd had a falling out. He'd been trying to help Sydney, but maybe it had come out wrong? He'd been going over and over what he'd said, trying to remember the *way* he'd said it as well as *what* he'd said, and he'd got angry at himself.

His patient rolled up her sleeve, staring at him, assessing him. 'She deserves some happiness, young Sydney. She's had her sadness, and she's paid her dues in that respect. Enough grief to last a thousand lifetimes. It's her turn to be happy.' She looked up at him and made him meet her gaze. 'And you could do that for her, Doctor. You and that little girl of yours.'

'Thanks, Mrs C.'

'Call me Elizabeth.'

He smiled and checked her blood pressure.

* * *

A bell rang overhead as Sydney walked into the charity shop. There was only one in Silverdale, and sales from it aided the local hospice. She hadn't been in for a long time, but was reassured to see a familiar face behind the counter.

'Syd! Long time, no see! How are you?'

Sydney made her way to the counter with her two bags of clothes. It wasn't much. But it was a start. 'Oh, you know. Ambling on with life.'

'We've missed seeing you in here. We could always rely on you to come in most weekends, looking for a new book or two.'

'I'm sorry it's been a while.' She paused for a moment. She could back out if she wanted to. She didn't have to hand these items over. 'I've…er…brought in a few things. Children's clothes.'

'Children's…? Oh, wait…not *Olivia's*?'

Her cheeks flushed with heat and she nodded. 'Just one or two outfits. Thought I'd better start sorting, you know.'

Lisa nodded sadly. 'Sometimes it's what we need to do, to move forward.'

She didn't want to cry. Wasn't that what Nathan had said in a roundabout way? And look at how she had treated him for it! Perhaps everyone had been thinking the same, but she'd been the only one not to know.

'It's all been laundered and pressed. You should be able to put it straight out.' She placed the two bags on the counter and Lisa peered inside, her fingers touching the fabric of a skirt that Olivia had worn only once, because she'd been going through a growth spurt.

'That's grand, Syd. I'll have a sort through and maybe make a window display with them. Launch them with style, eh?'

Unable to speak, Sydney nodded. Then, blinking back tears, she hurriedly left the shop.

Outside in the cold air she began to breathe again, sucking in great lungsful of the crisp air and strangely feeling a part of her burden begin to lift.

It had been a difficult thing to do, but she'd done it. She'd made a start. Hopefully next time it would be easier. But doing it in little instalments was better than trying to get rid of it all in one go. She knew that wasn't the way for her. Slow and steady would win this race.

But now she had a really hard thing to do. She had to see Nathan. Apologise. There was one last committee meeting tonight and perhaps there, on neutral ground, she could let him know that she'd been in the wrong. That it would be nice if he could forgive her. But if not...

She dreaded to think of *if not*...

Those hours in the attic—those hours spent sorting her daughter's clothes for donation—had made her begin to see just how much she had begun to enjoy and even to depend upon Nathan's friendship.

She'd been a fool to react so badly.

She could only hope he would forgive her in a way Alastair had never been able to.

It was the last committee meeting before the big day. The Christmas market and nativity—and the anniversary of Olivia's death—were just two days away, and this was their last chance to make sure that everything was spick and span and organised correctly. That there were no last-minute hiccups.

There was palpable excitement in the room, and Miriam had even gone to the trouble to supply them with chocolate biscuits to help fuel their discussion.

Sydney sat nervously at one end of the table, far from

Nathan, anxious to get the opportunity to talk to him and put things right. Her mind buzzed with all the things she needed to say. Wanted to say. She'd hoped she'd have a chance to talk to him before the meeting started, but he'd come in late once again and grabbed his place at the table without looking at her.

'The marquees are all organised and will be delivered tomorrow and erected on-site. Items for the tombola are all sorted, and Mike has promised us the use of his PA and sound system this year.' Miriam beamed.

'How are we doing regarding the food stalls? Sydney?'

She perked up at the sound of her name and riffled through her notes, her hands shaking. 'The WI ladies in the village are in full cake-making mode and most will bring their cakes down in the morning for arrangement. The manageress of The Tea-Total Café has promised us a gingerbread spectacular, whatever that may be.'

'Sounds intriguing. Any entries this year for the Best Pet competition?'

She nodded. 'The usual suspects. I'm sure Jim will be hoping to win back the trophy from Gerry this year.' She smiled, hoping Nathan would look at her so she could catch his eye, but he just kept gazing down at his own notes.

She could almost feel her heart breaking. Had she hurt him so much with her words the other day that he couldn't even *look* at her now? Was she shut out of his world completely? It hurt to think so.

But then he looked up, glanced at her. 'Can I enter Lottie?'

She turned to him and smiled hopefully. 'You can.'

Though they were seated two chairs apart, she itched to reach for his hand across the table. To squeeze his fingers. Let him know that she was sorry. That she hadn't meant what she'd said. That she'd had a knee-jerk reaction because she was frightened of letting go.

But then he looked away again as he scribbled something into his notes.

Her heart sank.

Malcolm filled them in on what was happening with the beer tent, the businesses that had applied to have a stall and sell their wares, who'd be covering first aid and said that licences for closing the road to the council had been approved.

'All that's left that's out of our hands is the nativity. Dr Jones, I believe your daughter is going to be the star attraction this year? Any idea how rehearsals are going?'

'Miss Howarth and Anna assure me that it's all going very well.'

'And I've arranged a small area for the donkey and other farm animals to be kept in whilst they're not performing,' added Sydney, hoping to join in on his contribution.

'Excellent, excellent!' Malcolm enthused.

Once the meeting was over Sydney quickly gathered her things and hurried out into the cold after Nathan. She *had* to catch up with him. She couldn't just let him go. Not like this.

The village had already gone full-force on Christmas decorations. The main street was adorned with fairy lights, criss-crossing from one side to the other, so as people walked along at night it was like being in a sparkly tunnel. Trees were lit and shining bright from people's homes, and some residents had really gone to town, decorating their gardens and trees into small grottos. It didn't hurt her any more to see it.

'Nathan!'

He turned, and when he saw her his face darkened. She saw him glance at the floor.

Standing in front of him, she waited until he looked up and met her gaze. 'Thank you for waiting. I...er...really need to apologise to you. For how I reacted—well, *overreacted* to what you said.'

He stood staring at her, saying nothing.

'I was so in the wrong. I wasn't ready to hear what you said, and I thought you were telling me I needed to be over Olivia's death, and...you weren't. You were telling me to focus on the good times and not the bad, and that was something completely different to saying, *Get over it Sydney!*'

She was wringing her hands, over and over.

'You were trying to help me. Trying to make me see that if I could just try and look at it in another way then it needn't be so painful. So sad. That it was trapping me in the past—'

He reached out and steadied her hands, holding them in his. 'It's okay.'

Relieved that he was talking to her, she had to apologise even more. 'It's not. I behaved abominably. I kicked you out of my house! You *and* Anna! I feel so terrible about that...so inhuman and abysmal and—'

He silenced her with a kiss.

It was so unexpected. One moment she was pouring her heart out, blurting out her apologies, her regrets for her mistake, hoping he would understand, hoping he would forgive her, and the next his lips were on hers. His glorious lips! Warm and tender and so, so forgiving...

She could have cried. The beginnings of tears stung her eyes at first, but then ebbed away as the wondrousness of their kiss continued.

He cradled her face in his hands as he kissed her and

he breathed her in. Sydney moaned—a small noise in the back of her throat as she sank against him. This was... amazing! This was what they could have had the other day if he hadn't thought otherwise and backed off. What they could have had if only she hadn't got angry or scared or whatever it was she had been, so that tricks were playing in her head.

Why had they delayed doing this? They fitted so perfectly!

His tongue was searching out hers as he kissed her deeper and deeper. She almost couldn't breathe. She'd forgotten how to. All she knew right now was that she was so happy he'd forgiven her. He must have done. Or surely he wouldn't be kissing her like this.

And just when she thought she was seeing stars, and that her lungs were about to burst, he broke away from her and stared deeply into her eyes.

She gazed back into his and saw a depth of raw emotion there, a passion that could no longer be bridled. He wanted her.

And she him.

'Drive me home,' she said.

He nodded once and they got into the car.

It didn't take them long to reach her bedroom. Once inside, their giggles faded fast as they stood for a moment, just looking at each other.

Had she ever needed to be with a man this much?

Sydney needed to touch him. Needed to feel his hands upon her. She knew that he would not make the first move unless she showed him that this was what she wanted.

She reached up and, keeping eye contact, began to undo the buttons of his shirt.

He sucked in a breath. 'Sydney...'

'I need you, Nathan.' She pulled his shirt out from his trousers and then her hands found his belt buckle.

Nathan's mouth came down to claim hers, his tongue delicately arousing as he licked and tasted her lips.

She pulled his belt free and tossed it to the floor. She undid the button, unzipped the zipper, and as his trousers fell to the floor he stepped out of them and removed his shirt.

'Now me,' she urged him.

She felt his hands take the hem of her jumper and lift it effortlessly over her head, and then he did the same with her tee shirt, his eyes darkening with desire as her long dark hair spread over her milky-white shoulders. His hands cupped her breasts, his thumbs drifting over her nipples through the lace, and she groaned, arching her back so that her breasts pressed into his hands.

His mouth found her neck, her shoulders, her collarbone, all the while causing sensations on her skin that she had not experienced for a very long time, awakening her body, making her crave his every touch.

He undid her jeans, sliding them down her long legs. His lips kissed their way down her thighs and then came slowly back up to find the lace of her underwear. Then he was breathing in her scent and kissing her once again through the lace.

She almost lost it.

When had she *ever* felt this naked? This vulnerable? And yet…she revelled in it. Gloried in it. She knew she needed to show him her vulnerability, show that despite that she still wanted to be with him. To trust him. After the way she'd treated him the other day, she needed him to know that she couldn't be without him.

'You're so beautiful…' he breathed, and the heat of his breath sent goosebumps along her skin.

His hands were at her sides, going round to her back. He found the clip on her bra and undid it. She shrugged it off easily, groaning at the feel of his hands cupping her breasts, properly this time, at the feel of his mouth, his kisses.

'*Nathan...*'

She could feel his arousal, hard against her, and she unhooked his boxers, sliding them to the floor.

As he lay back on the bed she looked at him in triumph. This beautiful, magnificent man was all hers. And she'd so very nearly cast him aside!

She groaned as she thought of what she might have lost and lay beside him, wrapping her limbs around him so that they were entwined as their mouths joined together once more.

All he'd ever done was listen to her. Understand her. Give her space and time to be ready to talk to him. Where else would she find a man that patient? That understanding and empathetic?

He rolled her under him and breathed her name as his hands roamed her body, creating sensations that she had forgotten she'd ever felt before. She needed him so much. Longed to be *part* of him.

She pulled him closer, urging him on as he began to make love to her.

This was what life was about! Really living. Being a *part* of life—not merely existing. It was about celebrating a relationship, sharing fears and desires and finding that one person you could do that with. About opening up to another person and being okay about that.

Nathan had shared his own vulnerability, his multiple sclerosis. It must have taken him a great deal of courage. And he had shared Anna with her. Letting her get to know his daughter. He couldn't have known that they would get on like this. Must have been worried that Sydney might reject them both once she got to know them.

I nearly did.

She suddenly understood how much pain he must have felt when she'd kicked him out and she pulled him to her once more, hoping as he cried out and gripped the headboard that he would finally see just how much he'd been right to trust her, after all.

She wrapped him safely in her arms and held on tight.

Afterwards, they lay in bed in each other's arms.

Sydney's head was resting in the crook of Nathan's shoulder and he lay there, lazily stroking the skin on her arms. 'I really missed you, you know...'

She turned and kissed his chest. 'I missed you, too. I hated what I did.'

'I understood. You were lashing out because what I said hurt you. You thought I was asking you to give up even *thinking* about your daughter.' He planted a kiss on the top of her head. 'I gave you the advice someone gave me once.'

She turned, laying her chin upon his chest and staring up into his face. 'What do you mean?'

'When I got my diagnosis I was in complete shock. It was like I was mourning my old life. The life in which I could do anything whenever I wanted, without having to think about muscle weakness or spasms or taking medication every day. I mourned the body that I thought would slowly deteriorate until it was useless, and I couldn't get over that.'

'What happened?'

'Anna was born. I was euphoric about that. But then I started thinking about all the ways I might let her down as a father. What if I missed school shows, or parents' evenings, or birthdays…? And then Gwyneth left, totally appalled by the fact that she'd got involved with someone with this illness, and that made me feel under even more pressure from myself. I *couldn't* let Anna down! She only had me to rely on. I *had* to be well. I *had* to be positive. But something kept pulling me back towards feeling sorry for myself. I'd lost my partner and my health and I couldn't get past that.'

She kissed his chest. 'I'm so sorry.'

'I went to a counselling group. It was led by a really good therapist. She helped me see that I was mourning a loss. I was mourning my future. She told me to look at it in a different way. Not to focus on what I'd lost, but on what I'd gained. I didn't necessarily have a bad life in front of me, that—I had a beautiful baby daughter who loved me unconditionally and I knew what my limits might be. But they weren't necessarily there. I had to celebrate the new me rather than mourn the old me. Does that make sense?'

She nodded, laying her head back down against his beautifully strong chest. 'It does.'

'Gwyneth leaving wasn't about me. It was about her and what *she* could deal with. I couldn't control her reaction, but I could control mine. And that's why I decided to focus on the good that was coming. On what I could learn about myself in the process. Discovering hidden depths of strength.'

'Did you find them?'

'Oh, yes!' He laughed, squeezing her to him. Then he paused for a moment and rolled above her, staring deeply into her grey eyes. 'Have you?'

She nodded silently, feeling tears of joy welling in her eyes.

'I think I'm starting to. Because of you.'

He smiled and kissed her.

CHAPTER EIGHT

IT WAS THE afternoon of the Christmas market and nativity and Anna was incredibly excited.

Nathan hadn't been able to get in touch with Sydney yesterday, being busy at work, but at least now he felt better about the direction they were heading in.

It was all going well.

When she'd slammed the door on the two of them and he'd had to walk away it had been the hardest thing he had ever done. Even harder still was the fact that Anna had been full of chatter about the kittens. When could she go and visit them again? Would Sydney mind if they went round every day?

He'd managed to distract her by getting her to read through her lines for her part in the nativity, and he'd been grateful when she'd gone quiet in the back of the car as she read her little script.

But now…? Everything was going well for them. He hoped he would get a moment to talk to Sydney, because he knew that this day would be hard for her.

She'd told him it was the anniversary of Olivia's death. That she'd always faced this day alone in the past. He tried for a moment to imagine what it would be like if he was mourning Anna, but it was too dreadful. He dashed the thought away instantly.

There was so much to do. He'd promised to help out with setting up the marquees and organising the stands, and said he'd be a general dogsbody for anyone who needed him.

Surely Sydney would be there too. She had stalls to organise. The Best Pet show to judge. He hoped he'd get a moment to talk to her, to make sure she was okay.

He parked in the pub car park and walked down to the square that already looked as if it was heaving with people and noise. Right now it seemed like chaos, but he hoped that by the afternoon, and for the nativity in the evening, it would all run smoothly and everyone would be entertained.

He searched for Sydney's familiar long chocolate hair in the crowd, but he couldn't see her amongst all the people bustling about.

This was his and Anna's first Christmas in Silverdale, and he was looking forward to making new connections with people that he'd only ever met as patients. He wanted to let people see him as someone other than a doctor. To let them see that he was a father. A neighbour. A friend.

Tonight was going to go really well. He knew it. And hopefully some of the villagers who didn't know him yet would get the opportunity to meet him and welcome him as a valued member of their community.

'Dr Jones! How good to see you. Are you doing anything at the moment?'

Nathan noticed Miriam, the secretary of the committee, loitering within an empty marquee that had tables set up but nothing else. 'No. How can I help?'

'I'm running the tombola, and all the donated items are in boxes in the van, but I can't lift them with my arthritis. Would you be able to?'

He smiled. This he could do. He was a strong man.

He could lift and carry whatever she asked of him and he would do it. 'A pleasure, Miriam. Where's the van?'

Miriam pointed at a white van parked on the edge of the barriers. 'You are a dear. A real bonus to our committee. We needed some new blood!'

He waved away her compliment. 'I'm sure Dr Preston is hugely missed. I just hope I can fill his shoes.'

Miriam beamed at him. 'You far surpass Richard Preston already, Dr Jones, just by my looking at you!'

Nathan grinned. 'If I was thirty years older, Miriam...'

'Thirty? Oh, you're too kind! *Much* too kind!'

Nathan headed to her van, opened it up and started pulling out boxes. Some were very light, and he assumed they were full of teddy bears and the like. But others were considerably heavier and he struggled to carry one or two.

Whatever were people giving away—boulders?

He lugged the boxes over to the marquee, and just as he set down the last one he heard Sydney's laugh.

Instantly his heart began to pound. She was *laughing*. She was *here*. She was helping out. Same as him. Just as she'd promised she would.

He looked about for her, and once he'd made sure Miriam was okay to empty out the boxes by herself found himself heading over to the pen that Sydney was building along with Mr Bradley from Wicklegate Farm—the owner of Bert the donkey.

'Sydney!'

She turned at the sound of his voice. 'Nathan!'

He kissed her on the lips in greeting—a gesture that earned a wry smile from Mr Bradley.

'How are you doing? I meant to call you earlier—'

'I'm fine!' she answered brightly.

'Really? You don't have to pretend. I know today must be difficult for you. I thought that—'

'Nathan... Honestly. I'm doing great.'

He tried to see if she was just being brave for him, but he couldn't see any deception in her eyes. Perhaps she *was* doing okay? He stood back as she continued to build the pen, fastening some nuts on the final fence with a spanner.

'It's for Bert and the goats and things. What do you think?'

'Erm... I'm no expert on animal holding pens, but these look good to me.'

She kissed him on the cheek. 'I've got lots to do. Off you go! I know you're busy, too. You don't have to hold my hand. I'm doing okay. I've got through this day before.'

He stilled her hands. 'You were on your own before.'

'And I'm not now. I promise if I have a problem, or get upset, I'll come and find you.'

'If you're sure...?'

'I'm sure.' She smiled at him. 'I appreciate your concern. Oh, I almost forgot—I have Olivia's costume for Anna.' She stepped out of the pen and over to her car, opening the boot and bringing back a small bag. 'It should fit. It's all loose robes, and she can tie it tighter with the belt.'

He nodded, accepting the bag. 'Thanks. She nearly had to wear what I'd made her.'

He would just have to trust her. She knew he would be in her corner if she needed him.

'I'm around. Just give me a shout and maybe we can grab a snack later? Before it all kicks off?'

She blew him a kiss. 'I'll come and find you.'

'I'll hold you to it.' He smiled and waved, and then, tearing himself away, headed off to deliver the costume to his daughter.

* * *

Sydney did as she'd promised. A few hours later, when the market was all set up and ready to open to the public, she sought out Nathan, She found him at the bakery tent, manhandling a giant gingerbread grotto scene to place it on a table, and they headed off to sit on the steps around the village Christmas tree.

Nathan paid for a couple of cups of tea for them both and then joined her, wrapping his arm around her shoulders in the cold evening air.

The Christmas market looked picture-postcard-perfect. The marquees were all bedecked with Christmas lighting, carols were being played over the PA system in readiness and—oh, the aromas! The scent of hot dogs, fried onions, candy floss, roasting chestnuts, gingerbread and freshly brewed coffee floated in the air, causing their mouths to water.

'Looks amazing, doesn't it?' she said, looking out at all their hard work. It felt good to be appreciating—finally—the magic of Christmas once again.

'It certainly does. Worth all those meetings we had to sit through.'

She laughed. 'When it all comes together like this it's hard to believe we managed to achieve it.' She paused. 'Did you get the costume to Anna? Did it fit?'

He nodded. 'Perfectly. Thank you.'

They sat in companionable silence for a while, sipping their tea and just enjoying the sensation of *being*. Enjoying the moment. It was nice to sit there together, watching everyone else beavering away.

Nathan took her hand in his and smiled at her as she snuggled into his arms. But then she sat forward, peering into the distance.

'Look! They're letting everyone in. Come on—we

have stations to man!' She tossed her paper teacup into a nearby bin and headed off to her first job of the evening.

Nathan watched her go.

Was she really as unaffected by this day as she seemed? He doubted it.

Frowning, he followed after her.

Silverdale was brimming with activity and the centre of the high street looked amazing. Sydney would have liked to truly immerse herself in the marvel of the beautiful fairy lights everywhere. To listen to the carol singers and their music. To taste the wonderfully aromatic food on display and talk to all the visitors and customers. Enjoy the floral displays.

But she couldn't.

She knew she had work to do, but she was beginning to feel guilty.

Was she really pretending that today wasn't *the day?* Had she deliberately tried to ignore it because she already knew how guilty she now felt? She hadn't mourned as much. She hadn't *remembered* her daughter the way she usually did today.

She felt bad—even if *'usually'* mostly involved staring at photographs all day and often ended with her being a crumpled, sobbing heap.

Her heart felt pained. Just breathing seemed to be exhausting. And yet she had to keep up a steady stream of false smiles and fake jollity for everyone she met or saw.

Was she lying to Nathan? Or to herself?

The stallholders were doing lively business, and she could see money changing hands wherever she looked. People she knew walked their dogs, or pushed buggies, or stood arm in arm looking in wonder and awe at their hard-worked-for Christmas Market. And now crowds were gathering at the main stage for the crowning glory of the evening—the nativity play.

She wandered through the tent with her clipboard, viewing the animals entered for the Best Pet competition. Their owners stood by, looking at her hopefully as she met each one, asked a little about their animal, remembering to remark on their colouring or lovely temperament and scribbling her thoughts on paper.

But she was doing it on automatic pilot.

Until she got to a black rabbit.

Lottie.

Lottie sat in her cage quite calmly, oblivious to all the hubbub going on around her. Her eye had healed quite well, and apart from a slight grey glaze to it no one would be able to guess that she had been attacked and almost blinded.

Sydney stared at the rabbit, her pen poised over her score sheet, remembering the first time Nathan had brought Lottie to her. How hard it had been to fight her feelings for him. How she'd tried to tell herself to stay away from him and not get involved. She hadn't listened to herself. He'd wormed his way into her affections somehow, with those cheeky twinkling eyes of his—*and, my goodness, it had felt so good to lie in his arms. Protected. Coveted. Cherished.*

And he was making her forget. Wasn't he?

No! Not forget. Just deal with it in a different way.

Losing Olivia had hurt like nothing she could ever have imagined. One minute her daughter had been lively, full of life, giggling and happy, and the next she'd wound up in a hospital bed, and Sydney had sat by her bedside for every moment, hoping for a miracle.

She'd felt so helpless. A mother was meant to protect her children—but how on earth were you meant to defend them against things you couldn't see? Bacteria. Viruses. Contagion. They were all sneaky. Taking hold of young, healthy, vital bodies and tearing them asunder. All she'd been able to do was sit. And pray. And talk to her daughter who could no longer hear her. Beg her to fight. Beg her to hold on for a little while longer.

It had all been useless.

She felt a bit sick.

What am I doing here?

'We need the result, Sydney. The nativity is about to start.'

Sydney nodded to Malcolm absently. She wanted to see the nativity. She'd promised Anna she would watch her and cheer her on as she rode in on Bert.

She marked a score for Lottie and then passed her results to Malcolm, who took them over to his small stand in the tent.

Pet owners gathered anxiously—all of them smiling, all of them hopeful for a win. There were some lovely animals, from little mice to Fletcher the Great Dane. Fletcher was a big, lolloping giant of a dog, with the sweetest nature.

Malcolm cleared his throat. 'In third place, with six points, we have Montgomery! A gorgeous example of a golden Syrian hamster.'

Everyone applauded as a little girl stepped forward to receive a purple ribbon for Montgomery.

'In second place, with eight points, we have Jonesy—a beautiful ginger tom.'

Again there was applause, and a young boy came forward to collect his ribbon.

'And in first place, with ten points, we have Lottie the rabbit!'

There were more cheers. More applause.

'Lottie's owner can't be here to collect her prize as she's preparing for her role in the nativity. So perhaps our judge—our fabulous Silverdale veterinary surgeon—would like to give us a few words as to why Lottie has won tonight's contest? Everyone... I give you Sydney Harper!'

Reluctantly, Sydney stepped over to address the crowd—a sea of faces of people she recognised. People she knew from many years of living in this community. There was Miss Howarth, Olivia's schoolteacher. And Cara the lollipop lady, who'd used to help Olivia cross the road outside school. Mr Franklin, who would always talk to Olivia as they walked to school each morning...

'Thank you, Mr Speaker.'

She tried to gather her thoughts as she stood at the microphone. She'd been in a daze for a while. Now it was time to focus. Time to ignore the sickness she could feel building in her stomach.

'There were some amazing entries in this year's competition, and it was great to see such a broad variety of much-loved animals, who all looked fantastic, I'm sure you agree.'

She paused to force a smile.

'I was looking for a certain something this year. I have the honour of knowing a lot of these animals personally. I think I can honestly say I've seen most of them in my surgery, so I know a little about them all. But Lottie won my vote this year because... Well...she's been through a lot. She went through a difficult time and almost lost her life. Instead she lost her eye, but despite that...despite the horror that she has experienced this year, she has stayed strong.'

Her gaze fell upon Nathan, who had appeared at the back of the crowd.

'She fought. And tonight, when I saw her in her cage, looking beautiful in her shiny black coat and with a quiet dignity, I knew I had found my winner. Prizes shouldn't always go to the most attractive, or the most well-behaved, or the most well-groomed. Animals, like people, are more than just their looks. There's something beneath that. A character. A *strength*. And Lottie has that—in bucketloads.'

She nodded and stepped back, indicating that she had finished.

Malcolm led the applause, thanked her, and then urged everyone to make their way to the main stage for the nativity.

Sydney waited for the main crowd to go, and when there was a clearing she walked out of the marquee, feeling a little light-headed.

She felt a hand on her arm. 'Thank you.'

Nathan.

'Oh…it was nothing.'

'Anna will be thrilled Lottie won. She didn't want to miss it, but she's getting ready for the show.'

'Make sure you collect your voucher from Malcolm later.'

'I will.'

'Right. Well…' She wanted to head for the stage. But it seemed Nathan still had something to say.

'You know, you were right just then.'

'Oh…?'

'About people having depths that you can't see. You know, you're a lot like that little rabbit. You have that inner strength.'

She didn't feel like it right now. 'We…er…we need to get going.'

'Wait!' He pulled something from behind his back. 'I got you this.'

He handed over a small parcel, wrapped in shiny paper and tied with an elaborate bow.

'It's for Christmas. Obviously.' He smiled at her. 'But I thought it was important to give it to you today.'

'What is it?'

He laughed. 'I can't tell you that! It's a surprise. Hopefully…a good one. Merry Christmas.'

Suddenly felt this was wrong. Much too wrong! She shouldn't be getting *presents*. Not *today*.

Nathan was wrong.

Today was the worst day to give her his gift.

'I… I don't know what to say.'

'I believe thank you is traditional.'

He smiled and went to kiss her, but she backed off.

'I can't do this,' she muttered.

'Syd? What's the—?'

'You shouldn't give me a gift. Not today. A present? Today? You know what this day is. You know what it means.'

'Of course! Which is why I wanted to give it to you now. To celebrate you moving forward, to give you an incentive to—'

It was too much. Sydney couldn't stand there a moment longer. She had to get away. She had to leave. She—

I promised Anna I'd watch her in the nativity.

Torn, she stood rooted to the spot, angst tearing its way through her as grief and guilt flooded in. This was *not* the way she should be on the anniversary of her daughter's death! She ought to be showing respect. She ought to be remembering her daughter. *Olivia.* Not Anna. Or Nathan. They couldn't be Olivia's replacements. They could never be what her daughter had been to her. Or mean as much.

Could they?

Her heart told her they might, even as the agony of this indecision almost made her cry out.

'Syd…?'

'Nathan, please don't! I can't do this. I can't be with you—'

'Sydney—'

'It's over. Nathan? Do you hear me? I'm done.'

He let go of her arms and stepped back from her as if she'd just slapped him.

She'd never felt more alone.

Nathan just stood there, looking at her, sadness and hurt in his eyes.

'You should remember what you said about Lottie. You're strong, too, you know… You've been through something…*unimaginable* and you're still here. But if you can't see it in yourself…if you can't feel it…believe it…then I need to keep my distance, too. I need to think about Anna. I can't mess her around. If you can't commit to us the way I need you to—'

'I never wanted to hurt you or Anna.'

'I know.' He looked away at the happy crowds. 'But… you did. Please let Anna see you before you leave.'

And he walked away.

Sydney gulped back a grief-racked sob, wondering what the hell she'd just done.

Sydney stood at the front of the crowd, waiting for Anna's big moment. She'd split up from Nathan as he'd headed backstage to give his daughter one last pep talk.

Guilt and shame were filling her. Today was the anniversary of her daughter's death. And she'd kept busy—tried her hardest not to think about her. She hadn't even gone to the cemetery to put down some flowers for her. She hadn't been for so long. Who knew what her daughter's grave looked like now? Mrs C had laid a flower there in November—was it still there? Dead and brittle? Covered by fallen leaves or weeds?

And she was here, waiting to applaud another little girl. What was she *doing*? She'd even given Anna Olivia's old costume. She'd be riding Bert, too. Saying the same lines. It would be too much to bear.

And now she'd hurt Nathan. Played around with that man's heart because she hadn't known whether she was ready to accept it completely.

Feeling sick, she was about to turn and push her way through the crowds when she noticed Bert the donkey come into view, with Anna perched proudly on his back.

Sydney gasped. She'd been expecting to be tormented with memories. But it was *so* clear now. Anna was *nothing* like Olivia. The shape of her face was different. She had her father's jawline, her father's eyes.

If I'd continued with Nathan I wouldn't have been just taking him on, but Anna, too. I'd have let them both down. And now I've broken his heart, and Anna's too...

Overwhelmed by shock and guilt, Sydney stood silently and watched. Suddenly she was smiling with encouragement as Anna's gaze met her own. She felt so proud of Anna. Almost as proud of her as she had been of Olivia, doing the same thing.

How can that be?

As she watched the little girl ride Bert over to his mark by the hay bale, dismount and then take the hand of her Joseph, Sydney felt sadness seize her once more. She could recall Olivia doing that very thing. She'd taken Joseph's hand and been led into the stable too.

'And Joseph and Mary could find nowhere to stay. The only place left to them was with the animals in the stable. And in the place where lambs were born Mary gave birth to baby Jesus…' A small boy at the side of the stage intoned his words into a microphone.

Anna reappeared, this time without her pregnancy bump and holding a doll, swaddled in a thick white blanket, which she lay down into a manger.

Why am I crying?

Sydney blinked a few times and dabbed at her eyes with the back of her hand. Was she being like the innkeeper of Bethlehem? Telling Nathan and Anna there was no room for them in her home? Her heart?

She'd felt there *was* room. It had been there. She'd felt it. Even now she could feel it.

Sydney turned and pushed her way through the crowds, tears streaming freely down her face, unable to look. Unable to face the future she would have had if she'd stayed with Nathan. Unable to believe that she had that inner strength Nathan had said she had!

It was too difficult to move on like this. Accepting Nathan and Anna would be like forgetting her own daughter, and she couldn't have that. Not ever.

Free of the crowds, she strode away from the nativity. She couldn't stay there any longer. She couldn't watch the end. All she wanted at that point was to be at home. To be surrounded by the things that made her feel calm again.

Back at her cottage, she threw her keys onto the table by the door and headed straight for the lounge, casting the still wrapped present from Nathan under the tree. She slumped into her favourite couch, settling her gaze upon her pictures of Olivia, on the one on the mantel of her daughter reaching up for those bubbles, which was now surrounded by Christmas holly and mistletoe.

She stared at it for a moment, and then sat forward and spoke out loud. 'She's not you. She could *never* replace you.'

Despite the heartache he was feeling at Sydney's abrupt departure, Nathan gave Anna a huge hug. She'd acted her part in the nativity brilliantly, and it had gone without a hitch. All those people who said you should never work with children or animals were wrong. Bert had done everything Anna had asked of him, and most importantly of all he had kept her safe.

Scooping her up into his arms, Nathan hitched her onto his hip and kissed her cheek. 'Well done, pumpkin.'

'Thanks, Daddy. Did you see me at the end? With my golden halo?'

'I did! Very impressive.'

'I made it in class.'

'It looked very professional.'

'I saw Sydney.'

He frowned, feeling his stomach plummet with dread. What had Anna seen? That Sydney had looked sick? That she'd run?

He'd almost gone after her. One moment she'd been there, and then the next...

'You did? She got called away, I think, towards the end. But she *did* see you, and she was smiling, so she was very proud.'

Anna beamed. 'I'm hungry, Daddy. Can we get something to eat?'

He nodded. 'Sure. I think the hot dog stand may just have a few left if we're quick.'

Putting her back down on the ground, he walked with her over to the fast food stall. He wasn't hungry. Not at all. All he could see was the look on Sydney's face just before she'd turned and bolted.

He'd been too far away to chase after her. Not that he could have done. He'd needed to be here for Anna, just as he'd promised. But he kept replaying in his mind the change that had come over Sydney's features. The brave smile she'd tried to give to his daughter before her face had fallen and she'd gone.

As they passed them various villagers stopped to compliment them and to tell Anna how well she'd done.

'Hey, guess what?' he said, determined to keep things happy and bright for his daughter.

'What?'

'Lottie won the Best Pet competition!'

'She *did*? Yay!' Anna jumped up and down with glee. 'Can we go and get her?'

'Let's eat these first.' He handed her a hot dog, covered with a healthy dollop of fried onions, ketchup and mustard. 'And then we will. Malcolm's looking after the pets at the moment, so she's not on her own.'

Anna bit into her hot dog and wiped her mouth when a piece of fried onion tried to escape. 'Did she get a ribbon?'

'I think she did.'

'And a prize?'

'I think so. She was very lucky, wasn't she?'

He was finding this difficult. Pretending everything was okay when all he wanted to do was sit alone and allow himself to feel miserable. Had he pushed Sydney too hard by giving her that present? Had he tried to make her accept things she wasn't ready to work through yet?

I should never have got involved! I should have kept my distance!

'We had the judge on our side.' Anna smiled and took another bite.

Did we? Maybe only briefly.

He bit into his own hot dog, but he didn't really want it. The smell of the onions only turned his stomach.

She'd not been gone long, but already he ached for her. Missed her. He'd thought for a moment that they had a future together. He'd pictured waking up in the mornings and seeing her next to him. Her grey eyes twinkling at him from her pillow. He'd imagined them taking country walks together, hand in hand, and having picnics in the summer—Sydney laughing in the warm sun, her hair glinting.

He'd imagined nights watching movies together and sharing a bucket of popcorn. Feeding each other tasty morsels and titbits from the fridge before running upstairs, giggling, as he chased her before they fell into bed. And then moments when they'd just talk. He'd hold her hand. Trace the lines on her palm. He'd imagined them making love. Maybe even having a family of their own together...

They could have had it all.

He'd had his heart broken again, and this time he felt even more distraught.

He'd known Gwyneth was selfish. Had always had to have things her own way. She'd always had the perfect life, and a disabled partner had not been for her. Even the promise of a new family, the child they'd made together, hadn't been enough for her. It had never been enough for her. His diagnosis had just been the last thing she'd needed before she walked away. He'd never expected that she would walk away from her own child, too, but she had.

Sydney was looking out for herself too, but in a different way. Her child—Olivia—had been the centre of her life. Her world. And her world had been taken from her. Her sun had been stolen so that she'd only been living in darkness.

Nathan had thought that he'd brightened that darkness for a while.

'Is Sydney coming to our house on Christmas Day?' Anna asked, finishing off her bun in a final mouthful.

'Er… I really don't know, Anna. She's a bit sad at the moment.'

'Because she doesn't have her little girl any more?'

Nathan looked at his daughter, surprised at her insight. 'Yes. I think that's it.'

But what if it wasn't just that?

'We could go to hers and try to cheer her up. It *is* Christmas, and Miss Howarth says it's the season of goodwill. We learnt that at school for the play.'

How simple it was in a child's world. Everything was so black and white. 'We'll see. You might be busy playing with all your new things.'

'Sydney could come and play with me.'

He sighed. 'I don't know, Anna. Perhaps we need to give her some space for a while.'

'I want to thank her for giving Lottie first prize. Can we go and see her now? Before Christmas Day? Before she gets sad?'

Nathan felt touched by his daughter's compassion. She was doing her best to understand. 'She's already sad. Maybe we'll see her in the village. Come on...let's get Lottie and go home.'

He took her sticky hand in his and together they headed off to the animal tent.

CHAPTER NINE

IT WAS CHRISTMAS MORNING. A day on which Sydney should have been woken by an excited child bouncing on her bed and urging her to go downstairs. Instead, she was woken by the sound of rain against her window, and she lay in bed for a moment, not wanting to move.

Christmas Day.

The house was full of decorations. Encouraged by Nathan, and feeling positive and optimistic, she had adorned the house throughout, sure in the knowledge that this season she would have a reason to celebrate. People she loved to celebrate *with*.

Only it hadn't worked out that way.

She stared at the ceiling and once again asked herself if she was really doing the right thing.

Nathan was a kind-hearted man. Compassionate, caring. And she felt sure he had strong feelings for her. Looking at the pillows beside her, she remembered that night they'd made love. How good he'd made her feel. The brief time that they'd had together had been exquisite. Being made love to, being cherished, being as *treasured* as he had made her feel, had made her realise all that had been missing from her life.

I'm alone.

He'd not come after her after the nativity. He hadn't

shown up in the few days afterwards either. She'd thought that he might, and she'd been prepared not to answer the door. To hide. But he hadn't come.

She'd always believed that by keeping her distance from romantic entanglements she was keeping herself safe—and, yes, she supposed she was. But she was also keeping herself in a prison of loneliness. It was a kind of solitary confinement. All she had was Magic, her cat. Her only interactions were with the people and the animals at work and the friendly faces she saw in the shops. When she returned home all she had left were herself and her memories.

Unless I choose Nathan's way of thinking.

Christmas was a time for family. She could be sharing the day with Nathan. With Anna. Darling, sweet little Anna, whom she also adored. And she was letting fear keep her away. Her fear of being vulnerable again. Of losing Nathan. Losing Anna. Of not being enough for either of them!

'I'm losing you if I do nothing!' she said out loud, angry at herself.

Putting on her slippers and grabbing her robe, she headed downstairs.

The Christmas tree twinkled in the corner, with just a few presents underneath it. There was that gift from Nathan. Something from her parents. A couple of gifts from faithful long-term customers at work. The gift she'd placed there in Olivia's memory.

There could have been more. There could have been something for Nathan. For Anna. There could have been happiness in this house again. The day could have been spent the way Christmas is supposed to be spent.

She could be cooking Christmas breakfast for them

all right now. Scrambled egg and smoked salmon. Maybe a little Bucks Fizz.

She sat by the tree and picked up the parcel from her mum and dad. It was soft and squidgy, and when she half-heartedly tugged at the wrapping she discovered they'd got her a new pair of fleece pyjamas. She smiled at the pattern—little penguins on tiny icebergs. The other gifts were a bottle of wine, some chocolates, a book…

All that was left was the gift from Nathan and the one for her own daughter that would never be opened.

She picked up the gift from Nathan and glanced at the card.

Merry Christmas, Sydney!
Lots of love, Nathan xxx

What would it be? She had no idea. Part of her felt that it would be wrong to open it now. They weren't together any more. He'd made that clear. She hesitated.

He'd wanted her to have it.

Sydney tore at the wrapping and discovered a plain white box. Frowning, she picked at the tape holding the end closed, getting cross when it wouldn't come free and having to use a pen from her side table to pierce it and break the seal. Inside, something was wrapped in bubble wrap.

She slid it out and slowly unwrapped the plastic. It was a picture frame, and taped to the front, was a small white envelope. There was something inside. A memory card…

It's a digital photo frame.

She plugged it into the mains, inserted the memory card and switched it on, wondering what there could be on it…and gasped.

There, right before her eyes, were pictures of Olivia

that she had never even seen before! Some were close-ups, some were group shots, some were of her with other people or children, most she recognised as people from Silverdale.

Olivia in a park on a swing set next to another little boy, who was grinning at the photographer. Olivia at a birthday party with her face all smudged with chocolate cake. Olivia in the front row of the school choir.

She watched in shocked awe as picture after picture of her daughter appeared on the screen.

Where had Nathan got these? They must have come from other people! People in the village who had taken their own photos and captured Olivia in them too. And somehow—amazingly—he had gathered all these pictures together and presented them to her like this!

Tears pricked at her eyes as she gazed at the beautiful images. And then it flicked to another picture, and this one was moving. A video. Of a school play. She remembered it clearly. It had been Olivia's first play and she'd been dressed as a ladybird in a red top that Sydney had spent ages making, sewing on little black dots and then making her a bobble headband for her antennae.

The video showed the last few moments. It captured the applause of the crowd, the kiddies all lining up in a row, taking a bow. A boy near Olivia waved madly at the camera, and then Olivia waved at someone just off to the left of the screen and called out, *'I love you, Mummy!'*

Sydney heard the words and burst into tears, her hands gripping the frame like a lifeline. She'd forgotten that moment. She'd been there. She remembered the play very well; she'd been so proud of Olivia for not forgetting any of her words, and she'd been a true actress, playing her part with aplomb. And at the end she'd seen Sydney in the crowd, and Sydney had waved at her madly and called out to her.

She pressed 'pause'. Then 'rewind'. And watched it again.

Sydney had always believed that she would never get any new photos of Olivia. That her daughter had been frozen in time. But Nathan had given her a gift that she could never have foreseen!

Surely he loved her? What man would do something so thoughtful and as kind as this if he didn't? He would have to know just what this would mean to her.

When the video ended and the frame went back to the beginning of its cycle of photos again, Sydney rushed upstairs to get dressed. She had to see him. She had to… what? Thank him?

'I don't want to thank him. I want to be with him,' she said aloud to Magic, who lay curled on her bed, blinking in irritation at her racing into the bedroom and disturbing her slumber. 'I've been so stupid!'

She yanked off her robe and her pyjamas and kicked off her slippers so hard they flew into the mirror on the wardrobe door.

She pulled on jeans, a tee shirt and a thick fisherman's jumper and twisted her hair up into a rough ponytail. She gave her teeth a quick scrub and splashed her face with some water. Once she'd given it a cursory dry with a towel she raced downstairs and headed for her car, gunning the engine and screeching off down the road.

She hadn't even locked her own front door.

But before she could go to Nathan's house there was somewhere else she needed to go first.

Silverdale Cemetery and Memorial Gardens was a peaceful place. But for a long time it had been somewhere that

Sydney had avoided. It had always hurt too much, and for a long time she hadn't come. She'd not felt she had the inner strength to get through a visit.

But today she felt able to be there.

She *wanted* to be.

Today she felt closer to her daughter than on any other day so far. Perhaps it had something to do with what Nathan had said. Perhaps it was because he had helped lift her guilt. Perhaps it was because he had given her that new way of thinking. But now Sydney felt able to go to the site where her daughter was buried, and she knew that she wouldn't stand there staring down at the earth and thinking of her daughter lying there, cold and alone and dead.

Because Olivia wasn't there any more. She wasn't in the ground, cold and dead.

Olivia was alive in her heart. And in her mind. Sydney's head was full of images long since forgotten. Memories were washing over her with the strength of a tsunami, pounding into her with laughter and delight and warm feelings of a life well-lived and enjoyed.

Olivia had been a happy little girl, and Sydney had forgotten that. Focusing too much on her last day. The day on which she'd been dying. Unconscious. Helpless. In pain.

Now Sydney had a new outlook on her daughter's life. And it was an outlook she knew Olivia would approve of. So the cemetery was no longer a place for her to fear but a place in which she could go and sit quietly for a moment, after laying some flowers. Bright, colourful winter blooms that her daughter had helped her to plant years before.

The headstone was a little dirty, so she cleaned it off with her coat sleeve and made sure her daughter's name was clear and bright. Her eyes closed as she pictured her daughter watering the flowers in the back garden with her pink tin watering can.

'I'm sorry I haven't visited for a while,' she said, her eyes still closed. 'But I got caught up in feeling sorry for myself. You wouldn't have approved.' She laughed slightly and smiled, feeling tears prick at her eyes. 'But I think I'm overcoming that. A new friend—a *good* friend—taught me a valuable lesson. I was stuck, you see, Olivia. Stuck on missing you. Stuck on taking the blame because I felt someone had to.'

She opened her eyes and smiled down at the ground and the headstone.

'I don't have to do that any more. I'm not stuck. I'm free. And because I'm free you are too. I can see you now. In my head. In here…' She tapped her chest, over her heart. 'I can see you so clearly! I can hear you and smell you and feel you in my arms.'

She paused, gathering her breath.

'You'd like Nathan. He's a doctor. He's a good man. And Anna…his daughter…you'd love her too. I know you would. I guess I just wanted to say that I… I *love* you, Olivia. I'm sorry I was gone for a while, but I'm back, and now I have someone looking out for me, and he's given me the ability to get *you* back the way I should have from the beginning.'

She touched the headstone.

'I'll be back more often from now on. And…er… I've put up a tree. I'm celebrating Christmas this year. There's something for you under it. You won't ever be forgotten.'

She sniffed in the cold, crisp December air and looked about her. Two headstones away was the grave of one Alfred Courtauld, and she remembered his wife telling her about how she'd once laid a flower on Olivia's grave.

Sydney picked up a flower from Olivia's bouquet and laid it on Alfred's stone. 'Thanks for looking after Olivia whilst I've been away.'

And then she slowly walked back to her car.

Nathan watched as Anna unwrapped her brand-new bike, her hands ripping off the swathes of reindeer-patterned paper that he'd wrapped it in, smiling warmly at her cries of joy and surprise.

'A *bike!*' she squealed, swinging her leg over the frame and getting onto the seat. 'Can I ride it? Can I take it outside?'

'Course you can.' He helped her take the bike out to the back garden and watched as she eagerly began to pedal, wobbling alarmingly at the beginning, but then soon getting the hang of it.

'Look, Daddy!'

'I'm watching, baby.'

He stood in the doorway, holding his mug of coffee, watching his daughter cycle up and down, but feeling sad that he couldn't give her more. He'd hoped this Christmas to be sharing the day with Sydney. To be opening presents together, giving Anna the feel of a *real* family, so the three of them could enjoy the day together because they were meant to be together.

But Sydney had kept her distance. She'd not dumped him as unceremoniously as Gwyneth had, but she'd still broken his heart.

It wasn't just Christmas he felt sad about. It was all of it. Every day. Christmas was a time for family, but so was the rest of the year. Waking every morning *together*. Listening to each other talk about their day each evening. Laughing. *Living*.

He'd hoped that Sydney could be in their lives, and he

knew that Anna still hoped for that, too. She'd kept going on about it last night before she went to bed.

'Will Sydney be coming tomorrow, Daddy?'

But, sadly, the answer had been no. She would not be coming.

As he headed into the kitchen to make himself a fresh drink he briefly wondered if she had opened his present. It had taken a lot of organising, but Mrs Courtauld had helped—reaching out to people, contacting them on her walks around the village with her greyhound Prince, asking everyone to check their photos and see if any of them had Olivia in them.

He'd dared to hope there would be one or two, but he had been surprised at how many they had got. Fourteen new pictures of Olivia and a video, in which she was saying the exact words he knew would gladden Sydney's heart.

Because that was what he wanted for her most of all. For her to be happy. For her heart to swell once again with love. He'd hoped that her love would include him, but...

His doorbell buzzed. *Who on earth...?*

It was Christmas morning. It couldn't be a door-to-door salesman, or anyone like that. Perhaps someone had been taken ill? Perhaps he was needed as a doctor?

He hurried to the front door, unlocked it and swung it open.

'Sydney?'

She looked out of breath, edgy and anxious. 'Can I come in?'

Did he want her to? Of course he did! He'd missed her terribly. But if she was just here to rehash everything they'd said the other night then he wasn't sure he wanted to hear it.

But something in her eyes—a brightness, a *hope*—made him give her one last audience.

He stepped back. 'Please.'

He watched as she brushed past and then followed her into the kitchen, from where she could see Anna, playing happily in the back garden.

'You got her a bike?'

He smiled as he looked at his daughter, happily pedalling away. 'Yes. It was what she wanted.'

Sydney turned to him. 'And what do *you* want, Nathan? For Christmas?'

Nathan stared at her, trying to gauge the exact reason for her turning up like this on Christmas Day. It wouldn't be a trick or a game. Sydney wasn't like that. *Had she opened his gift to her?*

He couldn't answer her. Couldn't tell her what he *really* wanted. So he changed the subject. 'Did you like your present?'

Tears filled her eyes then and she nodded, the movement of her head causing the tears to run freely down her cheeks. She wiped them away hurriedly. 'I can't believe what you did. How you managed that... I'm...speechless.'

He gave a small smile. 'I wanted to make you happy. Just tell me it didn't make you sad.'

'It didn't.' She took a quick step towards him, then stopped. 'I've come to apologise. I made a mistake.'

Nathan frowned. 'What do you mean?'

'Us. I made the wrong choice.'

He didn't say anything. He didn't want to make this go wrong. He needed to hear what she had to say.

'I got frightened. The day...the evening we were together I...panicked. And then, when I saw Anna on the donkey, I don't know what it was... I started feeling guilty. I felt that if I forgot Olivia on her most important day I would be losing her. But then today—earlier—I realised that it *wasn't* her most important day. The day she died. Her most important day was the day she was born! I can remember Olivia in a different way, just like you said, and by doing so I can also have a future. And so can she. Because my grief was trapping Olivia too. I kept her in pain all that time. Remembering the day she left me…when she was suffering. When I couldn't help her. I kept her there. Trapped in time. But not any more. Not any more,' she said firmly.

He shook his head. 'Love isn't what hurts people, Sydney. *Losing* someone hurts. *Grief* hurts. *Pain* hurts. But love? Love is the greatest thing we can experience.'

'I know. Because I feel love for Olivia. I feel love for…' She paused and stepped closer, laying a hand upon his chest, over his heart. 'For you. I've felt more helpless in the last few days being sat alone at home than I have ever felt. I need to be with you.'

He laid his hand over hers, feeling his heart pound in his ribcage as if it was a wild animal, trying desperately to escape. 'What are you saying?'

'I'm saying I want us to be together. You. Me. Anna. I think we can do it. I think that together we can be strong enough to fight whatever is coming in the future.'

'You mean it?' he asked, hope in his voice.

'I do. I've missed you so much! I've been in pain because I don't have you. I didn't realise what was missing from my life until I met you.'

Nathan smiled and kissed her, meeting her lips with a kiss that burned with fervour. Devouring her, tasting her, enjoying her with a passion that he could barely contain.

She wanted him! She wanted him back and she was willing to take a chance on their future.

It was all he'd ever wanted.

None of them knew what his future would be. How his disease would progress. Whether it would get worse. Just because that happened to a lot of people with MS, it didn't mean it would happen to him. He might be one of the lucky ones. It could stay as relapsing remitting. Who knew?

And even if it did progress he now felt braver about facing it. Because he would have Sydney at his side. And Anna, too. His daughter would not be burdened by carrying the weight of her father's illness all alone on her young shoulders. She would be able to share her worries. With a mother figure. With *Sydney*. And he knew Anna adored Sydney. They could be a perfect family. Or at least they could try!

They broke apart at the sound of his daughter's footsteps running towards the house.

'Sydney!' Anna barrelled into them both, enveloping them with her arms. 'Are you here for Christmas dinner?'

Sydney smiled at Nathan, and he answered. 'She's here for *every* dinner, I think. Aren't you?'

He looked into her grey eyes and saw happiness there. And joy.

'If you'll have me.'

Anna squeezed her tight and beamed.

Nathan pulled her close, so they were both wrapped in his embrace.

'Always.'

* * * * *

*If you enjoyed this story, check out these other
great reads from Louisa Heaton*

*SEVEN NIGHTS WITH HER EX
ONE LIFE-CHANGING NIGHT
A FATHER THIS CHRISTMAS?
HIS PERFECT BRIDE*

All available now!

MILLS & BOON®

MEDICAL ROMANCE™

THE ULTIMATE IN ROMANTIC MEDICAL DRAMA

A sneak peek at next month's titles...

In stores from 29th December 2016:

- **Falling for Her Wounded Hero** – Marion Lennox
  and **The Surgeon's Baby Surprise** – Charlotte Hawkes

- **Santiago's Convenient Fiancée** – Annie O'Neil
  and **Alejandro's Sexy Secret** – Amy Ruttan

- **The Doctor's Diamond Proposal** – Annie Claydon
  and **Weekend with the Best Man** – Leah Martyn

Just can't wait?
Buy our books online a month before they hit the shops!
www.millsandboon.co.uk

Also available as eBooks.

MILLS & BOON®

EXCLUSIVE EXTRACT

Saoirse Murphy's proposal of a 'convenient'
arrangement with paramedic Santiago Valentino
soon ignites a very inconvenient passion…

Read on for a sneak preview of
SANTIAGO'S CONVENIENT FIANCÉE
by Annie O'Neil

Saoirse went up on tiptoe and kissed him.

From the moment her lips touched Santiago's she
didn't have a single lucid thought. Her brain all but
exploded in a vain attempt to unravel the quick-fire
sensations. Heat, passion, need, longing, sweet and tangy
all jumbled together in one beautiful confirmation that
his lips were every bit as kissable as she'd thought they
might be.

Snippets of what was actually happening were hitting
her in blips of delayed replay.

Her fingers tangled in his silky, soft hair. Santi's wide
hands tugged her in tight, right at the small of her back.
There was no doubting his body's response to her now.
The heated pleasure she felt when one of his hands
slipped under her T-shirt elicited an undiluted moan of
pleasure. He matched her move for move as if they had
been made for one another. Her body's reaction to his
felt akin to hitting all hundred watts her body was capable
of for the very first time.

She wanted more.

No.

She wanted it *all*. The whole package. The feelings. The pitter-patter of her heart. Knowing it was reciprocated. Being part of a shared love. Not some sham wedding so she wouldn't have to live in a country where her soul had all but shriveled up and died.

She felt Santi's kisses deepen and her will-power to shore up some sort of resistance to what was happening plummeted. This felt so *real*. And a little too close to everything she'd hoped for wrapped up in a too-good-to-be-true package. That sort of thing didn't happen to her. And it wasn't. She'd started it, Santi was just responding. She heard herself moan and with its escape her resolve to resist abandoned her completely.

Don't miss
SANTIAGO'S CONVENIENT FIANCÉE
by Annie O'Neill

Available January 2017
www.millsandboon.co.uk

Give a 12 month subscription to a friend today!

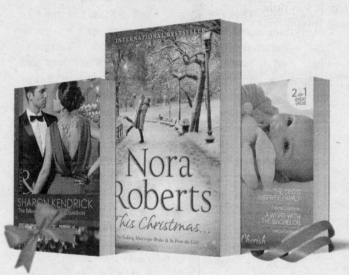

Call Customer Services
0844 844 1358*

or visit
millsandboon.co.uk/subscriptions